The diplomat De Puebla wasted no time. "My lady Princess," he said. "I have news which I thought I should impart to you without delay. I have this day written to your noble parents. The King. . . he is asking for your hand. . . ."

"For Prince Henry, I know. That has been decided."

"No. . . for himself."

Katherine stared at him and grew pale. "I can't believe this. . . . The Queen has not been dead two months!"

"The King is in a hurry." De Puebla smiled and moved closer. "He is obsessed by the need to get heirs."

"No! I shall never agree!" she cried, terrified. "No! Not that. . . anything but that. . ."

Fawcett Crest Books
by Jean Plaidy:

BEYOND THE BLUE MOUNTAINS

THE GOLDSMITH'S WIFE

THE LION OF JUSTICE

MYSELF MY ENEMY

THE PASSIONATE ENEMIES

THE QUEEN'S HUSBAND

THE PLANTAGENET SAGA

THE PLANTAGENET PRELUDE

THE REVOLT OF THE EAGLETS

THE HEART OF THE LION

THE PRINCE OF DARKNESS

THE BATTLE OF THE QUEENS

THE QUEEN FROM PROVENCE

THE HAMMER OF THE SCOTS

THE FOLLIES OF THE KING

THE VOW ON THE HERON

PASSAGE TO PONTEFRACT

THE STAR OF LANCASTER

EPITAPH FOR THREE WOMEN

UNEASY LIES THE HEAD

Jean Plaidy

FAWCETT CREST • NEW YORK

First American Edition 1984

A Fawcett Crest Book
Published by Ballantine Books
Copyright © 1982 by Jean Plaidy

Library of Congress Catalog Card Number: 84-11664

ISBN 0-449-20778-1

This edition published by arrangement with G. P. Putnam's Sons

Manufactured in the United States of America

First Ballantine Books Edition: May 1986

CONTENTS

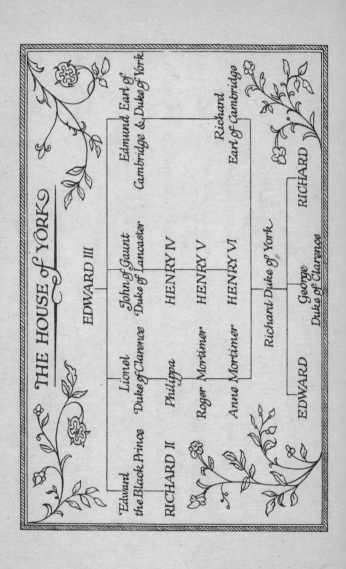

THE HOUSE of YORK

EDWARD III

Edward
the Black Prince

RICHARD II

Lionel
Duke of Clarence

Philippa

Roger Mortimer

Anne Mortimer

John of Gaunt
Duke of Lancaster

HENRY IV

HENRY V

HENRY VI

Edmund Earl of
Cambridge & Duke of York

Richard
Earl of Cambridge

Richard Duke of York

EDWARD

George
Duke of Clarence

RICHARD

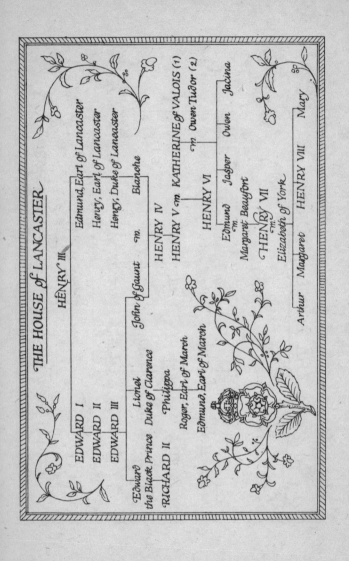

THE HOUSE of LANCASTER

HENRY III

- EDWARD I
- EDWARD II
- EDWARD III

Lionel, Duke of Clarence — John of Gaunt — m. — Blanche

Edmund, Earl of Lancaster
Henry, Earl of Lancaster
Henry, Duke of Lancaster

Philippa

Edward the Black Prince

RICHARD II

Roger, Earl of March

Edmund, Earl of March

HENRY IV

HENRY V — m. — KATHERINE of VALOIS (1) — m. — Owen Tudor (2)

HENRY VI

Edmund — m. — Margaret Beaufort

Jasper   Owen   Jacina

HENRY VII — m. — Elizabeth of York

Arthur   Margaret   HENRY VIII   Mary

'Uneasy lies the head that wears a crown.'
Shakespeare's *Henry IV*, Part 2.

THE BIRTH OF A PRINCE

There was great consternation in the Palace of Winchester on that misty September day, in the year 1486 for the Queen—who was not due to give birth to her child for another month—had started her pains.

It was extraordinary for only eight months had passed since the marriage. Everyone had been delighted by the Queen's promise of fruitfulness, and to have given birth nine months after the marriage would have been a most welcome sign, but to do so in eight months was a little disconcerting, though no one could believe for one moment that this might mean anything but the birth of a premature child.

Queen Elizabeth was sitting quietly with her sisters, Cecilia aged seventeen and Anne who was just eleven, working on an altar cloth which the King's mother, of whom they were in considerable awe, had decided was an appropriate occupation for them at such a time when all the favours Heaven could grant them were needed. Even Anne knew—for it was spoken of continually—that it was of utmost importance that the Queen should give birth to a healthy boy.

The Queen and her sisters had come through difficult times and still remembered them. They had been pampered and petted by their magnificent and all-powerful father but they had also suffered privations in the Sanctuary at Westminster when they had feared for their lives. If they had learned a lesson from life it must surely be that it was fraught with insecurity and could change drastically in the space of a few days.

At last Elizabeth was married to the King and although there had been a period when they had wondered whether Henry Tudor was going to honour his pledges, they now felt comparatively safe; and if the baby who was about to be born was a healthy boy, their chances of making good marriages and living in comfort—and perhaps even of survival—would be greatly increased.

As Cecilia stitched at the hem of the Madonna's robe in a silk

1

thread of exquisite blue she was wondering when *her* time to marry would come. She hoped her husband would be someone at the King's Court for she did not want to have to go away from home. At one time she had thought she was going to be sent to Scotland to be the Queen of Scots but that had come to nothing in the manner of so many of these proposed marriages. As for Elizabeth herself she had once been destined for the Dauphin of France and for a long time their mother had insisted that she be addressed as Madame La Dauphine. The fact was that one never knew where one would end up. Who would have believed that Elizabeth, after the humiliation of losing the Dauphin, would, through her marriage with Henry Tudor, become Queen of England?

Although one never spoke of it now the King should have been their brother Edward. But where was Edward? What had happened to him and their brother Richard? Some people said that both had been murdered in the Tower. It must be so for if they had not been, surely the King of England should have been either Edward the Fifth or Richard the Fourth—not Henry the Seventh.

Their mother had said: 'It is a subject which it is better not to discuss. We have to be careful not to upset the Queen who is in a delicate condition.'

Still it was strange not to talk of one's own brothers. What should one talk of? The weather? Whether Elizabeth would have a coronation when the baby was born? The christening?

'Don't talk too much about the baby,' their mother had warned. 'It might be unlucky.'

Then of what did one talk?

Cecilia was saved the trouble of searching for a suitable topic of conversation for Elizabeth suddenly turned very pale, put her hands to her stomach and said: 'I believe my pains are starting. Go at once to our mother.'

Cecilia dropped her part of the altar cloth and ran while Anne sat staring at her sister in dismay.

Queen Elizabeth Woodville, the Queen Mother, was alone in her apartments at the castle. She was longing for the next month to be over that she might hold her healthy grandson in her arms.

She was certain it would be a boy. If not her daughter Elizabeth must quickly become pregnant again. She had no doubt that Elizabeth would breed well, as she herself had.

She was congratulating herself on a return to prosperity. She and her family had passed through some very difficult times, during which she believed she had come near to disaster. King Richard had never liked her; he had always deplored his brother's marriage to a woman, as he would have said, of low quality. Naturally he had never dared say much against her when Edward was alive; and after Edward's death Richard had preserved his loyalty to his brother. Even when she had been caught with Jane Shore in conspiring against him, he had been lenient. Now everything was changed. He was dead—slain on Bosworth Field and the new King had become her son-in-law.

She was wishing Henry's mother was not in the castle. The Countess of Richmond with her quiet air of superiority irritated Elizabeth Woodville. It was true that Margaret Beaufort had royal blood in her veins, even though as Elizabeth often reminded herself it came from the wrong side of the blanket. Oh, everyone knew that John of Gaunt had legitimized his Beauforts but that did not alter the fact that they had begun in bastardy, and it was true that those who were unsure of their claims always asserted their rights to them most forcefully. She herself was one of those, for ever since King Edward had become so enamoured of her that he had married her and raised her to such dizzy heights, she had had to make sure that everyone remembered the respect due to her.

So it was with Margaret Beaufort, Countess of Richmond, and now that her son had become King this set her somewhat above the mother of the Queen, though, mused Elizabeth, none could doubt that the young Queen, as daughter of the late King Edward the Fourth, had more right to the crown than Henry Tudor who had won it by conquest rather than inheritance.

It was not a matter to brood on, for Henry now had the crown firmly in his grasp and he had fulfilled his contract to unite the houses of York and Lancaster, which he had done when he married Edward the Fourth's eldest daughter.

Such times we live through! the Queen Mother often thought sadly, dreaming of the days of her glory when an ardent young King had first seen her in Whittlebury Forest and pursued her with such fervent devotion that he had lifted her from her humble position and made her his Queen.

While he had lived she had been secure as Queen of England, surrounded by her family whom she had made prosperous; but alas he had died suddenly at the age of forty-four although he had seemed in almost perfect health up to that time. Then had come the greatest blow of all—the shattering declaration that Edward had been married to Eleanor Butler who was alive at the time when he had gone through a ceremony with Elizabeth—thus making her marriage no marriage at all and her children illegitimate.

And her dear little boys—young Edward, who had briefly been Edward the Fifth, and the little Duke of York . . . where were they now? It seemed they had vanished into obscurity. There had been rumours that their uncle, Richard the Third, had murdered them in the Tower. But why should he find that necessary? He had declared them illegitimate. Why should he have needed to murder them? Whatever had happened to them, they were lost to her . . . her little darlings. She mourned them deeply for although she might be a vain and selfish woman she was a good mother and had loved all her children dearly. There was mystery everywhere. She remembered long dreary days, cold sleepless nights in Westminster Sanctuary when she had not known from one day to the next what would become of her and her family.

Richard had not been unkind after a while. There had even been talk of his marrying young Elizabeth. It was not serious of course. How could an uncle marry his niece? However, young Elizabeth was destined to be the saviour of her family, now Henry, the new King, had married her. This meant that he did not consider her illegitimate . . . and yet if she were not, the young Princes also were not, and if they were alive . . . what right had Henry to the throne?

It was too complicated, too frightening to brood on. So she must put the past behind her. She must say: We have come so far and we are now as safe as any can be in this dangerous changing world. My daughter is the Queen of England. My little boys are lost to me forever. It might be true that Richard had murdered them in the Tower as one rumour had had it, yet why he should since they had been proclaimed illegitimate, she could never understand.

There was too much mystery; there had been too much misery; now they were moving forward into brighter times. She must forget the past.

If this child were a boy contentment would settle on the country. The new dynasty of the Tudors would be accepted and the child would be the vital link which bound the Houses of York and Lancaster together and settled their differences forever.

What was most important now was to care for the young Queen and to bring this all-important child into the world. There was a whole month to wait and waiting was so irksome.

Cecilia had rushed into the room. She was about to reprove

her daughter, reminding her that she must remember that she was not only the sister of the reigning Queen but also the daughter of great King Edward who was still mourned with such affection by his subjects. . .

But this was no time for a lecture on deportment. Cecilia was breathless.

'My lady . . . come quickly . . . it is my sister. . . She is in pain.'

The Queen Mother felt fear grip her.

'No . . . It cannot be . . .'

She was out of the room running as fast as she could to her daughter's apartment.

One look at Elizabeth was enough. 'Send for the midwife!' she cried.

Then with the help of her women she took the Queen to the lying-in apartments which by good fortune had already been prepared for her.

When Margaret Countess of Richmond heard that the Queen's confinement had begun she went at once to the lying-in apartments. She had prepared them herself so she knew that everything was in readiness and exactly as it should be.

Let there be no misunderstanding. This was the most important occasion the country had known since the crowning of the new King.

On the orders of the King's mother the lying-in chamber, which she had graciously allowed the young mother-to-be to choose herself, was hung with rich arras which was draped even over the ceiling. It hung at the windows, shutting out the light. This was fitting for a royal birth, said the Countess, and as the King accepted her word in all such matters, so must it be. Only women should be with the Queen at the time of the birth and the Countess had appointed members of her own sex even to such posts as butler and pages, positions usually occupied by men.

She knew that Elizabeth Woodville would have liked to countermand her orders; but she dared not. The King had no great liking for his mother-in-law, and the woman knew that she remained at Court on sufferance, because he could not ignore his wife's mother; even so she would have to understand that she must fall in completely with his wishes if she were to retain her place at Court, and that meant those of his mother also.

The Countess of Richmond was a very determined woman. She had been a beauty in her youth—not such a dazzling one as Elizabeth Woodville, but nevertheless a woman of striking good looks. Her features were regular, serene and so stern that they could be called frigid. She was a woman who kept her own counsel but there was one thing which was certain—and that was her complete devotion to her son.

She had been not quite fourteen years old when Henry had been born, already a widow for her husband Edmund Tudor had died in the November before his son was born the following January. The bewildered mother had been glad to retire to Pembroke Castle where her brother-in-law Jasper offered her a home. It was Jasper who became the guardian of the young baby and who had brought him through many dangers to his present position.

The Tudors were staunch Lancastrians and Margaret had watched the progress of the Wars of the Roses with alternate fear and hope. The deaths of Henry the Sixth and his son had made the way clear for Henry. How she had hoped and prayed for his success and naturally she had not been above a little scheming too; and at last her seemingly hopeless dream had become a reality. Her Henry—whose claim to the throne even she had to admit was a trifle flimsy—had landed at Milford Haven and from there marched to Bosworth Field where he had had the good fortune to put an end to the reign of the Plantagenets and begin that of the Tudors.

It was dramatic; it was the fortunes of war; and Margaret had played her part in it. Henry did not forget that and he deferred to her. She was glad of that. He was a serious young man, her Henry; she was convinced that he would make a good king. Of course he would. He would always be ready to listen to his mother.

Critically she looked now at that other mother. She had never approved of Elizabeth Woodville and had always thought King Edward must have been wanting in judgement when he married her. Of course everyone knew that he had been a lecher. All the more reason to wonder at his actions in marrying the woman. Still, it was all long ago and Edward and his Queen had given the country the present Queen, a charming girl who would do her duty and would not prove too difficult to handle, Margaret was sure. Moreover the girl, with Henry, had united the Houses of Lancaster and York thereby silencing those fierce Yorkists who might want to drive Lancastrian Henry from the throne. It had all worked out as well as could be hoped, thought Margaret.

But Elizabeth Woodville would have to realize that the King's mother was in charge of the King's household, and as the most important part of it at this time was the lying-in chamber, Margaret would be in absolute control.

'It is well,' she said, 'that we came to Winchester early as it is the King's wish that the child should be born here.'

'I should have preferred Windsor,' commented Elizabeth Woodville.

'It is of course the King's wish that must prevail in these matters. Great King Arthur built this castle.'

'Is *said* to have built it,' interrupted Elizabeth.

'King Arthur is an ancestor of the King.'

'Oh my dear Countess, there are so many who claim they have descended from Arthur.'

'That may be but the King has in fact. He always had a great admiration for King Arthur. When he was a boy he was constantly reading of his deeds and those of his knights; and when he knew he was about to become a father he said, ''I wish my son to be born in Arthur's castle.'' That is why the Queen is here.'

'We hope it will be a son. One can never be sure.'

'Your daughter will be fertile, I have no doubt. You yourself have been.'

Elizabeth smiled complacently. She felt superior to the Countess in that respect. For although Margaret might have had three husbands she had produced only one child. True, that child had become King of England, but so had Elizabeth's tragic little Edward the Fifth—if only for a few months before he retired into mysterious obscurity.

'There should be some light in the lying-in chamber,' she said.

'One window has not been fully covered. That will give her all the light she needs,' retorted the Countess.

Elizabeth was irritated. When she considered the number of times she had given birth she would have thought she knew more about it than the King's mother.

'When I think of my little son . . . born in Sanctuary . . .'

'I know, but the King's son will soon be born in Winchester Castle and that is what we must concern ourselves with.'

'My lady, is it not unlucky to talk of the sex of the child with such certainty?'

'I do not think so. I feel sure it is a boy the Queen carries. A little boy . . . who is so impatient to be born that he cannot wait his full time.'

'I trust Elizabeth will be all right. I do not like premature births. I almost wish that it was not premature . . . that . . .'

The Countess regarded her with horror. 'Do you mean that you would have the King forestall his marriage vows . . . You cannot mean . . .'

'Oh no . . . no . . . I am sure he would never do that. But if the baby comes before its time will it not be a little . . . delicate?'

'It is sometimes so, but Elizabeth is a healthy girl. I doubt not that if he should be born weakly we shall soon have him strong.'

'Well, she is young. This will be the forerunner of many it is to be hoped.'

Thus the two women talked while they waited to hear the first cry of the child. Elizabeth Woodville was hiding her apprehension. Her daughter had suffered recently from the ague and she was more worried than she would admit because the birth was premature. If Elizabeth died . . . No, she would not think of that. She had had too much bad luck with her beloved children. Elizabeth would survive. Elizabeth was the hope of the House of York. If she died, and the child with her, would the conflict begin again? The Yorkists would be ready to drive the Lancastrian from the throne. She knew that in some circles Henry was referred to as 'the impostor' and it was only this marriage with the daughter of the House of York which made him acceptable. Once the child was born—and pray God it should be a boy—that alone would seal the pact.

'Elizabeth, my darling daughter,' she prayed, 'live . . . live and give us a healthy boy . . . for the sake of the country, for the sake of us all.'

The Countess of Richmond was less confident than she appeared to be. Premature births were dangerous and it could not possibly be anything else but a premature birth. Elizabeth would never have taken a lover and Henry would never have forestalled his marriage vows. No . . . no . . . the child was coming a month before it was due. It had happened before. The main thing was that it should live and that Elizabeth should go on to give more children to the country. This conflict between York and Lancaster had to end. For thirty years—on and off—those wars had persisted. The strength of King Edward the Fourth had held them at bay but it had been seen how easily they had broken out when he had died. And now . . . Lancaster was in the ascendancy but the Yorkists were content because though the King was a Lancastrian the Queen was of the house of York. An ideal settlement, but it must stay firm. The Queen must remain the Queen and there must be a child.

It had all seemed hopeful until the Queen began to give birth prematurely.

If she died, thought the Countess, and if the child died . . . what then?

She had been watching Cecilia. The girl was comely—all Edward the Fourth's daughters were beauties, with that magnificent golden hair inherited from the mother. It was hardly likely that they could be other than handsome with parents who had been generally proclaimed as the best-looking man and woman in the country.

If Elizabeth died could Henry marry Cecilia . . . ? It would be tricky but it had always been the Countess's custom to be prepared for all eventualities.

Meanwhile the Queen was waiting the birth of the child. The pains were intermittent now. She felt very ill and wondered if she were going to die. She had been unprepared when the evidence of the child's imminent arrival became apparent and she was very alarmed. It could not be yet. It was not due for another month. They had brought her to this darkened chamber and she longed for more light but it was against royal etiquette, her mother-in-law had said—and it was the Countess who made the rules in this household.

The King deferred to the Countess and Elizabeth must defer to the King. She was not sure whether she loved her husband. He was not what she had imagined him to be. When the marriage had been suggested she had thought of him as a hero of romance. He was coming to protect her from her Uncle Richard—not that she had ever been greatly in fear of her uncle. She remembered his visiting her father when he was alive and what affection there had been between the two of them, though Uncle Richard had been quite different from her big, jovial, exuberant father. Quiet, retiring, speaking very little, being intensely serious—that was Uncle Richard. Yet Anne Neville had loved him; and Anne had been a good friend to her.

The truth was that she was in awe of her husband. He had shown her affection and stressed that he was delighted with his marriage but there was something she did not understand about him, something withdrawn . . . aloof. Behind those eyes were secrets she would never discover. Perhaps, she thought, it was better that she did not.

She was over anxious that she should produce a healthy boy because that was her duty. It seemed, looking back on her life, that it was what she had been born for. All her life she had been buffeted, it seemed, from this one to that. . . First one marriage was important . . . then another. At one time she had been offered to the son of Margaret of Anjou. That came to nothing because he was affianced to Anne Neville when Anne's father, the Kingmaker Earl of Warwick, turned his coat and went over to Margaret of Anjou, deserting his old friend and ally Elizabeth's father. Later she was destined for the Dauphin of France. What a grand opinion she had had of herself then. So had her mother, who had insisted that she be called Madame La Dauphine throughout the Court.

Then of course the King of France had decided to give his son to another bride and that, it was said, so shattered Edward the Fourth that it was one of the causes of his death. And eventually here she was. . . Queen of England.

At least that side of her life was settled. She would like to live quietly now . . . at peace . . . with many children to occupy her days. That was what she wanted and for once it coincided with most other people's wishes for her, so perhaps there was a chance of its coming to pass.

Perhaps she was wrong to be afraid of her cold-eyed husband. Perhaps she felt so because having lived close to a father like Edward the Fourth, she had expected to have a husband like him—full of good humour, full of laughter, handsome, dressed extravagantly, charming everyone with his smiles and well-chosen words. She remembered an occasion when the Lord of Grauthuse visited the Court and her father wished to do honour to him. There had been a great many entertainments and at one of the balls her father had led her out onto the floor and danced with her. She must have looked tiny beside his great bulk but how exalted she had felt—particularly when the dance was over and he had lifted her up before them all and kissed her. That must have been one of the happiest moments in her life. She remembered her mother, so beautiful that she seemed like a being from another world, looking on at the scene and smiling benignly—oh yes indeed, the happiest little girl in all the Court . . . in all the world perhaps. But one quickly learned that happiness was a fleeting moment . . . here . . . and gone . . . but it did leave something behind . . . a memory to bring out now and then and glory in.

Now, lying in her bed in this darkened room with so many people about her, listening to the whispering voices, waiting for the next bout of pain, events from the past would keep coming into her mind.

She was thinking of her young brother Edward's birth which

had taken place on a dark November day in the Sanctuary at Westminster where she with her mother and her sisters were sheltering from their enemies. She would never forget the exultation when it was learned that the new baby was a boy. Her mother had said: 'This is the best news the King could have. Now he will regain his throne.' She remembered the little boy's baptism in that grim place. There was no royal ceremony then, and yet that little boy was the King's son, the heir to the throne.

Little Edward, she thought. Where are you now? Where is my brother Richard? Little Edward, true King of England, what happened to you?

One must not think of the boys, her mother had said. They must have died . . . It is the only explanation.

Of course it was the only explanation, for if they lived and were not illegitimate as her Uncle Richard had proclaimed them to be, then Henry had no right to the throne and she was not the true Queen. And he must declare them legitimate for how could the King of England marry a bastard, for she must be one if her brothers were.

One certainly must not think of such things, particularly when one was about to bring a child into the world.

But the thoughts would keep intruding . . . terrible thoughts. There had been a rumour when her aunt, Queen Anne, wife of Uncle Richard was near to death that she, Elizabeth, and the King had conspired together to poison her. It was monstrous. It was absurd. Her Uncle Richard had never shown anything but devotion towards his wife and never never had she, Elizabeth, considered marriage to him. Her own uncle! It was criminal. And all for the sake of being Queen of England!

He must have felt the same horror for when the Queen died he sent her away from Court, and she had been more or less a prisoner at his castle of Sheriff Hutton in the North because he knew that there had been a secret betrothal to Henry Tudor.

That was her life—buffeted from one situation to another. Never was she consulted as to her wishes. They would do with her as best suited them. Received at Court one day, petted and pampered; and the next, banished to exile in what was more or less a prison.

At Sheriff Hutton she had been very much in the company of her cousin Edward, Earl of Warwick, who was the son of the Duke of Clarence—that brother of her father's who had died in the Tower of London by drowning in a butt of malmsey. Poor Edward, his lot had been very sad. He had been only three years old when his father had died; his mother was already dead and poor little orphan that he was he was happy for a while in the care of his aunt Anne, then Duchess of Gloucester soon to be Queen of England. There had been a time, after the death of King Richard's son, when Richard had thought to make young Edward his heir but the boy had continued at Sheriff Hutton, so that when Elizabeth had come there, she had found him already installed and a friendship grew up between them.

There they had been together at the time of the fateful battle of Bosworth which was to change the lives of so many, among them the two who were virtually prisoners at Sheriff Hutton.

Elizabeth had come to Court to marry the new King; and the young Earl of Warwick for no other reason than he was a threat to the new King's position was brought to London and lodged in the Tower.

Elizabeth was concerned for him; she would have liked to visit him, to ask her husband—or her husband's mother—for what reason her young cousin Edward was confined in the Tower. What had he done—apart from being the son of the Duke of Clarence who might be said to have claim to the throne?

When she had broached the subject with Henry, that cold veiled look which she was beginning to know so well had come into his eyes.

'He is best there,' he had said with a note of finality in his voice.

As the Countess of Richmond had said: 'The King will know how best to act.'

But it is wrong . . . wrong . . . she thought . . . to imprison him just because . . .

She tried not to think beyond that but the thoughts would persist: 'Just because he has a greater claim to the throne than Henry Tudor. . . After the sons of Edward the Fourth there is the son of his brother George Duke of Clarence. . . But where are the sons of Edward the Fourth? Where are my little brothers Edward and Richard?'

It was amazing how her thoughts came back and back to that question.

But the pains were starting again, and there was nothing else she could think of.

The King was out hunting when he heard the disturbing news that the child was on the point of being born. He was alarmed. It was too soon. Not only must this child be a boy, he must *live*. He was sure that if this could come about he would be secure upon the throne.

It meant everything to him. He believed he had all the gifts necessary to kingship. He believed he knew what England needed to make her a great country and he could bring this about. He hated war which he was sure brought little profit to any concerned in it. He had seen what the Hundred Years War and the Wars of the Roses had done to England. He wanted peace. He wanted trade. Edward the Fourth had seen the virtue of that and it was obvious that the country has prospered under him. He wanted to encourage the arts for he felt they enriched a nation; he wanted to accumulate wealth, for if the coffers of the exchequer were fuller a country lost its vulnerability and the money could be used to encourage commerce and exploration which would result in new markets; he could enrich the country through architecture and learning; the taxes enforced on the people should be used for its prosperity, not squandered on useless wars and other futile extravagances.

He knew what the country wanted and he knew he could give it. He knew too that he had reached the throne through good luck. The battle of Bosworth might so easily have gone the other way and probably would have done so but for the defection of his father-in-law's brother, Sir William Stanley. Then he had his mother to thank for so much. She should always be near him . . . cherished, revered. Well, here he was and here he intended to stay; but he must never forget that his position could not be firm, coming down through bastardy as it did. Many would say that his grandfather Owen Tudor had never been married to Katherine of Valois and therefore their children were bastards—part royal bastards though they might be. Then even his mother, daughter of John Beaufort, first Earl of Somerset, and his sole heir, descended from John of Gaunt, could not be completely free from the taint of bastardy. He would have been the first to admit that his claim to the throne was a very flimsy one, which was the reason why he must be very careful and ever watchful that those who might be said to have a greater claim were in no position to rise against him.

He was uneasy about Edward, Earl of Warwick, but he was safely in the Tower and there he must remain. It was fortunate that the only legitimate son of Richard the Third had died. The Yorkists would say that Elizabeth of York was the heiress to the throne. Well, she was his wife. That had been the only possible marriage for him and he had to thank his good fortune that he had been able to bring it about. Elizabeth not only had a claim to the throne but she was also a good wife. His mother had said: 'She will bring you great joy and little trouble.'

That was what he needed. So he had his gentle Elizabeth, the *legitimate* daughter of Edward the Fourth, who had already shown that she could be fertile.

There was the core of his anxieties. If she were legitimate then so were her brothers.

He did not want to think of those boys who had been lodged in the Tower. He kept telling himself that he need not worry any more about them. Richard had been a fool to remove them from the public eye after those rumours of their death. He had made one or two mistakes in his lifetime—the thoughtful Richard. Trusting the Stanleys was one—that had cost him his crown; and removing the Princes into obscurity had lost him his reputation.

'I am not by nature a cruel man,' mused the King. 'I am not a natural murderer. But sometimes what would seem to be evil deeds are necessary for the good of many. Then surely they cease to be evil. And what are the lives of two little boys compared with the prosperity, well-being and lives maybe of an entire kingdom?'

He must put unpleasant thoughts behind him. That would be easy enough if it were not for the constant fear that ghosts could arise from the past to confront a man when he least expected them; and if that man were a king, the results could be disastrous. But it was folly to see trouble where it had not yet raised its head. Time enough for that when the moment of danger arose.

There was one big threat to the throne and that could come through Clarence's son. Henry's enemies might decide to strike at him and use the boy as a figurehead. There would always be those to remember that Henry was a Lancastrian and the Earl of Warwick a Yorkist heir to the throne—providing the young sons of Edward the Fourth were truly no more. But unless it was absolutely necessary the boy must not die yet. There must not be too many deaths.

These were uneasy thoughts, but a king's thoughts were often uneasy, and he had always been prepared for that. Life had never been smooth. How many times had he believed his to be at an end? And how grateful he should be now that he had a chance to reach his destiny!

His good friend John Morton, Bishop of Ely, had assured him that God had chosen him. Morton should have the Archbishopric of Canterbury. He deserved it and Henry was going to bestow it on him next month. He owed his life to Morton and that was something he would never forget. He promised himself that he would be ruthless towards his enemies, but every man who had shown friendship to him should have his gratitude.

His Uncle Jasper and Morton were the best friends he had ever had—not counting his mother, of course, but complete devotion was something which came naturally from a mother . . . perhaps an uncle too. Morton though—without ties of blood—had been his greatest friend.

He did, however, owe a great deal to his uncle Jasper Tudor. Jasper had been true to the Lancastrian cause even when its fortunes were at their very lowest. His mother had told him how very alarmed she was to be left alone with a young baby and she could not imagine what might have befallen them but for his uncle Jasper.

'I remember the day he came to me,' she had told her son. 'He embraced me. He told me that he looked upon you as a sacred charge. The Tudors always stood together and as you had lost your father he was going to do for you all that a father should. I never forgot that. And he did, Henry. He carried out his word. Never forget what you owe to your uncle Jasper.'

No, he would never forget Jasper. As soon as he had come to power he had created him Duke of Bedford and made him a Privy Councillor; he had restored the earldom of Pembroke to him and made him Chief Justice of South Wales. No, he would never forget Jasper.

His education had been supervised by his uncle who had provided him with the best tutors.

'We have a boy here,' Jasper had said, 'who loves learning. It would be a sin not to let him have the best.'

His mother had fully agreed with these sentiments, so he had become immersed in his lessons, particularly stories about the Kings Arthur and Cadwallader whom he claimed as his ancestors. He had quickly become aware of the uncertainty of life, for his uncle Jasper was constantly engaged in battles as the war raged, with the Lancastrians victorious one day and the Yorkists the next. After one heavy defeat, when Henry was only five years old, Jasper had been obliged to fly to Scotland; the boy had been taken from Pembroke Castle to the fortress of Harlech where he had remained in Lancastrian hands until he was nine years old.

That had been a terrifying time. Henry hated war. He would do so all his life. He was not going to be one of those warrior kings like Henry the Fifth and the First and Third Edwards who, it seemed to him, sought to make war when it was not necessary to do so and when it would have been so much better for them and their countries to have lived in peace. He could not say the same of his family's arch enemy, Edward the Fourth, for he had fought only when war was forced upon him, when he had to make it or risk losing his crown. Henry could understand that a crown was something well worth fighting for.

When he was nine years old William Herbert had come and taken the castle of Harlech for the Yorkists—and young Henry with it. Then Henry had a new guardian and he was amazed that he could quickly grow fond of the Herberts, particularly Lady Herbert who treated him as he had never been treated before—as a child. Oddly enough he enjoyed that. She scolded him and looked to his comforts and was as affectionate towards him as though he were her own son. Lord Herbert had been given the title of Earl of Pembroke for this had been taken away from Jasper. Henry and young Maud Herbert did their lessons together, rode together, quarrelled together and in truth found each other's company very agreeable. Lady Herbert, watching, thought that one day they might enter into an even closer relationship. Then there had been a new development in the war. Fortunes had been reversed. The newly created Earl of Pembroke was killed in battle, the Lancastrians were restored to power, Edward the Fourth fled the country, and Uncle Jasper returned.

That had been a very important time in young Henry's life because he was taken to London and there presented to King Henry the Sixth, his father's half-brother, who welcomed him warmly, complimenting him on his handsome looks and musing in his somewhat absentminded way that it might well be that in time a crown would grace that head.

That was when young Henry first began thinking of the possibility of becoming a king. He had noticed the deference bestowed on the King; he was delighted to hear that he was related to him; he went back to Wales and read more and more of Arthur and Cadwallader. He was one of them. He could one day be a king.

Uncle Jasper had been full of high hopes at that time. The King was gracious to his Tudor kinsmen. It was clear that he had been impressed—as far as his addled mind could let him be—and had been struck by the looks and learning of young Henry.

'If he stays secure on the throne,' said Jasper, 'there will be a high place for you at Court, my boy.'

But poor mad Henry did not stay secure on the throne and it was not long before the mighty Edward returned to claim the crown and hold it with such firmness of purpose which, combined with the will of the people who had always loved him, showed quite clearly that York would be triumphant as long as the magnificent Edward was there to make it so.

Edward was shrewd. He did not like the thought of that boy being nurtured in Wales.

'It is clear that we are unsafe here,' said Uncle Jasper.

So they had left intending to go to France but a strong wind had blown them onto the coast of Brittany where they were cordially received by the Duke, Francis the Second.

It became obvious that it had been a wise action when Edward asked the Duke of Brittany to deliver young Henry Tudor to him. 'I do not intend to make him a prisoner,' Edward had declared. 'I would like to arrange a match for him with one of my daughters.'

Jasper had laughed aloud at that and decided they would stay in Brittany until what he called a more healthy climate prevailed in England.

Henry had often thought that one of the saddest things that could happen to a man or woman was to be an exile from his or her own country. Pray God it never happened to him again.

He would not be here this day if it were not for John Morton. What a good friend he had been—one who was ready to work for a cause and place his life in jeopardy! He had come through some difficult times, had John Morton. In spite of his Lancastrian leanings he had managed to win the confidence of Edward the King. What fools some men—even great men—were. Both Edward and Richard, whom he was ready to concede were wise in many ways, had been fools. They never seemed to doubt the loyalty of those about them; it appeared to be good enough for a man to profess friendship, for these Kings to accept his word. King Henry the Seventh would never be caught like that. He would trust no one who had not proved his worth—even then not too deeply. His mother he would trust with his life; and Morton, yes, but not even him completely. He would always remember Richard's trust in Stanley. How could he have been such a fool! That act of folly had lost him his crown—or contributed to it.

So Edward had trusted Morton and made him an executor of his will, and as Bishop of Ely Morton had been in a strong position when Edward died. Yet Richard had suspected him. Had he not been arrested at that famous council meeting in the Tower when Hastings had lost his head? But what had Richard done? Put the Bishop in the care of Buckingham. How could Richard have trusted Buckingham as long as he did!

The more he looked back to the past the more he saw that a king must be wary; he must be suspicious of all and he must not weaken in his vigil and his purpose and those who stood between him and the throne must in due course be eliminated. Not only for the sake of Henry Tudor but for the peace and prosperity of the land.

Be watchful then even of good friends like Morton who had once saved his life. He would never forget it; he would reward Morton; but he would be watchful of all men.

Yes, even Morton, though it was he who had sent warning to him when Richard was planning to capture him in Brittany, and so enabled him to escape to France in time. He owed his life to Morton. From Buckingham's care Morton had escaped to Ely and from there to Flanders where he had joined Henry with plans for the landing, for the conquest which should give Henry the Kingdom.

And now here he was . . . married to Elizabeth, heiress of York, awaiting the birth of his son.

Who knew, at this moment the child might have arrived.

He spurred his horse and rode with all speed to Winchester.

The Queen lay back exhausted and triumphant. It was over. She had heard the cry of her child, and the Countess of Richmond was at her bedside holding the infant.

'A boy!' she cried. 'Healthy enough . . . though small, as to be expected coming a month too soon.'

'A boy,' said the Queen, holding out her arms.

'Just for a few moments, my dear,' said the Countess. 'You must not tire yourself. We are going to get you well as soon as we can. That would be the King's command.'

'Where is the King?'

'He will be here soon. I long to see his face when he hears we have our boy.'

The Queen could see her mother standing there and she smiled at her.

'Dearest lady,' she said.

The Queen Mother was on her knees at the bedside. 'We have our boy, my dearest,' she said. 'A darling little boy. We must call him Edward after your father. And let us pray that he shall be such another as his grandfather.'

The Queen nodded and looked down at the child. But her mother-in-law was already taking him away.

'The Queen should have the baby for a while,' said Elizabeth Woodville. 'He will be such a comfort to her.'

'The Queen is comforted indeed by the knowledge that she has a son. She is exhausted now and it is best for her to sleep.'

The Countess signed to the nurse. 'Take the child now.' As the nurse did so she said, 'I hear sounds of arrival. The King is here.'

She hurried out of the chamber and went to greet him. She wanted to be the first to tell him.

There he was, eager and apprehensive. She bowed. She never forgot the homage due to the King. Elizabeth Woodvile had said that at every possible moment she reminded herself and everyone that he was the King and was warning all not to forget it.

He was looking at her expectantly.

'All is well,' she said. 'We have our child . . .' She could not resist holding back the vital information, perhaps because she felt that a few moments of anxiety would make the news more joyful.

'Healthy,' she said, 'strong, perfect in every way,' still prolonging the suspense. Then she let it out. 'A boy. My son, we have our boy.'

He was overcome with joy and relief.

'And all is well with him?'

'He is small . . . being a child of eight months. But we shall soon remedy that.'

'A boy,' he said. 'We shall call him Arthur.'

'A fitting name. The Queen's mother has already suggested Edward.'

The King shook his head. Edward? Never Edward. To remind everyone of that great handsome king whom they loved even more now that he was dead than they had when he was alive, although they had been fond of him even then! Edward, to remind them of that little Prince who had disappeared in the Tower!!

Never.

'I must see the boy,' he said.

'Come.'

She led him up to the lying-in chamber. To her annoyance the Queen had the baby in her arms. The Woodville woman must have countermanded her orders as soon as she went down to greet the King. She would have to do something about that but this was not the moment.

The King went to the bed and looked with wonder at the child.

The Queen was smiling at him. He smiled at her.

'I am happy,' he said.

'It is wonderful,' answered the Queen quietly. 'I dared not hope for so much joy.'

'We have our boy . . . our first boy. Now you must recover quickly.'

It was almost as though he were saying, We should have another soon, so don't waste time recovering.

His eyes were cold. She, who had grown up in a warmly loving family where displays of affection were commonplace, was repelled by her husband's coldness. Even at such a time he was in complete control of his emotions. He was delighted that she had come safely through and they had a son, but was that because it would have been extremely awkward if she had died; and of course a son and a living Yorkist wife were what he needed to make his position very secure.

She said: 'Is he not beautiful? He has a look of my father.'

The King shook his head. How could that red-faced wrinkled creature look in the least like the magnificent Edward.

'We should call him Edward,' said Elizabeth Woodville. 'It is a good name for the son of a king.'

'No, he is to be Arthur,' replied Henry.'He is born in Arthur's Castle. I am descended from Arthur. That is what my son shall be called. Arthur.'

'That,' said the Countess, 'is just what I thought. Come, little Arthur. Your mother must rest.'

With a triumphant look at the Dowager Queen the Countess took the child from his mother's arms and handed him to the nurse.

It was all very satisfactory. They had their son. The country would rejoice and Elizabeth Woodville and her daughter had learned yet again that they must obey the wishes and commands of the King and his mother.

THE BAKER'S BOY

Making his way through the streets of Oxford Richard Simon had often paused by the baker's shop to watch the graceful young boy helping his father there. Richard Simon, humble priest, disgruntled, inwardly complaining with much bitterness of the ill luck which had been his, often wondered what he could do to better his position. In the beginning he had had grand dreams. So many priests rose to greatness. One needed influence of course; that, or some great stroke of good fortune, and if only he could find it there was no end to what could happen to him. Bishoprics might come within his grasp and once he had got onto the first rung of the ladder to fame he would rise, he knew it.

He had ingenuity and imagination; he had courage . . . everything a man needed to rise; but as the years passed and he could not take that first step he was becoming more bitter and disillusioned every day.

In fact he was getting desperate. If good fortune would not come to him, he must go out to find it. There he was—personable and clever. He often thought he would have made a good Archbishop of Canterbury. There were some people who had the looks of distinction even though they were set in humble circumstances.

Take the young boy in the baker's shop for instance. He moved with a natural dignity. He fascinated Richard Simon. How did a boy like that come to be working in a baker's shop? That boy would have looked quite at home in the house of a nobleman.

He called in at the dwelling of a fellow priest and they sat together over a flagon of wine in a room which was darkened because the only light that came in came through the leaded windows. His own house might have been a replica of this one. It was a roof, a shelter, little more.

They talked of the country's affairs, of the new King, of the marriage of York and Lancaster, of the newly born Prince.

'It looks as if fortune is smiling on King Henry,' said Richard Simon's companion.

'Some are lucky. Look how he came to England. He defeated King Richard. Then he married King Edward's daughter and within eight months—eight, mark you—he has a child and that child a boy. Does that look like fortune smiling on him? Why, Providence even cut short the time of waiting and made his son in eight months instead of the customary nine.'

Richard Simon's lips curled with bitterness. There was nothing he would like better than to see the luck of Henry the Seventh change drastically. He would like to see him brought low . . . lose everything he had gained. Not that he cared which king was on the throne. He just hated the successful because he was a failure.

His companion admitted that it certainly seemed as though God were smiling on King Henry. 'He is a man to wipe away all obstacles,' he said.

Richard Simon's eyes narrowed: 'Like King Richard . . . the little Princes . . .'

'King Richard was slain in fair combat and it was Richard who disposed of the Princes in the Tower. They were killed long ago.'

'It was rumour. Why should Richard kill them? They were no threat to him. And if they were bastards as Richard would have it, does that not make the Queen herself one since she came out of the same stable.'

'You talk rashly, Richard my friend.'

'I speak as I find. I wonder what happened to those boys . . .'

'There is a tale going round that they escaped from the Tower and are living somewhere . . . in obscurity.'

'Yes . . . I had heard that . . .' Richard narrowed his eyes. 'It could be true. They must be somewhere . . . I remember that story about King Richard's wife, the Lady Anne Neville . . . Clarence wanted to get rid of her and wasn't she working in a kitchen somewhere? She, a high-bred lady, a kitchen maid. That was a story you'd scarce believe.'

'Yes it was true enough. It was well known at the time so my father told me.'

'So you see, there's no end to what can be done.'

Richard Simon rose and said he had business to attend to. He went back to the baker's shop. The boy was serving a customer. He might be listening to a petitioner, thought Richard Simon. He has all the grace of royalty.

He went into the shop. The baker came out rubbing his hands, smiling at the priest.

He had come for a cob loaf, he said.

'Lambert,' called the baker. 'Get a cob for the gentleman.'

He watched Lambert. How gracefully the boy moved, how delicately he took the loaf and wrapped it. There was a diffidence about him and great dignity.

'Thank you, my boy,' said Richard.

Lambert inclined his head. Where did he learn such manners? Richard wanted to linger, to ask questions. He could scarcely say to the baker, How did you come to sire such a boy as this?

'I hear your bread is of the best,' he said to the baker.

The baker was smiling broadly; he rubbed his hands together: 'You're not the first who has heard that, Father. I've a reputation hereabouts. Have you ever tried my simnel cakes?'

'No, I have not.'

'Then you must. Then you must.' The baker leaned forward smiling broadly. 'I'm so noted for them that they've called me after them.'

'Oh . . . what do you mean?' Listening to the father's chatter he was still watching the boy.

'I'm known as Baker Simnel. That's after my cakes, wouldn't you say?'

'I would indeed. And your boy is a great help to you, I'm sure.'

'Oh he's young yet . . . coming up for eleven. Still he'll be useful when he's a year or so older.'

One couldn't spend the whole afternoon chatting over one cob loaf. Reluctantly Richard Simon left the shop.

He walked thoughtfully to his lodging.

The boy haunted him. What if it were really true that the Princes had not been murdered after all, that they had escaped . . . or perhaps been taken away and hidden somewhere . . . and where would be the best place to hide a Prince? Where it would be least expected to find him. Clarence had made Anne Neville a kitchen maid. She might never have been found but for the determination of King Richard. Just suppose that boy Lambert Simnel was either King Edward the Fifth or the Duke of York. And suppose he, Richard Simon, humble priest, had found him. Suppose he restored him to the throne. The luck of King Henry the Seventh would change then would it not, and so would that of Richard Simon.

It had become an obsession. He went to the baker's shop whenever he could, where he engaged young Lambert in conversation. The boy did not speak like a royal prince—as soon as he opened his mouth it was apparent that he was a baker's son. But speech was something that could be changed. How long could he have been with the baker? Three years? A boy could change a great deal in that time. He was on the point of questioning the baker, but that would have been folly. There was no doubt that the baker would have been paid well to take the boy but he would never admit that he had; moreover, and perhaps this was the real reason for his hesitation, the baker might call him mad and prove without a single doubt that the boy Lambert was his. The dream would be shattered. Richard Simon could not bear the thought of that. He had been happier since wild schemes had been chasing each other round in his head than he had for a long time. Perhaps he only half believed them. It did not matter. They were there; they were balm to his bitterness. He saw himself being graciously received by the King whom he had restored to the throne. Whether it was Edward the Fifth or Richard the Fourth he was not sure. That did not matter. The King was there; the upstart Henry the Seventh was deposed.

'I owe it all to my newly appointed Archbishop of Canterbury,' he heard the new King saying.

'What I did, my lord, was what any of your loyal subjects would have done had God favoured them with the good fortune to see the truth.'

He saw himself riding into Canterbury, the Archbishop who had saved the throne for the rightful king and rid the country of the impostor.

But these were only dreams—pleasant to indulge in for a while but insubstantial. There must be some action some time.

He visited his friend frequently and often he was on the point of telling him of his discovery, but he refrained from doing so. He was afraid of bringing his theories into the light of day because he greatly feared they would immediately evaporate.

Instead he talked of events of the days of great Edward and the accession of Richard.

'The Tudor has a very flimsy claim to the throne,' he insisted.

His friend always looked furtively over his shoulder when he talked like that. He was a timid man. 'It is of little concern to us,' he said. 'What difference does it make to the life of a humble priest what king is on the throne?'

'I like to see justice done,' said Richard piously.

'We all do as long as it doesn't do us any harm. We know it could have worked so differently. As you say, Richard might not have died at Bosworth. He might have lived to have sons. Or there might have been others to come to the throne. There's young Edward of Warwick and his sister Margaret. They are children, I know. But there is John de la Pole, the Earl of Lincoln. They say that Richard made him the heir to the throne . . . in case he didn't get children of his own . . . on account of the Earl of Warwick's being but a boy.'

'The King has young Warwick under lock and key in the Tower, which shows he's afraid of him. What has this young boy done . . . a boy of ten years or so, to deserve imprisonment? Why he's as innocent as . . . as . . .'

A vision of the young Lambert Simnel came into his mind. He must be about the same age as the imprisoned Earl of Warwick.

'I wonder,' he went on, 'why some of them don't rise up and er . . . do something about it.'

'Oh, Henry Tudor is safe on the throne, particularly now he's married Elizabeth of York . . . uniting the houses . . . and as they've got a son . . . young Arthur . . . well, he's safe enough now.'

'But I reckon some people feel angry about it. I reckon there's the Earl of Lincoln for one . . .'

He was excited. He wanted to get away to think. He had to be practical. What hope had a poor unknown priest of bringing about a rebellion? Why hadn't he seen before that he needed help? He was reluctant to share the glory but, on the other hand, shared glory was better than no glory at all.

Suppose he went to the Earl of Lincoln. Would the mighty Earl receive a humble priest? But perhaps he would want to see a priest who believed he had made a great discovery.

And then it seemed to him that he had a sign from Heaven.

It was his friend who imparted the news to him. He had been wondering how he could find the Earl of Lincoln when his fellow priest said: 'Have you heard the latest news? They say that the young Earl of Warwick has escaped from the Tower.'

Richard's heart began to hammer against his side. Escaped from the Tower! When? It could have been some time ago because such news took a long time to get around.

The young Earl of Warwick was aged about ten. He must look rather like the boy in the baker's shop.

Now he must act. This had decided him.

It was not easy to get an audience with the great Earl of Lincoln but when Richard Simon eventually succeeded in doing so what he had to say received the Earl's full attention.

John de la Pole was about twenty-three years old. He deeply resented what he called the usurpation of the Tudor. In his view Richard the Third had been the undoubted King and he believed that the children of Edward the Fourth were illegitimate which made the Earl of Warwick the heir to the throne. Nobody wanted a child king; nothing was worse for the stability of the country; therefore the Earl of Lincoln himself was the one who should be wearing the crown. His mother had been Elizabeth, sister to Edward the Fourth, and therefore he considered his claim indisputable. Richard the Third had thought so too, for he had named him his heir.

'I was struck by the looks of this boy called Lambert Simnel as soon as I perceived him,' said Richard. 'He quite clearly did not begin his life in a baker's shop.'

'But you do not know what the Earl of Warwick looks like.'

'That is true, my lord, and my first thoughts were that here was one of the Princes . . . son of Edward the Fourth.'

'They are illegitimate. They haven't the same claim to the throne as the Earl of Warwick.'

'And now that we hear he has escaped from the Tower . . .'

The Earl nodded.

'Has he the looks of an earl? Has he the manner?'

'He has indeed, my lord.'

'And have you spoken with him?'

Richard hesitated.'His speech is a little rough . . . like that of apprentices in the streets of London.'

'Not like an earl . . . eh, and a royal earl. Of course speech is acquired and if he has been long in the baker's shop, it would be natural for him to adopt that method of speech.'

'So thought I.'

'The people would not accept him unless he appeared perfect in every respect. There would be those who would call him an impostor even though he were proved conclusively to be the Earl of Warwick.'

The Earl of Lincoln was thoughtful. Then he went on: 'There would be many who would support the Earl of Warwick against the Tudor.'

'I know that well, my lord. There are many who murmur against Henry Tudor. One hears whispers in the streets.'

'It is among people in high places that we should look to support this cause. When we have that, the people in the streets may flock to our banners.'

'My lord, I would do everything within my power to see this wrong righted.'

The Earl nodded. 'The Irish have alwas supported the House of York,' he said.'They deplore the coming of the Welshman. My aunt, King Edward's sister, the Duchess of Burgundy, would help us I know. I have a feeling that the Dowager Queen is not very happy even though Henry Tudor has made her daughter Queen. I will leave England and sound out these people. In the meantime it would be well for you first to have an audience with the Queen Dowager, sound her. She could be a very good ally in the very centre of Court itself.'

Richard's heart was bursting with pride. His wildest dreams were becoming realities. He, to have an audience with the Queen Dowager! It was beyond belief. But he would do it. He would bring this about. The Archbishopric of Canterbury was not far off.

'Then,' went on the Earl of Lincoln, 'you must get the boy and bring him to Ireland. There we will make sure that he has forgotten none of those customs and modes of speech which would be becoming in the Earl of Warwick.'

It was very irksome for Elizabeth Woodville to be frustrated at every turn by the Countess of Richmond. She wanted to shout at her: 'I am a Queen. What are you? A Countess! Your husband was the son of a bastard; and you yourself come from the bastard Beauforts. I am a Queen I tell you. I reigned with Edward. He was my devoted husband until the day of his death. My daughter is now Queen of England. How dare you adopt this patronizing manner towards me!'

It had been worse since the baby had been born. It was the Countess of Richmond who gave orders in the nursery. What did she know of the care of children? She had been thirteen when her son was born . . . the only one too, and when Elizabeth considered her own brood—most of them healthy—she wondered how Margaret Beaufort had the impertinence to try to tell her what should be done.

Little Arthur was not exactly robust. How could one expect an eight-month child to be? He needed very special care. He needed a little coddling. But the Countess would have none of that. She wanted him to grow up sturdy and strong, she said. 'And I', had retorted Elizabeth Woodville, 'want him to grow up!'

It was frustrating and the Queen seemed very much in awe of both her husband and her mother-in-law. How things were changed since those days when Edward was alive and she had managed to get her own way, which he was prepared to grant providing she did not interfere with his love affairs. Not that she ever attempted to for she had been secretly glad that there were other women to cater for his insatiable sexuality. They were the good days. How different it would be if the Countess of Richmond were not here! Then she, Elizabeth, could step into her rightful role as grandmother to the heir to the throne. Dear child. She was sure he had a look of Edward. He should have been called Edward of course. Arthur! What a name for a king. He would be constantly compared with the mystic Arthur and that was not going to be of much help to him. Every time anything went wrong the magical name would be recalled. Oh no, Arthur was not going to find life easy with a name like that and it was a great error of judgement to have saddled him with it.

If only they had taken her advice . . .

But they would never do that.

She was in a very disgruntled mood when she heard that a priest was asking for an audience with her. He came on the recommendation of the Earl of Lincoln.

The Earl of Lincoln had been a firm adherent of Richard, and she was not sure how he regarded her. One of the most shocking moments of her life had been when she heard that Richard was declaring her children to be illegitimate. He had revived that absurd story of Eleanor Butler's marriage with Edward and as Eleanor Butler had been alive when he had married her, Elizabeth, that meant *their* marriage was invalid and her children illegitimate.

Nonsense! Nonsense! she had wanted to cry; but it had been accepted as fact and Richard therefore became the King; he had behaved as though her two sons, young Edward and Richard, did not exist as claimants to the throne. He had considered Clarence's son, the young Earl of Warwick, as his heir but because he was only a boy and the country needed a strong man he had named Lincoln.

She could imagine how Lincoln was feeling now . . . ready for revolt against the Tudor, she did not doubt.

Well, that gave them something in common for she felt the same.

Therefore she was ready to receive the priest who was Lincoln's protégé.

Richard Simon was overawed. Elizabeth Woodville could be very regal when she wished; but that she was eager to hear what he had to say was clear.

He came quickly to the point and told her that he had seen a boy whom he had reason to believe was the Earl of Warwick. He was at the moment working in a baker's shop. He had reported his discovery to the Earl of Lincoln who, as she knew, had suggested that the matter be imparted to her. The Earl had left for the Continent. He was going to see the Duchess of Burgundy, so strongly did he feel that this matter should not be brushed aside.

The priest was aware of a terrible fear in that moment. There was a cold glitter in the Queen Dowager's eyes. What a fool he had been to come! True, she was of the House of York, having married the great Yorkist King—but her daughter was now the wife of Henry Tudor. Would she work against her own daughter?

For a few moments he visualized himself seized, dragged away to a dungeon, tortured to reveal things which he did not know. Fool . . . fool that he had been to deliver himself right into the lions' den.

But he was wrong. Elizabeth Woodville had always revelled in intrigue ever since she and her mother had plotted to entrap Edward in Whittlebury Forest. She was furiously angry with the Countess of Richmond who treated her as though she were of no account at all. Her daughter, Queen Elizabeth herself, was treated as though she were merely a puppet by these Tudors.

Of course Henry was an impostor. What of her own little boys? Where were they? Sometimes she dreamed of them at night. They were stretching out their arms to her, calling for her. She kept thinking of the last time she had seen the younger of them, little Richard, who had been taken from her to join his brother in the Tower. "I should never have let him go.' How many times had she said that?

And where were they now? She never mentioned them to their sisters. The Queen never wanted to talk of them. There was that horrible slur of illegitimacy which King Richard had laid on them and which Henry had ignored. And if he ignored it. .. then the true king was little Edward the Fifth. But where was he? And where was his brother?

When she thought of her boys she thought of Henry Tudor and that he had no right to be on the throne. If he had been humble, a little grateful because she had allowed her daughter to marry him, she would have felt differently.

But every day the Countess of Richmond gave some indication that the King and his mother were the rulers while the Queen and her mother did as they were told.

An intolerable situation and if she could make trouble for Henry Tudor—no matter with what consequences—she was ready to do so. Moreover life was dull nowadays; she thought longingly of the intrigues of those days when she was the King's wife and had ruled him in many ways of which he was ignorant.

So now she was ready for a little divertissement. It would be welcome.

'And how did you discover this boy?' she asked.

'Strangely enough, my lady, I went into the baker's shop to buy a cob loaf. I noticed at once his grace, his dignity. It was unmistakeable.'

'Have you spoken to him of these matters? Have you spoken to the baker?'

'My lady, I have spoken only to the Earl of Lincoln. He is convinced that this boy is the Earl of Warwick. He was most anxious that he should have your approval of this matter before proceeding. It is dangerous, he said. I know if we went to the King and laid the matter before him we should be clapped into prison and never heard of again.'

'That is very likely,' said the Queen, and Richard Simon began to breathe more easily.

'So the Earl suggested that we come to you.'

'What help does he expect to receive from me?'

'He wants your approval, my lady. He wants to know whether you would consider it wise to pursue this matter.'

'He asks me?'

'He remembers your judgement . . . when you were able to give it. He remembers how you were of such help to our great King Edward.'

'Ah,' she sighed. 'There was a king. We shall never see his like again.'

'It is true, my lady, but we must needs make the best of what is left to us. The Earl wished to know if you thought it wise for us to take up this boy, to discover more of him. And if he did indeed prove to be the Earl of Warwick, attempt to get him to that place where he belongs.'

The Queen nodded slowly. 'The House of York would be reigning again. The House of Lancaster was never good for this country.'

'My lady.' He had lifted his eyes to her face and they were full of admiration for her beauty, of course. Elizabeth Woodville had been used to such looks all her life—though they came more rarely now. She had never grown tired of them and never would. 'I shall proceed with a good heart. My plan is to take the boy to Ireland.'

'The Irish were always friends of York.'

'So said my lord of Lincoln. He is on his way to Burgundy.'

To Edward's sister Margaret, of course, the forceful Duchess. She had always been a strong adherent of the House of York and had like all the family idolized her magnificent brother Edward. Naturally she would want to see a member of her family, her own nephew on the throne; she hated the usurping Tudor.

'I should be kept informed,' she said.

'We shall see that you are, my lady. And you will be here in the Court. You will be able to keep an eye on what is happening here. The Earl was most anxious that he should have your approval. I think if he did not have it he would want to go no further in this dangerous matter.'

She was delighted. She would keep her eyes open. She would be watchful and any discovery she made would be passed on to the Earl of Lincoln or her sister-in-law of Burgundy.

The priest left her. She felt as though she were alive again. Something was happening and if this were successful she would be the recipient of much gratitude. Land perhaps . . . wealth . . . and above all the opportunity to show the Countess of Richmond that she was not nearly as important as she had believed herself to be and indeed must now be subservient to her arch enemy Elizabeth Woodville.

The next step was to get possession of the boy. Richard Simon strolled along to the baker's shop. Baker Simnel recognized him at once as the priest who came in now and then for his cob loaf.

'There it is, Father,' he said. 'All waiting for you. Don't stand there like a zany, Lambert. Wrap it for his lordship.'

Richard watched Lambert wrap the loaf. Then he turned to the baker.

'I would like to have a word with you. Is there somewhere where we could go in private?'

The baker looked alarmed. He immediately began to search his mind, wondering if he had said or done something which could be brought against him. The priest had seemed very interested in his shop for some time.

'Oh yes . . . yes . . .' he said. 'Come this way. Take charge of the shop, Lambert. And call me if I'm wanted.'

Richard followed him into a dark little room at the back in which were two stools. Richard took one and the baker the other.

'This is good news for you, my friend,' said the priest. 'It concerns your boy.'

'Lambert? Why so, Father? What has he done?'

'He has done nothing for which he can be reproached. He is an unusual boy.'

'He's not so bad, you know. Not as bright as some you might say but he'll improve, I shouldn't wonder. He is getting quite good in the shop.'

'He is amazingly handsome.'

'Oh yes, a good-looking boy. He takes after his mother. 'Tis a pity she went . . .'

'Went?'

The baker raised his eyes. 'She was took to Heaven seven years since. It was when our other boy was born.'

'So you have another son.'

'Bright he is . . . brighter than Lambert . . . He'll be coming along.'

'I'm glad to hear it because I am going to ask you to let me take Lambert into my service.'

'Into your service . . . but for what purpose?'

'He has an air of dignity which is appealing. I think he might be trained for the Church.'

'Trained for the Church? My Lambert? Why he's not . . . well . . . you don't know it, Father, because why should you . . . but Lambert is what we say here, one groat short.'

'You mean he is different from the rest of you. I perceived that.'

The baker tapped his forehead. 'A good boy, mind you . . . but well, shall we say somewhat simple.'

'Nothing that a little learning wouldn't put right, I'd say. In any case, if you are willing I will take the boy into my household and have him taught. I am traveling to Ireland very soon and should like the boy to be one of my party. There will be little duties for him to perform but if he shows the slightest aptitude he could go far.'

The baker was bewildered. If the man had been any but a priest he would have been highly suspicious. Of course it had been known for some young apprentice to catch the eye of a nobleman and be taken into his service. Why shouldn't this happen to Lambert?

'Send for the boy,' said the priest.

The baker hesitated.

'On second thoughts,' went on Richard, 'let us discuss this matter first. Let us work out a plan. Then it can be presented to the boy and if he agrees we will go ahead.'

'Lambert will do as I say.'

'So much the better for I see that you are a wise man. You will know what is best for the boy and let me remind you this is an opportunity such as will never come his way or yours again for as long as you live. I promise this boy a good future if he is ready to learn.'

'I think if he had opportunities to learn, he would.'

'That is well. He would have a good future. He could become affluent, a comfort to his father in his old age.'

'Tell me more of this.'

'I should like to take him on trial. He will come away with me and soon we will sail for Ireland. He will be taught to read and write and speak like a gentleman. Then he will be ready to study for his profession.'

'You choose Lambert for this? Lambert who is a little . . . simple, you must understand. My other boy . . .'

'No, it is Lambert or no one.'

'I admit the boy has a way with him. I sometimes wonder how I and his mother got him . . .' The baker laughed sheepishly. 'Though she was a good-looking woman, I will say that for her . . .'

'Well, what is the answer?'

'Lambert shall come with you.'

'Good. I will call for him this day . . . when the shop closes. Say nothing of this to anyone. There are such rumours nowadays.'

The baker swore secrecy and later that day Lambert Simnel left his father's house in the company of Richard Simon.

Richard Simon quickly realized that he could not have chosen a better subject for his purpose. He had not been mistaken in Lambert. He had a natural dignity, a graceful deportment and dressed in appropriate clothes could indeed pass for a boy of high degree. Richard Simon had immediately tackled his speech, which was halting and carried the accent of the streets.

He was sure that could be remedied. It was true that Lambert was simple, but that in itself proved an advantage. He did not question very much. Simon was amazed at the calm way he accepted his transition from his father's household to that of the priest. It was as though he thought it was the most natural thing in the world for bakers' sons to be whisked away from their natural environment to become someone else.

He had a natural gift for mimicry and in a matter of days his speech had improved. The Earl of Lincoln had supplied Richard Simon with funds and Lambert was fitted out in a velvet coat which reached almost to his heels and which had elaborate hanging sleeves slashed to show an elegant white shirt beneath it; he had grey hose and pointed shoes and a little hat with a feather. He was delighted with his appearance and moved and walked with even greater grace so pleased was he.

Richard Simon devoted the first few days in teaching him to speak. That was the most important. He must also learn to read a little and write a little. Not much would be demanded in that respect but of course he must have some ability in these arts.

When a few days had passed, Simon was delighted with his

results and the more he was with the boy the more pleased he was by his simplicity.

It would have been impossible to impress on a normal boy that he was something other than he actually was. It was different with Lambert. That which his father called simple meant that his mind was pliable.

Simon realized this as soon as he tested him.

'You were not born in a baker's shop,' he told the boy.

Lambert opened his eyes very wide.

'No. You were born in a noble palace . . . in a castle . . . and your father was not the humble baker. He was a great duke.'

Lambert still continued to stare. Oh yes, it would not be difficult to mould him.

'The great Duke of Clarence. When you were three years old your father died. He was drowned in a butt of malmsey when he was a prisoner in the Tower.'

'The Tower.' He knew the Tower. Like other inhabitants of the capital he saw its grey walls often. It was regarded with a mixture of awe, apprehension and pride. It was one of the landmarks of London. He knew that terrible things happened there. Far away in the maze of his mind he remembered hearing something about a duke who had been drowned in a butt of malmsey.

'Yes, your father was the Duke of Clarence. Your mother was the Lady Isabel. She was the daughter of the Earl of Warwick who was known as the Kingmaker. Your mother died before your father . . . So you see you soon became an orphan.'

He was still wide-eyed, taking it all in, not questioning what the priest told him. Priests often told of strange happenings . . . the resurrection . . . the Holy Ghost visiting the disciples . . . things such as that, and compared with them the fact that he was in truth the Earl of Warwick did not seem so strange. He had his velvet coat; he wore pointed shoes. They showed that he was different.

'The man who now sits on the throne is a usurper. That means he took what did not belong to him and when that is a throne all good and true men want to take from him that which he has stolen and put it back where it belongs.'

The boy nodded.

'My dear little lord, the crown belongs on your head, not that of the wicked Tudor who now wears it. Do you understand?'

The boy nodded vaguely. 'Well,' went on Simon, 'there is no need to . . . yet. There is much to be done. We are ready now to sail for Ireland. You must work at your words. You must throw off the accent you acquired while working in the baker's shop, where the wicked Tudor put you.'

Lambert could not remember the wicked Tudor putting him in his father's shop. He thought he had always been there, but if the priest said he hadn't then he supposed it was right. Priests always spoke the truth. A boy had to listen to them and obey them, otherwise he would not go to Heaven.

So before they reached Ireland Lambert was speaking with a dignity which matched his deportment and he already believed that he had been a prisoner in the Tower of London and had been taken out by the wicked Tudor and placed in a baker's shop.

So smoothly was everything working out that Richard Simon was certain that God was on his side. The Archbishopric of Canterbury was coming very near.

The King was disturbed. This was the most ridiculous assertion he had ever heard and yet it made him very uneasy. He had no doubt that he could quickly deal with this trouble but it was a warning to him. He was sure that throughout his life he would be beset by such annoyances.

There would always be those who sought to rebel against him for it was invariably so when one was not the direct heir to the throne. He would be the first to admit that he lacked that personal charm, charisma, aura of royalty, whatever it was which Edward the Fourth had had in abundance. Henry the Fifth, Edward the First and Edward the Third had had it. Was it something to do with making war? It might well be. It was more than that. It was the power to make men follow. But whatever it was, he lacked it.

He prided himself on facing facts. He knew that he would be a good king . . . if the country would let him. And after a few years, here was the first rebellion.

It was a foolish assumption. The Duke of Warwick masquerading under the name of Lambert Simnel who was the son of a baker! Ah, not the son of a baker was the rumour. The son of the Duke of Clarence and daughter of the great Earl of Warwick . . . the next in line to the throne.

Nonsense. A boy of eleven or so. Moreover he was in the Tower at this moment . . . a prisoner.

Yet . . . the people who were behind this rebellion alarmed him. There was the Earl of Lincoln whom Richard the Third had named as heir to the throne; there was Margaret of Burgundy, a formidable woman with vast forces at her command; there was Francis Lovell, a former adherent of Richard the Third. Well, how could they say they had the Earl of Warwick when the real one was in the Tower . . . his prisoner?

But rumour knew how to lie. Even though he proved to them that he had the Earl of Warwick in the Tower, even though he showed the boy to the people, there would still be some to say that this Lambert Simnel was the true Earl and that the boy the King was showing to the world was some creature he had set up in his place.

His mother came to him. She knew of his trouble. She had her ear to the ground, as she said, and she was ever watchful.

'You are uneasy about this Lambert Simnel,' she said. 'It is the most arrant nonsense. You have young Warwick in the Tower. How can they have the effrontery to say he is with them.'

'It's true. I must have the young Warwick paraded through the streets.'

'That will settle the matter once and for all.'

'Nay, my dear lady, not so. There was a rumour some time ago that young Warwick had escaped. That will be believed, you will see. It will be said that the boy whom I shall parade through the streets is a substitute. I know it is nonsense . . . but there will be some to believe it. My enemies will make all they can of this.'

'They will not succeed.'

'They must not succeed. Imagine if they did. This baker's son would be set up as the King . . . oh, only a figurehead of course . . . but Lincoln would be there to govern the country . . . and you can imagine Margaret of Burgundy dictating what should be done. Men like Lovell will support them. No, my lady Mother, it is nonsense, I grant you, and I shall overcome it, but in the meantime I like it not.'

'Who does like these disturbances? I hear it is an unknown priest who has started all this—a certain Richard Simon.'

'It is. But I daresay it is taken out of his hands now. They have dared crown this Lambert Simnel in Dublin.'

'That is impossible.'

'Alas, not so. They have support from Margaret of Burgundy and two thousand German troops with them. The Germans are good fighters.'

'And what do they propose to do?'

'You can imagine. They will land here and we shall have to do battle. I thought the Wars of the Roses were at an end.'

'They are at an end. They must be at an end. You and Elizabeth have joined up York and Lancaster. There shall be no more wars.'

'That is my fervent hope. But we must always be wary of troublemakers like this upstart priest.'

'Richard Simon . . . why he came here once!'

'Came here!'

'Why yes, to see the Dowager Queen.'

Mother and son looked at each other intently.

'So Elizabeth Woodville is concerned in this,' muttered Henry. 'The Queen's mother! It seems incredible.'

'I would believe anything of that woman. You have given her so much but she is quite ungrateful. I am sure she tries to manage everything here in the Queen's household and because she cannot, will turn the Queen against you.'

'I have no fear that I shall not be able to influence the Queen.'

'Elizabeth is a good creature, I grant you. I have no complaint of her. She will be a docile wife and she admires you and is of course grateful because of what you have brought her. But I have never liked Elizabeth Woodville, an upstart from the beginning. I should like to see her removed from Court.'

'If she is involved in the slightest way with this affair of the baker's son then she shall most certainly be removed from Court.'

'My son, leave this to me. I shall discover and when I do I shall ask for the privilege of dealing with the woman. You know you can trust me.'

'I never was more certain of anything,' answered the King. 'I leave the matter of the Dowager Queen in your hands.'

The Countess found the Dowager Queen in her apartments surrounded by her women. One of them was reading while the rest of them worked on a piece of tapestry.

The Countess said: 'I wish to speak with the Queen Dowager alone.'

The women immediately arose and, bowing, began to retire.

'Wait,' said Elizabeth in her most imperious manner. 'I feel sure that what the Countess has to say to me can be said before you.'

'I do not think you would relish that, my lady,' said the Countess grimly, and Elizabeth felt a shiver of apprehension. She knew that preparations were going ahead on the Continent, that Lambert Simnel had been crowned in Dublin, that Margaret of Burgundy had decided to support the boy whom she called the son of her beloved brother Clarence, and that Lincoln had succeeded in getting an army of Germans together to fight the Tudor. It was satisfactory progress, but all the same she hoped that Henry had not discovered too much for he might resort to all kinds of drastic conduct if he knew how far this plot had gone against him.

She did not stop the women's leaving and when they had gone she said with a strong resentment in her voice: 'Countess, it is my place to give orders to my servants.'

'I am of the opinion that they might not be your servants much longer.'

'I do not understand. Are you suggesting that you will choose my attendants for me?'

'I am suggesting that you may not be here at Court much longer.'

Elizabeth laughed. 'I am sure my daughter, the Queen, would not wish me to leave her.'

'I think she will when she knows what you have been doing.'

'You had better explain, Countess.'

'On the contrary it is you who should explain. Of what did the priest Richard Simon speak to you when he came on the instructions of the Earl of Lincoln to visit you?'

Elizabeth turned pale. So they knew. It was inevitable. The King would have his spies everywhere. Did it matter? He would soon know when the troops landed.

Elizabeth decided to be brazen. She was the mother of the Queen, so they would not dare harm her.

The Countess was saying: 'It is no use denying that Simon came here. He is now in Ireland with that foolish baker's boy whom they have had the temerity to crown in Dublin.'

'You mean the Earl of Warwick.'

'You know the Earl of Warwick is in the Tower.'

'I know he *was* there, poor child. Put there as my own sons were because of their claim to the throne.'

'You speak treason, Elizabeth Woodville.'

'I speak truth, Margaret Beaufort.'

'The King and I have a way of dealing with traitors.'

'I know you have a way of dealing with those whose claim to the throne is greater than that of fhe Tudor.'

Elizabeth felt reckless now, which was rare with her. But she believed Henry Tudor was no fighter and there were many in the country who resented him; they had accepted him because they wanted an end to the war, but no one could say that his claim to the throne was very strong.

Now was the time to take sides.

'You admit that you are involved in this nonsensical conspiracy?'

'I admit that the priest came here. I admit that I know the Earl of Warwick escaped from the prison in which your son had put him—poor child, little more than a baby and his only fault being that he had a greater claim to the throne than Henry Tudor.'

'You go too far, Elizabeth Woodville.'

'Well, what is it to be? The Tower? Do you think the Queen will allow that? And what do you think the people will say when they hear that the Queen's Mother is sent to prison merely for saying the Tudor has a very shaky claim to the throne? If you imprison people for saying that, you will have the whole country in captivity.'

'Silence,' cried the Countess. 'You are to leave for the nunnery at Bermondsey without delay.'

'A nunnery! I am not ready for that.'

'You will have a choice. It is the nunnery or the Tower. If you go to the nunnery it can be said that you go for your health's sake. The King and I give you this chance.'

'You and the King do not wish the country to know that I believe the boy Lambert to be the true Earl.'

'That matter will soon be settled. Prepare to leave for the nunnery.'

'I will see my daughter first.'

The Countess lifted her shoulders.

'You must be ready to leave before the end of the day.'

When she was alone Elizabeth felt deflated. The victory was theirs, but she was sure it was a temporary one. Power was in their hands now. It was true they could have sent her to the Tower and she was not so popular with the people that they would greatly care what became of her.

To be sent to the Tower, put in a dark cheerless cell—those places of doom in which a prisoner spent long days and nights, to be forgotten and remembered only when he or she was no longer there and none could be sure how that prisoner had died and none cared.

My little boys, where are you? she wondered. Do *your* ghosts roam the Tower by night?

And what of the Earl of Warwick? Had he really escaped? Had he gone the way of the little Princes? Who could say?

The Queen came to her. She looked disturbed. So the Countess had told her what was planned.

She went to her daughter and took her in her arms but the Queen was somewhat aloof. The Dowager Queen had never been demonstrative . . . not like King Edward, and it was not possible to become so just when the moment demanded it. It would be so easily detected as forced.

'They are asking me to leave for Bermondsey,' she said.

'I know. You have been involved in this foolish uprising . . . if that is what it will come to. How could you!'

'How could I? Because that boy in Ireland whom they have crowned has more right to the throne than Henry Tudor.'

'How can you say such foolish things! Henry is my husband. I am the Queen. Our marriage has put an end to the Wars of the Roses. York is honoured in this marriage as much as Lancaster.'

'Is it? You are the King's puppet. You do as he says. I am treated as of no importance. Lancaster is in the ascendant. Where is York now?'

'My son is of the houses of both York and Lancaster. Henry is going to make this country great. He knows how to do that but he must have peace. We want none of these foolish troubles . . . and this is a particularly stupid one. I am surprised that you received that priest. I think that Henry is being very lenient in sending you to Bermondsey.'

Elizabeth's spirits sank. They had taken her daughter from her. They had made her one of them. Perhaps she had been foolish to become involved in this affair. After all would it be so good for her if the young boy was on the throne when her own daughter was Henry's Queen? But Elizabeth was too meek. She was already one of them. She was on their side against her own mother.

Elizabeth Woodville began to realize that she was lucky merely to be banished to Bermondsey.

There were crowds in the streets of London watching a young boy on a white horse. He was some twelve years old, very pale, for he had been a prisoner in the Tower since the King's accession and before that had lived in some restraint at Sheriff Hutton.

He was a little bewildered now and looked about him with a kind of dazed wonder as the people pressed round to look at him. He was on his way to St Paul's Cathedral where he could hear Mass and confess his sins which would not take long for there were few sins a prisoner of twelve years old could commit.

The people studied him intently. Was he the real Earl of Warwick as the King said he was? Or was he a substitute? Who could say? Important and influential people said the true one was in Ireland now. . . coming to England to claim the throne.

Who could know the truth?

The King and the Queen were present and the Earl rode close behind them. Looks of recognition passed between the young boy and the Queen, and they shared memories of Sheriff Hutton where they had both been in restraint before the battle of Bosworth. Both had been buffeted from one position to another and all because of who they were.

The young Earl knew why he was in the Tower. His father had died in the Tower, killed they said on the orders of his own brother the great King Edward, to whom Clarence had been a menace. That was the trouble, they were all menaces if they were in the line of succession to the throne—except Elizabeth. She had other uses. She was a Princess and by marriage had joined the Houses of York and Lancaster.

The boy looked at her pleadingly. She understood. He was saying: I should like to be free again. I should like to go into the country, to ride out, to smell the grass and the trees. Freedom is the most important gift in the world and one which is not appreciated until it is lost.

He was hopeful. Elizabeth was kind and she was the Queen now. She would remember their friendship at Sheriff Hutton. Perhaps she could persuade the King to let him go free. If he could only be released he would promise never to try to gain the throne. He would barter all his claims . . . for freedom.

So he rode through the streets where the heralds proclaimed him—Earl of Warwick, son of Clarence . . . alive and well and lodging at the Tower.

The people had seen him. They should know now that the boy those traitors were threatening to bring to England was an impostor.

At least, thought the young Earl, I have had one day of freedom because of him.

So from St Paul's he went back to his prison in the Tower.

Elizabeth Woodville was at Bermondsey; the young Earl of Warwick was back in the Tower; but this was not an end to the matter. It had gone too far and there were too many powerful people at the centre of it.

The Earl of Lincoln had joined the not inconsiderable army gathered together in Ireland and they were ready to cross the water and make good their claim.

Young Lambert had almost forgotten the days when he had worked in his father's baker's shop. He had been an earl and now he was a king. People bowed to him, spoke to him with respect and all he had to do was smile at them and obey his good friend Richard Simon. He was always a little alarmed when Richard Simon was not there. The Earl of Lincoln and Sir Francis Lovell were very respectful to him but they frightened him. He need not be afraid, Richard had told him; all he had to do was speak as he had been taught to and do exactly as they told him. Then he could keep the beautiful crown which had been put on his head.

He had learned to ride and rode at the head of all the soldiers. The Earl of Lincoln was on one side of him and Sir Francis on the other. He was a little nervous because Richard Simon was some way behind. 'Don't be afraid,' Richard had told him. 'I shall be there.'

So they boarded the ships and crossed to England with all the men in their splendid uniforms and all the beautiful horses. They landed near Furness in Lancashire and then they started to march.

'The people will flock to our banner,' said the Earl of Lincoln. 'They are weary of the Tudor and they know he has no right to the throne.'

But by the time they had reached the town of York it was realized that the people were quite indifferent to their cause. It might be that the Tudor's claim was slight but they had had enough of war. They had thought the royal marriage had put an end to that and now here was some remote member of the House of York trying to start it all up again.

The Earl of Lincoln grew less optimistic, especially when he heard that the King's forces were on the march.

The opposing armies met at Stoke and battle ensued. The Germans fought valiantly and, professional soldiers that they were, came within sight of victory; but the King's forces were too much for even them and gradually they had to face defeat.

The Earl of Lincoln was slain; Lovell managed to escape and Lambert Simnel and the priest Simon, who were not actually involved in the fighting, were surprised together in a tent and taken prisoner.

'It is all over,' said Richard Simon fatalistically. He would never be Archbishop of Canterbury now. He visualized the terrible fate which was customarily meted out to traitors, and for the first time Lambert saw him without hope. The boy was frightened. He did not quite understand what had happened but he did know that something had gone terribly wrong.

They put him on a horse and he rode to London. Richard was on another horse beside him. He supposed now that they would send him back to his father's baker's shop. Now, that former life seemed more real to him than what had happened since the soldiers had come to the tent.

The King had expressed a wish to see the traitor priest and the boy who had dared pose as the Earl of Warwick and they were brought to the palace of Shene on the river's edge where the King was staying at that time. They stood before Henry Tudor—the shivering priest who had been too ambitious and the bewildered boy who even now was not quite sure what this was all about.

Henry looked at them coldly.

'So you, sir priest, thought to replace me with this boy?' said the King.

Richard Simon fell on his knees. He could not speak; he could only babble. The boy watched him in bewilderment. He put out a hand to touch him, to try to comfort him in some way. He was less overawed than the priest by the cold-eyed man who was watching him so closely. That was because he did not know the magnitude of what had happened and his part in it. Perhaps it was because the King did not look as splendid as the Earl of Lincoln had when he had first seen him. Perhaps he had grown accustomed now to seeing important men. But the King was by no means the most impressive of these.

'What have you to say, boy?' asked the King.

Lambert looked at him and did not know what to say. They had always told him what to say. Now there was no one to do so.

'Speak up,' said the King.

The priest spoke then: 'My lord King, it is no fault of the boy. He did as he was told.'

'So thought I,' said the King. 'They took you from your baker's shop, eh boy? They set you up as their puppet. That was it. I knew it. You admit it, eh?'

The boy still looked dazed.

'He is a simpleton,' said the King. 'What folly was this! Lincoln dead. I am sorry. I should have liked to ask him what foolishness could have possessed him to pass off this half-witted creature as the Earl of Warwick. Take them away . . . both of them.'

So they awaited their sentence. The King was smiling which was something he rarely did.

He was not sorry that this had happened. He would show the people how he would keep order. There had been this uprising . . . yes . . . with a disgruntled earl and a boy from a baker's shop. He had quickly suppressed that. He had shown them how he would deal with these impostors.

The ringleaders were dead or in flight and he had only the priest and the half-witted boy to deal with.

It should be a traitor's death for them both. No. They were not important enough for that. He would show mercy to them both. The priest should be imprisoned for life because he had plotted against the King and might well take it into his knave's head to do it again. The boy . . . well he was very young; moreover he was addlepated. How could one punish a boy like that? It was no fault of the poor half-witted creature. He had been plucked out of his father's baker's shop because of his pleasant looks which the King admitted was all he had to recommend him.

He should go into the King's kitchen. That would best suit him.

'Let this Lambert Simnel become one of our scullions,' said the King. 'I doubt not he will soon forget his grand aspirations there.'

So Richard Simon, congratulating himself that he had escaped the barbarous traitor's death, lived on in prison—a contrast to the archbishop's palace of which he had dreamed; as for Lambert he was happy in the King's kitchens. His fellow workers laughed at him but without malice so Lambert laughed with them; and he worked hard and well. He was happier there than he had been sitting on an uncomfortable but very grand chair with a crown on his head.

In the streets they laughed at the story of Lambert Simnel—which, said the King to his mother, was the way he had hoped it would be.

CORONATION

Although People laughed to think of the leader of a rebellion now working as a scullion in the King's own kitchens, Henry himself did not dismiss the matter so lightly. He talked it over with a young man whom he had recently made one of his Privy Councillors and towards whom he had felt especially drawn. This was Edmund Dudley, a lawyer in his twenties who was showing characteristics which were not unlike the King's own.

Henry wanted to gather round him men of his own choosing. No king should inherit statesmen for they would most certainly compare the present master with the previous one and as the departed always gained in stature such comparisons put the living at a disadvantage.

Henry's early life had made him suspicious and cautious and acceding to the throne had not lessened these traits in his character. Edmund Dudley who had studied law at Gray's Inn and had later become Sheriff of Sussex was a man with whom he felt immediately in harmony; also Dudley had an associate, Richard Empson, another lawyer, educated for the Bar, who had already shown himself to be an astute lawyer. These were the kind of sharp minds Henry needed around him; and he had already shown favour to these two.

So now as they walked down to the river's edge in the grounds of his favourite Palace of Shene and they talked of the rising of Lambert Simnel, Dudley commented that it was a sobering thought to contemplate how many Lincoln had been able to rally to his banner.

'And what do you think this indicates?' asked the King.

Intercepting the look which passed between Dudley and Empson, Henry knew that they had discussed the matter together.

'Come, speak up. I shall not be offended by truth.'

'Sire,' said Dudley, 'the people approve of your marriage and the uniting of York and Lancaster, but they are saying that York does not receive its dues.'

'What do they mean by this?'

'That Lancaster is in the ascendancy.'

'It must be so since I am the King.'

Dudley hesitated and Empson nodded to him.

'My lord,' he said, 'you have taken the throne, you have an heir in Prince Arthur, you have been crowned King of England, yet the Queen has not been crowned.'

'Ah,' said the King. 'You think a coronation would please the people?'

'Coronations are ever a source of delight to the people, Sire,' said Empson. 'Free wine in the streets . . . celebrations throughout the country. . . . They love their ceremonies. But we were thinking of the Yorkists who might have reason to complain.'

The King nodded, giving an approving look to his two advisers. He could trust them to come up with a tangible suggestion.

'Perhaps the time has come then for the Queen to have her coronation,' he said. 'Her mother is a source of irritation. I never trusted that woman. People say it was sorcery which enabled her to ensnare the late King.'

'She has outstanding beauty,' commented Dudley. Again he looked at Empson.

'And not too old for marriage I dareswear,' he said.

Henry was alert. 'Could you by any chance be thinking of the King of Scotland?'

'He has just lost his Queen.'

Henry gave one of his rare smiles. 'There is nothing I would like better than to send my mother-in-law over the Border.'

'It would certainly rid us of the unpleasantness of having to keep her under restraint, which is another reason why the Yorkists might be restive,' commented Dudley.

'I shall send an ambassador to Scotland without delay,' said Henry.

'Perhaps we should also inform the Dowager Queen of the intention?'

Henry was silent. 'She is an obstinate lady, I fear.'

'My lord, surely she would consider very favourably changing a prison for a crown.'

' 'Tis scarcely a prison at Bermondsey. I'll swear my lady mother-in-law reminds them every hour of the day of her rank and is treated there with the utmost respect.'

'Nevertheless the match could scarcely be made without her consent.'

Henry agreed and the two matters of importance were decided on. Elizabeth Woodville should be offered to the King of Scotland and the Queen should have her coronation.

*   *   *

It was true that Elizabeth Woodville suffered no harm in Bermondsey. She had her own apartments and her own servants there and apart from the seclusion of the life she might have been in her own palace. It was tiresome of course to be shut away from the world; but no less frustrating than being at Court where she was continually finding the interference of the King's mother so irksome.

When she heard that her daughter was to have a coronation she remarked that it was time she did; then she regretted that she would not be there. It was monstrous. The mother of the Queen and more or less in restraint because of that upstart Tudor!

If only Edward had lived. If only her fair sons were with her! It was at times like this that she thought of them and wondered again what had happened to them in the Tower. She longed to see her little grandson. Dear Arthur. Though what a ridiculous name! It should have been Edward of course. However she was glad it was not Henry.

She longed to see her girls. Not that Elizabeth had much time for her mother nowadays; she had been completely subjugated by those Tudors. It was right of course that a woman should cling to her husband but when that husband showed himself the enemy of the mother who had cared for her through all the difficult years . . . it was cruel and unnatural.

Dear Cecilia had more spirit than Elizabeth. She fancied that Cecilia was very interested in Lord John Wells. She had intercepted glances between them. It had made her a little uneasy at the time for although John Wells was a worthy man, and quite a favourite of the King, he was not a suitable husband for Cecilia. He was twice her age to begin with.

Nothing would come of that. She could dismiss it from her mind. But she did remember a certain defiance in Cecilia which had been lacking in her elder sister.

She often wondered why Henry had not found a husband for Cecilia. At one time she suspected he had planned to test out Elizabeth and if she did not produce the heir . . . or died . . . he would try for Cecilia. She suspected Henry of all sorts of devious scheming. One could be sure there would be some motive behind everything that he did.

One of her servants came to tell her that a nobleman saying he came from the King wished to see her.

Ah, she thought, he has come to tell me that I shall be released for the coronation. He will realize that the people will notice my absence. It is only right and fitting that the mother of the Queen should be present on such an occasion.

The nobleman was brought in. He bowed with all due deference.

'Pray be seated,' she said. 'You come from the King?'

'I do, my lady. He wishes to have your views on a matter of some importance.'

'I am honoured that the King should seek my opinion,' she replied with a hint of sarcasm.

'My lady, it concerns you deeply and it is for this reason. The King of Scotland has been recently bereaved. He is of a mind to remarry. The King thought that if you were of like mind, negotiations could begin to bring about a union.'

'Between myself and the King of Scotland? Why he is half my age!'

'It is always said that you have the looks of a lady half your age.'

She was pleased. She could not help it. She had not thought of marriage for herself. She had never wanted much from men except power. That was why she had made a success of her marriage with Edward. She had never shown any jealousy of his countless mistresses; she had never sought to restrain his activities with them; it was for that reason that he had loved and admired her and she had been able to keep her hold on him. But the King of Scotland! Well, to be a queen again . . . a reigning queen, that was a great consideration. And to exchange this . . . well, retreat, one might say . . . for palaces and castles. It was rather a pleasant idea.

'I can see that the idea is not repulsive to you, my lady.'

'These proposed marriages often come to nothing,' she said. 'My daughter was to have married into Scotland. How strange that the offer should now be made to me.'

'The King feels sure that James of Scotland will be overjoyed at the prospect.'

'We shall see,' said the Queen and graciously inclined her head to indicate that the interview was at an end.

She wanted to be alone to consider the suggestion. She had not really committed herself. She could always abandon the project if she had a mind to. At the moment it added a certain spice to life. Queen of Scotland! She was amused to contemplate the trouble she could bring to the King of England if she were ever in that position.

Elizabeth the Queen came riding into London with her sisters

Cecilia and Anne. They were all excited because Elizabeth was about to be crowned.

'A queen is not a real queen until she is crowned,' said Anne. 'You will be a real queen now, Elizabeth.'

'I wonder why it has been delayed so long,' added Cecilia.

'The King has his reasons,' replied the Queen serenely.

That is the answer her mother-in-law has taught her, thought Cecilia, and it applies every time the King's conduct is questioned. Since her marriage Elizabeth has become a shadow of the King and his mother. I should never allow that to happen to me.

No indeed she would not. She was thinking of John Wells. She knew that he was a good deal older than she was, but she did not care. In his company she felt elated yet at peace; she felt contented and had a great desire to be with him. Was that love? She believed it was. She had explained her feelings to him and he had confirmed this. Moreover he felt the same contentment with her.

She knew that he was the husband she wanted. Her mother had often said that the King would soon be marrying her off and she would not be surprised if Cecilia was soon making some alliance which the King thought would be good for him. I won't be, thought Cecilia. Elizabeth married him. That is enough. Elizabeth doesn't mind being married to him. She is ready to agree that everything he does is right. That is good enough; she has done the family duty towards him. I will marry where I will.

She shuddered to think that she might now be miles away from John Wells. She might be in Scotland for they had once wanted to marry her to little Prince James of Scotland. And now there was rumour that her mother was being offered to that little Prince's father. We are bandied about like a parcel of goods with no thought for our feelings, she thought. We are unimportant. . . Well, some of us are. They will find the Princess Cecilia different.

They were to stay first of all at the Hospital of St. Mary in Bishopsgate from where, the Queen told them, they would watch the King's entry into the capital.

'It will be a triumphant march,' said Anne, 'because the King has defeated the scullion boy. Shall we ever see him, do you think, Elizabeth? I should very much like to see him.'

'It seems hardly likely that you will,' replied the Queen. 'And if you did you would find he looked exactly like every other little scullion.'

'I think he would look a little different,' said Cecilia. 'After all he must have had something about him for them to decide to use him in the first place.'

'Let us not discuss the silly boy,' said the Queen. 'I find it all most distasteful. The King has shown his contempt for him and was it not benevolent of him to let him go free?'

Cecilia was silent. She was thinking: I shall marry John. What will the King say then? Whatever it is, Elizabeth will tell me it is right. I shall not care if we are banished. I am sure John will not either.

'After the coronation,' said Elizabeth, 'I shall be more often in the company of the King.'

'Rendered worthy by the act of crowning,' added Cecilia. 'Yet *you* are the daughter of a King whereas he . . .'

'He is descended from the great kings Arthur and Cadwallader. Do not forget that.'

Dear Elizabeth, thought Cecilia. She is bemused. Not by love of the King I'd swear. By a love of peace. A desire that everything shall go smoothly around her. That is good enough when one has everything one wants. Perhaps I shall be like that when I am married to John.

'I have heard it whispered,' Anne was saying, 'that the House of York is not treated with the same respect as that of Lancaster.'

'You should not listen to whispers,' the Queen told her.

The people of London were growing vociferous in their welcome of Elizabeth. She made a charming picture riding with her two sisters who were as good looking as she was herself, and the cheers were prolonged. The Queen bore a striking resemblance to her dead father. Her long golden hair hung loose about her shoulders in the style which showed it to its best advantage; her oval face was a little on the plump side which with her pink and white complexion gave her a look of glowing health; her forehead was high like her father's; if she was not quite as beautiful as her mother had been she lacked Elizabeth Woodville's arrogance and that gentle, rather self-deprecating, smile appealed to them. There was more warmth in it than her husband could ever show them. The fact was the people were pleased with Elizabeth of York. 'Long live the Queen!' they cried.

They liked her sisters too—beautiful girls both, with the same high foreheads and long flowing golden hair. Their beloved King Edward had indeed passed on his handsome looks to his family. It was to be hoped that the children of this noble lady would take after her family rather than that of the Tudor.

Not that they were against their King. By no means. He appeared to be strong and they knew a strong king was what the country needed. He had settled this unfortunate rebellion of Lambert Simnel and had amused them by making the leader of the insurrection a scullion in his kitchens. In fact the story provoked laughter whenever it was mentioned. They merely liked the rosy handsome looks of York rather than the dour ones of Lancaster. And this was a great occasion. The crowning of their Queen.

Seated at a window of St. Mary's Hospital the Queen, with her two sisters beside her, watched the King's entry into the City. He came as the victor of the battle of Stoke where he had annihilated the rebels, and his triumphant procession through the capital was meant to tell the people that they could hope for peace in his time. He was going to be a strong ruler; he was going to put an end to wars; and although this last little fracas was a contemptible effort to break the peace he had quickly suppressed it. Moreover he had not wanted revenge. He would be a strong but benevolent king; they would realize that when they considered his treatment of Lambert Simnel.

'It is sad that our mother is not here,' murmured Anne. 'I wonder what she is thinking in Bermondsey.'

'That she was foolish to plot against the King, I doubt not,' said Elizabeth.

Cecilia thought: She is no longer like our sister. She has become merely the King's wife. They shall never mould me as they have her. I will do as I please. I *will* marry John.

'The King has taken her estates from her,' she said. 'She will be so sad for they meant a lot to her. And it was only last year that the lordships and manors were granted to her.'

Anne murmured softly: 'Waltham, Magna, Badewe, Mashbury . . .'

'Dunmow, Lighe and Farnham,' finished Cecilia. 'I remember how elated she was when they were granted to her. She kept repeating them over and over again as though to learn them by heart . . . which we did, too.'

'She was very unwise to receive that priest,' said the Queen severely. 'The King reluctantly decided that she must be taught a lesson.'

'I could almost believe,' said Cecilia, 'that it is the Countess of Richmond sitting there and not our sister.'

The Queen shrugged her shoulders impatiently. It was nearly time for the King to arrive and she could hear the tumult in the streets a little way off.

The King came into Bishopsgate and when he reached the

Hospital of St. Mary he paused and looked up at the window at which the Queen sat with her sisters.

He gave Elizabeth one of his rare smiles and she returned it with a look of genuine love which delighted the crowd. He could trust Elizabeth to do what was expected of her.

The crowd roared its approval. Henry acknowledged the cheers and passed on.

He was thinking that Empson and Dudley were right. The coronation of the Queen was what the people wanted. Now they were going to have it. Moreover if he could bring off this marriage of Elizabeth Woodville with the King of Scotland he would have rid himself of that most tiresome woman.

The King conducted the Queen to Greenwich Palace leaving her there while he returned to the Tower of London. In accordance with tradition she must come without him to the capital for the ceremony of crowning and he must be at the Tower of London, waiting to welcome her when she arrived.

She must sail down the river with the most glorious pageantry which could be devised. It would be an expense, Empson had said, and he, no less than the King, deplored expense; but there were occasions when rules of economy must be waived and reasonable sums laid out if the result of spending money was to have the desired effect.

It was a misty November day when the Queen left Greenwich, but no one seemed to care very much about the weather. The people were determined to enjoy themselves and they set about doing so with gusto, for here was their handsome Queen at the centre of one of the colourful pageants which they had grown accustomed to during the reign of that incomparable monarch King Edward the Fourth.

Elizabeth was seated in her barge with her sisters and some of her ladies, there were craft of all description on the river that day; moreover people had massed on the banks to witness the progress of the pageant as it sailed along the Thames. The civic companies all had their barges on the river but what gave especial pleasure to the Queen was the presence of the students of Lincoln's Inn in the Barge of the Bachelors, for they had decided to do honour to the House of Tudor and Elizabeth realized how this would delight the King. He was always gratified by such gestures although he did not show it. But there were those rare occasions when the people seemed really glad to welcome the Tudor; and that was what the Bachelors were doing now for they had erected a red dragon in their barge and on his side was a notice that he was the Red Dragon of Cadwallader. Henry of course prided himself in his descent from Cadwallader so this could only be construed as a special tribute to him. The people thoroughly appreciated the dragon and roared with delight as fire spouted from his mouth and fell into the river. Moreover as the Barge of the Bachelors sailed along close to that of the Queen several students strummed their lutes and others sang songs of Wales.

'The King will see that when we approach the Tower,' said the Queen to Cecilia. 'It will put him in a good humour.'

'He should already be in that,' said Anne. 'He should be pleased because at last it is his Queen's coronation.'

Poor Anne is a little put out because our mother is not here, thought Elizabeth. But she would have been if she had not angered the King by seeing that foolish priest. The Countess is right, she does interfere too much. And it makes us all unhappy because she is more or less in restraint. It will be good for everyone if this Scottish marriage comes about.

But she was a little sad thinking that she might have to say goodbye to her mother. Theirs had always been a close family and it was hard to remember always that she must not allow her mother to guide her when she had the very excellent Countess to do that.

She must not have sad thoughts on her coronation day so she must remember that if her mother was in her present position it was due to her own fault.

Now she could see the grey walls of the Tower. Soon the King would be greeting her. She would rest in the Tower for the night and from there she would go to Westminster and the ceremony of coronation.

Her sisters were with her when she was dressed for the journey from the Tower to Westminster Palace where she would spend the night and from there, on the next day, go to the Abbey.

She looked beautiful and remarkably like her mother had at her age, except that there was a humility about her which Elizabeth Woodville had never possessed even before she rose to a throne.

Already the crowds were gathering in the streets. The people of London were anxious to see more of her. They had grumbled because, although she was the Queen, they believed the King had contrived to keep her away from them. But it seemed that they had misunderstood. She had become pregnant immediately after her marriage and often ladies did not wish to show themselves in that state and this would seem particularly true of such a modest one as the Queen obviously was. It was not so long since little Arthur had been born, and now she was emerging. They would see her often with the King now, and today they would watch the procession to Westminster Palace and the next day the coronation itself.

There she was in her kirtle of white cloth of gold and her mantle of the same material edged with royal ermine; and her beautiful golden hair was caught in a golden caul and about her brow was a simple gold circlet.

She might not have the perfect features of her mother but she had a warmth which that arrogant lady had lacked. Moreover she managed at the same time to have a look of her royal father and that was enough to endear the people to her.

As she left the Tower her train was carried by her sister Cecilia who, some said, was even more beautiful than the Queen; she certainly had the same golden looks and magnificent long flowing hair. Walking beside the Queen was the King's uncle Jasper Tudor whom Henry had made Grand Steward, so eager was he to do him honour; and there was Lord Stanley, husband of the Queen's mother-in-law who had now been created Earl of Derby and whose brother Sir Wiliiam Stanley had played such a decisive part at the battle of Bosworth by changing sides at the crucial moment. A not very noble act, but it had brought about peace and what the people of London wanted more than anything now was peace.

There might be many staunch Lancastrians but York was represented too. The King had not been so foolish as to leave them out; and even the Duchess of Suffolk was there, which was an indication of how merciful the King could be, for it was her son, John de la Pole, Earl of Lincoln, who had sought to set up Lambert Simnel and who had been slain at Stoke.

For the rest of the journey the Queen was to travel by litter and this was brought forward. She sat in it smiling at the people as she passed through the streets under the canopy which was held by the four knights of the Bath whom Henry had recently created.

It was comforting to Elizabeth to see how the people liked her. They had hung out gaily coloured material from their windows; they leaned forward to strew leaves and sweet-smelling herbs in her path; and every now and then the procession was halted while bands of children stepped forward to sing her praises.

It was very gratifying; and tired but exalted, she reached Westminster Palace.

There she could spend a quiet night in preparation for the next day's ordeal.

Cecilia was with her when they dressed her.

'You look very grand,' she said. 'Not like our sister any more.'

'I am the same beneath all these fine robes, Cecilia.'

Not quite, thought Cecilia. You are the King's wife now.

Did Elizabeth still remember those dreary days in Sanctuary at the time when Richard had taken the crown, when they had not known from one day to the next what their fate would be? Had she forgotten how even their father had had to fight to keep his crown . . . and that it was always the Lancastrians against whom he fought? Now she was one of them. Of course that had to be and marriage between the two houses was better than war. But Elizabeth seemed to have changed sides. In fact she could see no point of view but that of the King. Had it something to do with the mystic ritual of the marriage bed?

I shall find out, Cecilia told herself. And she knew then that she was going to marry John . . . in secret of course, for to announce her intentions openly would most certainly mean that they would be frustrated.

How beautiful Elizabeth looked in her kirtle of purple velvet edged with ermine with her magnificent hair loose, flowing from the circlet of gold studded with pearls and stones of several colours which they had placed on her head.

She looks so serene, thought Cecilia, as though coronations were commonplace with her. She has no will of her own, now; only that of her husband and her mother-in-law. They decided what she must do and Elizabeth mildly did it. Perhaps that was a happy state to be in. Elizabeth certainly looked happy. Did she ever think of anything but pleasing her husband, submitting to his embraces in order to do her duty and produce one child after another, for that was how it would be, Cecilia was sure.

They had entered Westminster Hall, there to wait that moment when they would set out for the Abbey. The way from the Hall to the Abbey was carpeted with striped cloth which the people regarded as their own perquisite, for after the Queen had walked on it they were at liberty to cut off pieces which would then be theirs.

So eager were the people to get their pieces of the material that no sooner had the Queen walked over it with her trainbearers than they dashed forward and started to cut the cloth. The ladies who were following were terrified to find themselves surrounded by the rush of people, shouting, abusing each other and even trampling those who had fallen under foot. Fortunately some of the lords, having seen what was happening, rushed forward to rescue the ladies, which they did just in time.

Cecilia, going ahead with the Queen, looked back and to her horror saw what was happening. Elizabeth knew something was wrong but she went serenely on. Nothing must mar this day. The King would expect her to play her part like a queen.

Cecilia was deeply disturbed; she knew she would never forget that brief glimpse of those people who were descending on the cloth like so many wild animals.

Every vestige of the cloth had disappeared in a very short time, but those who had fallen in the affray had to be carried away as unobtrusively as possible while in the Abbey the ceremony continued. The King with his mother was watching from an enclosed box between the altar and the pulpit. He had said that he wished to witness the ceremony but in no way did he want to take attention from the Queen.

So was Elizabeth of York crowned Queen of England and so, said many, were the Houses of York and Lancaster entirely united forever.

The company then returned to Westminster Hall where the banquet was to be held. The King and his mother did not join the Queen at table but, as they had in the Abbey, watched the proceedings from an enclosed box.

That, thought Cecilia, was taking it a little far. Was it implied that the people would be so overawed by his presence that they would forget the Queen? She did not think that likely. In fact it seemed clear that although the King was accepted, the Queen's popularity was greater than his. Perhaps that was why he wished to hide himself.

With the King one could never be sure.

She was certain that she must marry John before the King had knowledge of it, for who knew what devious methods he might employ to prevent it if he knew in advance.

She had persuaded John that if they were to marry they must do so in secret.

'I do not think that I am of such great interest to the King now that my sister has borne him a son,' she insisted.

Lord Wells was deeply enamoured of the young Princess, and somewhat surprised that she should feel the same about him. He was not a young man but Cecilia was a serious-minded girl and she was determined to choose her own husband.

He was in favour with the King for his family had always been ardent supporters of the Lancastrian cause. His father had died with the Lancastrian army at Towton and at that time his estates had been confiscated by Edward. John's elder brother Richard was killed during Warwick's rising leaving John the heir to the estates should they be released. Edward had been notoriously lenient to his enemies and John somehow came into favour during the years of peace. He was present at the coronation of Richard the Third but had never favoured that monarch and had been a firm supporter of Henry for there was a family connection with the Countess of Richmond.

Henry had not forgotten his services when he came to the throne and had given him two castles and several grants of manors; moreover the family estates had been restored to him; he had been given the title of viscount and the King clearly trusted him.

It was for this reason that he believed Henry might not frown too deeply on the marriage once it was accomplished although, as Cecilia said, if his permission were asked it would very likely not be given and then marriage would be quite out of the question.

So Cecilia and he were married secretly and gave themselves up to the joy of being together; but of course the marriage could not remain a secret and Cecilia decided that she would tell her sister and ask her to pass on the news to the King.

Elizabeth was in a very happy mood. The coronation had been a great success; she found the King less formidable than he had seemed at first. He appeared to be growing fond of her. She adored her little Arthur though she saw very little of him; she was less worried about her mother now that a match was proposed for her, and there was an atmosphere of peace and serenity all about her.

Cecilia came to see her. There was a change in her. She seemed as though she were very happy about something, and yet at the same time a little apprehensive.

'I wanted to talk to you . . . as a sister,' she said.

'My dear Cecilia,' replied the Queen, 'am I not always your good sister?'

'You look very happy today.'

'I am. Henry was so pleased with the coronatiion . . . apart from those people who got crushed to death.'

'Imagine risking your life for a piece of cloth!'

'I suppose it meant something more than that to them. Cecilia,

Henry has been so generous to me. He has given me a grant of seven lordships and manors.'

'Seven. Why it was seven he took from our mother.'

'Our mother forfeited the right . . .'

'I know. I know.'

Cecilia looked at her sister intently. 'He has given you Waltham . . . has he?'

Elizabeth nodded.

'Waltham, Magna, Badewe, Mashbury. Dunmow, Lighe and Farnham.'

Cecilia began to laugh. 'He has given you those which he took from our mother.'

'Why should he not? They were available.'

'No reason at all. But it is all so neat. And it keeps them in the family.'

'I think it is very good of the King.'

'To take them from our mother?'

'Our mother was fortunate. She could have been accused of treason. I consider he has been most generous . . . to us both.'

Cecilia thought: Be careful. Don't alienate her. You need her help.

'Elizabeth,' she said. 'I have something to tell you. I want you to do something for me.'

Elizabeth smiled. She really is a sweet-natured and generous creature, thought Cecilia. I should remember that when I criticize her.

'If it is possible . . .' began Cecilia.

'Tell me.'

'I . . . want you to speak to the King on my behalf.'

Little lights of alarm were in the lovely eyes; they were no longer quite so serene.

'Oh sister, what have you done?'

'I have married.'

'Cecilia!'

'Yes, you may well look shocked. I was determined to marry where I wanted to and I have done it.'

'But . . .'

'I know as the Queen's sister . . . sister-in-law to the King . . . I should have had his consent. Well, I did not, Elizabeth.'

'But why . . . ?'

'You may well ask. For the simple reason that I feared that consent might not have been given if we asked for it.'

'Who is it?'

'Lord Wells.'

Elizabeth looked faintly relieved. 'The King has a good opinion of him.'

'And should have. His family have firmly supported Lancaster for years. Elizabeth, will you please speak to the King for me? Will you plead for us? Tell him that we love each other, that no other will do for us, and that he must approve of what we have done.'

Elizabeth was uneasy. The King was not going to like this, and she was to be the one to tell him. How could Cecilia? Why did she not wait? She had always been so firm in her opinions; it had never been possible to shift her from them—for Elizabeth at least.

Elizabeth was sorry for her sister. She was fond of her family. They had been a very loving community. Deep in her heart she was worried about her mother. She fervently wished that people would live in peace with each other and not do things which were a source of irritation to others. She had to hide her anxieties about her mother . . . and now here was Cecilia. She did not know how the King would deal with the matter. She was afraid to anger him—although she had never seen him in anger. She remembered the violent rages of her father. They had not happened often and they were soon over, but he did have more than a touch of what was called the old Plantagenet temper. Henry had none of that. He was always calm, cold almost. She often felt that he considered carefully everything he said before he uttered it.

How he would feel about Cecilia she was not sure. She had had a notion that he was not anxious for her to marry. He had never mentioned a husband for her since their own marriage; and she had noticed that there was never any special place for Cecilia at functions.

Cecilia was now looking at her anxiously. She could see that she would have to take this matter to the King and it would be better for him to hear quietly through her than through any other source for it would not be easy to keep such a matter secret for long.

She said: 'I will tell him, Cecilia.'

Cecilia had taken her hand and was looking at her earnestly.

'And you will explain that we love each other . . . that John wanted to ask the King but I would not have that. It was I who thought that if we were married first it would be too late to stop us.'

'I will tell him that, Cecilia. I will try to explain.'

'Thank you, sister.'

Cecilia kissed the Queen on the forehead.

She said: 'It is almost as though we were little again. You and I were always good friends, Elizabeth. Do you remember . . . how we thought the others were such babies?' Elizabeth nodded. 'And now you are Queen. It is strange but we always thought that Edward . . .'

Elizabeth flinched. It was foolish to bring up their young brothers at this time. Perhaps at any time. Nobody wanted to think of them now. Their disappearance must remain a mystery. To try to solve it might bring forth some evidence which certain people might find embarrassing.

Cecilia went on: 'I know the King will listen to you. I am sure he must love you dearly.'

'He does,' said Elizabeth firmly. At another time Cecilia might have said that he loved the alliance they had been able to make between the two houses, but not now. This was not the time.

It seemed only in the bedchamber that the Queen could be alone with the King.

Elizabeth's women had departed. She was in her long white nightgown, her golden hair in two long plaits giving her a childish look. Soon the King would come in and she was preparing what she would say to him.

When he came there was that somewhat forced smile on his pale face. He was always gentle and kind; it seemed to her that he was grateful for his good fortune in becoming King but was always on the alert lest someone should take the crown from him. He was fond of her. She had in certain moments of self-revelation wondered how fond, or whether his fondness was for what she stood for, not for her person.

She had asked for nothing for herself. She did not want jewels or extravagant pageants. Moreover she knew that Henry would never have given them. He had explained to her that the exchequer was in an unhealthy state. Her father had been extravagant but because of the pension he had had for some years from the King of France he had made the country prosperous. But that pension had stopped before his death. Uneasy times had followed his death; the perpetual unrest culminating in the Battle of Bosworth had impoverished the country. He was determined to crush extravagance, and she would not dream of asking for unnecessary luxuries.

But she would have liked to ask for her mother to come back

to Court, though she accepted the fact that it would be impossible because her mother had really committed an act of treason.

Now there was this matter of Cecilia's marriage.

He came to her smiling. He would lead her to the bed and they would make further attempts to get another child. It was the ritual when they were together. She believed that Henry had no greater liking for the act than she had for they were both aware of a certain relief when it was over, though it brought with it a sense of achievement which they hoped would be rewarded and a certain respite gained. Sometimes she thought of her father and all his mistresses. How different he must have been!

'Henry,' she said, 'there is something I have to tell you. I hope it will not anger you.'

He was alarmed. She sensed that rather than saw it. He never showed his feelings but she was aware that she had made him uneasy.

She said quickly: 'It is my sister, Cecilia. I am afraid she has acted rather foolishly.'

'How so?' he asked.

'She has married.'

He looked puzzled. But she could not tell whether he was angry or not.

She said quickly: 'To Lord Wells.'

He remained silent for a few seconds. Cecilia married to Wells! He was not at all put out. He had been watchful of Cecilia. In his mind had been the thought that he might have had to put her in Elizabeth's place. He was a man who calculated all eventualities. Life had made that necessary in the past and once a habit was formed with him, it generally continued. Moreover it was as necessary now as it had ever been. He had visualized Elizabeth's dying in childbed as so many women did and perhaps the baby with her. Then there would have been no alternative but marriage with Elizabeth's sister Cecilia. Cecilia was the one. The others were too young. So therefore he had kept Cecilia in the background. He had made sure that she should not be offered on the marriage market. He had looked upon her as a reserve. And now . . . she had married John Wells.

Wells came of a family which had always been loyal to him. He liked John Wells.

'You do not speak,' said Elizabeth, watching him fearfully.

'I am taken by surprise.'

'Of course it was very wrong of them.'

'But natural I suppose. We have been inclined to think of Cecilia as a child. She has shown us that she is not that.'

'Oh Henry . . . are you . . . ?'

He said: 'What's done is done.'

He was thinking: I am safe now. I have Arthur. As long as I have an heir who is half York and half Lancaster all is well. It is a pity Arthur is not more robust. However, it is no use thinking of Cecilia now. There is Anne. . . Very young as yet. But Elizabeth is still here . . . and strong . . .

He had always kept a firm control on his emotions and that habit never failed him. Always he liked time to think: What is best for Henry Tudor? What is safe for Henry Tudor? while his quick shrewd mind worked out the answer for him. He believed that he had come as far as he had because of this.

He said now: 'Why are you trembling, Elizabeth? You must not be afraid. You are not afraid of me, are you?'

She lowered her eyes. She could not tell a blatant lie.

'You must not be. You did right to tell me. I should not have liked to hear this from another source. But it is done. I trust John Wells. He has always been a good servant to us. Perhaps I shall tell him that he has been a little hasty. You may like to tell your sister that. Well, then let us wish them happiness and a fruitful marriage, eh . . .'

'You are so good,' she said with tears in her eyes. 'I shall never forget that scullion boy . . . and now Cecilia.'

'Lord and Lady Wells would not relish being compared with Lambert Simnel, my dear. Now . . . let us to bed.'

THE DEATH OF A QUEEN

In her nunnery at Bermondsey Elizabeth Woodville heard of her daughter Cecilia's marriage and that the King had accepted it with a philosophical shrug of the shoulders.

This meant, Elizabeth knew, that he felt secure now Arthur was progressing well. Oh why should she be kept from her grandchild! Why should she be kept here? What an end to a career of such brilliance! But looking back there had been many times like this when she had had to remain shut away from the world as the only way to preserve her life. She was tired of it. If the Queen could persuade the King to accept Cecilia's marriage why could she not bring her mother back to Court?

The answer was simple. The first did not affect the King one whit; the second might. Henry Tudor will always take care of Henry Tudor, thought Elizabeth bitterly.

Every day she expected to hear news of Scotland. That James would agree she had no doubt. She had at one time been reckoned to be the most beautiful woman in England and beauty such as hers did not disappear; it became a little faded—a little subdued sounded better—but she was still a very beautiful woman and with the right clothes and environment could toss aside the years as though they were tennis balls.

To Scotland! She had heard the climate was dour and the manners of the people not the most gracious in the world, but it would be better than remaining here, shut away from the Court, living in a kind of disgrace and with the knowledge that the King would always be suspicious of her if she went back to Court, and she could be sure that mother of his would never be far away.

Scotland was the best she could hope for, and why should she not make a success of her new role? She was not young but nor was the King of Scotland. She calculated that he would be just under forty. Mature, very glad no doubt to have for his wife a beautiful woman who had been a Queen of England.

She would try to forget her family here. Elizabeth who had become the Queen; Cecilia who had married Lord Wells and now, she heard, had retired with him to the country; Anne who was just thirteen and who would soon be having a husband found for her; Catherine who was but eight years old and Bridget who was a year younger and destined for a nunnery. All girls left to her and two little boys lost forever. No, she must stop herself trying to solve that mystery. It would bring no good. All this she must forget. She must put the past behind her. She must think of the new life in Scotland.

It would be entirely new . . . a new world to conquer. Her spirits were lifted considerably. She felt almost as she had that day when she, the desperately impoverished widow, mother of two boys by the dead John Grey, had gone out to Whittlebury Forest and made a name for herself in history.

Now . . . here was another chance. Queen of Scotland. The more she thought of the past, the more she considered her prospects for the future, the more she felt that her salvation was in Scotland.

She read of Scotland; she studied the history of Scotland; and what a tumultuous history it had! The Scots seemed to be more warlike than the English and one noble house was forever at odds with another.

It would be primitive of course. The Scottish castles were as draughty as the English ones and there was a colder climate with which to contend. She would need fur cloaks and rugs; she visualized great fires roaring in the rooms of the castles; she could bring a more gracious way of life to that unruly race.

Each day she became more and more eager to leave. She knew that the delay in receiving an answer from James was probably due to the fact that he was now engaged in a war.

She would try to teach them that diplomacy worked so much more effectively than bloodshed. She would introduce a little culture into the Court. She would have friends visiting her from England.

One afternoon a visitor called at the nunnery. She was wrapped in a concealing cloak and she had two ladies with her. The Queen Mother was called down to greet the visitors and when one of them stepped forward and threw back her hood, she saw that it was no other than her daughter, the Queen.

She gave a cry of joy and ran forward to embrace her.

The young Queen was almost in tears.

'Dear mother,' she said. 'I am so happy to see you. I trust you are well.'

The Queen Dowager said that she was well indeed, and would be quite fit to travel when the time came.

'Dear lady,' said the Queen, 'I would speak with you alone.' She signed to her attendants to fall back, which they did, and Elizabeth Woodville took her daughter to her apartments. There she dismissed her servants and the two Queens sat down to talk.

The young Elizabeth seemed as though she did not know where to begin and her mother said: 'Have you news of Cecilia?'

'Only that she is well and happy and enjoying life in the country.'

'She has been fortunate in escaping the wrath of the King. Not like her poor mother. It was a very rash and reckless thing she did.'

'But it harmed no one,' said the young Queen firmly. 'Dear lady, there is news from Scotland and that is why I felt I must come to you with all speed.'

News from Scotland. James was waiting for her. How soon could she set forth? In a week . . . Not less, she supposed.

'Well?' she prompted, for her daughter seemed to find it difficult to proceed.

'James is dead, my lady. He was killed in battle.'

'God has indeed deserted me.'

'Oh my dear mother, did you so long to go to Scotland?'

'Who does not wish to escape from prison?'

'But you have your comforts here.'

'I lack freedom, my daughter.'

'It will not always be so.'

'Have you spoken to the King?'

'He believes that it is for your own good to be here.'

'Henry believes what is for his good is always so for that of other people.'

'You must not talk thus of the King. You will want to hear of the sad end of the King of Scotland?'

'Slain in a battle, you say?'

'Yes . . . in a way. There was a revolt of the feudal houses.'

'There were always revolts.'

'I fear so. There were powerful men in this one . . . Angus, Huntly, Glamis. . . They met the King's forces and defeated him. He was in retreat with a few of his followers and went to a well for water. While they were there a woman came with her bucket and James could not resist saying to her: ''This morning I was your King.'' He told her that he was wounded and wanted to confess his sins to a priest. He begged her to find one and send the man to him, and she promised to do this. But what she did was to inform the townsfolk that the King was at the well and wanted a priest. There were some of the enemy forces in the town and one of these disguised himself as a priest. James was waiting at the well when the bogus minister arrived. The King fell on his knees and entreated the priest to shrive him, whereupon the man drew his sword and saying,"I will give you short shrift,'' slew the King. That is the story, my lady.'

'So I have lost my King,' said Elizabeth Woodville.

'Dear lady, do not be so sad. You never knew him.'

'He was to be my salvation.'

'Oh come, dear mother. If you truly repent of what you did I am sure the King will forgive you. You are happy here. Why you live as luxuriously as you would at Court. It may be that in time the King will find another noble husband for you. But it will not be Scotland now.'

'Adieu Scotland,' said the Queen Mother slowly. 'Adieu my King whom I never knew.'

She looked about her apartments.

'I have a feeling that I shall end my days here,' she said.

The King was feeling a little melancholy. He had just received the members of the embassy he had sent to Spain; they had been cheerful, optimistic, certain that their efforts would bear fruit, but Henry had never been one to deceive himself. He knew that whatever compliments had been paid and promises hinted at, nothing had really been achieved. He knew the reason why and it was that reason which he found so disturbing.

Arthur was at the very heart of his safety. He had thought himself the luckiest man in England when he had defeated Richard at Bosworth—or at least his armies had. Henry himself was no great general. His strength lay in his ability to govern rather than wield a sword—which men of good sense should know was more important for a king. They did not seem to, though—and if the time came for him to protect his kingdom he would need to shine on battlefields as well as in council chambers. That was what he dreaded.

He was never sure from one moment to the next whether someone might leap out to kill him. Every rustle of a curtain set him wondering; every time there was a knock on his door he wondered who would enter. It would get better when he felt more secure on his throne. It must be thus with all those who are not strictly in the line of succession.

The Lambert Simnel affair had worried him far more than he would admit. Not because it had had much hope of success—not because the baker's boy could have been anything but an impostor—but because it showed how easily these rebellions could arise and how many people—even with only the flimsiest causes—would rise to support them.

And now here was the embassy from Spain. If it had brought back results—a signed agreement . . . something like that, he would have had an indication that he was accepted as a King of England, likely to remain firm on his throne. But it was not so. The embassy had come back empty handed.

The fact was that Ferdinand and Isabella of Spain had a family—one son and four daughters; and the youngest of these daughters was Katharine who was a year older than Arthur. Henry believed fervently in alliance between powerful countries, and a marriage of the children of the rulers was the best safeguard for peace. It had seemed to him that if Ferdinand and Isabella would give their daughter Katharine in marriage to his son Arthur, it would show the world that the monarchs of Spain believed in the stability of the King of England. Moreover Spain and England would be powerful allies against the King of France. This might appeal to Ferdinand and Isabella; it was the fact on which he had pinned his hopes. But he knew that the sovereigns would not want to form an alliance with a king whose grip on his crown was far from steady.

So he had listened to his ambassadors newly returned from Medina del Campo with gloomy attention and nothing they could say of the lavish Spanish hospitality, the gifts they had brought back with them, could dispel his melancholy.

Isabella and Ferdinand would not commit themselves to an alliance between Arthur and Katharine because they were not convinced that Arthur's father would be able to keep his hold on the throne.

'Let us face the facts,' he said to John Dudley. 'We have wasted the money we have spent on this embassy.'

Dudley was not sure of that.

'At the moment,' he said, 'they are unsure. They will have heard of the Lambert Simnel affair and it has shaken them.'

'To think this could have come about through that baker's boy!'

'It is not exactly through him, Sire. It is the fact that Margaret of Burgundy supported him . . . among others . . . and the indication that there are people who are ready to rise against you.'

The King nodded gloomily. 'As I say, we need never have wasted the money.'

'It may not have been wasted. We have sown a seed. It may well be that later, when they see you have come to stay, they will change their minds. The children are so young yet and therefore marriage could not take place for several years. So much can happen in even a short time. And, Sire, we are going to show them that in spite of Lambert Simnel and any like him, King Henry the Seventh is here to stay.'

'You are right, of course, my lord. But it is a disappointment. I should have liked Arthur to be betrothed to Spain.'

'It will come, Sire. Wait. Let us be watchful and patient. Let us be ready for these troubles when they arise. Lambert Simnel has done us no real harm. You have shown the people that you can quell a rebellion, and it was a master stroke to send the boy to the kitchens. We need patience. Let us not be unduly troubled by the evasiveness of the Spaniards. The money has not really been wasted. The idea is sown in their minds. What we have to show them is that your throne is secure. Then we shall have them suing us for the marriage.'

Henry knew Dudley was right. With luck he would succeed. The result of his careful policies would soon be evident; and if he could get another son he would feel very confident in the future.

In the late spring there was good news. His efforts with the Queen were rewarded. Elizabeth was once more pregnant.

At the end of October Elizabeth the Queen went into retirement in the Palace of Westminster to prepare for the birth of her child. It was not due for another month but in view of Arthur's early arrival it had been thought wise for the Queen to be prepared.

Margaret Countess of Richmond had arranged the household as she had for the birth of Arthur, and this time she was not harassed by the presence of Dowager Queen Elizabeth Woodville who, to the Countess' great satisfaction, was still confined at Bermondsey.

The Countess had made a list of all her requirements.

'There must be two cradles,' she had told Elizabeth, 'the cradle of state decorated with cloth of gold and ermine and that other in which the baby will sleep.'

Elizabeth listened contentedly. She was delighted to have her mother-in-law to rely on; and as she never questioned any of the Countess' requirements there was perfect amity between them.

'We must have a good wet nurse . . . that is most important—a strong, healthy young woman and her food shall be considered most carefully so that she can give the baby all due nourishment.

Then we need a dry nurse, sewers, panterers and rockers of course.'

'As with Arthur,' said the Queen.

'Exactly so. Oh my dear Elizabeth, if this proves to be a boy I shall be overjoyed. Now I have arranged for a physician to be in attendance with the wet nurse at all her meals. That is most important for the health of the child.'

'How good you are.'

'I long to see you with a family of children . . . boys and some girls . . . for girls have their important parts to play in affairs of state.'

'I do agree.'

'I have my eyes on a good woman. She will give birth at the same time as you do. She is a respectable woman and this is not her first child. She has remarkably good health and has reared other children most satisfactorily. Her name is Alice Davy. The day-nurse will be Alice Bywimble. She is a good woman and I have two very good rockers. I have prevailed upon the King to pay them three pounds six shillings and eightpence a year. He thought it a great deal of money for such people but I have impressed on him the need to pay these people more than they would get in an ordinary household to make them realize the importance of serving a royal child.'

'And did he agree?' asked the Queen, wondering for a moment whether she would have to take sides with the King against her mother-in-law and thinking how awkward that would be.

'Oh I brought him round to my point of view,' said the Countess complacently, implying that she could always do that—even with the King.

Elizabeth was relieved. She reached out a hand and took that of the Countess.

'My lady, I thank you. I am so grateful to have you here to take care of these matters.'

'My dear dear daughter, you cannot be happier than I. You know what my son means to me . . . apart from the fact that he is the King and ruler of us all, and I will say this—that although you come from a house which has for so long been the enemy of my own, there is none I would rather see my son married to than you.'

Elizabeth was deeply moved.

It was so easy to remain in loving friendship with her mother-in-law. All she asked was agreement in everything she did and as she was a very wise woman, this worked out ideally for Elizabeth.

The days began to pass at Westminster. It was quite clear that the new baby was not going to make a premature appearance, but arrived on the night of the twenty-ninth of November of that year 1489, which was exactly the time it was due.

The child was rather disappointingly a girl. But a strong, healthy girl—more lusty than Arthur had been.

The Queen requested that she should be called after the King's mother to whom she owed so much, and the King was most graciously pleased to agree.

So in due course the Princess Margaret joined her brother Arthur in the royal nurseries.

It was pleasant to retire to Greenwich. There she would stay until the birth of the child, for Elizabeth was once again in what people who do not have to endure it call a happy condition.

The nursery now contained Arthur who was five years old and Margaret nearly two. Arthur was a gentle, serious child, already showing an interest in his books. Perhaps this was because he was a little delicate. The King watched him anxiously. He was afraid something might happen to Arthur who was more than a son to him; he was one of the chief reasons why the people wanted him to remain King.

Minors were a menace. That had been the lesson of the ages. What the people always wanted was a strong king who had a son or sons in his youth, so that by the time he died, there would be someone strong to take his place.

'How I do hope this one will be a boy,' prayed Elizabeth.

Margaret was already showing herself to be a somewhat forceful little creature. She wanted her own way all the time and invariably got it, for she had grown out of the childish way of screaming for it and employed more devious methods to cajole the guardians of the nursery. The only person of whom Margaret seemed to feel some awe was her grandmother the Countess of Richmond, for the child was shrewd enough to recognize that there was a lady to be obeyed, and although she avoided having to comply whenever she could, she did know when it would be expedient to do so.

Elizabeth prayed that Arthur's health might be improved and Margaret's temper controlled and contemplated what the new one would be like.

She enjoyed being at Greenwich—less important of course than Winchester, the birthplace of Arthur, or Westminster, that of Margaret. But this one after all was but a third child.

There was a peace here among the green fields with the river meandering through them. She was not surprised that the Romans had called it Grenovicum when they had seen it and later the Saxons had named it Grenawic—the Green Town. It had been a royal residence since the days of Edward Longshanks and it had become increasingly popular ever since. Henry had enlarged the Palace and because the river was encroaching had added a brick wall along the water front. The tower in the Park had been started years ago and not finished until Henry had it completed. He was now talking about building a monastery for the Grey Friars who lived in the district. It seemed strange that Henry should consider spending money on such things for he was usually so careful and hated to see it, as he always said, 'wasted.' But this was different. This was adding to the wealth of the country. He said: 'It is important that we preserve our buildings.'

She was glad. It was lovely to see the old Palace as it should be. The people at Greenwich were pleased, too, and they were delighted that she had come here for her accouchement.

It was hot that June; she found the room stifling but of course it had to be closed in. These were the orders of the Countess of Richmond who said they must always comply with Court etiquette.

'Leave everything to me,' said the Countess. 'All you have to do, my dear, is produce a healthy boy.'

'Pray God I do,' she replied fervently.

In London the sweating sickness was plaguing the people and the King had been very anxious that she come quickly to the cooler, fresher air of Greenwich, so here in this Palace with the tall mullioned windows and the lovely shade of terracotta in the tiled floors, she felt comfortable and secure. All she had to do was stay in her apartments with her women around her and wait.

It was comforting to know that the Countess of Richmond was at hand.

Oh God, she continued to pray, let this one be a boy.

And on a hot June day her prayers were answered.

Her child was born; strong, lusty, informing the castle of his arrival within a few minutes of his birth by his piercing cry.

The King came to Greenwich. This was a happy day. The new baby was of the desired sex and he seemed as healthy as his sister Margaret was proving to be. Another addition to the nursery and a boy! It was something to thank God for.

His birth was, of course, not of the same importance as Arthur's but he was the son of the King, and although while Arthur lived he would be of secondary importance it was always wise to have some boys in reserve.

The King was therefore pleased, and although the festivities in honour of the child would not compare with those which had announced the birth of the heir to the throne, they should be commensurate with his rank of second son to the King.

It was decided that the boy should be baptized only a few days after his birth which was always a wise procedure, for so many healthy-seeming children died suddenly for no apparent reason. Bishop Fox came to Greenwich expressly to perform the ceremony and the Church of the Observants there had been specially decorated. The King had ordered that the font be brought from Canterbury for the occasion and there were carpets on the floor—a very special luxury and a wonder to those who beheld them and who were accustomed to seeing rushes there.

The little boy was discreetly divested of his garments and carried to the font into which he would be dipped, and all present marvelled at the size of the baby and remarked that he was perfect in every way.

Bishop Fox proclaimed to all those present that he named the boy Henry.

Henry. It was a good name—his father's name.

Only the child was indifferent and in spite of his extreme youth he appeared to look on at the scene with calm aloofness.

After being wrapped in a white garment he was taken from the church back to the Palace, with the musicians marching before him playing their trumpets and drums, to the Queen's presence chamber where Henry and Elizabeth—who had not attended the ceremony in the church—were waiting to receive the procession.

The child was carried to the Queen, who took him into her arms and murmured a blessing. Then the King took the child and did the same.

All those present looked on smiling.

'Long live Prince Henry,' murmured the Countess of Richmond and the cry was taken up throughout the chamber.

Life had not gone smoothly for the Queen Dowager since she had lost the King of Scotland. She had suddenly realized that her days of power were over. It was scarcely likely that the King would find another husband for her now. She could not reconcile herself to spending the rest of her life in a convent. Yet it seemed that that was the intention of the King and his overbearing mother; and if it was their wish it would be very difficult for her to evade it.

She spent most of the days in dreaming of the past. It is a sorry state of affairs when a woman who once enslaved a king has come to this, she thought.

She was not so very old. It was true that she would not see fifty again, but she was still beautiful and she had always been mindful of her outstanding beauty and had sought to preserve it. If she were fifty-five years of age she certainly did not look it. And yet of late she had begun to feel it. She experienced unaccountable little aches and pains, an inability to breathe easily, the odd little pain here and there.

Age! How tiresome it was. If only she were young as she had been when she had gone into Whittlebury Forest. But she must stop brooding on the past. But could she when the past had been so thrilling, so exciting, so adventuresome . . . and now . . . what was she? A queen still, mother of a queen . . . but a queen who had become the tool of a cold stern man who was quite immune to the charms and wisdom of his mother-in-law.

Of course it is that woman, she thought. Surely the mother of the Queen carries as much weight as the mother of the King . . . or should do when the Queen had far more right to the throne than the King had, who in fact had acquired it largely through his marriage with the daughter of Elizabeth Woodville.

It was old ground and perhaps she shouldn't go over it perpetually. And yet how could she help it? What was there to do in her nunnery except relive the glories of the past?

One morning when she awoke she began to cough and during the day found great difficulty in breathing. Her attendants propped her up with cushions and that eased her a little but by nightfall she felt very weak.

She thought: Is this the end then? Is this how death comes?

She thought of Edward the King who had been so strong and well one day and then had had that fit of apoplexy, which she was sure had been brought on by the shock of hearing that the King of France had broken his treaty with him, and their daughter was not to be Madame La Dauphine after all. But he had recovered from that and seemed well . . . but soon afterwards quite suddenly he had died after catching a cold when he was out fishing.

It was better if death came swiftly. Who wanted to outlive one's power? Certainly no one who had enjoyed so much as Elizabeth Woodville. But the thought of death was sobering when one brooded on all the sins one had committed, all the things one should have done and those which had been left undone.

A woman has to live . . . to fight her way through, particularly if she has after much success been visited by adversity.

But she had outlived her power . . . and her wealth. She had very little left for herself after having supported her girls. It would have been different if her son had come to the throne . . . little Edward the Fifth. Little son, what happened to you there in the Tower? What dark secret is hidden from me? You were the delight of our lives when you were born in Sanctuary, your father overseas, striving to come back and claim his throne. You were delicate. I know you suffered some pain. I was glad you had your brother Richard with you in the Tower. You wanted him to be with you so much. Yet if I had not let him go to you . . . perhaps he would be with us now.

In her heart she admitted that she had let him go for the sake of her freedom. It was an ultimatum they had delivered to her. Suppose she had held Richard back? Would he have been King now? Never. The Tudor would have come just the same and taken the throne.

If Edward were living today what would he think? The first thing he would do would be to take up arms and drive the Tudor from the throne. He would see the red rose trampled in the dust, the white triumphant.

But the white rose lived on in Henry's wife, the present Queen. That was the irony of it. Lancaster and York reigning side by side—but it was only token power for York. It was Lancaster through Henry Tudor who wielded the real power.

The pain in her chest was growing worse.

'I should like to see my daughters,' she said.

Cecilia was the first to come. She knelt by the bed, alarmed to see the beautiful face so pale and sunken.

'Dear mother,' she said, 'you must get well.'

'I feel I never shall again, my child,' said Elizabeth. 'This is the end. Do not look so sad. We all have to go sometime and I have had a good life. Where is the Queen?'

'She has taken to her lying-in chamber. Her time is very near.'

'She does her duty by the Tudor. I hear young Henry flourishes.'

'Indeed, yes. He and Margaret are fine healthy children. I wish I could say the same for Arthur.'

'I never believed in that closed-in room, but the Countess insisted.'

'Margaret and Henry were born in the same conditions,' Cecilia gently reminded her. 'Dear lady, should you not rest?'

'There is a long rest ahead of me. Cecilia, I am glad you are provided for. Is Lord Wells a good husband?'

'The best of husbands.'

'Then you are fortunate. And you lack for nothing, I believe. He is very rich.'

'We are very comfortable and happy, my lady.'

'I wish the others had been a little older so that I could see them settled.'

'Elizabeth will provide for them.'

'She must when I can no longer do so. I have very little to leave, Cecilia. You find me in dire poverty. I have been growing poorer and poorer.'

'But our father left you well provided for, did he not?'

'When York lost to Lancaster . . . I lost much of what he left to me. Your father's personal property is in the hands of your grandmother. Cecily of York is one of the most avaricious old women I ever heard of.'

'Think not of money now, dear mother. Rest your voice.'

The Queen Dowager smiled and nodded. 'Sit by my bed, dear child,' she said. 'Hold my hand. I loved you all dearly . . . far more than I ever showed you.'

'We were so happy when we were children, dear mother. You and our father were like a god and goddess to us. We thought you perfect.'

'Neither of us was that, dear child, but whatever else we were, we were loving parents.'

Seventeen-year-old Anne arrived next with her sisters Catherine and Bridget, the youngest, who had come from her convent at Dartford to be at her mother's bedside. Anne was a source of anxiety to the Queen Dowager because she was seventeen years old, ripe for marriage. Who would look after her now? Elizabeth the Queen must do that. Catherine was eleven; there was time yet for her. Bridget was the only one whose future was assured for she was preparing herself to take the veil.

Elizabeth looked at them through misty eyes. Her beloved children. Was it only eleven years ago that Edward had been alive and they had rejoiced at the birth of this daughter?

She held out her hands to them. The younger girls looked at her with alarmed dismay. They had never seen her like this before, poor children, thought Cecilia. She looks so ill. I really believe this is the end.

'Bless you, dear daughters,' said the Queen Dowager. 'I think I shall be gone before Whitsuntide.'

'Where shall you go?' asked Catherine.

'To Heaven, I hope, sweet child.'

Then the little girls began to weep and Bridget knelt down by the bed and prayed as she had seen the nuns do.

'Goodbye, my dear ones. Remember this. No parents ever loved their children more than the King and I loved you. Sad events have fallen upon us but we must make the best of them . . . Your sister, the Queen, will care for you.'

Catherine said: 'Dear mother, I think I should send for the priest.'

On the following day Elizabeth Woodville died.

It was Whit Sunday when the Queen Dowager's body was taken along the river to Windsor.

There was a very simple funeral. Only the priest of the college received the coffin, and some Yorkists who had come out to see the end of great Edward's Queen murmured together that such a hearse was like those used for the common people.

Was this the way in which King Henry honoured the House of York? What was all this talk of the roses entwining—the uniting of white and red—when a Yorkist queen was buried with no more ceremony than the humblest merchant?

On the following Tuesday the daughters of Elizabeth Wood-ville—Catherine, Anne and Bridget—came to Windsor. Cecilia was at the time unwell but her husband Lord Wells came in her stead.

The burial itself was performed with as little expense as possible. Even black clothes had not been provided for those who had been engaged to sing the dirges and they appeared in their working garments. This was unheard of for a royal personage—and a queen at that.

There was a great deal of murmuring. 'The Queen should have provided proper mourning for her mother,' said many.

'The Queen has no power and the King is a miser.'

But at least she was buried where she would have wished to be—in St. George's Chapel beside her husband, King Edward the Fourth.

Henry was relieved. He had always been uneasy concerning his mother-in-law. He had never trusted her and in his suspicious mind he saw the possibilities of her being at the centre of an intrigue to drive him from the throne. The animosity between Elizabeth Woodville and the Countess of Richmond had been more than feminine bickering. The Countess had seen danger in the woman, for like her son's, her own life had prepared her to look for trouble.

But now Elizabeth Woodville was dead; the Queen was deliv-ered of another child—a girl, Elizabeth, this time and delicate like Arthur. The King was thankful that he had the robust Henry and Margaret to show they could get healthy children. Four was a goodly number and the Queen was still young, and if a little delicate that did not seem to impair her ability to bear children.

He fancied, too, that on the continent they were beginning to regard him as a formidable figure in world politics. The King of France had just shown a healthy respect for him; and he was delighted because he was going to be spared the necessity of going to war.

He had been drawn into an agreement with the Holy Roman Emperor Maximilian, and Isabella and Ferdinand. He was particularly eager to have the friendship of the Spanish monarchs because he saw through an alliance with them a bulwark against the perennial enemy, the French, and he was still hoping for a marriage between their daughter Katharine and his own Arthur. He hated war, seeing it as senseless and costly, but he had come to the point where he had found it impossible to back out.

Dudley and Empson had said that it would be necessary to raise the money from the people. It was a strange and sobering fact that while the people were reluctant to pay taxes in order to increase industry they were ready to do so to go to war, and there had been many a squire who had sold part of his estates in order to equip himself for war. Why? Did he think the spoils he would bring back would compensate him, or was it just the lust for conflict? War was no good to anyone, was Henry's theory; and he could not understand why, when this had been so well proved through the ages, men still wanted to indulge in it.

But because it had been impossible to evade it he had landed an army in France and laid siege to Boulogne, and although this had not proved outstandingly successful as the town was very well fortified, the French King sued for peace—offering to pay Henry's expenses and a sum of money if he would retire from the field.

The acquisition of money had always been a pleasure to Henry and to get it without the loss of men or equipment seemed to him a heaven-sent opportunity.

There were people to murmur against it, for operations like this, while so profitable to the leaders, were scarcely so to those who had sold part of their estates to enable them to join the expedition and then returned empty-handed.

However Henry was delighted. He accepted the offer, made peace and came back to England.

It was while he was congratulating himself with those devoted and efficient statesmen Dudley and Empson, that he received news which shattered his peace.

A young man had presented himself to the peers of Ireland with the story that he was Richard Duke of York, second son of King Edward the Fourth, whose disappearance with his brother had caused such speculation some years before.

His brother—who was in truth Edward the Fifth—declared this young man, had been murdered. But he, the second son, had escaped. He had called himself Peter Warbeck and had remained in obscurity until the time was opportune for him to take the throne.

He was now gathering together an army—he had the support of some influential people including the Duchess of Burgundy—and was coming to take the throne from the usurper Henry Tudor who now occupied it.

Henry's peace of mind had completely deserted him. Here was another of them. It was lies . . . lies. None knew that better than he did.

Richard of York—the second of the Princes in the Tower—was dead, he knew that. But how could he explain to the country why he was so sure?

And was this another Lambert Simnel? No . . . indeed not. Lambert Simnel had been doomed to failure from the first.

Something told Henry that this was a far more serious matter, and he knew that his enemies would be preparing to strike at him.

He had constantly to look about him for where the blows would come.

He had not thought that it could be through one of the little Princes in the Tower.

PERKIN

Peter had been ten years old when the Framptons came to Flanders. He was a bright boy, tall and handsome with abundant golden hair and very alert blue eyes. His father, John Warbeck, was a customs official and his mother Katharine was a clever woman. They had several children, otherwise they would have been able to do more for Peter; as it was he was put into several noble houses there to learn how to be a good squire.

After the Battle of Bosworth when there was a turnabout in England and the House of Plantagenet, which had reigned since Henry the Second came to the throne in the year 1154, was defeated and replaced by the Tudors, among those who felt it was necessary to leave England were Sir Edward and Lady Frampton. They were staunch supporters of the House of York—so much so that they were committed to help bring that House back to power if it was at all possible for them to do so.

When they settled at Tournay in Flanders they had been able to bring much of their wealth with them and they were made very welcome and took several people into their household.

Peter's good looks and amazingly pleasant manners secured him a place and very soon he became a favourite of Lady Frampton.

'You remind me,' she told him, 'of our great King Edward. He was exceptionally handsome. The people loved him. It was the greatest tragedy that could befall England when he died. And, Peter, you have a look of him.'

Peter was flattered and was eager to discover all he could about the handsome King to whom he bore such a strong resemblance.

Lady Frampton was always ready to talk to him. When she rode out Peter would act as her groom and she often sent for him in the house so that she could chat to him.

It was very pleasant for her to have such an attentive audience and she was only too glad to speak of the past because the present seemed so hopeless.

'If only,' she was fond of saying, 'by some stroke of good fortune, we could drive the usurping Tudor from the throne.'

Peter asked a great many questions about the late King Edward to whom he bore such a resemblance.

'I suppose,' said Lady Frampton, 'the King was in Flanders at some time. I'd be ready to swear, Peter, that he was interested in some Flemish maid and that you were the result.'

'My mother is a very virtuous wife.'

'I know . . . I know. But sometimes those whom we believe to be our parents are not. You understand what I mean, Peter? Suppose the lady you think of as your mother was asked to care for a child . . . a child who came rather mysteriously into the world. Suppose that child was the result of a liaison between some persons who dared not divulge their identity.'

If it was an absurd supposition, Lady Frampton refused to accept the fact. Edward had many bastards but he had never made any secret of the fact. He had no one to answer to and even his Queen had been aware of his activities in that field and knew she must turn a blind eye to them.

Still, it was interesting to talk and the boy was very pleased at the prospect of having a king for a father. He wanted to know about the sons Edward had had by the Queen and why they didn't rise up and take the throne away from this obnoxious Tudor.

'They disappeared. . . It is most mysterious for none so far as I have heard have an answer to the question. Richard the Third declared the children illegitimate. The two boys were put into the Tower of London. They have never been seen since.'

'Did King Richard murder them?'

Lady Frampton was indignant. 'Richard was a good Yorkist king—brother of Edward. He would never murder his own nephews. It was the Tudor. You see while they lived they were a menace to him. The elder of the boys was Edward the Fifth; his younger brother was Duke of York. And if Edward died there was still Richard of York to come before this Tudor.'

'So he kept them imprisoned in the Tower.'

'Yes . . . and no one knows what became of them.'

'If they were alive would they not show themselves?'

'It may be that they will one day.'

'And I look like them, you say, my lady?'

'Very much so. They had long blond hair . . . just like yours. And a certain bearing . . .'

Peter was very proud. He was very careful of the way he

looked, the way he walked; he studied noblemen and imitated them.

Lady Frampton remarked to Sir Edward that the boy grew more royal-looking every day.

When the Framptons left for Portugal, Peter went with them. He had a great desire to see the world. Lady Frampton's talk of his resemblance to the Princes had set ambition growing in him and he had a feeling that he might become the centre of great events. He dreamed about himself and there were times when his dreams seemed more real than his everyday life.

He had not been long in Lisbon when he made the acquaintance of a knight called Peter Vàrz de Cogna—a somewhat battlescarred gentleman who had lost an eye and who seemed to young Peter one of the most interesting people he had ever met. The Knight, too, noticed the royal looks of young Warbeck and he talked to him a great deal about the recent uprising headed by Lambert Simnel.

'It is clear that the Tudor is uneasy on the throne of England,' he said. 'And it is not to be wondered at, considering he has very little right to it.'

Peter liked to hear how Lambert Simnel the baker's son had been taken from his father's shop by the priest Richard Simon and had come within a short distance of taking the throne of England.

'A baker's son!' cried Peter, aghast. 'How did he manage to pass himself off for the Earl of Warwick?'

'He had such good looks . . . and a manner of carrying himself. They say he looked the part and when they had taught him to speak . . . as an earl would speak—well, it might have been an earl himself.'

'And now he is just a scullion.'

'Some would say he has been lucky.'

'Of course he might have succeeded. And if he had . . .?'

'He could not succeed because the real Earl of Warwick lives and is the King's prisoner in the Tower.'

'Because,' said Peter, 'he has a greater claim to the throne than the Tudor. I find it of great interest.'

'I'm not surprised. With looks such as yours you might be one of the sons of Edward yourself.'

'Would it not be strange if I were?'

'It is said that he had children all over the place. He was that kind of man.'

'I should like to go to England.'

'You would have to learn the language.'

'I do speak a little. It seems to come naturally to me and Lady Frampton has taught me a good deal.'

'You should go to Ireland first.'

'Why Ireland?'

'They have always supported the Yorkists. They would like the look of you. They would think the young Edward the Fifth or his brother of York had come back to life.'

It was not long after this that a Breton merchant came to Lisbon and stayed a while at the house of Peter Varz. He was, he told them, on his way to Ireland where he would do business. At the mention of Ireland, Peter Warbeck's eyes sparkled.

'It is a country I long to see,' he said.

Peter was thoughtful. Could it be possible? He did not see why not. Peter Varz would not stand in his way. He told him of his great desire to see Ireland and the Breton merchant replied that there was no difficulty about that. He was sailing for Ireland shortly and there would be a place for Peter Warbeck on his ship.

It seemed to the young man that there was some Divine purpose in all this. First he had been endowed with these marvellous looks; secondly he had met the Framptons; and now here he was on his way to Ireland.

The Breton merchant was proud of the interest his protégé aroused.

'They say he is one of the sons of Edward the Fourth,' he told people; and it was not long before Peter was invited to call on Lord Desmond.

Lord Desmond was an influential Irish peer and the Irish had always believed that they could expect better treatment from the Yorkists than from the Lancastrians. They wanted home rule and there had once been a hint from a Duke of York that he believed this might be brought about. That it would never be granted by Henry the Seventh they were certain. It might be another matter if there was a Yorkist king on the throne of England, and they would like to see this come about.

They had supported Lambert Simnel although it must have been clear that he was an impostor, but Lambert had managed to make trouble for the English and that was what the Irish liked to do beyond anything.

The Earl of Desmond was delighted by Peter Warbeck.

'Why, you have the Yorkist look. I could easily believe you are one of Edward's sons. Tell me about yourself. From whence do you come?'

'I was in Tournay with people whom I had always believed to be my parents.'

'And they were not . . . ?'

Peter passed a hand across his brow. Lord Desmond noticed how graceful were his gestures.

'It is a little hazy . . . I remember being in a prison . . . with my brother . . . There was some trouble. . . . I cannot remember . . . although sometimes flashes of it come back to me.'

Lord Desmond was excited.

'I should like you to stay here for a while. There are people whom I would like to meet you.'

Peter felt a sense of mingling excitement and apprehension. He knew that he had stepped over the dividing line between fantasy and reality.

It was Lord Desmond and the Irish peers who had changed him. He had been through a great experience, he told himself. It was natural that he should feel as he did. The past was beginning to emerge and it was becoming increasingly difficult to tell the difference between what had actually happened and what he wanted to have happened.

That he was of noble birth everyone was ready to accept. Lord Desmond was teaching him to speak fluently in English and with an acceptable accent.

The Irish peers discussed the boy.

'He could not be the son of Clarence because he is still in the Tower,' said Desmond, 'where he has been languishing since the accession of the Tudor—for no other reason, of course, than that he has a stronger claim to the throne than Henry. But he could be one of the sons of Edward the Fourth . . . those Princes who were kept in the Tower. No one knows what became of them.'

That seemed very likely. Could he be Edward the Fifth? Was he old enough for that? It seemed far more likely that he was the younger brother, Richard Duke of York.

Now if he were the young Duke of York he was, in fact, the true King of England, providing his brother Edward the Fifth was dead.

It was an exciting project. It was just what the Irish peers were looking for. They wanted a Yorkist claimant to the throne; they were always ready for a fight; and there was nothing they liked better than bringing trouble to the English King.

Moreover, let them produce the true King of England, let them lead a rebellion against the Tudor, set the young King on the throne, and he would not forget what he owed to Ireland.

Lord Desmond was constantly in the company of Peter Warbeck. They conversed together of the affairs of England and Ireland and they decided that what had happened was that Peter (his real name was Richard Plantagenet) had been put into the Tower by his uncle Richard the Third. When Henry Tudor won the Battle of Bosworth Field he planned to murder the two little boys—which he must do, for he was to marry their sister; which he could not do if she were illegitimate (as Richard the Third proclaimed the family to be) and if she were not illegitimate then her brothers were not either; and if they were not then they were the true heirs to the throne. So here, according to Peter Warbeck, was what had happened.

The two little Princes had been taken out of the Tower and given to certain gentlemen who had orders to kill them. This was carried out in the case of the elder—King Edward the Fifth. His brother, Richard Duke of York, fared differently. The gentleman who had been selected to kill him found that he could not commit so foul a deed, for he was deeply moved by the boy's guilelessness and could not bring himself to destroy such innocence. He had paid two men to take the boy away, strip him of his identity, give him a new name. 'Swear that for eight years you will not divulge his story,' they were told. 'On this condition only can his life be spared.'

So the boy was taken abroad; he wandered around and was finally taken into the house of the Warbecks who accepted him as their son.

It was a likely story—at least it was good enough to start with.

There came the day when Peter's speech and manners were so perfect that Lord Desmond thought they should move into action. He proposed to send messages to the sovereigns of Europe announcing the fact that the younger son of Edward the Fourth, about whose death—with that of his brother—there had been a longstanding mystery, had come forth and was about to lay claim to the throne of England. His brother had been murdered, but by a miracle Richard Duke of York had escaped. As true King of England he asked those whom he was sure were his friends and would wish to see justice done, to aid him to get what was his and drive the usurping Tudor back to Wales and obscurity where he belonged.

There was immediate interest. Henry Tudor was known to be insecure on the throne; the King of France and the Emperor Maximilian would not be averse to a little trouble in England. It was always wise to keep kings engaged on their own doorsteps. It prevented their meddling in the affairs of others.

The King of Scotland sent a warm invitation for Peter to visit him; but before he could reply there was another invitation—this time from the King of France.

This was too important to be dismissed and Peter set out for France without delay.

It was at this time that Henry heard what was happening and knew that he had to discover all he could about this Peter Warbeck who called himself the Duke of York. That the man was a liar Henry was well aware. He could have told the world that it was quite impossible for him to be the Duke of York. But how could he be so sure? they would ask. There was the crux of the matter. Henry *was* sure, but he did not want the reason for his certainty to be known.

He sent spies to the Continent to find out how far this matter had gone and who was involved in it.

He remembered how his contemptuous treatment of Lambert Simnel had reduced the boy to a figure of fun. It showed the people how those who set out to take a crown from a king could end up watching the spits in that king's kitchen.

He talked not angrily of this impostor but slightingly, giving him the nickname Perkin which was sometimes given to those called Peter.

In Court circles and in the streets they talked of Perkin Warbeck and the name Henry had given him did surprisingly diminish his stature.

Henry was getting very concerned when he heard through his spies that the King of France had received Perkin Warbeck with honour as though he were indeed visiting royalty. He knew that his enemies on the Continent were just waiting to see him fall. It was a perpetual nightmare. During his early years he had been striving for the throne and when he eventually achieved it he discovered that his real troubles had begun. To be ever watchful of enemies, wondering constantly who was plotting against him, to be in constant dread of assassination . . . was this what he had dreamed of all those years in exile?

But he was committed now. He had to hold his throne for the sake of his son, King-Arthur-to-be, for the sake of the House of Tudor.

Some might have shrugged aside this ridiculous impostor, have told the world that he was liar and cheat—and the reason why it was a certainty, if necessary.

Sometimes it was in the interests of peace that murder should be committed. Henry could assure himself that only in such circumstances would he be guilty of it. He wanted to be a good strong king; he wanted to bring prosperity to England; he wanted to leave a great country behind him when he died. He wanted Arthur to have an easier life than he had. Was that wrong? What happened to countries ruled by minors? There was always trouble. Looking back over history this was a lesson which stood out clearly. He had come to the throne through conquest. He did have a claim. He was descended from great British Kings Arthur and Cadwallader—his mother was descended from John of Gaunt and his grandmother had been Queen of England and daughter of the King of France. Was that not good enough?

The people would realize in time that a serious-minded king who sought to do what was best for the people was more worthy to rule than some little boy with pretty manners—even if he were the true son of Edward the Fourth, which this ridiculous young Perkin was most definitely not.

There was one ray of light. The French King was eager to complete the Treaty of Etaples and Henry would refuse to sign until Charles had promised that he would give no aid or shelter to pretenders to the English throne.

At least that was a small victory.

Charles signed the treaty and the result was that Perkin Warbeck with his adherents was asked—very politely—to leave France.

This Perkin did but he had already received an invitation to visit Margaret Duchess of Burgundy.

The Duchess of Burgundy, the sister of Edward the Fourth, was a forceful woman who had on the death of her husband become a very powerful one.

She was devoted to her family. Like all of them she had adored her eldest brother Edward and one of the great sorrows of her life had been the quarrel between Edward and their brother George Duke of Clarence, which had ended by Clarence's being drowned in a butt of malmsey in the Tower. It was said to have been an accident because he had been a heavy drinker and it was assumed he had fallen into the butt during one of his bouts of drunkenness. Margaret did not know whether to believe the story or not, but she suspected George had become a menace and that Edward had removed him for that reason.

That saddened her. Families should cling together. She could not blame Edward of course, for she knew George would have been a danger to him but she did mourn him sadly. She turned her attention to developing the arts and to encouraging the printer

Caxton in his works, later sending him to Edward to print books in England. She had obtained licences for the English to export oxen and sheep to Flanders and also wool free of custom duty. She had wanted friendship and trade between Flanders and England; and because of her relationship she had got it.

And then the Tudor had come. He had killed her brother Richard and that had been the end of the House of Plantagenet, which to her had been heartbreaking. To think that the noble House to which she had belonged had been set aside for that upstart Tudor was intolerable. She hated Henry Tudor. He was mean and grasping; he was the complete antithesis of her brother Edward. Edward had been generous-hearted, romantic, handsome, pleasant . . . a perfect man. And this Tudor was a miser who thought of little but hoarding money. He was slight in stature whereas Edward had been a man of bulk as he grew older, but when he had been young he had had the figure of a god. She had never seen Henry Tudor and did not want to, but she had heard many descriptions of him—pale dry skin, greyish eyes, cold as a wintry sea, and reddish-brown hair. Not a handsome man, but one who could be ruthless if crossed.

I will cross him, thought Margaret. If I had a chance I would drive him from the throne.

There was, moreover, a personal grievance, for when he had seized the crown, Henry had confiscated the greater part of the dowry which Edward had bestowed on her when she married the Duke of Burgundy. It was maddening to think that what should be hers was in the hands of that man; and she made very welcome at her Court all the dissatisfied Yorkists who came from England. They all hated the Tudor monarch and were ever seeking means to overthrow him and they could be sure of finding a sympathetic listener in the Duchess of Burgundy.

Thus when Perkin Warbeck arrived she was ready for him.

She embraced him affectionately, then held him at arm's length that she might see him better.

'My nephew,' she said. 'We have often wondered what became of you. You are so like your father, I weep to look at you. I am thankful that you have come to me. It may not be long now before you have that which is your rightful due. You will find friends here who are only waiting for the opportunity to help you.'

So at the Duchess' Court Perkin was treated as though he were indeed her nephew. He told his story of his wandering after the man selected to murder him had allowed him to go free. He talked of the Framptons who had befriended him and first made him realize that he should do something and save his country from the Tudor rule.

'That shall be done,' said the Duchess firmly. 'We will raise an army. You will find that you have many to help you.'

She kept him beside her. Everywhere she went she presented him as the White Rose, Prince of England, King Richard the Fourth. She talked to him continually of her brother King Edward, of how he had lived; she told him everything she knew of that king's family and it seemed to Perkin that the life of Richard of York was more real to him than that of Perkin Warbeck of Tournay. He began to believe he had really been in Sanctuary with his family; he could almost remember being sent to the Tower to join his brother; he could see his mother's face distorted with grief; he could feel her tears on his face as she kissed him and gave him over to his jailers.

With Margaret he *was* the Duke of York. Peter Warbeck was just an identity he had assumed while he was waiting to declare himself.

Henry, watching events very closely, was getting more and more disturbed.

He must take some action. It was no use asking Margaret of Burgundy to give up this ridiculous charade. She wanted him off the throne, he had always known that; and what could suit her better than to set up her own puppet?

He could bring trouble to Flanders, and against his better judgement he decided to do so. He forbade all contact between England and Flanders and expelled all Flemings from England.

It was a mistake and enraged the people of London. Riots were narrowly averted but it taught Henry how easily the people could be persuaded to rise against him and that any one of these pretenders with no claim to the throne whatsoever could ruin himself and the country.

'It is no use shrugging aside this Perkin,' he said to his Lord Chamberlain Sir William Stanley. 'He is more dangerous than Lambert Simnel. It is all very well to talk slightingly of Perkin as we did of the scullion now in the kitchens, but they make trouble, these petty adventurers.'

'Indeed it is so, my lord,' said Stanley, 'but this fellow is a nobody and most people know this.'

'My good Stanley, you give the people credit for too much good sense. There are people who will support a cause however flimsy because they take a delight in discord. One is never quite sure where trouble will come from next.'

'Sire, you are firm on the throne now. It would take a mighty force to shift you.'

The King smiled at Stanley. He wished he had his confidence. Good Stanley. He owed a great deal to him and had recently made him a Knight of the Garter. He doubted whether but for Stanley he would be where he was today. Stanley was in a way a member of the family, for his brother had married the Countess of Richmond thereby becoming Henry's stepfather. It was Stanley who at Bosworth Field had deserted Richard the Third and brought his men over to Henry's side at a vital moment. One could say he had helped put Henry on the throne and Henry liked to have such men about him, being haunted as he was by the fear of assassination or the rising of those who would try to take the crown from him.

They were joined by Empson and Dudley, who were so good at thinking up taxes which could be legitimately imposed on the people and thus adding to treasury funds.

They were smiling. They had brought him good news of large sums of money which had recently been added to the exchequer. But the King could not be weaned from his melancholy mood.

'It is no use amassing wealth and creating a prosperous country if all our efforts are to be squandered in wars to suppress pretenders.'

'No one can really believe that Perkin Warbeck is the Duke of York,' said Empson.

'We know that, my friend,' replied Henry, 'and my enemies on the Continent know it as well as we do, but it suits them to set him up, to provide him with that which he needs to come against me. I have a suspicion that he is not without friends in this country.'

'That cannot be,' cried Dudley, aghast.

'Impossible!' echoed Stanley.

'I have not your trusting natures, my friends,' said the King. 'There are certain people about me whom I know to be loyal . . . who have proved their loyalty . . . but beyond that.'

He was looking with approval at the three men who nodded sympathetically.

'We must be on the alert,' said Stanley. 'We shall increase our vigilance and may I say, my lord, that this project of yours for Prince Henry will be an answer to these people on the Continent.'

'I thought so,' said the King.

'We will try to make it not too costly,' said Empson.

'On an occasion such as this will be, in my opinion, one should not give an impression of parsimoniousness,' Stanley said. 'As a matter of fact, my lord, I have come with suggestions for the tournaments which must necessarily follow. And the Prince will need his special garments.'

'We will discuss these matters,' said Henry, 'and when we have decided we will pass over the accounts to our good friends here . . .'

Empson and Dudley bowed their heads and, realizing that their presence was not needed while the arrangements were discussed, asked leave to retire and left the King alone with his Lord Chamberlain.

Later Henry recalled his lawyer financiers to discuss the cost of the ceremonies he was planning and when they had glanced through the suggested expenditure the subject of Perkin Warbeck arose again. Indeed it seemed one which the King found impossible to leave for long. It was clearly very much on his mind.

'The more I think of it the more certain I am that we have enemies in our midst,' he said. 'It may well be that they are planning to help Perkin when he attempts to land.'

His ministers looked grave.

'If we could find out who they are . . .'

'I intend to,' said the King. 'That is why I am setting spies along every road that leads to Dover. I am having all travellers searched. In this way we shall ourselves receive messages which are intended for our enemies.'

'A big task, Sire.'

'We are constantly confronted by big tasks—and this happens to be a very important one . . . for us all. The Londoners are already up in arms because of the cessation of trade with Flanders.'

Both Dudley and Empson were silent. They did not think that was a very good measure to take merely to upset Margaret of Burgundy. England herself had suffered from the loss of trade which was the last thing the King wanted. It showed how deeply he feared this Perkin Warbeck.

'And have your spies on the Dover road discovered anything?'

'Not yet. But I am hopeful.'

He was right to be hopeful for within a short time his spies found what they were looking for. When he read the letters which were being brought from Flanders for Lord Fitzwalter he was horrified.

The letters were written by Sir Robert Clifford, a man whom he knew and whom he would have trusted. He had been with the army in France, spoke the language fluently, and had acted as an interpreter. Henry would have vouched for his loyalty. It was a terrible blow to discover that he did not know in what direction to look for his enemies.

Clifford had written: 'I have been in contact with the Pretender. He is so like the late King Edward the Fourth that he must be his son. I have no doubt whatsoever that the man who is contemptuously called Perkin Warbeck by Henry Tudor is in truth Richard the Fourth.'

The letters went on to state that plans were going ahead for the invasion. It was necessary to have friends whom they could trust in England so that when the invading forces landed they would know where to look for supporters.

This was worse than Henry had feared. The correspondence revealed names in the most unexpected quarters. There was Lord Fitzwalter, a man whom he had made steward of his household during the first year of his reign and later joint steward of England with Jasper Tudor. He was deeply wounded by the perfidy of such a man. What had he wanted? More honours? Or did he genuinely believe that Perkin Warbeck was Richard of York? Who could say? The mysterious disappearance of the Princes would go on reverberating through the ages. If the truth could be told. . . No! The truth must never be told. But his concern of the moment was to bind his friends to him and to cut off his enemies for ever.

Sir Thomas Thwaites, Sir Simon Mountford . . . traitors all of them. Men close to him, men whom he had believed to be his friends! And this was not all, there were three members of the Church involved in the conspiracy—and important ones at that. The Dean of St. Paul's himself and the Prior of Langley as well as the Provincial of the Black Friars.

He was cold with fear and rage.

He sent for his guards.

'Arrest these men,' he said.

So now he knew the extent of the conspiracy. He had been wise to intercept the messengers.

He thought constantly of Sir Robert Clifford. He knew the man well, remembering him from the days in France. He was not a man whom he considered would be distinguished for his bravery, and it occurred to the King that Robert Clifford might be very useful to him. The men whose names had been revealed were not of any great importance perhaps. They were not the leaders of the conspiracy and Henry's natural suspicions led him to believe that there might be men close to him who were working against him. They were the ones he must try to catch.

He made a decision. Could he use Robert Clifford to work for him as an informer, a counter spy? It seemed possible. He immediately sent one of his spies to Flanders in the guise of a merchant with the instructions that he was to seek out Robert Clifford, sound him, offer him a pardon, offer him money, if he would work for Henry instead of for this Pretender whose claims he must know were as spurious as those of the scullion Lambert Simnel.

Henry eagerly waited for the response. It came quickly. Robert Clifford was ready to work for Henry Tudor.

Henry was pleased. Robert Clifford should be given a free pardon—he had the King's word for that. When it should be ripe for him to return to England he should have a grant of five hundred pounds; and there should also be a free pardon for his servant Richard Waltier who would also be expected to serve the King in this matter of revealing those who worked against him.

This was a wise move. Henry now began to realize how deeply the dissatisfaction had gone in England. He was amazed at those who were ready to listen to this preposterous claim of young Perkin and moreover dally with the possibility of betraying their crowned King.

HENRY DUKE OF YORK

In the nurseries at Eltham Palace the royal children played their games and grappled with their lessons unaware of the fact that their lives could drastically change within a few days if their father's enemies were successful.

In spite of the fact that he was the youngest and only three years old, Henry was already making his presence felt. Arthur, five years his senior, was a quiet and studious boy, rarely asserting himself and leaving his sister Margaret and young Henry to fight together for supremacy. Five-year-old Margaret was showing signs of a forceful personality which was matched by that of three-year-old Henry who would send his bronze horse on its squeaky wheels shooting across the nursery in pursuit of any who offended him. He loved that horse for on it sat a knight with a lance and a shield and Henry had always seen himself as that knight, fearless, ready to attack his enemies, and at the same time it offered a certain comfort in the dark. Margaret had complained many times to Anne Oxenbrigge, whose task was to watch over Henry, that her brother had grazed her legs with his silly old horse.

Anne would scold Henry in a mild way which was no real scolding. Henry knew he only had to bury his face in her skirts and look woeful and she would pick him up and cuddle him. He liked cuddling Anne; she was warm and soft with enormous bosoms from which he had sucked his milk when a baby. She had been chosen because she was young and healthy, large of hip and bosom with a red and white complexion which showed good health. Henry knew of course that she was only a nurse and that his mother was a queen, but a lady so noble that she could not be concerned with children in nurseries. But children in nurseries grew up and when they did they became important as his mother and father were.

He must wait for that day. In the meantime he had to rule the nursery. It would not have been difficult but for his rival Margaret who could scream as loud as he could, kick and cajole as effectively. He did not have to worry about Arthur. Although he was big and old he never listened to their quarrels, and never took part in any; he was always meek and anxious to do his lessons.

Anne said: 'Your brother Arthur is a good boy. Now why don't you try to be more like the Prince of Wales?'

'*I* should be Prince of Wales,' said Henry.

'Now, now, that's silly. Arthur is older than you. It is his right.'

'It's my right *really* . . .'

'The pride of him!' said Anne, kissing him. 'Now you try to be a good boy and don't send that horse of yours crashing into Margaret. You hurt her badly.'

'I'm glad.'

'Now that is really wicked.'

'I *am* wicked. I want to be wicked. I am going to hurt Margaret with my horse. My knight doesn't like her. He doesn't like Arthur. He thinks I ought to be Prince of Wales.'

'Tut! tut!' said Anne; he heard her say afterwards to one of the maids: 'Our young Henry has a fine conceit of himself. I fancy he is jealous of his brother. I'm always telling him he ought to be more like him. I thank the Virgin that he is not.'

Henry was all ears. The perfidy of women! Wasn't Anne always telling him that he should be good and quiet like Arthur, studying his lessons—and now she was thanking the Virgin that he was not! This was interesting.

'Delicate,' whispered Anne. 'Takes after his mother.'

'Don't suppose he'll make old bones.'

'It wouldn't surprise me at all. It's a good thing we have young Henry.'

'There's a sturdy little fellow for you. They say he takes after his grandfather King Edward. I never saw him but I hear he was big and tall and more handsome than anyone ever before.'

'I reckon that's about right and young Henry will be such another. It's a pity he wasn't born first . . . What a king he would have made!'

'Well . . . who knows . . .'

'Hush! We shouldn't talk like this. The Queen would think we were illwishing her eldest.'

'God forbid. He's a dear boy.'

'Easier to manage than young Henry I can tell you.'

'Ah well, he's a boy to be proud of . . . though a handful.'

The 'handful' went off brooding on what he had heard. A resentment had started to grow in his heart. It was rather unkind of God not to have made him the eldest—more than unkind, foolish, for it was clear that he would have made a much better king than Arthur.

He was growing fast and he was a big child. He was secretly delighted to realize that he was catching up on Arthur. Arthur was a little thin and weedy; Henry was sturdy rather than plump; he had a cherubic face with a pink and white complexion, whereas Arthur's face was thinnish and rather pale; Henry's reddish hair was thick and plentiful, Arthur's was inclined to be less vital. Margaret was very like Henry. Vociferous and demanding, there was bustle surrounding her always and she was constantly in some argument with the nurses because she wanted to do something which was forbidden.

Henry felt the nursery would have been a happier place without Margaret—without Arthur too for that matter. He would have liked a nursery where he was the eldest and perhaps one or two brothers and sisters who looked up to him as though he were already a king.

He liked to leave the Palace, which he had done on one or two occasions when he had been to see his parents at Westminster. He had ridden on his palfry—led by a squire—and the people had liked him. They had cheered him wildly—him more than the others he was sure—and he had smiled at them and waved and he fancied his father had been rather pleased with him. He thought it was a shame that they had to come back to Eltham; it was a pleasant palace but away from everything that was especially exciting. Although it was only eight miles from London it was shut away. He felt when he was crossing the drawbridge over the very deep moat that he was leaving the exciting world behind. The walls were so high, the archway so lofty, he felt shut in by all those grey stones and he longed to be older that he might go to Court and hear the people cheer him.

He sat at table with his brother and sister.

Arthur was constantly told: 'Now you must eat that, my lord. You'll never grow into a big strong boy if you don't.'

No need to tell Henry. He could always eat all the beef or mutton which was put before him; he always asked for his pewter tankard to be refilled with the ale which they were given to drink. They never had water; it could be dangerous. He liked good spiced meat far better than that salt fish they had on Fridays and in fact he disliked Fridays because of the fish, for food meant a great deal to him.

Meals were quite a ceremony. They were presided over by squires well suited to the task, for princes must be taught to conduct themselves in a seemly fashion at the table and not fall on the food like ravenous wolves. They must not show too great an interest in the food—because that was what the needy would do. They must wash their hands both before and after a meal; they must eat with a knife gracefully and use the correct fingers for holding the food. Even the washing of hands was a ceremony, for one of the carvers would bring the bowl, then kneel and pour water over Henry's hands while another servant stood by with a towel to dry them.

The most difficult part was to show indifference to the food. That was something Henry could not feel for he was invariably ravenously hungry.

It was September, about three months after Henry's third birthday, when messengers arrived at the Palace. They came to announce that in a few days the King and Queen would be visiting Eltham.

The household was in a twitter of excitement, which was mainly apprehension. They were all very much in awe of the King, for although he rarely spoke to any of them, if he noticed anything of which he disapproved there would be a complaint and the fact that it would not be made in the hearing of the one to blame made it worse because there was no chance of answering the charge.

The Queen was a beautiful, gentle lady, but it was the King who counted.

Henry was at the nursery window with Arthur and Margaret when the cavalcade rode into the great courtyard. He saw the magnificently caparisoned horses and the servants of the King in their green and white livery mingling with those of the Queen's purple and blue. It was exciting. Henry jumped up and down in his glee.

'Be still, Henry,' admonished Margaret. 'You are behaving like a stable boy.'

Henry's little blue eyes narrowed. He would have liked to send his bronze horse and knight rushing straight at her. But this was not the time for retaliation so he merely scowled at her which did not bother her in the least and she laughed at him saying, 'Now you look really ugly!'

As though he ever did! As though he ever could! How often had he heard the servants say he was the image of his grandfather Edward and *he* had been one of the most handsome men in England.

Anne Oxenbrigge was running into the nursery casting an anxious eye over them all. Arthur's tutor was there with other attendants and servants because now was the time for the children to go down and greet their parents.

Arthur led them into the great hall.

They knew what they had to do. They must bow to the King and Queen and wait until they were spoken to.

The King was a disappointment to Henry. He did not look like a king. Henry would have liked to see his father in purple velvet and ermine with a golden crown on his head.

When I am King . . . he thought . . . and then with a guilty look at Arthur . . . *if* I am King I shall always look splendid. My father might be just a squire or a lord . . . out for a day's hunting. The Queen was beautiful though—like a picture, rather remote, with her plump rather expressionless face and a certain longing in her eyes which the children did not understand.

The King watched them to make sure they behaved in the correct manner and when the first ceremony of greeting was over they were all a little more comfortable.

Refreshment was immediately brought for the party and Arthur served the King and then the Queen with wine and cakes. The Queen kept Margaret and Henry with her . . . one on either side, and Henry thought how beautiful she was and was proud of her. He kept comparing her with Anne Oxenbrigge. Anne was by no means as beautiful . . . but somehow he would hate them to send Anne away whereas when the Queen went he would not mind so very much after the first day or so, and then he would only mind because it meant that all the excitement of a royal visit was over.

The Queen asked questions about what they did. Margaret tried to talk all the time but Henry was not having that. There was quite a little babble about the Queen which was different from what was happening with the King and Arthur, who seemed to find it difficult to keep their conversation going.

Finally that ceremony was over and the King and Queen went to their apartments while the children returned to the nurseries, there to wait the next summons which would be for dinner; as they would take this with their royal parents their mentors hoped they would remember all they had been taught about the washing of hands and the correct method of eating.

Arthur was given precedence of course; he it was who held the basin while the King's hands were washed; then he sat beside the King and there was more of that uneasy talk. Poor Arthur, he was wishing that the ordeal was over.

They were all glad when the tumblers who travelled with the King and performed for his entertainment were brought in. The

King's stern face relaxed into a smile as he watched them and young Henry was so excited he leaped up and tried to imitate them which caused a great deal of amusement and even made the King laugh aloud.

Then there was the King's fool called Patch who said a lot of things to make them all laugh and was really quite disrespectful to the King which Henry could not understand until he learned afterwards that this was a special privilege for fools whom nobody took seriously.

If I were a king, he thought, I wouldn't allow anyone to speak disrespectfully of me, fool or no.

Ever since he had overheard that conversation he was thinking more and more of what he would do if he were king.

He was surprised when the King told him to come and sit beside him. His father studied him very carefully.

'You may have been wondering why the Queen and I have come to Eltham.'

'To see me . . . and Arthur and Margaret.'

'Yes, that is so. But there is a rather special reason and it concerns you, my son.'

Henry's eyes were bright with excitement; his little mouth turned up in a smile.

'I am going to honour you, Henry. I am going to give you a title. You must be worthy of it.'

'I will, my lord,' said Henry firmly.

'I believe you will. You are going to be the Duke of York.'

'Couldn't I be Prince of Wales?'

'What do you mean? Arthur is the Prince of Wales.'

'He doesn't like being Prince of Wales very much. I should . . .'

The King's smile was a little wintry. 'You must not say such things. There is a Prince of Wales and he will remain Prince of Wales until he becomes the King. You will have to understand these matters. You will be Duke of York which is next in rank and honour to the Prince of Wales.'

Henry was subdued. He had betrayed his dreams. That was silly. Although he hoped that one day he would be the King, he knew that he must never tell anybody.

'What must I do, my lord?' he asked.

'You will be told and have time to learn what you have to do. It is a most important ceremony and I want you to be worthy of it.'

Henry nodded gravely.

'There, my son,' said his father, 'that is the purpose of our visit . . . to honour you.'

That was very pleasant, but for just a fleeting moment Henry wished that his parents had come to *see* him . . . rather than just to tell him of something he had to do, even though it was such an honour.

The King dismissed him and he went back to his place beside the Queen. Margaret was watching him jealously, and he could not resist crying out: 'I'm going to be Duke of York. I'm going to be honoured.'

He looked up at his mother. On impulse he buried his face in her skirts. He felt cool hands taking hold of him. It was one of the carvers. His mother was smiling but she made no attempt to touch him. Margaret was looking pleased which meant that he had behaved in a manner which was quite incorrect. The King was pretending not to see what he had done, but the King saw everything. He would hear more of this.

His pleasure was dampened. He knew then that he wanted his mother to ruffle his hair as Anne Oxenbrigge did, to pick him up and hold him against her breast, to tell him that for all his impudence he was only a baby.

He was glad when the tumbling and antics of the fool ceased and he could go to the nurseries. Anne was there waiting. He ran to her and caught her by the knees.

'Anne, Anne, I'm going to be Duke of York!'

He was picked up, held in the strong arms. He buried his face into her large soft breasts.

'Well, well,' she said, 'you'll have to mind your manners, won't you?'

She was laughing. He said: 'Are you glad, Anne? Are you pleased?'

She was silent for a while. Then she said: 'No . . . I expect I want you to stay my baby . . .'

Then he put his head down on her breast again and clung to her. He was comforted.

It was a golden October day when they came to prepare him for the great event. He was dressed in velvet with a cap on his abundant reddish hair, and they put a heavy gold chain round his neck; his cheeks were even rosier than usual, for he was very excited.

His riding master had had some qualms. He was very young to ride but it was believed he was proficient enough to manage a small quiet horse; and the people would of course be delighted with him. The King had said that this was the time to show them that there was one Duke of York and one only, and he was the son of Henry Tudor here in London, and not a lying impostor skulking on the Continent.

So young Henry came riding into London where the Mayor, the aldermen and dignitaries from the city companies were all waiting to greet him. The people had crowded into the streets and when they saw this beautiful little boy sitting so confidently on his horse and returning their greetings with such royal gravity they roared their applause.

At Westminster the King was waiting to receive his son and when he saw him he congratulated himself on this move. Few could have done more for him than this beautiful child at this dangerous moment when the news from the Continent was growing more and more grim and it was certain that people in England were concerned in the conspiracy. A glow of affection showed in his eyes but young Henry was too concerned with his own role to notice it.

He had been drilled constantly for the last week so that he should not fail to do what was expected of him and he was thoroughly enjoying it all. This was his day. And although Arthur might be the Prince of Wales, the most important son of the King at this time was Henry.

His first task was to join in the ceremony of washing the King's hands. It had been decided that he should be the one who stood by with the towel. But he must kneel when offering it and he was a little unsteady. However the King smiled at him and he believed he had performed that duty with grace. Now he could sit down and eat—being very careful how he did so—and even at such a time his appetite did not fail him.

Afterwards he was taken away to a small room where he was stripped of his clothes and placed in a warm herb-scented bath. This he knew was the ceremony of purification which all knights had to undergo.

He sat in the bath and listened to the injunctions which were read out by Lord Oxford, explaining to him what knighthood demanded. He must remain faithful to the Church; he must protect widows and maidens; and above all he must love the King and serve him with all his heart.

The King put his hand in the water and making the sign of the cross on young Henry's body, kissed the spot.

Then the boy was taken from his bath and dressed in a robe made of coarse stuff which irritated his skin. He was then allowed to go to his apartments although the rest of the knights who had joined in the ceremony would spend the night praying in the chapel.

He was glad to cast off the coarse garment and delighted when the following day they dressed him in silken clothes which in comparison seemed deliciously soft. In the chapel the knights were waiting to conduct him to the Star Chamber where one of them, Sir William Sandes, lifted him and carried him to the King's Hall where the King was waiting.

The King then commanded two of the most noble peers in the land to put the spurs on the little boy's feet, so the Duke of Buckingham fixed the right one and the Marquis of Dorset the left, while the King himself put on the boy's sword. There he was equipped like a knight—though a diminutive one, but he felt very proud.

The King kissed him and said: 'Be a good knight, my son.' Then he picked him up and put him on a table and as he stood there with his newly acquired sword and spurs everyone cheered.

He was now a Knight of the Bath.

But it was the greater title which the King wished to bestow on him and the following day there was another ceremony.

This was far more impressive because the King wore his robes of state and his crown and he himself wrapped young Henry in the velvet cloak of deep crimson edged with miniver and put on his coronet and sword.

He was now the Duke of York.

After that it was rather disappointing because although there were tournaments and entertainments to celebrate his elevation, the adults seemed to have forgotten that he was the centre of it all and now that he had actually gone through his performance he was once more regarded as a little boy. It was true he was allowed to sit in the royal box and watch the knights tilt against each other, but Margaret and Arthur were there too; and when the prizes were distributed to the successful knights it was not he who awarded them but Margaret.

How self-satisfied she was when the knights came up one by one and knelt to her. She could not resist glancing over her shoulder to make sure that Henry was watching. It was as though she said: 'I know you went riding through the city and everyone cheered you, but watch me now. They are all *kneeling* to me.'

It was irritating and he scowled at her, but try as she might she could not take from him the memory of all those people smiling at him and cheering him and so obviously thinking how important he was.

He wanted that adulation to go on and he grew more and more sorry that he had not been born the eldest. He was sure the people would have preferred him to Arthur.

How could fate have been so blind?

It was just after Christmas when Sir Robert Clifford arrived in England and called on the King at the Palace of the Tower where he had taken up residence at that time.

As soon as he knew that he had arrived Henry received him.

The man bowed low.

'So,' said the King, 'you have returned.'

'My lord, I can do no more in your service. I am of the opinion that the conspirators have become aware of my actions and I have news of one near to you who is a traitor and I believed that I had something to say to you which could not be trusted to paper.'

'I see,' said the King. 'Go on.'

'I would remind you, Sire, of your promise to me.'

'Yes, yes, a free pardon. It is yours.'

'And five hundred pounds for my services.'

'It shall be yours. Tell me of this traitor.'

'I fear you will be inclined to disbelieve me for it concerns one very close to you . . . even related.'

The King tapped his fingers impatiently but still Sir Robert hesitated, whether to give his revelation more momentum or whether he feared the King's wrath over what he was about to reveal, Henry was not sure.

'Come, come, Clifford. Speak up.'

'My lord, Sir William Stanley is in league with Perkin Warbeck.'

'Stanley! Impossible.'

'I feared you would feel so, my lord. But it is the truth. I have evidence. Letters in his handwriting. He is ready to offer his help to the impostor when he lands in England.'

Henry was silent. He would not believe it. Not William Stanley . . . brother of his father-in-law! Heaven preserve him, how deep had this thing gone! He had scarcely had a night's sound sleep since he had heard the name of Perkin Warbeck.

'Allow me, Sire,' said Clifford. 'I can give you irrefutable evidence and knowing that you would find it difficult to believe in this man's perfidy I have brought you that evidence.'

The King held out his hand.

He stared down at the paper. Stanley's writing. Stanley's treason! There could be no doubt of it.

He felt sick with disgust and anger. Had he not seen it with his own eyes he would never have believed it. Stanley! What would his mother say? What would his stepfather say? This was terrible. This was treachery of the worst kind.

'My lord, you believe me now?'

'I believe you, Sir Robert. You have done good work. It is a pity that you were ready to betray me in the beginning.'

'A mistake, Sire, for which I crave the pardon which you have already granted me. I realized my mistake and I wished to rectify my errors . . . which I am sure with your love of truth and justice you will readily agree that I have done.'

For five hundred pounds and a free pardon! How uneasy is he who is a king! Must it always be so? Must those whom he most trusts betray him?

'You have done well,' he said. 'You shall be paid your five hundred pounds. Leave these papers with me. . . You may go to my treasurer and take an order from me for your five hundred pounds which shall be paid to you at once. Then you may go.'

'Thank you, my lord. It has been my pleasure to serve you.'

'Go now,' said the King coldly.

He sat silent for a few seconds. Somewhere in this very palace Sir William Stanley would be preparing for the evening's entertainment, little guessing that his perfidy was revealed. Henry was glad that he had come to the Tower. Stanley could be taken to his cell without undue fuss.

He sent for the guards.

'Arrest Sir William Stanley,' he said, 'and have him conducted to a dungeon. Make sure that he is well guarded.'

The men-at-arms were astounded. They hesitated, wondering if they had heard correctly.

The King said, and his voice was very cold: 'Those are my orders. Sir William Stanley is to be conducted without delay to a dungeon. He is under close arrest.'

The men bowed and went out. Henry sat for a few moments staring into space, his face creased into lines of desperate unhappiness.

The King signed to the jailer to open the door of the cell. He went in. Stanley turned sharply and let out a cry when he saw who his visitor was. He went onto his knees and tried to take the King's hand.

'My lord . . . Sire . . . I do not understand.'

'Get up, Stanley,' said the King. 'Alas, I understand all too well.'

'My lord, I pray you tell me of what I am accused.'

'Of treachery, Stanley.'

'Treachery? I . . . Your faithful servant . . .'

'My unfaithful servant, alas. Have done with pretence. I know that you have been in correspondence with the impostor Perkin Warbeck. I have seen your letters . . .'

Stanley's shocked silence would have proclaimed his guilt if that had been necessary. It certainly was not. Henry had no doubt of it. It had been made quite clear to him.

'My lord . . . I thought . . . to discover more of this man . . .'

An old excuse! It never worked. He was going to say: I was pretending to be with the other side in your service. I wanted to find out what they were planning so that I could present my findings to you.

'It is useless, Stanley, I know all. Do you imagine that while you have your friends over there I have none? My good servants were working for me, Stanley, while my unfaithful ones were working against me. I could not believe it at first. You . . . Stanley. . . Your brother my own stepfather. My mother will be quite distressed. I should think your brother will be ashamed.'

Stanley covered his face with his hands. 'As I am, my lord . . . as I am . . .'

'Perhaps I should have suspected you. You were ever a turncoat.'

Stanley spoke with some spirit. 'Ah, my lord, you owe something to that. Have you forgotten Bosworth Field?'

'I do not forget, Stanley, that you started out with Richard and when the battle turned against him you changed sides.'

'And decided the day for you, my lord.'

'There could be something in that. But one should never trust a turncoat. So now you are ready to give your services to Perkin. Has he promised to pay you well? I rewarded you did I not? Did I not acknowledge my debt to you? You were my Lord Chamberlain. Knight of the Garter. Did I not give you estates in Wales? And yet, and yet . . .'

Stanley was silent.

The King looked at him steadily. 'I just wondered why, Stanley. You must have been promised a great deal. I know your love of possessions. I have heard that you have many treasures stored away in Holt Castle. Alas, Stanley, you cannot take them with you.'

'My lord . . .'

'You shall be tried, Stanley. Never fear—it shall be a fair and just trial. And if you are found guilty . . . as it would seem you cannot fail to be . . . you will pay the penalty demanded of traitors. Goodnight, Stanley. I think you should begin to make your peace with God.'

The King went out. A terrible melancholy possessed him. He felt that he would never trust anyone again.

Sir William Stanley was brought before his peers in Westminster Hall, where he was accused of falsely plotting the death and destruction of King Henry the Seventh and attempting to overthrow the kingdom.

In vain did he protest his innocence. He had been maligned, he insisted; his enemies had trumped up evidence against him; but even he knew that none would believe him. He had been a fool. He had gambled too far. He had always been an adventurer. As a Yorkist during the reign of Edward the Fourth he had enjoyed many favours; he had professed friendship for Richard the Third but when he had seen an opportunity of finding favour with Henry he had blatantly deserted Richard and as it happened swung the battle in Henry's favour. He had often congratulated himself on going over at precisely the right moment. Henry had been grateful, had rewarded him. But perhaps Stanley was adventurous by nature; perhaps the thought of this young man on the Continent had fired his imagination. It was possible that he was one of the Princes in the Tower, for the question of what had happened to those Princes had never been satisfactorily answered.

However, whatever motives had led him to this, he was here and he had come to the end. He knew now there would be no adventures, no more plots and counter plots.

He must now say: It is over, and prepare himself for his fate.

'Guilty of treason' was the verdict and he was condemned to the traitor's death.

The traitor's death! It was the most barbarous act which could befall a man. To be dragged through the streets on a hurdle, to be hanged, cut down before death put a merciful end to suffering, cut open and one's entrails burned until one could endure no more.

Every man dreaded it. To be a traitor men needed the utmost courage and yet . . . so many of them were ready to risk this terrible death for something they believed in.

Did Stanley believe in Perkin Warbeck? Not in his heart. He knew Warbeck was another Lambert Simnel but more polished, more prepared. He had the other to draw on for a lesson.

That he, William Stanley, should have come to this was hard to believe. He had brought disgrace on his brother, but the Countess would protect her husband from the King's wrath against the family. Perhaps Henry was not the man to visit the sins of one man on another just because they happened to be brothers. Henry was a just man. He was not revengeful. He would eliminate people—coldbloodedly as some thought, but that would only be because he felt it necessary to do so. Any violent deed which he condoned would not be done in hot blood or vengeance. It would be because it was expedient to do it.

It was no use asking for clemency, for Henry would reason that it would be unwise to grant it. Sir William Stanley was a traitor and the King must give a lesson to all would-be traitors.

Henry was more concerned about Stanley than he cared to admit. There must always be men who worked against a leader, he supposed, because men were envious by nature, and if a man was up, there would always be those who wanted to bring him down, for no other reason than that he was up . . . and perhaps they thought they had more right to be where he was. That he accepted. But not the treachery of close friends—men whom he had trusted. This was the blow.

He was shut in with his melancholy. To whom could he talk of these depressions which obsessed him? Not to his mother—she was too close and she would be particularly disturbed because the criminal was her husband's brother. No, he could not distress her more by revealing his grief to her. To Elizabeth the Queen? No. He never talked to Elizabeth. She knew him as a kind and gentle husband but he had never shared a state secret with her and he had never talked to her of the affairs of the country. Arthur was a child. He wished his children were older. How comforting it would have been to discuss this matter with a son. Arthur was grave and serious. He had high hopes of Arthur . . . but as yet a boy of eight.

The King felt desperately alone.

It was not only Sir William Stanley who had been exposed as a traitor. There were many more. It was disturbing that there should be others but Stanley was the one on whom he brooded.

Not one of them must be spared. There must be public executions. The people must be made fully aware of the dreaded fate in store for traitors.

People crowded the streets. Executions were like public holidays. Crowds massed outside Newgate to watch the prisoners brought out and taken to the place of execution. Those of higher rank were taken from the Tower but the place was of little importance to the condemned. They were all to meet the same fate.

Henry spared one or two of them at the last minute, just as

they were preparing themselves for the axe. This created drama, as the King intended it should. A messenger would arrive at the last moment and there would be an announcement from the scaffold that the King had decided on a reprieve for this particular criminal because he considered he had been led astray by evil counsellors. The reprieved man would go back to prison where in due course he might earn his liberty.

This made the executions almost like a play. At every one of them the people waited expectantly for an announcement. It was obvious in the faces of the condemned that they too were waiting.

There would be a hush in the crowd and a watchfulness for the messenger waving the King's pardon. Though it came rarely the expectation was always there; and when the axe finally descended there would be a deep sigh from the crowd.

Henry decided that he could not submit Sir William Stanley to the indignity of the traitor's death and at the last moment the sentence was changed to beheading, so on a bleak February day Sir William was brought out of the Tower to Tower Green and there in the presence of a large crowd he laid his head on the block and paid the penalty for his treachery to the King.

The city was now adorned with the heads of traitors, but the King did not want to disgrace the Stanley family in this way, so he decreed that William Stanley's head should be buried with his body at Sion on the Thames.

Young Prince Henry, Duke of York, knew that something was happening and he was frustrated because no one told him what it was.

Margaret pretended to know but he was not sure that she did. Arthur of course knew, but would not talk of it. It was maddening.

And following so soon after his elevation particularly so, for Henry had realized during that ceremony that he was, if only a child, a very important one and he wanted everyone around him to remember it.

It was all very well for Anne Oxenbrigge to call him her baby. There were times when he wanted to be just that but even she must remember that he was also the Duke of York and although he might like to cuddle up against her warm and cosy bosom, he was still a very important boy, only slightly less so than Arthur.

'Where is Sir William Stanley?' he asked Margaret.

He had seen a great deal of Sir William before that splendid ceremony when he had been the centre of attraction. He wanted Sir William to bring him some more silken garments and to arrange more pageants in his honour.

'You are not to know,' retorted Margaret. 'You are too young.'

'*I* am the Duke of York,' he told her proudly.

'You are not four years old yet.'

'I will be in June.'

'But it is not yet June and you are only three. Fancy being only three!'

Henry was furious. He hated Margaret. If I were the King, he thought looking at her venomously through narrowed eyes . . . What would he do to Margaret? Send her to the Tower.

Arthur was kind. He asked him. His elder brother hesitated.

'It's of no moment,' said Arthur gently. 'I hear you have a new spinning top. Does it go well?'

'I whip it hard,' said Henry with satisfaction.

'You must show me.'

'First I want to know where Sir William Stanley is.'

Arthur thought: He will have to know sometime. There was no point in keeping it secret.

He said: 'He is dead. His head was cut off because he was a traitor.'

Henry's little eyes opened wide, and the colour rushed into his cheeks. He was trying to visualize Sir William Stanley without his head.

'There is a wicked man on the Continent who says he is the Duke of York.'

'*I* am the Duke of York.'

'Yes, this is a spurious one.'

Arthur used long words, forgetting that others couldn't understand them, because Arthur was supposed to be very clever with his books, and Henry was not going to admit that he didn't know what spurious was. It was clear that it was something wicked.

'What about him?' asked Henry eagerly.

'He wants to take the crown from our father.'

'Why?'

'To wear it, of course. Oh you are too young . . .'

'No, no, Arthur. I am growing up more every day. I wish I was older. I wish I were older than you.'

'Then you'd be Prince of Wales, brother.'

'You wouldn't like that.'

Arthur hesitated again. He was always hesitant, weighing everything up before he answered. 'I shouldn't mind,' he said slowly. 'In fact perhaps I might be rather glad.'

A wild excitement possessed Henry. Arthur didn't want to be Prince of Wales. Perhaps they could change places. He cried: 'I'll be it for you.'

That made Arthur laugh. 'Thank you, little brother, but it is not possible.'

Little brother! He had betrayed his youth again. It was maddening.

'Tell me about Sir William,' he said.

'It's merely that he was corresponding with Perkin Warbeck who pretends he is our uncle who disappeared in the Tower, and if he was alive would be King.'

'King? Then our father . . .'

'Oh you have a lot to learn, Henry.'

Henry was bewildered, raging against his youth and inexperience.

He was going to find out though and if it was ever possible, he was going to change places with Arthur.

Whenever they rode out from Eltham to join their parents at Westminster or Shene he saw heads on poles. They fascinated him.

'Whose heads are they?' he wanted to know.

The heads of traitors, he was told.

That was the right way to treat traitors. Their heads should be cut off and put on poles for everyone to see. The thought of someone taking his father's crown away frightened and angered him, for if his father were no longer King, Arthur would not be Prince of Wales—then how could Henry Duke of York change places with him when the time came?

There was more talk of Perkin Warbeck that summer, for the young man had taken an action which implied that he was very determined in his attempt to get possession of the throne.

News spread throughout the country that a fleet of ships led by the Pretender had appeared off the port of Deal.

The people of that town crowded onto the beaches to watch them, fearing that war was inevitable and that they were in the front line. And where were the King's forces and how long would it take them to reach the coast?

Some of the spirited members of the community of Sandwich, a town a little way along the coast, gathered together a fighting force. After all the executions which had taken place not so long ago they were not going to be accused of conspiring with the invaders.

Coming in close to land Perkin saw the hostile crowds assembled there and decided that he would not risk all of his troops. It would be difficult to land and he could see that while this operation was in progress he could be attacked and lose many of his men and much equipment.

He decided therefore to land a few men who could persuade the people that they came to deliver them from one who had no right to the throne while he, the true King, Richard the Fourth, was preparing to come and be their good lord.

But the people were not to be persuaded. The Mayor of Sandwich was there to meet them as they attempted to land. 'We want none of you Pretenders here,' he declared. 'We're content with what we have and that's an end to fighting. We're not having that on our soil.'

Perkin's troops realized that they were at a disadvantage and many of them rowed back to the ships. The others who had landed were immediately taken prisoner and their equipment captured.

When Henry heard what had happened he was delighted with his good people of Sandwich and Deal. They had taken over a hundred and sixty prisoners to send him, and the rest of the invading force at sea decided to give up the attempt, for the time at least, and make other plans for landing which might have a chance of success.

The people of Sandwich excitedly tied up their prisoners and sent them on to London in carts where they were received into the Tower and immediately sentenced to hanging. That the country might realize what happened to men who indulged in such actions against the King, they were publicly hanged in the coastal areas and from London to as far as Norfolk.

It was unfortunate that Perkin was not among them, but he had sailed on to Ireland.

Am I never to be free of this Perkin Warbeck? wondered the King. It was four years since he had first heard that name and it had haunted him ever since.

When would it end? Perhaps more important still, where would it end?

That September a sad event took place in the royal nurseries. The little Princess Elizabeth died. Young Henry had never taken much interest in her. She was a year or so younger than he was and that made her quite a baby. She was delicate and had to be specially taken care of, which to one in his robust health seemed a little contemptible.

The Queen came to Eltham—beautiful and remote. She was clearly very distressed by the state of her little daughter's health. Henry wondered why, because she saw very little of her. It was

Anne Oxenbrigge who made such a fuss, going about with red eyes and turning away every now and then to choke back her sobs.

Death! He knew it happened to traitors. He had seen their heads on poles. He used to count them when he rode through the streets from Eltham to Westminster or Shene. But that death should come to the royal nursery, that was different.

There were physicians everywhere. His father and his mother were in the nursery together. The rest of the children were sent out. They waited in an ante room; and then Arthur was called in.

'She is dying,' said Margaret. 'We shall have no sister now.'

'I have one,' said Henry.

'I haven't,' she said. 'But I have two brothers. You only have one.'

'I don't want two brothers.'

'You're only a baby yet.'

How she liked to taunt him with that. It was because she knew it was what he hated more than anything.

'I don't want any sisters either,' said Henry ominously.

'And I only want one brother . . . dear Arthur who is the nicest brother. I don't want a silly baby brother . . .'

Henry flew at her. He already showed signs of possessing a quick temper, which alarmed Anne Oxenbrigge.

It was Anne who came in now.

'For shame!' she said. 'Fighting when your little sister is dying. What do you think the King and Queen would say to that?'

'They won't know,' said Margaret slyly.

'God will,' Anne reminded her.

Both children were silent, contemplating the awfulness of God's watching them.

'So,' went on Anne, having made her point, 'you should be very careful.'

They were subdued. Henry whispered a prayer: I didn't mean it, God. It wasn't my fault. It was Margaret. You know what a silly girl she is.

He had made up his mind that he was always going to do what God would like, for he had heard it said that a king needed good allies and Henry had reasoned that God was the best ally any man could have.

The Queen had come out of the nursery. She came to the children and embraced them solemnly. They knew what that meant. Then Arthur came out with the King, and the King said very quietly: 'My children, you have no sister Elizabeth now. She has gone to live with God and His angels.'

Elizabeth was buried in the new chapel her father had built in Westminster Abbey.

THE SCOTTISH COURT

In the great hall of Stirling Castle the Scottish King was seated at the table, his favourite mistress Marion Boyd beside him. Everyone was drowsy as was invariably the case after they had feasted well. Several of the highest nobles in the land were present, among them Lennox, Huntly, Bothwell and Ramsay . . . all friends now, thought James, until they decide to revolt against me. What a crowd! He could not trust them any further than this hall. The only one he could really rely on was Marion—and perhaps her father Archibald Boyd of Bonshaw . . . solely because of his association with Marion of course.

James was cynical. How could he be otherwise? His countrymen must be the most quarrelsome in the world—with the exception of the Irish who might be said to be even worse; and another thing they had in common was perpetual hatred of the English. No matter what truces they made, no matter how many treaties were signed, how often they exchanged the kiss of peace, the antipathy was always there. It was as natural as breathing. The people below the Border were regarded as enemies by every Scotsman living above it.

He twirled a lock of Marion's hair. She was pregnant. That was pleasing. He liked children; and it was comforting to know how virile he was. He had several bastards for he was a man who found feminine society irresistible, and it had been so ever since he had come to the throne as a boy of fifteen, seven years ago. He wondered whether the child would be a girl or boy. He wouldn't mind. He would be proud of a boy but he had a greater fondness for the girls.

'Perhaps we'll call in Damian,' he remarked.

'What to tell us?' asked Marion idly.

He touched her protrusion playfully. 'A little girl or a little boy?' he said.

She took his hand and kissed it. 'Let's wait and see,' she said.

'I should like to see the fellow. He says very soon he shall be able to fly.'

Marion laughed. She did not trust the wily Abbot of Tungsland, who had leaped into favour with the King when he had declared that he possessed supernatural powers. James was intrigued. He had always listened to soothsayers—and relied on them perhaps too much.

Marion would not complain. James had been faithful in a way. That was if one did not mind his dallying now and then with other women. He could not help that. It was the nature of James. But his best-loved mistress could hold her place. None of them had ever had reason to complain of his meanness for he was very generous with those who pleased him—and beautiful Marion did that.

She had of late seen his eyes stray to Janet Kennedy. There was a beautiful woman if ever there was one. However she was the mistress of Archibald Douglas, and even James would think twice about upsetting the great earl.

Round the table several of the men had fallen asleep—they had slumped forward in their chairs, some snoring. Others sat with their women caressing them, perhaps rather too intimately for polite society. Not that James cared. They were Scots and would act in the Scottish way. The English who came to the Scottish Court were shocked by what they called the coarseness of the manners there. As for the elegant French they were amazed.

Let them be. It was Scotland for the Scots, said James.

George Gordon, Earl of Huntly was present with his eldest daughter Katharine—a very beautiful girl, James thought her. Her mother had been a daughter of James the First so there was a family connection. If he had not been so deeply involved with Marion—and Katharine was not the kind of girl with whom he could carry on a light intrigue—he might have been tempted. Perhaps it was better as it was. There was a puritanical streak about Katharine—young as she obviously was—and James had never been attracted by puritans. Connoisseur that he was, he had discovered that hot-blooded women were the most satisfactory partners.

Marion followed his gaze round the table and said: 'It is different at Westminster, I'll be bound.'

'You're right, my love. Henry is a very virtuous man. I have never heard one whisper that he is unfaithful to his Queen.'

'Perhaps people are afraid to whisper.'

'I think not. They whisper of other things. They say that his heart beats faster when he tots up a column of figures and sees what profits he has made than it ever could in the most appealing bedchamber in the world.'

'I see he has not your tastes, James.'

'You should thank Heaven for that, Madam.'

'I do . . . I do. But you are a little afraid of Henry Tudor are you not?'

'Dear Marion, my ancestors have been afraid of the rulers on the other side of the Border since the beginning of time. Trouble in England therefore means rejoicing in Scotland.'

'And the other way round?' suggested Marion.

'Don't upset me, woman. I have trouble enough as you know. I wonder how many of these who call themselves my friends, snoring and eating here at my tables, fornicating or committing adultery in the rooms of my castles . . . would as lief thrust a knife in my back as kneel to me in homage.'

'You must keep them in order, my King.'

'One thing is sure: they will always follow me when I make war on the English. That is the common enemy. We can all be friends hating them, but when the English are not coming against us then forsooth we must go against each other.'

'So it is in your interests to preserve your old enemy,' said Marion lightly.

'I hear that he is in a state of panic at this time.'

'Which pleases you mightily?'

'How did you guess? His throne trembles under him, you know.'

'I know. This fellow on the Continent . . . is he really the Duke of York, Edward's son?'

'Where is Edward's son? Where are Edward's sons? Two little boys in the Tower, and they disappear. Where to? Can people disappear in that way?'

'Easily if their throats are cut or they are stifled as I have heard these boys were . . . stifled by downy pillows . . . poor little mites. Did Richard do it as some say?'

'Why should he? He said they were bastards. But Henry has married their sister. He couldn't marry a bastard . . . which she must have been if they were. It sounds reasonable to me. Henry takes them from the Tower in secret . . . puts them out to be murdered far from the spot. Someone takes pity on the younger boy . . . and there we have our Perkin Warbeck.'

'Reasonable,' she admitted.

'And a great anxiety to old Henry. You can picture him—

trembling on his throne. There are many in Europe who are ready to rise up and help the young man fight for his crown.'

'Richard the Fourth. Would Scotland be happier under Richard the Fourth than under Henry the Seventh?'

'Scotland asks only to have an English king to fight. What his name is is of no matter. Scotland asks to harry the English King and if it can be done by making him change his name from Henry to Richard so much the better. Scotland is happiest when Englishmen are fighting against Englishmen because it saves the Scots the trouble of fighting them. I like to see my poor old enemy Henry being frightened out of his wits by this young man from Flanders.'

'Is he frightened? He seems to be holding his crown rather well.'

'Who can say, little love? He has to be continually on the alert. That has to take his mind from his money bags. And he won't like having to spend some of those contents on war, will he?'

'James, you are malicious.'

'I am indeed where Henry is concerned . . . but kind and loving to my friends, do you not agree?'

'I would agree with that.'

'I am thankful to have your approval. I fancy I don't have Huntly's at this moment. He is wondering whether his daughter Katharine should be in such company.'

'My lord, I trust you will keep your eyes from Katharine. She is not for you.'

'Well I know it. Huntly need have no fears for his virtuous daughter. We must find a worthy husband for her. That I assure you is the reason why he has brought her to Court. Now what say you to sending for Damian?'

'If it so please my lord, then let it be.'

'I'll send for him tomorrow. Now my bed calls . . . and it would seem it does for many of our friends.'

The King stood up and the company rose with him.

He bade them all a good and safe night; then with Marion he went to his bedchamber.

Damian appeared the next day. The Abbot of Tungsland had come far since he had attracted the attention of the King and this he had done through what he proclaimed to be knowledge of the art of magic.

He was an astrologer, but there were other astrologers. Damian had special gifts. He could tell the King what was about to happen. He could tell him what to avoid. He had had some luck in those respects and James, who wanted to believe, was inclined to pass over Damian's mistakes and remember his successes.

Marion had once said: 'You help Damian when he is groping for messages and things from the unknown. You supply him with little bits of information which help him make the right guess.'

James had been really displeased. Easy-going as he normally was he could be angry if anyone spoke disparagingly of something so near his heart as the effectiveness of the occult. Marion was quick to learn lessons. She would have to be careful; her association with James had been dangerously long and she saw the look in his eyes when they strayed to Janet Kennedy—mistress of old Bell-the-Cat though she might be. Kings were not all that averse to taking what Earls regarded as theirs; and James in his passionate pursuit of a mistress would be more determined than he had shown himself to be pursuing an enemy in war.

So Marion said no more about Damian and feigned an interest in his work which she did not really feel, and when Damian arrived she was with the King.

'Damian . . . my good friend,' cried the King, embracing the abbot. 'I am right glad to see you here.'

'My lord's wish is his command as far as I am concerned. I am always at your service, Sire.'

'Well, have you looked at the stars of late?'

'I search them continuously.'

'On my behalf I hope.'

'My lord King is never far from my mind.'

'Well, Damian, well . . . what sex is the child my dear Marion carries so proudly? Is he the King's son?'

Marion cried: 'James! How could he be another's!'

'Impossible, impossible dear lady. All know your fidelity to their sorrow . . . some declare I am sure. I was about to say, is he the King's son . . . or daughter?'

This was the sort of question which Damian liked least. One could so easily . . . and so quickly . . . be proved wrong. If one predicted some things it was easy to adjust one's meaning if the need arose, but the sex of a child—a plain yes or no—that was tricky.

He placed his hands on the girl. She was large. The manner in which she carried the child indicated it might be a boy. The last was a girl. What the King wanted to hear was that it was a boy and his reward would probably be greater if he made the King happy. It was a chance he had to take in any case, so why not take the happy chance?

'I think I can say with certainty that the child my lady carries is a boy . . . and your son, my lord.'

'Bless you, Damian. That's good hearing, eh Marion?'

'The best, my lord.'

'And will he grow up to be a good boy to his father?'

'He will,' said Marion. '*I* shall see to that.'

'There, Damian, you have a rival. The lady is looking into the future and finding the answer before you do.'

'The lady will indeed do all she says. I can confirm that.'

'What a pair of comforters I have! Now tell me of my old enemy below the Border. What trials can you search out for him, Damian?'

'He is beset by them. His eldest boy is sickly.'

'Is he going to die?'

'Not yet . . . but later . . .'

'Ah, there's another though. A sprightly little fellow by all accounts . . . recently made Duke of York by his doting father.'

'To show, my lord, that there should be but one Duke of York.'

'Well, there is eh? The other is the true King of England.'

Perkin Warbeck. Here was dangerous ground for Damian. He was always very well informed of affairs so that he knew exactly what was happening. That enabled him to give a considered judgement and once again he had been lucky in being right more often than wrong.

He had the gift of making his prophecies vague. That was the secret. A good sorcerer couched his words in clever obscurity so that when a certain thing happened people said, 'Oh that was what Damian meant!'

It was very helpful.

He said now: 'A visitor will come to your shores, my lord.'

The King was alert. Was he expecting someone? wondered Damian. It was always wise to say a visitor was coming because visitors came so often to a king. Damian knew that the French were eager to see Perkin Warbeck harry the King of England and that Margaret of Burgundy was helping him, and he knew that the Irish had helped in the past. It was very likely that some messenger would come to Scotland from one of these sources. So it was safe to mention a visitor.

'And how could I receive this visitor?'

'Receive him well. Listen to what he has to say. He will ask your help. Give it.'

That was wise. It was always good to listen and people usually came in supplication. It was never a bad thing to give help when it was asked. This was easy. It was the direct questions such as the sex of a child that made him uneasy.

The Abbot joined the courtiers at the dinner table that day. They all fired questions at him which amused the King.

And while they were at the meal one of the servants came running into the hall; his face was red and he was almost inarticulate in his desire to impart his startling news.

'A fleet of ships has been sighted off the coast of Scotland, my lord. They are saying it is Perkin Warbeck who comes to you.'

The King rose excitedly. Warbeck! The man who was claiming the English throne. It would be very amusing—and perhaps profitable—to have the man under his roof.

He looked at Damian who was smiling with satisfaction.

'Blessings on you, Damian, here is your visitor. Why the words were scarcely out of your mouth . . .'

'I did not know that he would be here so soon, my lord,' said Damian modestly.

'You excel yourself, Damian; now I have only to wait for the birth of my son.' He turned to the company. 'I think we should prepare to greet our guest,' he said.

James received Perkin Warbeck at Stirling Castle. Perkin had lived as a royal personage for four years and having been schooled in the part by none other than the Duchess of Burgundy, he had come to believe that he was the son of Edward the Fourth. So many times he had told the story of his being handed over to a man who was too soft-hearted to murder him and had set him free to roam the world for a few years before disclosing his identity that he believed it.

To converse with grace, to accept the homage due to his assumed rank, to behave with the manner of a courtier—this was all second nature to him.

Some of the noblemen of the Scottish Court were ready to laugh at his dandified manners because his gracious and graceful behaviour made them feel uncouth.

When he had the throne of England, he told James, he would remember those who had helped in his need. He had made many friends during this period of waiting and they could rest assured he would not forget them.

James said he was welcome and offered him a residence and one thousand two hundred pounds a year. Damian had said he should make his visitor welcome and this was surely that visitor.

Letters arrived from Ireland from Lord Desmond telling James that the Irish would support Richard the Fourth and drive the usurping Tudor from the throne. Moreover James took a fancy to Perkin. The young man talked well and seemed in no great hurry to go to make war into England. He was quite content to dally at the Court; he danced well, sang well; indeed he was a gracious courtier and James could well imagine how concerned the Tudor must be below the Border. The last place he would want his enemy to be was plotting with that other ever-present adversary. Moreover it would be easier to march into England over the Border than it ever could be by sea from the Continent. That was a hazardous matter, but to creep over the Border, to plant the flag on English soil—that had been done many times and would be done again.

But not yet. They would wait until the time was ripe. Let them have help from overseas. Let the Tudor fret in his bed at night . . . just a little longer.

In the meantime Perkin had noticed beautiful Katharine Gordon. That was interesting. A lovely girl—cousin of the King, Huntly's daughter. Perkin looked high . . . that was if he were only plain Perkin. Of course if he were indeed the true King of England it would be an excellent match for Katharine Gordon.

Marion's child was born. It was a son and so Damian had scored again.

Marion was delighted and so was James. He said the child should be called Stewart after his father. Alexander Stewart. None could doubt with a name like that that he was a true Scotsman.

Damian was clever, Marion agreed, crowing over her little son. He had been right about the child and the visitor.

'And he said that I was to welcome him,' said James. 'None can say I have failed as a host. And did you notice, Marion, that our gallant gentleman is casting eyes on Katharine Gordon?'

Marion had noticed. She was ever watchful of Katharine Gordon.

'It would not surprise me,' said James, 'if he should ask for her hand.'

'You'll grant it?'

'Huntly will have to be asked. But if he is indeed the true King of England he should have a bride with royal blood.'

'So you'll give your consent.'

'I might . . . when it's asked. I wonder what the Tudor will have to say about his rival's marrying into Scotland.'

'For that my dear, we must wait and see,' commented Marion.

'And you, my very dear, are as usual right,' said James. He was laughing. He was glad Perkin had come to Scotland. Perhaps soon they would make warfare over the Border. It would be pleasant to see the Tudor ousted and a beautiful Scottish lassie on the throne of England.

Perkin Warbeck was in love.

She was a very beautiful girl, this Katharine Gordon, daughter of the great Earl of Huntly and cousin of the King himself.

She was gracious to him. After all he was an honoured guest at the King's Court. They called him the Duke of York . . . heir to the throne of England . . . more than that, rightful King of that country. He had come a long way from the Warbeck home in Flanders. Fleetingly he thought of John and Katharine Warbeck whom he had believed to be his parents before he learned the fantastic story. What would they have said if they could see their son—or so-called son—now, honoured guest in all the courts of Europe, awaiting the moment when he should regain his throne.

He did not want to think too much of those early days in Flanders; they had been put away in some quiet recess in his mind—not to be disturbed, to be left there until they crumbled away into forgetfulness. Especially now he must not remember. What would these people say—the King, and the Earl of Huntly—if they thought a humble Flanders adventurer was asking for the hand of Katharine Gordon.

And Katharine herself? The manner in which she returned his glances, the flush which came to her cheeks at the soft pressure of his hand was enough to tell him with a girl like Katharine. She was not like so many women at James' Court. To tell the truth its crudity after the elegance of the Court of Burgundy had shocked him. The women were bold and brazen and the men openly coarse. That did not appeal to Perkin. He was immediately attracted to Katharine because she was different from so many of the others.

He contrived to be near her when possible, to talk to her, to attempt to assess what her feelings would be if he were to ask for her hand. The Huntlys were powerful noblemen; they lived close to the King. But the King had shown him the utmost friendship ever since he had arrived in Scotland. He could but try. It would be strange if having done so much for ambition he should falter in love.

In the dining hall of Stirling Castle he contrived to seat himself beside her. From the end of the table he was aware of James watching him and he could swear there was a glint of amusement in his eyes. If he was against a match between them would he allow them to be so much in each other's company? The Earl of Huntly was present also and he showed no objection.

Beside the King was his mistress Marion Boyd—very sure of herself now that she had a son as well as a daughter and both without doubt the King's.

Perkin deplored such conduct. The King should marry and settle down and make his Court respectable. If he must have mistresses he should have them in private. Perkin had heard there were negotiations for marriage going on between him and Spain. This showed something of the devious natures of the Spanish Sovereigns for there were similar diplomatic missions in progress between them and Henry Tudor for the same purpose. It was clear that Isabella and Ferdinand were playing one off against the other.

If the Spanish Sovereigns would aid him, with the help of Margaret of Burgundy and perhaps the King of France, he could be certain of achieving his goal.

There were times when he wondered whether that was really what he wanted. He tried to see himself as a king and could not quite manage it, for he knew there was more to governing a kingdom than riding through the streets in purple and gold and smiling at the people while one acknowledged their cheers. He had managed the speech and the manner very well, but he was not quite sure how he would emerge from the other. In the meantime this dalliance was very pleasant particularly now he had met Katharine.

He turned to her and said: 'You must forgive me for staring at you.'

'Were you?' she asked.

He smiled. 'Ah, you are so accustomed to people gazing that you do not notice. In truth they cannot keep their eyes from you, for they all admire you as I do.'

'Thank you,' she murmured. 'You are kind to say so.'

'I say only what I feel. If you but knew what I feel for you . . . well, I hardly know what you would say.'

'If I knew, you might have an opportunity of finding out.'

She was smiling at him, encouragingly surely, but if he asked her to marry him and she refused . . . that would be the end. He wanted to go to James and say, 'The Lady Katharine Gordon and I love each other, I beg you to give your consent to our marriage for that reason.' But what if she didn't? He realized that he was afraid. That was why he did not want events to go farther. He wanted to stay just as he was . . . pretender to the throne . . . accepted by important people talking constantly of the day he would be a king. He did not want to think beyond that. The future yawned before him like a dark pit and he was afraid to step into it lest he should fall into darkness. At the moment he was happy in the sunshine. He wanted to remain there.

He prevaricated as he did so often.

'You look so serenely beautiful; you are so young and when the sun shines on your hair it is like gold. I never thought to see such a perfect being.'

'I fear you do not see very clearly if you consider me perfect. I am far from that.'

'You have everything. Your family is a great one, you are rich, you are beautiful, above all you are good. I have been your slave . . . from the moment I saw you.'

'Have you?' she replied smiling. 'I did not know.'

'You mock me.'

'In truth, no,' she said. 'How could I mock one who pays me the sort of compliments which anyone would want to hear?'

'I would speak seriously to you,' he said, 'if I dared.'

'I did not expect you to be a fearful man, my lord Duke.'

'In one respect . . . yes . . . where you are concerned.'

'Afraid of me! Oh no, that is not possible.'

'Katharine, you must know my feeling for you. Ever since I set eyes on you I have thought of little else.'

'You should be thinking of regaining your crown.'

'I could regain it I know . . . if I could but have this dearest wish of all granted me.'

'And you ask me to grant it?'

'You are the only one who can. I know I have to regain my crown. I know my future is insecure. . . Perhaps I should not have asked you until I have that in my grasp . . .'

'You do me an injustice,' she said, 'if you think that I would say no if there were no crown and say yes if there were one.'

'Then you know of what I speak.'

'My lord, you are taking such a long time to say it that I must say it for you, since you are meandering back and forth from the point in such a manner that you leave me no alternative but to guess.'

'Katharine . . .'

'Duke Richard, ask me . . . if that is what you want.'

'Will you marry me?'

'Yes,' she said.

'I cannot believe it.'

'Of course you know full well . . .'

'I know now that I am the happiest man on earth.'

'You will have to get the King's permission.'

'And that of your father.'

'The one would follow the other.'

'I feel James will be sympathetic towards lovers.'

'I feel that too.'

'Oh Katharine, I would we were alone that I might kiss your lips.'

'You will speak to the King?'

'At the first opportunity, which I shall now seek. Katharine, you will be the Queen of England.'

'I hope there will not be a lot of fighting. I would rather stay here . . . at James' Court all our days. Perhaps we could escape often to the country . . . and be by ourselves.'

'I cannot wait to speak to him.'

'He is in a good mood now. He is pleased with Marion but I believe he is glancing far too frequently at Janet Kennedy, but speak to him soon . . . speak to him tonight.'

'I will.'

He did. The opportunity occurred that very night.

The company was dancing and James, who had drunk a great deal of wine, seemed drowsy. Perkin went to him and asked permission to sit beside him which was readily given.

'Sire,' he said, 'I want to speak to you of a matter which is very important to me. May I do so?'

James smiled and nodded. 'Though I'll take a guess first. It concerns a lady.'

'You are so shrewd, Sire.'

'Where ladies are concerned, yes. And the Lady Katharine is a beauty. I grant you that.'

'We love each other, Sire.'

'Love indeed! A beautiful emotion. Nothing like it. What do

you wish, my lord Duke? You can't make a mistress of a girl like Katharine. Huntly has her at Court to find a husband for her.'

'That is what I want to be, my lord.'

'Ah, marriage to Huntly's daughter. Well if you are going to be King of England that will be an honour which even Huntly can't refuse.'

'It is your consent I am asking for.'

'You have it, my lord Duke. I will speak to her father. I will point out to him the advantages of such a match for his daughter.'

'You have earned my endless gratitude. But you had that already. I cannot tell you what your kind acceptance of me at your Court has meant to me. And now . . . and now . . .'

'There, my lord Duke. That is enough. I wish to help you. I see no reason at all why the fair Katharine should not be yours and I shall see that Huntly feels the same. What of the lady herself?'

'She loves me . . . even as I love her.'

'That is charming. That is delightful. I like to see people around me happy. Now, my lord Duke, you have deserted her too long. Let me see you lead her into the dance.'

When he and Marion were alone that night in the royal bedchamber, James was overcome by mirth.

'This is a fine state of affairs,' he said. 'This is going to set the Tudor ranting . . . if he ever rants. I doubt he does. He is a very self-contained man who never shows his anger. But just think what he will say when he hears that Perkin Warbeck is marrying Lady Katharine Gordon . . . my cousin . . . I can tell you this is going to madden him.'

'It pleases you,' said Marion.

'My dear, have you only just learned that what infuriates Henry Tudor is most certain to give me the utmost pleasure?'

'I hope it works out well . . . for the Lady Katharine,' said Marion.

So they were married and because of the rank of the bride and the expectations of Perkin they were given a royal wedding. James took a gleeful delight in behaving as though Katharine Gordon was marrying into the royal family. She was royal herself. 'A fitting bride,' said James, 'for the future King of England.' He was maliciously wondering what was happening below the Border.

The bride and the groom gave little thought to anything but each other, and as the weeks sped by their happiness grew for they were more in love every day. Katharine was all that he had believed her to be—gentle yet strong; modest yet proud of her family and of him; pliant and yet firm; fun loving and yet she could be serious. These were the happiest days of Perkin's life and he wanted them to go on forever. The thought of leaving Katharine to go and fight for his throne horrified him. In his heart he did not really want the throne. He wanted to live in peace with Katharine for the rest of his life.

She admitted that she wanted the same. It was amazing how they thought as one person.

He realized during those weeks of marriage that he had never really wanted a throne. It was people around him who had selected him because of his appearance and his natural grace to fill a role for which they sought a character to fit.

He began to see that he had been used.

But he dismissed that flash of understanding. He could not bear to examine it. He had become adept at pushing aside the truth and supplanting it by a picture of his making—or perhaps that of those around him.

All he knew now was that he wanted to go on like this. He wanted to make his home here in Scotland, to go on living under the protection of the King and the powerful family into which he had married, but into the halcyon contentment of those days there crept the fear that they must be transient. At any time the call would come. They would raise an army for him and send him to gain that to which they said he had a right.

'I don't want the crown,' he said to Katharine. 'I just want to stay here with you.'

She held him tightly against her. 'If only it could be,' she said.

'Do you want to be Queen of England?'

She shook her head. 'Not if it means your going away, risking your life. No . . . Let us hope we can stay here. Why should we not?'

He shook his head. 'They will never allow it. Oh, I wish . . .'

What did he wish? That he had never left the home of John Warbeck? But if he had not he would never have met Katharine. Anything was worth that.

But it brought him back to where he had started. Here he was . . . blissfully happy, except when he remembered, then living each day in terror that suddenly the call would come.

Katharine added to his bliss when she told him that there would be a child. He wanted to weep with happiness . . . but it was a happiness quickly tinged with fear.

When the call came, there would be even more to leave . . . and perhaps lose.

TYBURN AND
TOWER HILL

When Henry heard that James of Scotland had allowed the Lady Katharine Gordon to marry Perkin Warbeck he was deeply disturbed.

'This means that James really accepts the impostor!' he cried to Dudley and Empson whom he had summoned because he knew that he would have to consult them as to how to raise money for war.

That seemed inevitable now. James would never have allowed such a marriage if he had not made up his mind to help Perkin Warbeck fight for the crown of England.

'He must be mad!' said Empson. 'Does he want war then?'

'He is bent on making trouble. It's a Scottish custom,' said Henry bitterly. 'It will mean raising money for an army, which is the last thing I wanted to do. It is infuriating to see money wasted in this way.'

'It will be necessary to tax the whole country,' murmured Dudley.

'We must be in readiness for war,' agreed the King.

'The Spanish emissaries have arrived in England, Sire,' Empson said. 'They will have heard of this marriage. It will not please them.'

'The French will be delighted. Do you think they intend to give him their support?'

'Who can say with the French! They are involved in their affairs.'

'But *I* am their affair, Empson,' said the King. 'If they can do anything to harm me, you may be sure they will. A curse on these pretenders! First Simnel . . . now this one. If ever I get that fellow into my hands, I'll put an end to this once and for all.'

Dudley looked at him in silence. He thought: Is that possible while the disappearance of two little Princes in the Tower remains a mystery? Will there not always be men to rise up and say, 'I am Edward the Fifth.' 'I am Richard Duke of York.'

Within a few days Don Pedro de Ayala arrived from the Court of Spain. He had a proposition to make. His Sovereigns wished Henry to join the Holy League for keeping the French out of Italy and if he was to be free to do this, it was rather important that he was not engaged in hostilities with Scotland.

'The Infanta Katharine is promised to my son, Arthur,' Henry pointed out. 'But I hear that the Sovereigns are offering one of the Infantas to the King of Scotland as a bride. It would seem that Spain is seeking an alliance with Scotland as well as England.'

'My lord,' cried Don Pedro, 'there is no intention of a marriage between Spain and Scotland. I have been instructed to lay these suggestions only before you. You yourself have a daughter. Would you consider offering the Princess Margaret as a bride to James? This would be a way of preventing hostilities between your two countries.'

Henry was silent. What he wanted more than anything was peace. And the idea of having to spend money to go to war he found completely frustrating. He did not want war. He had always seen the folly of it. England wanted a peace. That was what he prayed for, a spell when he could work for the good of the country, curb extravagance, develop trade. He wanted all Englishmen to realize that the harder they worked, the more closely they were united with one aim in view, the richer they would all be. But that aim was not war. It was peace.

Oh yes, Henry wanted peace.

He would willingly give Margaret to Scotland for it. Why not? That was what daughters were for . . . to make alliances between hostile countries and bring about peace between them. Yes, Margaret could be the bride of James the Fourth of Scotland.

But there was one other factor. Perkin Warbeck must be delivered to him.

Until that was done there could be no talk of a marriage between Margaret and James—no talk of peace.

There could no longer be reason for delay. James was ready and eager to advance on his enemies below the Border.

He sent for Perkin and told him gleefully that soon he would be crowned at Westminster, so Perkin could do nothing but feign an eagerness, while there was nothing he longed for so much as to be left to live in peace with his wife and his newly arrived daughter.

But this was what he had come for. This was the price he had to pay for all the grand living, all the splendour, all the adulation he had enjoyed for so many years and now he had become accustomed to it. But just at that time he would have given a great deal to be living with Katharine in a small house in Flanders—two humble people of whom no one outside their immediate circle had ever heard.

Katharine knew of his feelings. She shared them. She did not want a throne any more than he did and would have been perfectly content with that humble home in Flanders.

He could have wished that all this had never happened to him, that he had never gone into Lady Frampton's service and attracted her by his good looks—but for the fact that through it he had met Katharine. More and more he was remembering those early days and there were times when he was on the point of making a confession to Katharine. He did not though; he could not bring himself to do it, even to her; and now the time had come when he must leave her and go marching into England.

'I shall send for you as soon as I am settled,' he told her.

'I know. I know.'

'What I don't know is how I shall bear the separation.'

'You will be too busy to miss me,' she told him, 'whereas I shall have to wait . . . and pray.'

'I shall need your prayers, Katharine. Pray I beg you that it shall not be long before you are beside me.'

'That is what I shall pray for.'

'I would give up everything I ever hoped to have not to leave you now.'

She nodded. She understood. Perhaps deep in her heart she knew that he had never been that little boy in the Tower of London.

James reviewed his troops and at Holyrood he made offerings to the saints and ordered that masses be sung for him and when Perkin joined him there he greeted him with pleasure.

'Now,' he said, 'we shall see men flock to your banner. They have had their fill of the Tudor impostor. We will harry the Border towns and carry off spoils and see what effect this has on the Tudor. Meanwhile we will issue a proclamation in the name of Richard the Fourth, King of England and when you have thousands welcoming you . . . that will be the time to march south.'

Meanwhile they went to Haddington and across the Lammermuir to Ellem Kirk. They crossed the Border and raided several towns, but there was no response at all to the proclamation and it was very soon clear that the Englishmen of the Border were not interested in driving Henry Tudor from the throne and setting Richard of York up in his place.

James and Perkin laid siege to one or two towns. The expedition was taking on the nature of one of the Border forays of which there had been hundreds over the years, and James was getting bored. Moreover to march south without the support of the people of England for the new King would be folly.

He began to think that Perkin was not exactly a great leader of men and he would need a very big army if he were going to gain the crown. James had no intention of providing that, even though Perkin had promised him a good many concessions when and if he were successful.

James was wanting to be back in Edinburgh. He was making good progress with Janet Kennedy in spite of Archibald Douglas. It was true that he was tiring of Marion Boyd, although she had been a good mistress to him, but if she would understand his need to wander far afield, he would not mind keeping her on and visiting her occasionally. But it seemed to him that Janet would be the sort of woman who might absorb all his interest, in which case it would have to be goodbye to Marion.

Who wanted a rough camp bed when he could be in a luxurious four poster with a glorious red-headed woman to comfort him? It was true Perkin had made great promises. It was very easy to make promises when one still had to gain a victory before he could redeem them; afterwards the promises could be forgotten for they might not be so easy to carry out.

He went to Perkin's camp. The young man was sunk in melancholy.

'You do not look happy, my friend,' said James. 'Are you missing your warm marital bed?'

' 'Tis so, my lord.'

'Ah, I miss my own bed. I tell you that.'

'I am troubled because the blood we are shedding is that of Englishmen . . . my own subjects,' said Perkin. 'I cannot sleep at night for thinking of it.'

He cannot sleep at night because he wants his Katharine! thought James. He cannot sleep at night because he knows that Englishmen do not want King Richard the Fourth, and they will stay with Henry Tudor rather than fight. Well, it is a pleasant and human excuse and it will help to get me back to Edinburgh.

James nodded. 'That is no mood in which to go to war, my friend.'

'I agree,' Perkin answered eagerly.

'Well, we have done our little foray. Perhaps we should think of returning to Edinburgh.'

Perkin felt as though a great weight had been lifted from his shoulders.

He was going home to Katharine and the baby.

There was murmuring throughout the country because Dudley and Empson were endeavouring to raise money for the Scottish war. The people were being asked to pay heavy taxes because a certain Perkin Warbeck was attempting to wrest the throne from Henry Tudor.

To the people of Bodmin in Cornwall this seemed a matter for kings to decide among themselves. What did it matter to them what king was on the throne? When did they ever see him? King Henry or King Richard . . . what did Cornwall care?

Lawyer Thomas Flammock felt very strongly on this issue. He went into the market square and talked to the people about it. They gathered round listening intently. There was not a man present who had not been harassed by extra taxes.

'My patience me,' grumbled the blacksmith Michael Joseph, ' 'tis hard enough for the likes of we to put bread in our mouths and those of our childer . . . are us going to stand by and pay like helpless fules? Don't 'ee think we should up and do som'at about it?'

Joseph was a powerful speaker. In his forge he talked what the King would call sedition but what to the people of Bodmin seemed sound common sense.

'Where is the fighting?' asked Thomas Flammock. 'It's on the border between Scotland and England, there's where it is. They've been fighting there for hundreds of years and they'll go on fighting for a hundred more. Why should we be asked to pay for their quarrels?'

'But what do we do about it, eh, lawyer?' shouted a voice in the crowd.

'That is what I want to suggest to you,' said Flammock. 'We can march to London. We can present a petition to the King and ask him to get rid of his evil advisors. If the King wants to wage war it is not for us . . . the people of Cornwall . . . who know no difference, wars or no wars . . . it is not for us to pay for it.'

The crowd cheered loudly.

'And who will go to London with this petition?' asked the man who had spoken before.

'We must all go, my friend. If one or two of us go . . . we'd not be received most likely. We've got to show them that we mean what we say. We must go to London in a body . . . march to London . . . show that we mean what we say: we will not pay these taxes for a fight which does not concern us.'

'We would want someone to lead us,' said the man. He pushed his way to the spot where Flammock was standing with Joseph. 'Friends,' he cried, 'here's two good Cornish men. Shall we ask them to lead us to London and the King?'

There was a shout from the crowd.

'Lawyer Flammock and Blacksmith Joseph! Our leaders . . .'

There was wild enthusiasm, but Flammock lifted his hand for silence.

'I will lead you,' he said. 'And you, Michael?'

'Aye,' said Michael. 'I'll come along.'

'We will lead you until we can find someone more worthy to be your leader.'

'Ain't no one more worthy than 'ee, lawyer,' shouted a voice.

'Someone of the nobility would carry more weight. But we shall not delay. We shall set out for London . . . Tomorrow at dawn . . . we'll assemble here and those who can, must come with us. The more men we have the more likely we are to make our point. Is that agreed?'

There was a roar of approval in the crowd. The next morning at dawn, Flammock was amazed at the numbers who had assembled in the square. They were carrying bows and arrows and billhooks. He was a little alarmed for he had meant this to be a peaceful demonstration.

By the time they reached Taunton their numbers had grown and Flammock was a little dismayed for he had been joined by ruffians whose intent he knew was to rob and pillage. This was the last thing Flammock had had in mind, and he began to wonder whether it would not have been better to have selected, say, a dozen men, all worthies of the town of Bodmin, and with them gone to London to present the petition.

The crowd was getting out of hand. This was proved when the Provost of Taunton came out to remonstrate with them, for some of the men were overrunning the town and helping themselves from the shops.

Flammock was horrified to see the Provost lying in a pool of blood. The man was dead.

He managed to get them out of the town quickly. There he spoke to them. 'That was a regrettable incident,' he said. 'Now we have a man's blood on our hands. To kill is not the purpose of this expedition. I want no more scenes like that. We have not come to rob and murder but to talk to the King about harsh taxes. There must be no more killing. God help us for we have slain a man who was doing nothing but his duty.'

At Wells they were joined by James Touchet, Lord Audley. Audley was very dissatisfied with the King. He had been in France with Henry and he felt he had not been given his dues. He was therefore feeling extremely disgruntled and when he saw the large numbers of men descending on Wells he rode out to speak with their leaders.

He found Thomas Flammock a reasonable and educated man and he agreed with him that it was insupportable that the King should demand such high taxes from people who were not in a position to pay them.

In a rather rash moment he offered to accompany them.

Seeing an opportunity of shifting responsibilities, Flammock was delighted.

'My lord,' he said, 'you are a nobleman of high degree. It is for you to take over the leadership of our party.'

Audley saw the point of this.

So, with Audley at their head the Cornish rebels marched to London and on a hot June day, weary but expectant, they arrived at Deptford Strand.

Henry was furious. This was what he had always feared. A dissatisfied people no doubt fired by this impostor in Scotland now saw fit to rise against him.

The nightmare had become a reality.

His forces were concentrating in the North to deal with the Scottish threat. And now here was trouble from the West.

He hastily sent messengers to his armies on the way to the North. They must send a considerable force up to the Border it was true; but he must have forces in the South to meet the rebellious Cornishmen.

Lord Daubeney, who had only just set out for the North when the call came, turned back and made his way to Deptford Strand. The Cornishmen had become somewhat disheartened by the indifference of the people through whose towns and villages they had passed and who were clearly of the opinion that to start a rebellion would bring them more trouble than paying what was asked.

In vain did Flammock attempt to explain that it was merely a petition he had set out to take to London. He was learning that it was impossible to prevent such an undertaking assuming an uglier aspect.

He was dismayed when the King's forces had come into

contact with some of the marchers and the Cornishmen had a momentary victory, taking a few prisoners. There was one of these who was obviously of high rank and when he was questioned it was discovered that he was none other than Lord Daubeney himself—the leader of the King's army.

Audley and Flammock conferred together.

'We must release him at once,' said Audley. 'Otherwise we shall be called rebels and accused of treason. This is not a rebellion. It is a deputation to protest against the high taxation.'

Daubeney was brought in and Audley explained this to him.

Overcome with shame at being captured by rebels and guessing how this would lower his prestige with the King, Daubeney hid his fury and embarrassment and pretended to understand.

He was immediately released with the other prisoners.

But Daubeney was not going to allow this insult to pass. He immediately planned to attack the Cornishmen and this he did, taking them by surprise at Blackheath. They, with their arrows and billhooks, were no match for the King's trained soldiers and the battle was over almost before it had begun, and Daubeney had the satisfaction of taking the rebel leaders, Audley, Flammock and Michael Joseph, alive.

So that little flurry was over, thought Henry; he could be grateful for that. He wondered how best to act. He wanted to show the people his leniency and on the other hand he must make them realize that no one could rise against him with impunity.

The Cornishmen themselves—the humble artisans from Bodmin—should have a free pardon. They could go back to their remote town and talk of the benevolence of the King.

The leaders should not get off so freely. Men like Flammock and Joseph were dangerous. Moreover, but for them this disturbing affair would not have taken place.

The people must be shown that the Flammocks and Josephs among them were dangerous men to follow. This time, because the King was merciful they had been forgiven and had escaped the punishment they deserved—but it must not happen again.

Audley was considered the chief offender. It was men such as he who were the real danger. He forgot his position in the country when he placed himself at the head of a rabble and he must pay the penalty. He was brought before the King and condemned to death. As he was a nobleman he should be beheaded and not suffer the barbarous penalty which befell lowborn traitors, but he must be shamed first. He was put into a

paper coat which showed that he had been stripped of his knighthood, being no longer worthy of it, and was led from Newgate to
Tower Hill where the executioner with his axe was waiting for
him.

When his head was separated from his body it was stuck on
London Bridge—a warning to all who thought they might play
the traitor.

Flammock and Joseph were less fortunate. They suffered the
traitor's death. They were taken to Tyburn where they were
hanged, drawn and quartered; and their limbs were displayed in
various parts of the city.

This was what happened to traitors, those who in moments of
folly lightly undertook to plot against the King.

Henry was satisfied. He had dealt with the matter in his usual
calm way; and no one could say he had been unduly harsh.

Many a king would have slaughtered hundreds of them. But
not Henry. He could always calmly decide what was best for
Henry Tudor, and that was not to murder for murder's sake. He
did not want to do so for revenge even. He was rarely in a hot
rage about any matter and therefore always had time to calculate
which would be the most advantageous way to act.

Reluctantly he had decided on the traitor's death for the three
ringleaders. He must give no one an impression of weakness.
No. He was not weak. He was stern perhaps, but just—always
just.

He could congratulate himself that he had dealt very properly
with the Cornish rebels.

There still remained Perkin Warbeck to haunt his days and
turn pleasant dreams into nightmares.

James was growing rather tired of Perkin Warbeck. The expedition into England had shown clearly that the people were not
going to flock to his banner, and James was not going to beggar
himself by supporting another man's cause—and a possible King
of England at that! No, indeed not. Perkin must fight his own
battles and the more thought James gave to the matter the more it
seemed to him that it would be better for Perkin to fight somewhere which did not involve Scotland.

Not that James gave much thought to the matter. He was
inclined to let it slide out of his mind, for he was deeply
involved at this time with the most beautiful woman he had ever
seen. She was delightful, gentle, loving, passionate, outstandingly beautiful and everything which he liked best in a woman,
and as he liked women better than anything else on Earth and

had had great experience of them, this was saying a good deal. For the first time in his life—although he had often imagined himself to be in the condition on other occasions—James was truly in love.

The lady was Margaret Drummond, daughter of John, first baron Drummond, a very able man who had been raised to the peerage for his services to Scotland some ten years before. He was a Privy Counsellor and justiciary of Scotland as well as the Constable of Stirling Castle, and his offices brought him to Court. With him came his beautiful daughter—a fact which caused the King to rejoice.

Marion Boyd, Janet Kennedy—delectable wenches both of them—could not compare with Margaret Drummond.

James paid constant visits to Stirling Castle where Margaret lived in the care of Sir John and Lady Lindsay. It had not taken him long to woo Margaret. Gentle, virginal . . . a little over-whelmed by so much royal favour, she had quickly fallen under the spell of the King. But perhaps, James thought ruefully, it would be more correct to say that he had fallen under hers. He could think of little else, so it was small wonder that whenever the name of Perkin Warbeck was spoken to him he felt a mild irritation.

He wanted nothing to come between him and his pursuit of Margaret. His thoughts were completely occupied by the possi-bility of seeing her. There was no reason why they should not be openly together. The whole of the Court knew of his infatuation—including Marion and Janet—and it was easier to face the whole of his Court than those two, particularly fiery Janet.

Who wanted war? Women were so much more enjoyable. And while Perkin Warbeck remained in Scotland he represented a threat. Henry had demanded that the young man be delivered to him. That, James had refused to do of course. Perkin had promised to restore Berwick to Scotland when he came to the throne, in payment for James' hospitality. That would be good. Berwick was one of the most important Border towns. Certainly he wanted Berwick . . . and all the other concessions which Perkin had promised.

But promises! . . . What did they come to if wars had to be fought for the hope of their fulfilment?

No, he wanted no more now that he and Margaret had dis-covered each other.

He broached Perkin when they met at Linlithgow.

'It seems to me, my lord Duke,' he said, 'that you are achieving little here. You do not wish to fight these people in the

North . . . your own subjects, you say . . . men who had never heard of Richard Duke of York . . . or perhaps Henry Tudor.'

'I could not bear to see the blood of my own subjects shed,' said Perkin.

'I understand that well. So this is not the place for you. You have your friends in Ireland. I'll tell you what I am going to do, my lord Duke. I am going to give you a ship. You can sail from Scotland to Ireland, taking Katharine and the baby with you. I have no doubt that the Irish will rally to your cause. You will have more chance there than here in Scotland.'

Perkin was left in no doubt that this was James' diplomatic way of telling him to leave and he had no alternative but to accept the offer of the ship and prepare to depart.

If Katharine was sad to leave her native land she did not show it.

'We are together,' she said. 'That is all that matters.'

Perkin was apprehensive. He could no longer prevaricate and he had an idea that the easy life was over. He would have to make some attempt to wrest the crown from Henry Tudor and if he achieved it then his difficulties would begin. In his heart he knew he was unfitted to rule a country. He was frightened by the enormity of this matter which had come about in the first place through a love of adventure, and an excitement because people noticed his royal looks.

Still it had led him to Katharine, for if all this had not happened he could never have met her.

As he stood on the deck watching the coastline of Ireland grow nearer he could echo her words: 'We are together.'

Lord Desmond was dismayed. Life did not stand still, he pointed out, and in spite of the rebellions Henry Tudor still had a firm grip on the crown. People were beginning to like his rule apart from one thing—the exorbitant taxation, and they blamed Empson and Dudley for that. Those two were the most unpopular men in the country and the fact that they did not regard Henry himself entirely responsible was an indication of how he was beginning to be accepted as a good king.

The fact was that Desmond did not want to have anything to do with the rebellion. He could see that Henry's calm wisdom would inevitably make him the victor.

He said: 'The Irish are an unpredictable people. They sway one way and then another. There has been a rebellion in Cornwall. Now that is where you would find your supporters.'

'Henry suppressed that rebellion.'

'Because it was just a rabble. Audley was there to give it some standing, but they were not trained soldiers. No. It would have been different if they had been. After all, they captured Daubeney in the first place. Think what they could have done if they had had some backing. No, the West Country is your hope, my lord. You should go there and raise an army.'

It was quite clear that Desmond did not want to be involved.

Scotland had rejected Perkin, and now Ireland. So there was nothing for it but to take ship to Cornwall.

There his spirits rose.

From the moment he landed at Whitesand Bay Perkin was warmly welcomed and he rode in triumph to Bodmin where memories of the recent march to London were still vivid.

'Good Flammock,' they said. 'His parts exposed all over London! And him always such a modest man. That they could do such a thing to Lawyer Flammock is past belief.'

'And don't 'ee forget Joseph. There's none could shoe a horse like that 'un . . . And to think of 'ee . . . Oh it be past thinking of.'

They were smarting from the humiliation levied on those two worthy men.

'But the rest of 'em just came back. Don't 'ee do it again . . . that's all they did say.'

'Well, stands to reason, they couldn't do to us all what they did to good Flammock and Joseph.'

'I'd think not. Cornwall wouldn't stand for that.'

'Aye, and 'e do know it, King or not. He couldn't treat us Cornish like that.'

And now here was the handsome young man.

'Reckon he could show old Tudor a thing or two . . .'

'He could and all . . . if he had Cornishmen to back him.'

Perkin's spirits rose.

'This is different from our reception in Ireland,' he said.

The Mayor proclaimed him in the square as 'Our King Richard the Fourth.'

The Cornishmen were with him. They were going to have a king of their own choosing and it was going to be this handsome young man, and his beautiful wife who should reign beside him.

'I shall win this time,' said Perkin, trying to bring enthusiasm into his smile.

'I shall be near by,' said Katharine.

Perkin shook his head. 'I want you to be safe . . . you and the baby.'

She shook her head but he would not listen.

Men were flocking to his banner. They all wanted to go and fight the Tudor. It was an adventure and if all went well they would have put a new king on the throne and if it did not . . . well, they would just come back as their friends had done when they had followed Flammock and Joseph to London.

Three thousand men had rallied to his banner. This was success. He believed that when he was on the march with such a following more men would fall in behind him.

'I must go,' he told Katharine. She was in tears. Perhaps she who loved him knew that, good husband that he was, he was no leader of men. But it was true, he did seem inspired. If it should happen that he gained the throne she must stand with him, reign as his queen. She fervently wished that it could be happily settled and that they could go away and live in obscurity and leave Henry Tudor his throne.

'They tell me that you will be safest on St. Michael's Mount,' he told her.

'It will be so far from you.'

'I shall not rest happy unless I know you are in a place of safety.'

'Do you think I can rest happy anywhere until you are back with me?'

He kissed her fondly. 'It will not be long,' he promised her.

But she did not believe him. Sadly they parted—she going westward with her child, he marching on to Exeter.

It was true that men fell in with his army. They liked the look of him. He was so handsome; he had the Plantagenet look; he had the appearance of a king—more so than Henry who never smiled and whom they said had aged twenty years since he took the throne.

It was not so easy as he marched on. Exeter stood out against him so he had to put the town under siege. But he was no soldier. He could only be strong when he faced the weak. As soon as he heard that the Earl of Devonshire with other noblemen of Devon were on the march against him, knowing he could not stand a chance facing a professional army, he gave orders to retreat and fell back to Taunton. There worse news awaited him: Lord Daubeney had reached Glastonbury and was marching onward.

'We cannot stand against him,' he said. 'We have not the experience to face a professional army. There is nothing for it but to get away.'

'What will the men say?' he was asked.

He was frightened as he knew he would be. This was not what

he wanted. He wanted people to say, 'Here is Richard the Fourth. Let us make him our king.' But to fight for the crown . . . he could not do it. He did not want to fight. All he wanted now was to go back in peace to Katharine.

He could not take his army with him. They would never get away, so he selected sixty of his men and together they left Taunton. But even sixty horsemen found the going difficult. People came out in alarm to watch them, and there was not enough food in the inns for sixty.

Perkin said: 'This will never do. We shall be captured at once if we go about in such numbers.'

He selected three men from the sixty and said to them: 'When night falls, we will steal away. It will be easy for four of us to make our escape. It is impossible with sixty.'

So the four of them slipped away in the darkness and in due course they arrived at Beaulieu in Hampshire where they found an empty house and there took refuge.

What Perkin wanted to do was lie low until the hue and cry had died down, then make his way back to St. Michael's Mount, get a ship and take Katharine and the baby, where . . . ? Perhaps they could go to Flanders. Perhaps he could find John and Katharine Warbeck, those parents whom he had denied. Then perhaps they could all live happily together again.

He wanted no crown. He just wanted to live in peace with Katharine.

He lay on the floor, his companions beside him.

Perhaps he should leave them . . . slip away. He could disguise himself as a peddler . . . work his way back to the Mount. He and Katharine could hide themselves away until they found a ship to Flanders . . . .

Not yet. It was unsafe as yet. He must be careful to preserve his life because Katharine needed him.

Somewhere in the darkness he heard a sound. He raised himself.

Was it the sound of distant horses' hoofs? Perhaps. Some traveller out late.

He lay down and thought of Katharine. Yes, he would find his way back to her. They must hide themselves and plan to get away.

She would agree. Her wish was the same as his—that they should be together.

Again that sound . . . nearer now . . . perhaps . . . He looked at his sleeping companions. Should he rouse them? No. It was only a traveller in the night.

And then . . . the noise was nearer. Not one horseman but many. He stood up. His companions were awake now. They went to a window.

'We are surrounded,' said Perkin.

There was nothing to do but to surrender. Perkin and his companions were taken back to Taunton by the King's guards, and for the first time Perkin came face to face with the man whose right to the throne he had challenged, the Tudor himself. So Henry had thought the matter of sufficient importance to see his captive in person.

At first Perkin thought: Why, he is an old man! He seemed so to Perkin. Old and grey. He was in truth forty years of age but looked ten years older. Slight with greying hair, light blue-grey eyes and a pale complexion. But there was a certain strength about him and it was impossible to be in his presence without being aware of it.

Perkin was overawed by the pale, ageing man. If he had shown anger he would have been less afraid of him. It was the calmness of the Tudor which unnerved him, the almost blank expression which nevertheless suggested that it was merely a mask to hide his thoughts which he was determined to keep to himself.

'You are Perkin Warbeck,' said the King.

Perkin started to say: 'I am King Richard the Fourth . . . I was taken from the Tower . . .'

'Nonsense,' said Henry Tudor. 'I know who you are. You are Perkin Warbeck, son of John Warbeck, customs man of Tournay in Flanders.'

Perkin drew himself up to his full height. He must remember what he had learned from Lady Frampton and the Duchess of Burgundy . . . from Lord Desmond. He wished that he could forget that house in Flanders, but somehow with this stern cold-faced man looking at him so penetratingly as though he could read his thoughts he found it difficult.

Henry said: 'I have sent for your wife, Perkin. We knew she was at St. Michael's Mount.'

'No . . . I beg of you . . . Do not harm her. She is not to blame.'

'We know that. She has been deceived as others have. Do not disturb yourself. I am not a monster. I do not harm innocent women.'

Perkin was immensely relieved. Henry was observant. He

cares for her more than for his aspirations, he thought. A senti-
mental fellow. He will not be difficult to handle.

'Now, Perkin,' he said. 'You have caused us a great deal of
trouble but I know you are just the tool of certain men . . .
enemies of my country. I know you are a foolish young man
from a humble family in Flanders and have been used by these
people. I am not a cruel man. I have a reputation for being
lenient . . . a lover of justice. I do not blame you so much as
those who have used you. I shall not harm your wife. I know she
is a highly born lady. I shall have her sent to my Queen where
she will be accorded the honour due to her rank.'

Perkin put his hands to his face. He was weeping with relief.

'Oh I thank you, my lord, I thank you with all my heart. She
has done no harm. She believed . . . with the rest . . .'

Henry smiled. It was going to be very easy to get a confession
from this boy. He was glad. He hated the clumsy work of
torturers, and the information they got was always suspect.

'So,' he went on gently, 'you can rest assured your wife and
child will be well treated. Now as for you . . . well, you have
offended us greatly. This nonsense about your identity. You
know full well who you are and it is not Richard of York. That's
so. Is it not?'

Perkin was silent.

'Oh come. Do not be foolish any more. I tell you your wife is
safe. You must be grateful for that. Are you?'

Perkin nodded dumbly.

'I understand. I have heard of your devotion. You see, I hear a
great deal about you, Perkin. There was another like you who set
himself up. Lambert Simnel. He has worked well in my kitchens. I have just promoted him to become one of my falconers.
He is a good servant . . . very grateful to his King for having
spared his life. Poor simple boy. He knows he deserved to lose it
. . . as you do, Perkin, as you do. But I do not propose to put
you in my kitchens. All I ask you to do is to make a full
confession. If you do this, I shall spare your life. I have sent for
your wife. You must confess in her presence. And if you do that
I shall send you to the Tower of London where you will be my
prisoner for a while but I have no doubt that if you behave with
propriety . . . well, I am not a vindictive man and it might well
be that in due course . . . you could join your wife . . . if she
still wants to be the wife of a Flemish adventurer after she
thought she had a royal Duke of York.'

Perkin could not speak. He had not imagined it would be like
this at all.

Henry rose. 'I will give you a little while to think. And when your wife arrives you shall make your first confession . . . to her.'

Perkin was taken to Exeter where Henry had gone and it wasn't long before he was summoned to the King's presence.

As soon as he entered the chamber he saw Katharine.

He gave a cry of joy and would have rushed to her but he was restrained by guards. Eagerly he studied her. She was not harmed in any way. She looked at him in a bewildered fashion as though she was seeing him afresh. He could not bear that.

'Katharine . . .' his lips formed the words and she smiled at him.

'Husband . . .' she whispered, and he knew that she loved him still.

The King said. 'Give the Lady Katharine Gordon a chair, and place it here beside me.'

This was done and Katharine sat down.

'Now, my lady,' said Henry, 'your husband wants to tell you who in truth he is. He will explain everything. I thought it right that you should know and hear it from his own lips. Proceed, Perkin.'

He tried to speak but he could only look at her. He wanted her to run to him; he wanted to put his arms about her; but she only sat there looking at him with those beautiful appealing eyes begging him to speak.

He had to tell the truth and it all came back so vividly now.

'My father is John Warbeck. We lived in Tournay. He was a controller of customs.'

She stared at him disbelievingly. He should never have lied to her. He should have explained everything before they married. But at that time he had for long periods believed it was true that he was Richard Duke of York. That story of being with his brother in the Tower, of being handed over to the man who could not murder him had seemed far more real than his father's house in Tournay.

But he must go on. He must preserve his life. He must try to make Katharine understand. He could not bear to see her look at him like that.

He went on: 'I was put into several houses. I served there in various capacities . . . in exchange I was given some education. Then the Framptons came to Flanders. They had been supporters of the House of York and they had to leave when King Henry came. They saw my resemblance to the Duke of York and they convinced me that I was one of the Princes who disappeared in the Tower. I passed from one household to another . . . I went to the French Court and the Court of Bordeaux . . . I was learning all the time . . . You know the rest. I passed myself off as Richard Duke of York, second son of Edward the Fourth . . . and therefore since Edward the Fifth was dead, heir to the throne.'

The King was watching Katharine closely during this confession. He said: 'You see, my lady, how you have been deceived like so many others.'

Still she was silent, looking at Perkin with disbelief in her eyes.

'My lady, you shall go to the Queen. I have asked her to care for you and treat you as a sister. You will understand I cannot free your husband. I shall not treat him harshly for I see full well that he has been the tool of others. Now he will go to London and you shall go to the Queen. I will leave you for ten minutes to take your farewells of each other and to say what you wish to.'

With those words Henry rose and walked slowly out of the chamber.

Perkin rushed to Katharine. He knelt at her feet and buried his face in her skirts. For a few seconds she did nothing; then he felt her fingers in his hair and he lifted his face to hers.

'Is it true?' she asked. 'Is it something they have made you say under threat?'

He shook his head. 'It is true . . . alas. Lady Katharine Gordon has married the son of a customs official.'

'I married *you*,' she said.

He had risen and taken her into his arms and they clung together for a moment.

'Oh . . . my love . . . what will they do to you?' she asked.

Joy flooded over him. In that moment he did not care. All that mattered was that she cared.

'They say the King is lenient . . .'

She thought of the stories she had heard of Flammock and Michael Joseph. What had they done? Not nearly so much as her husband. He had raised a revolt, headed an army, called himself true king.

'He will send me to the Tower,' he said. 'But he has hinted that in time I might be free.' He took her face in his hands. He said: 'Katharine, I don't think I wanted to go on with it . . . after I found you. But if I had never started it I should never have met you. Marriage between us would have been an impossibility . . . but once I had you . . . and the baby . . . I just wanted to go back . . . back into obscurity . . . to Tournay . . . in a little house . . .'

She said: 'I know.'

'And what will you do?'

'It has been decided for me. I must go to the Queen.'

'Katharine . . . in time . . .'

She said: 'Let us pray it will be soon.'

'Oh God bless you. You are even more wonderful than I ever thought you could be.'

'I did not love a crown,' she said. 'I loved you.'

'And you still do?'

'I do not change,' she told him. 'I think perhaps I knew . . . I could never see you as King of England and myself as Queen . . . I shall pray that the King frees you . . .'

'And then, Katharine?'

'We shall go away . . . right away . . . where no one knows us.'

'You will want that?'

'There will be the two of us . . . the three of us . . . perhaps more children. We will make a home for ourselves . . . and over that will hang no shadows . . . no fears of going to war . . . no crowns which have to be won.'

'Oh Katharine . . . it's strange but I feel happier than I have for a long time.'

The guards had come. It was time for Perkin to go to London and for the Lady Katharine to be taken to the Queen.

Henry was not quite as lenient as he had first implied he would be. He did not feel vindictive towards Perkin, but he wanted everyone to know the extent of his folly.

Therefore Perkin must ride through the streets of London that the citizens might come out of their houses to look at the man who had tried to be their king. Some of them threw mud at him. He was crestfallen and humiliated.

'King Richard,' they called after him derisively.

After that he was lodged in the Tower.

Several weeks passed and one day a man in the green and white livery of the King's household came to him and told him he was free to leave his prison providing that he went immediately to the King's Court where he would remain for a while under surveillance.

His spirits rose. He was on the way to freedom. He was sure that after a while he would be able to go to Katharine.

He came to Court. The King watched him with amusement

and so did others. 'The man who would be king!' they said. Well, they had to admit that he had a certain grace, his manners and speech were impeccable. He had clearly had some very good tutors.

Desperately he tried to get news of Katharine. She was with the Queen whose health was not of the best which meant that she spent a great deal of time away from the King's Court. She had given birth to a daughter the previous year. Little Mary was a strong and healthy baby; but the following year Edmund had been born and by all accounts he was sickly. The Queen's health was a matter of concern to the King and he allowed her to live in a certain obscurity provided she showed herself from time to time to let the people know that their royal marriage was a felicitous one. They had two daughters and a son Henry who were all pictures of health and enough to delight the hearts of any parents. If Arthur and Edmund were not as healthy as they might be, that was sad, but as their nurses said, they would grow out of it. There had been the death of little Elizabeth but Henry felt secure in his family. Therefore he was pleased with his Queen and as long as she continued to add to their brood she could live as she wished.

This made it impossible for Perkin to see Katharine unless he left the King's Court or she came to it from the Queen's. But although the Queen treated her as a sister, she was still her attendant and it was obvious that Henry did not want the husband and wife to meet. It may have been that he feared they might plot, or people seeing the handsome pair together might think they would well grace a throne.

However they did not meet and there came a time when Perkin could endure this state of affairs no longer.

He was going to see Katharine, no matter what the consequences.

It was folly of course. He was too closely watched, and he had not gone very far when he realized that he was being followed.

He rode with all speed to the monastery at Syon and there sought refuge but the King's men were immediately on his trail.

He must give himself up, he was told. It was the only way he could hope to save his life after this. He had been treated well by the King and he had broken his solemn word never to leave the castle or palace where he was in the King's custody, and he had done so.

'There is no help for it,' said the King. 'The man is not to be trusted. Take him to the Tower. I have no wish to harm him. He is a foolish fellow . . . a little brighter than Lambert Simnel but still a fool. Let him stay in the Tower until I decide what we shall do with him.'

The King did decide. Perkin had tried to escape. For what purpose? To attempt to rally men to a cause that was so absurd it was lost before it started?

No. The people must realize what Perkin stood for, and the best way to treat him was to humiliate him. Let the people laugh at Perkin. The more they jeered the less dangerous he became.

'Let him be placed in the stocks by Westminster Hall,' said the King. 'There he shall repeat his confession of fraud. I want the people to know that off by heart. Then let him do the same in Chepeside. We will have his confession printed and circulated throughout the country. When this is done I think we shall have clipped his wings.'

So Perkin suffered the humiliation of the people's ridicule.

After that he was taken back to the Tower.

He felt desperate. He was sure Henry would never give him the opportunity to escape again.

Henry was not seriously concerned with Perkin Warbeck, for it had been so easy to prove him to be the impostor he so obviously was; but that did not mean this matter gave him no uneasiness. Even Lambert Simnel had done that, and the reason was, of course, that these men were products of a shaky throne. Henry was a strong king; he was a born administrator and men would learn in time that this was what a country needed. He could make England great, if he could but be allowed to reign in peace. These impostors might well go on springing up and the reason was of course that so many English resented his kingship simply because they did not believe in his claim to the throne.

He himself knew that the sons of Edward the Fourth were dead. If only he could make this known to the people it would help a lot—but not of course if they must also know the manner of their dying. It was better to let Richard the Third bear the blame for that. Alas, there was so much evidence against the theory of Richard's removing them, that the matter must be wrapped in mystery. The fact remained that they were dead. But there was one still living who had a greater claim than Henry— and that was Edward, Earl of Warwick whom he had kept in the Tower ever since he had come to the throne.

It had not been so difficult in the beginning but that was fourteen years ago when the young Earl had been but ten years old. To take the boy into his care as he called it seemed a reasonable thing to do and if that care was a prison in the Tower no one dared to protest. The boy had no close relations; he was too young to attract ambitious men. He was easy prey.

But now the Earl was twenty-four years of age and there must be many who remembered that he was in fact heir to the throne. His father, the brother of Edward the Fourth, had been judged a traitor and met his death ignobly in a butt of malmsey, but that did not mean his son was not next in line of succession.

Henry had long been uneasy about that young man. And when he received dispatches from Spain his thoughts turned even more urgently towards him.

Henry desperately wanted alliance with Spain. Since the Sovereigns had married, since they had turned the Moors out of Spain, and joined Castile and Aragon, they had become very powerful indeed.

If Henry could bring about that alliance between Arthur and their daughter Katharine he would be very happy. He would feel much safer on the throne; he would have friends to stand with him against France and all those who might come against him. He must get the marriage solemnized as soon as possible.

But as he read these dispatches, cordial as they were, he was shrewd enough to read between the lines.

The Sovereigns were uncertain about the alliance. They did not want to see their daughter married to a deposed king. They were very uneasy. Lambert Simnel and Perkin Warbeck might be impostors but they would never have arisen if the throne had been secure; and while there was this uncertainty others might rise against the King of England and perhaps be more successful.

There was only one person who had a true claim, and that was the captive Earl of Warwick. If he could be disposed of, thought Henry, there would be no real claimant to come before me.

The matter tormented him, disturbing his dreams, presenting itself at all hours of the day; making him furtive, watchful of those about him. Every time a man entered his presence Henry found himself wondering whether that man carried a concealed dagger.

He could have had the Earl murdered. He could have drowned him in a butt of malmsey, had him suffocated in his sleep. It was not as though he had to catch the Earl. He was there in the Tower, the King's prisoner. It shouldn't be difficult.

But Henry was eager to have the approval of his subjects. He did not hope for their love; he knew well enough that he was not the type to inspire that. But he wanted them to see him as a just—if stern—king, as a man who was determined to make England great. They knew this in their hearts even though they were continually grumbling about the high taxes which had been imposed during his reign. They blamed Dudley and Empson more for this than they did Henry, which was unreasonable for they were only carrying out the King's commands. The royal exchequer was growing. England was becoming rich. He had brought this about in fourteen years, pulling the country away from bankruptcy, making her prosperous.

But he did not want to be known as a murderer of those who stood in his way. At times a certain guilt came over him but he could remind himself that he had done what he had, not only for his own good, although he had to admit this was part of it, but for the good of England. The kingship of minors invariably meant disaster. It was better to remove minors than, by letting them live, risk the lives of thousands. That was how he had reasoned and he had always been able to convince himself that he had good sense on his side.

What was done was done. His immediate problem was the Earl of Warwick.

While the Earl lived—a perpetual threat with a greater right to the crown than Henry himself—there could be trouble, and Isabella and Ferdinand would not wish their daughter to make an alliance with a Prince who might never reach the throne.

He had to be rid of Warwick . . . and soon. But how?

Then suddenly an idea struck him.

Perkin Warbeck was in the Tower. Perkin Warbeck was longing to be with his wife, and it was certain that if he was not reunited with her soon, he would make an attempt to reach her and plot to escape.

Suppose Warbeck and the Earl of Warwick occupied cells close to each other—two prisoners of the King, one with a spurious claim to the throne, the other with a real one? They should have something in common.

It was a chance.

Henry sent for the Constable of the Tower.

He said: 'I wish Perkin Warbeck to be moved. Place him close to the Earl of Warwick, and let both young men know that they are near to each other. It might provide some comfort for them. Who are your most trustworthy guards . . . I should like to see them . . . not yet, not yet. In due course . . .'

Henry was smiling. He would not hurry the matter. The whole point was that everything should appear to have happened naturally.

Perkin was getting desperate. He began to feel that he would never get out of this place. He had had no news from Katharine.

He did not know that the King had given instructions that no letters from his wife were to be delivered to him. Henry wanted him to get desperate and Henry was succeeding.

His guards were friendly. They lingered often in his cell and talked to him; they had made his life more tolerable than it might have been; his food was good and well served and he believed this was due to the guards.

But sometimes he was in acute despair.

'If only I could get out,' he would say. 'I'd go away. I'd leave England. I should never want to see this place again.'

The two guards were sympathetic.

'Well, there is the poor Earl just there.' The guards pointed vaguely at the wall. 'He's been here for nigh on fourteen years. Think of that!'

'For what reason?'

One of the guards lifted his shoulders and coming a step closer whispered: 'For no reason but that he is the son of his father.'

'Oh . . . of the Duke of Clarence, you mean?'

'Died in this same place . . . Drowned in a butt of malmsey . . . helped himself . . . or others helped him to too much wine.'

Perkin shivered. 'And his son has been here ever since the King came to the throne?'

The guards were becoming very confidential. 'Well, he's got a right, hasn't he?'

'A right?'

One of them made a circle around his head and winked. 'Wouldn't do for him to be around having more right to it . . . some say. Well, it stands to reason . . . He has to be kept away . . . under lock and key, don't he?'

Perkin was thoughtful. Only a short distance from him was a young man who had a real claim to the throne. He had made no attempt to rise against the Tudor . . . and yet here he was . . . condemned to be a prisoner all his life maybe.

All his life! Perkin grew cold at that thought. Was that what was intended for him?

'You and the Earl,' said the guard, '. . . you'd have a lot in common wouldn't you? If you liked to write a note to him . . . I'd see he got it.'

'What should I write to him about?'

The guard shrugged his shoulders. 'That's for you. I thought two young men . . . here . . . so near and can't see each other. I reckon the Earl would like to get a note from you . . . and you'd like to get one from him.'

Perkin shook his head.

The guard went out. His fellow guard was waiting for him.

'He don't take to the idea,' he said. 'He'll need a bit of working on.

But Perkin did take to the idea. He thought about the lonely Earl and he felt that if he could pour out his thoughts on paper it would relieve his feelings considerably. He would like to tell someone who could understand, how he had been drawn into posing as the son of a king and how he might so easily have become a king if his luck had gone the other way. It was not that he wanted to be a king; all he asked now was to rejoin his wife and child. That was all he asked but the King would not grant it and kept them apart. If Katharine could come and live with him in the Tower he was sure she would.

He asked the guard for paper and a pen to write. He should have been suspicious of the alacrity with which it was produced.

The Earl was equally glad to enliven his days in correspondence with his fellow prisoner. He told Perkin that he had heard something of him. News came now and then to the prisoners in the Tower—snippets of it . . . and then long silences so that one never really got the real story. Perkin told him what had happened to him and the Earl was eager to know more. Poor young man, he had been so long in the Tower that he knew very little of the outside world.

Perkin wrote of the freedom he longed to obtain, of Katharine waiting for him. All his thoughts were of freeing himself and getting away. . . Escape from this fearful place, he wrote. Freedom. That is what I crave.

The Earl craved it, too. 'Am I to spend *all* my life a prisoner?' he wrote.

The guards who read the letters and gave them to the constable who showed them to the King before they were passed on to the intended recipient, said: 'We are getting somewhere.'

They were right. In time the two young men began to write about means of escape. How could they achieve it? 'The guards are friendly,' wrote Perkin. 'I have an idea that they would help us. There must be many prisoners in the Tower—many of them guiltless. It might be possible to get them to help us . . . It would be freedom for them as well as for us.'

The Earl was inclined to leave the planning to Perkin who had had adventures in various places, who had actually gone into battle. What could a young man who had been a prisoner since he was ten know of these matters?

Planning made the days pass pleasantly. Perkin had a grand plan for seizing the Tower, they would get the guards to help. Warwick must not forget he was the true heir to the throne. He had the right to command. Perkin was only a humble citizen but he would admit he had experience.

They grew excited. They drew plans. It was all in the mind. Both of them knew what they wrote about would be impossible to put into action.

But it was far more serious than they realized and they were to pay dearly for their diversion.

One day the guards came into Perkin's cell. He looked up eagerly thinking they might have brought him a communication from the Earl.

The guards looked different; they were no longer smiling conspiratorially, no longer asking for the latest communication to the Earl of Warwick.

'Perkin Warbeck,' said the senior of the guards. 'You are to be tried at Westminster on the sixteenth day of November.'

'Tried! But I have already been judged.'

'This is another matter. You will be tried with the Earl of Warwick for treason.'

Perkin did not understand.

'Plotting against the King's person. Plotting to take possession of the Tower.'

'You mean . . .'

'You won't get away with this one, I can tell you. It's all there . . . in the letters.'

'My letters to the Earl . . .'

'And his to you . . . You're in trouble, you and the noble Earl.'

Perkin understood then. This had been their plan. The friendly guards were the sinister spies of the Tudor King and he was in trouble . . . moreover he had involved the Earl of Warwick with him.

Henry was gratified. His ruse had worked. Perkin was of no importance to him, but the Earl of Warwick had fallen into his hands.

The two men had written to each other of escaping from prison. It would not be easy to condemn Warwick to death for that. People would say, for what reason was he in prison? Wasn't it the most natural thing in the world that he should plan to escape?

That would not do.

He consulted with Lord Oxford who was the High Constable of England. The Constable knew what his wishes were and why. It was imperative that the match with Spain be made without much more delay. If the matter was allowed to drift the Spanish Sovereigns might well betroth their daughter to someone else.

'It would seem,' said the King, 'that the Earl of Warwick was not planning merely to escape. His idea was to gather an army about him. That is quite clear.'

It was not. But the Constable knew that the King was commanding him to make it clear.

Henry was right. Oxford saw that. While the Earl lived there would be no peace in the kingdom. At any moment someone would arise and use him as a figurehead. There must be peace. What was the life of a young prince compared with the terrible revenge of war? It was the good of the country against an innocent young man.

'It must be made clear,' said Oxford.

Henry nodded.

The Earl was bewildered to find himself in the midst of so much excitement. Up to now he had spent his days in the quietness of his prison. He knew little of the world. Vaguely he remembered life at Middleham with the Duchess of Gloucester who had afterwards become Queen Anne. She had been kind to him—she had been his mother's sister and she used to talk to him about her childhood when she and Isabel his mother were together at Middleham with Richard whom she married and George whom Isabel had married. 'They were brothers,' she had said, 'we were sisters . . . daughters of Warwick the Kingmaker who married the sons of the Duke of York.' It had all been very interesting. Then she had died and King Richard had been killed at Bosworth and that was when life changed completely and he became a prisoner in the Tower. For what reason he had never been quite sure. Now he was beginning to understand. It was because his father was the brother of King Edward and King Richard and because King Edward's two sons had disappeared in the Tower and Richard's son had died and there was only himself left.

And because of this he had plotted against the King. Had he? He had not known that. He had merely wanted to be free.

The Earl of Oxford visited him. 'Yes,' he said, 'you wanted to be free so that you could take the crown.'

The young man looked puzzled. 'I wanted to be free,' he said.

'You have been here a long time.'

'I came when I was ten years old. I am now twenty-four. More than half my life I have been King Henry's prisoner.'

'Oh . . . not a prisoner,' said the Earl of Oxford. 'You were put here for your protection.'

'Did I need it for so long?'

'The King thought so. And because your father was the Duke of Clarence you thought you had more right to the throne than he had.'

'I had more right to the throne.'

The poor innocent boy. He did not realize that he was signing his own death warrant. It was so easy to trick him . . . this innocent. How could he be otherwise, having spent so many years shut away from the world?

'I have come here to help you,' said the Constable of England. 'It would be better for you if you confessed that you know you have more right to the throne than the King and you wanted to depose him.'

'I have more right to the throne . . .' began the boy.

'Ah, that is what I said. Confess your guilt and the King will doubtless forgive you as he did Perkin Warbeck.'

'Oh, he is free then?'

'He is not free now. I was referring to what happened when he was captured and brought to the King. The King was lenient to him and at first forgave him . . . but he tried to get away and only then did the King put him into the Tower. Confess to your guilt and the King may well be lenient with you.'

The young Earl was persuaded and the Constable went in triumph to the King.

'He should be tried and condemned at once. Warbeck too.'

'They will both be found guilty,' commanded the King. 'Warbeck is unimportant. He has been proved to be a fraud. But I have had enough of the ungrateful fellow and he could have a following and one can't be found guilty and pay the penalty without the other.'

So Perkin and the Earl of Warwick were tried, found guilty of treason, and both condemned to death.

The King did not wish to take revenge on either of these traitors. They were young and foolish, he said; but they had made trouble and for the good of the country this time he intended to act. He had been lenient before; but he had been answered by ingratitude.

Perkin Warbeck should be taken to Tyburn and hanged; the Earl of Warwick should be beheaded on Tower Hill.

*　　　*　　　*

In their cells in the Tower the two men awaited the death sentence.

Perkin was resigned. He would never see Katharine again. He wondered what her life would be like without him. It was true that they had been separated for some time while he was imprisoned. But there had alwys been hope.

This was the end then—all those grandiose schemes were to end up at Tyburn.

There was no hope now. Waiting for them to come and take him he wondered if there was some point where he could have altered the course which had led him to this day. He did not know and it did not matter now.

The people had crowded into the streets to see his last moments. It was a holiday for the spectators. He heard their shouts as he was drawn along. He did not care that they jeered at him, that they had come to witness his last humiliation.

As they put the rope about his neck he was murmuring Katharine's name; and he hoped that she would recover from the desolation he knew this day would bring her. He was praying that she might find some happiness after he had gone.

This was the end then. He, Perkin Warbeck, had come to the end of the road.

At Tower Hill there was another spectacle. The young Earl walked out of the Tower and felt the cool air on his face; the mist was on the river; it was a bleak November day. But it was a great experience to walk out from those grey walls. He wondered what his life would have been like if he had been at liberty for those fourteen years he had spent in prison.

But the time had come for him to lay his head on the block. He did so . . . feeling almost indifferent. Why should he regret leaving a life of which he knew so little?

One swift stroke and it was over.

They brought the news to the King: Warwick is dead.

Henry nodded. Now he was sure the negotiations with Spain would be delayed no longer. He had removed the only claimant he had to fear.

THE SPANISH PRINCESS

The Court was at Richmond. Prince Henry with his sisters Margaret and Mary had ridden in the day before from Eltham; everyone was excitedly talking about the imminent arrival of the Infanta from Spain.

Prince Henry was now ten years old, and more resentful than ever because he had not been born the eldest. It was small consolation that when he and Arthur rode together he was the one people cheered and he knew their eyes were on him. When he remarked with a certain modesty—he thought—that he could not understand why the people stared so: was there anything wrong with him? his sister Margaret who had a very sharp tongue, retorted: 'Yes, a great deal.'

Mary would snuggle close to him and say that it was because he was so much prettier than Arthur, which was what he wanted to hear—though he would have preferred handsome to pretty. He must tell Mary that boys were not pretty.

Mary was very ready to learn. She admired him and thought he was the most wonderful person at Court. Margaret, who did not share their sister's views, said that Henry had too great a conceit of himself.

He and Margaret were not good friends; Henry never liked people who were critical of him—except perhaps his tutor John Skelton who was constantly laughing at something in a way which was not exactly complimentary. Henry did not know why he bore John Skelton no resentment—perhaps it was because he amused him and wrote such witty poems. But no one else must criticize him—except, of course, his father whom he could not prevent doing so and whose cold looks were a continual criticism. Henry had known from his early days that his father was one of the few people who preferred Arthur. It was because Arthur was the eldest, the Prince of Wales, the King-to-be. The odd thing was that Arthur didn't seem to be greatly impressed with his superiority.

It was late summer when they rode into Richmond Palace.

Henry never passed under the gateway without remembering that day just before Christmas three years before when Shene Palace had been burned down. It had been nine o'clock at night. He had been in the nursery apartments he shared with Margaret and Mary when he had been roused from his pallet by his sister Margaret shouting to him. Leaping out of bed, he had smelt the strong acrid smell of smoke and immediately the children had been surrounded by excited men and women and were marshalled together and taken to their parents. The fire had started in the royal apartments; the rushes were aflame in a very short time and before anything could be done to save the palace it was burning fiercely. Beds, hangings and tapestries were destroyed on that night. The King had been desolate, thinking of all the valuable things which had been lost, but everyone was safe, which was a consolation; and his father had immediately ordered that a new palace should be built on the ruins of the old. Thus old Shene had become Richmond Palace, always a favourite of them all because of its nearness to London—that most exciting city—and the view from the front, of the River Thames. Henry liked its long line of buildings with their towers both circular and octagonal topped by turrets, though Skelton said that the chimneys looked like pears turned upside down. It was his father's favourite residence, perhaps for the reason that he had rechristened it Richmond after one of the titles he had had before he became King. So they were there very often.

Henry was beginning to believe that his father was not always so calm and self-assured as he tried to pretend he was. Henry sensed quickly that though the people accepted his father as their king they did not like him very much. Their cheers were not spontaneous as they were for him. He always hoped when they were riding in procession that his father would notice how they smiled and waved and called for Prince Henry. He knew how to make them like him. He waved and smiled and sometimes blew kisses—which delighted them. His father had said to him afterwards: 'The people like you, yes, but it will be well for you to remember that you are not the Prince of Wales.'

'I know my lord that I am not. It is my brother who is he.'

'Remember it,' was all his father said.

The King was a man of few words, and those words did not always express what he was thinking. Henry liked to watch his father; his little eyes would narrow in speculation. Henry knew about Lambert Simnel and Perkin Warbeck. He had exchanged words with Simnel about his falcon, for Simnel was a good falconer and very pleased when Henry asked him questions. It was impossible to believe that he had once thought he would be king. Perkin Warbeck was different. He had paid the price of his ambitions. His head had been killed, which was the best way of treating traitors. Skelton talked about Perkin Warbeck. There was no subject about which Skelton could not be lured to talk. Skelton thought Warbeck was probably a natural son of Edward the Fourth because he was so like him.

'Your noble grandfather was in Flanders some months before the birth of Warbeck. And I can tell you this, my young lord, where Edward was there might well spring up little bastards . . . He was a great man. Great in all ways . . . as you will be, my young bantam lord. Oh yes, I see another such as great Edward strutting there.'

It was disrespectful talk. His father would not agree with it, but Henry liked it. It was pleasant to think he was going to be like his maternal grandfather. Skelton remembered the late King when he was a man of forty and said his years had sat lightly on him. 'Even the men cheered Edward,' Skelton went on. 'It seems they liked him to admire their wives . . . and as his admiration was of a practical nature if you know what I mean . . .' He nudged young Henry who laughed with delight. 'Then you do know what I mean!'

Skelton was a wonderful tutor, for he was a clever poet, a man of education who had studied the classics and French literature; he had translated Cicero's Letters. That he was ribald and bawdy was accepted because of his achievements and Henry would not have changed him for anyone else. He attended to all aspects of Henry's education and gave him not only an appreciation of the arts, but of women. Sometimes he talked to the boy as though he were a man. Henry liked it. He could never bear anyone to refer to his youth.

At that time Henry was destined for the Church.

He disliked the idea but Skelton laughed at him. 'A very good time can be had in the Church, my lord. Particularly for one of your rank. I swear you'll be Archbishop of Canterbury before you are very old. Think of the power you'll have.'

'I do not wish to go into the Church.' Henry's eyes were narrowed. But at the same time he looked up at the sky to placate an angry God who might be listening, for what he feared more than most things was heavenly vengeance. 'At least . . .' he added. 'At least . . . if I can serve my country in any other way. I do not think I am suited to the Church.'

'Nor are you, my lord, but wise men fit the post to themselves not themselves to the post. And think of our illustrious Pope

Alexander the Sixth . . . otherwise known to the world as Rodrigo Borgia. He manages to live a very full and varied life . . . Church or not. Don't tell me my lord that you as an Archbishop of Canterbury cannot be as clever as the Pope of Rome.'

That was how Skelton talked—laughing, irreverent, full of anecdotes. A very exciting person to be with.

Skelton was glad he was not Arthur's tutor. 'There would be no fun with our Prince of Wales,' he said. 'He is a very serious young gentleman. Not like you, my lord of York . . . ah, my lord of York, my Prince Henry, my willing pupil . . . there is a man . . . a man who was born to be king.'

Skelton should never leave him if he could help it.

Henry thought a great deal about his father and he came to the conclusion that he did not really enjoy being a king, which was strange because to Henry that seemed the ultimate achievement— that was happiness and contentment.

The King acted very strangely now and then. Henry remembered something which had happened not very long ago which gave him a certain insight into his father's nature.

It had happened at the arena. The King kept a large menagerie and he was very fond of sports in which the animals took part. Young Henry believed that his father was always trying to make the people like him. He showed them how lenient he was to his enemies; they were always present at tournaments and shows in the arena. But he always looked so stern and he rarely smiled. If only he would smile, speak to some of them in a friendly way, he would have been liked so much more than because he forgave Lambert Simnel, and Perkin Warbeck, too . . . for a very long time. If I were the King . . . Henry thought. It was a recurring observation.

But on this day in the arena the King's lion was brought out. He was a fierce and splendid animal and when the dogs were set on him he was always the victor. His name was Rex which meant he was the King.

On that day four mastiffs were set against him. Never had the dogs beaten Rex, but they did that day. Young Henry loved the dogs and they put up a magnificent fight against old Rex. They were battered and wounded . . . but the dogs won in the end and it was Rex who lay dying in the centre of the arena.

Young Henry's impulse had been to shout with excitement but he had caught the stern looks of his father, and his mother, who sat beside the King, was watching Henry and her look begged him to restrain his high spirits. Then he realized that the King saw something significant in this episode. The King had been set on and killed. Poor Rex was king of the animals no more.

It was a symbol. These mere dogs had set on the king of the beasts and killed him. Rex was the King. Henry saw it clearly when John Skelton pointed it out to him.

The King had left the arena in silence. People had thought it was because he had loved his lion. But it was more than that. Before sunset those four victorious mastiffs were brought out from the kennels and hanged on gibbets in the arena. Their bodies dangled there for two days so that all might see them.

It was a symbol and a warning to all would-be traitors. The mastiffs had killed the king of the beasts. Therefore they were traitors.

Henry was a little bewildered. He talked over it with Skelton.

'But it wasn't the fault of the dogs. They were put in the arena to fight Rex,' he pointed out.

Skelton said: 'One does not have to be at fault to be hanged as a traitor.'

'Then how can they help it?'

'They cannot. Young Warwick couldn't help it, could he? He was born to what he was . . . so he was a potential traitor if another should take over the throne.'

'Warwick wanted to take my father's place,' said Henry.

Skelton bowed low. 'Ah, the noble Tudors. Bless me, I had forgot. They have a right to the throne. The rank of Lancaster! Of course. Of course. York must stand aside for the Tudors.'

Henry laughed as he often did at Skelton. But he would not repeat quite a lot of what Skelton said because he knew that if he did he would his lose his tutor and who knew—his tutor might lose his head. But he did know, through Skelton's innuendoes, that his father was very much afraid that someone would rise up and take the throne from him.

There was another occasion when the King had one of his best falcons killed. This amazed young Henry. He loved his own falcons and he could not understand why the very best one of all should be destroyed.

The falcon had matched itself with an eagle, he was told. And it had bettered the eagle. All knew that the eagle was the king of the birds as the lion was the king of the beasts.

The King had said: 'It is not meet for any subject to offer such wrong to his lord and superior.'

Henry was bewildered. He came to Skelton for explanation.

'It's a parable, my lord. Your noble father is fond of parables. That is because he sees himself as our god. He wishes it to be remembered that he will brook no traitors. Any who threaten his throne will go the way of the mastiffs and the falcon. Poor innocent creatures who must be so sadly used in order that the King's human subjects be provided with a lesson.'

'I would never destroy my best falcon,' said Henry.

'Let us hope, dear lord, that if you should attain the throne you would never find it necessary to teach us all such a lesson.'

'I should just wait until I had real traitors and then cut off their heads.'

'Ah, if my Prince ever came to the throne then the heads would begin to roll, would they?'

'Traitors' heads would.'

'And traitors would be any who opposed my lord's will. Ah, but such talk is treason . . . to our lord the King and to the Prince of Wales. I must take care or I shall find myself hanging beside the mastiffs.'

'I would prevent that, good Skelton,' said Henry.

Skelton laughed and coming close to Henry whispered in his ear: 'Ah, but my lord Prince, you are not the King . . . yet.'

'You say yet, good Skelton . . . as though . . . as though . . .'

Skelton laughed. 'Life is full of chances,' he said. 'You are at the moment second in line . . .'

'Skelton, have you been seeing the soothsayers and wise men?'

Skelton shook his head. 'The wisdom comes from inside this head, my lord. And it tells me that . . . there is a chance . . . Of course when our Prince of Wales has sons . . . then, my lord of York, your chances fade with the birth of each one.'

'Arthur is not very strong. Do you think he will be able to do that which is necessary to get children.'

Skelton looked slyly at his pupil. 'There is only one, my lord, who can answer that question.'

'Who? Where is he? Find him . . .'

'I do not have to. He is here with us now.'

'Whisper his name.'

Skelton put his lips to the ear of the Prince and said: 'Father Time.'

Henry was irritated and slunk away in a temper, cross even with Skelton.

Now he looked from the windows—a dull and misty October day. He liked the spring—the lovely season when the world refreshed from the winter started to burgeon again. The spring, the hot summer . . . journeys into the country to be cheered by the people, to let them see what a fine son their King had got for them. 'Alas,' he imagined them saying. 'He should have been the firstborn.'

He ran an impatient finger along the ledge of the window seat. It was decorated with roses. Tudor roses they called them. It was roses everywhere. Red roses the most prominent of course because the red rose of Lancaster was slightly superior to the white rose of York. They were entwined now; and he liked to remember the white rose. His glorious grandfather had proudly worn it. He was the one who impressed Henry—not the obscure Tudors. In the gardens some of the roses lingered on as though loath to go. In the summer they made a colourful display. He liked to run across the grass past the statues to the end of the garden where that building which was called The Houses of Pleasure was situated.

There it was possible to play games at which he was beginning to excel. He had real mastery at tennis and he loved the game. Arthur would never play with him. But he played with others and he almost invariably won. Sometimes he wondered whether they allowed him to because he could be rather angry if they didn't. He never said so but he tried not to play with the winner again. Skelton noticed—Skelton noticed everything.

'It is all very well to hate to be beaten. Natural, right and proper, but to *show* you hate it . . . now that is quite another matter.'

There were times when he wished Skelton were not so perceptive. Sometimes they played chess together.

'Now, my lord Duke,' Skelton had once said, 'how is your mood this day? May I beat you? Or would your temper not stand it?'

'Skelton you rogue,' he said, 'the better man will win.'

'Oh that is how you wish it, is it? Very well. I just wished to know whether I was to consider my lord Duke's skill or his temper.'

He saw too much, knew too much. There were times when he felt he would have rid himself of the man if he could. But he knew he never would. Skelton was too clever, too entertaining.

He would like to play a game of tennis and he was in no mood to be beaten, so he selected one of his squires who had not the skill to beat him even if he did not know it was impolitic to do so.

'Come,' he said. 'I would to the tennis court. We can get a game before it is dark.'

So they went and while they were playing a barge drew up at

the river bank. Henry dropped his racquet and ran to see what this meant.

'What news?' he cried. 'What news?'

'I must see the King,' said the messenger.

'I am the Duke of York,' said Henry.

'My lord.' The man bowed. 'I must see the King with all speed.'

Henry was sullen. His squire was watching. He had thought the messenger would be so impressed by meeting the son of the King that he would immediately tell his business. But it was not so.

One of the King's attendants had seen the messenger approaching and came hurrying out.

'I have news for the King,' said the messenger.

'Come this way.'

Henry followed. The King, aware of the arrival of the messenger, was already in the hall. The man approached him and fell on to his knees.

'Your Grace. The Infanta of Spain is in England. She has arrived at Plymouth.'

'Good news! Good news!' said the King. 'We must thank God for her safe arrival.'

He noticed his son standing there but gave him no greeting.

Then he said: 'I will go to tell the Queen this good news.' And to the messenger: 'Go to the kitchens where you will be refreshed.'

Henry looked after his father as he left the hall.

He felt angry and frustrated. Arthur would be summoned. This was his bride.

Oh why did I have to be the second son? he thought, with more bitterness than usual. He wanted a bride. He wanted a marriage. It was true he was only ten—but he was so advanced for his age.

It was maddening, frustrating. He would have suited the occasion so much better than pallid Arthur.

He was excited when a short while after he was summoned to his father's apartment.

When he arrived his mother was already there.

He went forward and bowed as he had been taught to do. He noticed his mother's eyes on him with a certain pride and satisfaction which pleased him.

'Henry,' said the King, 'there are going to be some splendid celebrations. This marriage with Spain is very dear to my heart and to that of your mother.'

The Queen nodded in agreement. She would always agree with her husband.

'Your brother Arthur is a very fortunate young man,' said the King.

Henry smiled almost imperceptibly. Arthur was in Wales and Henry wondered how he would receive the news of his good fortune. He was now fifteen, pale and more like his father than his mother; he was gentle, hated great ceremonies in which he had to play a part, and he would be very apprehensive about those which would inevitably be the result of his 'good fortune.'

'The Infanta is on our shores. There can be no hitch now. The marriage will most certainly take place and when it does we shall have a powerful ally. This is a happy time for us all.'

'Henry will have his part to play,' said the Queen, smiling at him.

The colour rose to Henry's cheeks touching the normal healthy pink to rosy red—the colour of a Lancaster rose. His eyes sparkled. He was going to enjoy these celebrations if he could forget that they were for Arthur's wedding, for Arthur's bride, and that Arthur would be at the centre of them.

'And,' went on the Queen, still smiling, 'I am sure he will play it well.'

'What must I do?' asked Henry eagerly.

'I have decided that you shall bring the Infanta into London. You shall be her escort companion when she enters the capital.'

'Oh thank you, my lord.'

'You are pleased?' said the King.

'Oh yes, indeed I am. I would I could do more.'

'That will be enough,' said his father. He was trying not to compare the boy with Arthur. Henry was tall for his age and he had bulk too. His skin was glowing with health; he was vigorous and excelled at games, archery, horsemanship; and Skelton said he was good with his books too. He should have been the first born, of course. But they had Arthur. The King was fond of his eldest son in a way which he had not believed he could be fond of anyone. Arthur was so vulnerable. In Arthur he saw something of himself. Long ago Henry had dreamed of kingship. In his Welsh stronghold his uncle Jasper had primed him, and the thought had been constantly with him in exile: 'One day you will be King.' It had seemed the ultimate goal, the end of the road. Now it was here he was tortured by anxieties, not knowing from one day to the next when some Pretender would arise to claim the crown on which he seemed to have such a light hold. Arthur was uneasy too. Prince of Wales . . . accepted successor . . .

and the longer Henry remained on the throne the more firm his seat would be. But he could see that Arthur was afraid of the future, even as he was. Arthur did not want this grand marriage; he did not want the crown.

Had it been young Henry, how different it would have been.

'Very well my son,' said the King, 'you must prepare yourself for this duty. You will have to ride through the streets of London with the Infanta. I know you can manage your horse as well as our best knights. But it will be more than that. You will have to treat her with the utmost courtesy. Remember she is a Princess of Spain and she will be one day Queen of England. Now you will show her the utmost respect. I do not know yet how you conduct yourself with the ladies.'

'I am very gallant with them, my lord.'

The Queen's lips curved in a smile but the King regarded his son sternly.

'You have a good opinion of yourself, Henry.'

'One must have, my lord, for if one has not a good opinion of oneself who else would have one?'

That was pure Skelton. It amused the Queen but the King showed no sign of mirth.

'A little more than gallantry will be required,' said the King. 'I will have you taught what you should do. The Infanta has to come from Plymouth. That is a long way off so you will have plenty of time to learn how to conduct yourself. Now you may go. We have matters to discuss which do not require your presence.'

He left a little dispirited in spite of the prospect ahead.

He went to the nurseries. His sisters Margaret and Mary were there. Margaret was drawing and Mary, watching her, was saying it was beautiful and Margaret was very clever.

Mary was so young and naively admired her brother and sister so much because they could do things which she could not.

Margaret said: 'Have you seen the messenger?'

'I have been with our father,' replied Henry grandly.

'Oh Henry . . . have you really!' cried Mary. 'What did you talk about?'

'This coming marriage,' said Henry importantly. 'The Infanta is at Plymouth. She will have to be met and brought to London. I suppose I shall have to lead her into the city.'

'A little boy of ten!' cried Margaret.

'I tell you I am going to do it. I have just told our father that I will.'

'She is grown up. She is sixteen . . . even older than Arthur. You will look such a baby beside her.'

There were times when he would have liked to strike Margaret. There would be terrible trouble if he did. It would be quite against the rules of chivalry. They might even prevent him from taking part in the wedding celebrations, so he kept his temper, which was not easy.

'I shall look what I am—a Prince of England,' he said.

'Well I think you will look very silly,' said Margaret.

'I think you will look nice,' murmured Mary who always took his side when she was there.

'I shall look just as a Prince should look and the Infanta will wish that I was the one she is to marry.'

That made Margaret laugh still louder. 'You marry. . . That won't be for years. I am to be married soon.'

'Into Scotland. It is a land of barbarians.'

'I shall be the Queen of Scotland.'

'I hate the Scots,' declared Henry.

'You will have to learn to love them when they are part of our family . . . through this marriage.'

'At least,' said Henry his eyes narrowed to slits, 'I shall be grateful to the King of Scotland for taking you away.'

'And I shall be grateful to him for relieving me of your company.'

'Please don't quarrel.' Mary had slipped her hand into that of Henry. 'It's so exciting . . . with Arthur's wedding and then Margaret's . . . don't spoil it, Henry, please . . .'

He stooped and kissed the beautiful little face turned up to his. Mary flushed with pleasure and Henry's good humour was restored.

'Come with me, Mary,' he said. 'And I'll tell you all about what I shall do when the Infanta comes to London. I am to lead her in. You may be able to see me. Let's leave Margaret . . . and we'll sit together . . . and talk.'

Mary nodded. Margaret watched them with a curl of her lips.

'Boast away,' she shouted. 'All the boasting in the world won't make you the Prince of Wales. You'll never be the King . . . though that's what you want. You're wicked . . . You wish Arthur was dead . . . yes you do . . . yes you do . . .'

Henry turned and looked at her; for once his rage was cold rather than hot.

'How dare you say such a wicked thing!' he cried.

'I didn't mean it,' said Margaret, suddenly contrite. It was unlucky to talk of death outright in such a way. Many times she had heard the vague comments of the attendants, the innuendoes about Arthur's not making old bones . . . but that was different.

She should not have mentioned Arthur's dying. What if Henry told their parents!

Henry said: 'Come on Mary. We will leave this wicked girl alone.'

Margaret, subdued, muttered something and turned away and Henry and Mary went to the window seat and sat down.

He started to tell her what a glorious pageant it would be. He described others he had seen but this one would be different because he would be at the centre of it.

Suddenly Mary said in a whisper: 'If Arthur died would you marry the Infanta, Henry?'

'Hush,' he said. 'You must not speak of death.'

Then he went on to describe what he thought the wedding would be like and when he did so he was not seeing Arthur as the bridegroom, but himself, miraculously grown a little older, as old as Arthur . . . old enough to be a bridegroom.

The picture made him very excited. It was nonsense, of course, just a dream, a fantasy; but it was very enjoyable.

And oddly enough he could not dismiss it from his mind.

When the Spanish Infanta stepped ashore at Plymouth with her duenna beside her, she was warmly received by the dignitaries of Plymouth. They had been warned of her arrival and had been awaiting it for several days and when the ship appeared on the horizon the call had gone up: 'The Spanish Princess is here.'

The King had given orders that she was to be royally entertained. He would be sending Lord Brook the steward of the royal palace to look after her; he himself could not be expected to make the three-week journey to Plymouth, but he was determined that she should be entertained in accordance with her rank and that her parents should have nothing to complain of in the treatment she received in her new country.

Catalina herself was bewildered. It had been a frightening journey although she had set off from Granada in May and had not embarked at Corunna until August; but even then the ship in which she had set out had been forced back to the coast of Castile because of gales and storms. She had been so ill when she landed that she had not been able to set out again until September. Then her father had ordered that the finest ship he owned—one of three hundred tons—should be put at her disposal. This was a great deal more comfortable than the previous vessel and on the second of October when Plymouth was sighted, Catalina felt that she had been travelling for months.

'Catalina,' her mother had said, 'you will have to learn the language of your new country and you will no longer be called Catalina. In English it is Katharine. But what is a name? You will still be my good Catalina whatever they call you.'

Was it so important to change a name? Only because it was a symbol. Everything would be different now. She had to learn. She had to be a credit to her parents. She had been told that often enough.

How desolate she had been when she stood on deck watching the green land come nearer! Only her strict upbringing had prevented her from turning to Doña Elvira Manuel and begging to be taken home to her mother.

What foolishness that had been! She had left Spain for ever. Whatever anyone had said to comfort her she knew that and the fear that she might never see again her beloved mother was what hurt her most.

She had known for a long time—since she was ten years old, and she was now sixteen—that it had to happen. A similar fate had overtaken her sisters Maria and Juana. They had left Spain—lost to their home forever. Her eldest sister Isabella and her adored brother Juan had been even more irrevocably dealt with, for Death had taken them.

How often had she asked herself during that long and exhausting journey why life had to be so cruel. If only time could stand still, and they remain children, all happy together, for they had been such a happy family and it was their mother who had made them so. She had loved them all dearly and if they had—every one of them—been in awe of her, they had loved her with a devotion which had made them desperately unhappy to leave her.

People were crowding round her. They were speaking and she could not understand what they were saying, but she knew these smiling cheering crowds were telling her that they liked her and that she was welcome on their shores.

She was taken into a small mansion and there conducted to an apartment where she might wash and rest before food was served. What she wanted more than anything was to be alone, but she knew that she could not hope to be without her duenna.

'I am thankful we have come through the journey safely,' said Doña Elvira. 'I thought it was the end for us . . . but the saints preserved us and before anything else we should give thanks to them.'

Queen Isabella had chosen Doña Elvira to conduct her daughter to England because she had faith in her trustworthiness and religious principles. Elvira watched with hawklike eyes and Catalina knew that if she did anything which was not correct according to strict Spanish etiquette, her mother would hear of it.

'You look too sad,' said Doña Elvira. 'You must not look so. It is not good manners. You must show these people that you are happy to be here.'

'But I am not, Doña Elvira. I am most unhappy. I hope the Prince doesn't like me . . . and sends me home.'

Doña Elvira clicked her tongue in exasperation. 'And what grief would that cause your gracious mother? And your father would be angry and only send you back again and then we should have to face those terrible seas once more.'

'It is just that I keep thinking of the past . . . when I was little . . . when we were in the nursery together . . . Juan, Maria and Juana . . .'

'Childhood does not last forever.'

'They have all gone, Doña Elvira . . . My dear dear brother . . .'

'He is with the saints . . .'

'And Isabella . . . She didn't want to go back to Portugal. She had married once for state reasons. That should have been enough. It was strange how she was so unhappy about going to Portugal but she loved her husband in time. I think she was fond of both her husbands, though she loved Alfonso most. But Emmanuel was very kind to her and she was grateful for that.'

'That is how it should be. That is how it will be with you, my lady Catalina. But I must call you Katharine now . . . It is not so easy to say. But we must all learn to change.'

'If that were the only thing one had to learn it would be easy. Katharine seems different. Catalina was the girl who was so happy. When we were young I was so proud, Doña Elvira . . . proud to be the daughter of the Sovereigns who had driven out the Moors and united Castile and Aragon . . .'

'So you should have been . . . and still should be. Never forget who you are, Catalina . . . Katharine.'

'But we soon learned that Spain was more important than any of us. The greatness of Spain. The glory of Spain. That was what mattered. That was why Isabella had to go back to Portugal and marry Emmanuel . . .'

'Who had loved her ever since she set foot on Portuguese soil to marry Alfonso, and was a good husband to her.'

'But she didn't want to go back. I remember her sadness so vividly. I was only ten at the time . . . but I remember. They

sent her back and she died . . . and now Maria has had to go to
marry Emmanuel . . . because friendship with Portugal is important to Spain.'

'Perhaps you should rest. You are talking too much.'

'It relieves me to talk. I must talk to you. These people here
don't speak our language. I wonder what Arthur will be like.'

'He is to be your husband. You will love him because it will
be your duty to do so.'

'I wonder if Juana loves her husband.'

'There has been enough of this talk. Now you are going to lie
down for twenty minutes. I shall awaken you at the end of that
time and you must prepare yourself to meet the important people
whom the King will send.'

'Will the King come himself?'

'Of course the King will come. He will want to show how
grateful he is to be able to welcome the daughter of the Sovereigns of Spain.'

'I hope they will like me.'

'What nonsense is this! How could they fail to like the daughter of King Ferdinand and Queen Isabella? Now rest. You are
wasting the time in idle talk.'

She allowed her veil to be taken off and lay back on the cool
cushions. She closed her eyes and tried to shut out the future by
looking back over the past.

Did Juana love her husband? She couldn't stop thinking of
her. The truth about Juana had come to her suddenly. It was after
one of those distressing scenes in the nursery when Juana had
suddenly begun to dance wildly around and climbed onto the
table and danced and when their governess tried to stop her she
had clung to the arras hanging on the walls, swinging there.
Their mother had been called and she had ordered that Juana be
seized but none could take her because she kicked at them as
they tried, and all the time she was laughing wildly.

Then Queen Isabella had said, 'Juana, listen to me.'

And that had made Juana stop laughing.

'Come,' the Queen had gone on quietly. 'Come down to me,
my darling.'

Then Juana had come down and flung herself into her mother's arms and her wild laughter was substituted by sobbing which
was as wild.

The Queen had said quietly, 'I will take the Infanta to her
apartments. Bring one of her potions.' She had led Juana away
but as she left, the Queen had seen the wide frightened eyes of
Catalina. She touched her on the head caressingly and passed on.

It had been later when the Queen had sent for her. They were alone together. Those had been the occasions which meant so much to Catalina. Then Queen Isabella was not so much the great Sovereign—greater even than Ferdinand, many said—she was the fond mother.

'Come to me, Catalina,' she had said, holding out her hand and the child had run to her, clinging to her. The Queen had lifted her youngest daughter onto her lap and said: 'You were frightened, my child, by what you saw today. Juana is not to blame. She is not wicked. She does not do these things to grieve us. She does them because they are a compulsion . . . do you understand? Sometimes there is a little seed in families which is passed on . . . through the generations. Be kind always to Juana. Do not provoke her. Juana is not the same as we are. My mother suffered from the same affliction. So you see what has happened to Juana has come to her through me. You understand why I wish us to be very very kind to Juana.'

She had nodded, happy to be nestling close to that great queen who was also her dear mother.

She had never forgotten that. She had never provoked Juana, and had always tried to follow her mother's wishes and keep Juana quiet.

But even if Juana had been different from the others she still had to play her part. Insane or not she must marry for the glory of Spain; and a grand match indeed had been found for her—no less than the heir of the Hapsburgs, Philip, son of Maximilian—and so she would unite the houses of Hapsburg and Spain.

It had been a match which made King Ferdinand's eyes sparkle, and the alliance had been even stronger when Margaret, Maximilian's daughter, married Juan.

Dear dear Juan, who had been so beautiful and so good. No wonder they said of him that he was too good for long life. The angels wanted him for themselves, that was what Catalina had heard someone say. And there had been that terrible time at Salamanca when the town was *en fête* to welcome Juan and Margaret his bride and the news that Juan was dead had come to them. There seemed no reason . . . except, as they said, that the angels wanted him in Heaven.

Catalina remembered her mother's grief. She suspected that loving all her children as the Queen did, Juan was her favourite, her beloved son, her only son. That was a melancholy time of mourning. Margaret, his new wife, was heartbroken because, being Juan, he had already charmed her.

Doña Elvira was at the side of her couch.

'Is it time then?' she said.

'I gave you a little longer, so we must hurry now '

It was no use thinking of the past. She had to face the future. Catalina was left behind in Spain. Katharine was here . . . in England.

It seemed that they were not to meet the King and Prince Arthur at this stage, but were to begin the journey to London without delay. Doña Elvira was a little put out. She thought that the bridegroom at least should have been waiting at Plymouth to greet his bride.

'I am not sorry,' said Katharine. 'It will give me time to know a little of this land . . . and to see the people . . .'

She was feeling better as the effects of the sea journey were wearing off, and was making an effort to stop grieving for her family and feel an interest in the new sights which presented themselves.

How green was the grass! What a number of trees there were! 'It is a beautiful green country,' she said to Elvira. She liked the villages through which they passed—the gabled houses which clustered round the church, the village greens. 'Always green,' she said. 'It is the colour of England.'

It was only when they came to Exeter that she saw crowds again. They had come to look at her, the Spanish Princess, the Queen-to-be. 'She is so young,' they said. 'Only a child. Well, Arthur is the same. It is better for him to have someone of his own age.'

But they were disappointed because she was veiled and they could not see her face clearly.

'Is there something wrong that we are not allowed to see her?' Her hair was beautiful—long and luxuriant, hanging down her back, and there was a glint of red in it.

At Exeter, Lord Willoughby de Broke was waiting to greet her.

He was charming. The King would soon be on his way, he told her. In the meantime he had the King's express command to make sure that everything which could be done to make her comfortable was done.

She thanked him and said she had been made very welcome.

'You will discover how delighted we are to have you with us,' he told her. 'I am the High Steward of the King's Household and he has sent me from Westminster to make sure that nothing is left undone. The Spanish ambassadors are here in Exeter and they will be calling upon you soon, I doubt not. They will want to make sure that you are well cared for and if there is anything that does not please you, you must tell me and I promise you it shall be rectified.'

Katharine assured Lord Willoughby de Broke that she was well cared for. He was able to speak a little of her language and she was grateful for that. She realized that she would have been wiser to have spent the time when she was waiting to come to England in learning the English language. It was going to be very difficult for her to understand and make herself understood. She wondered why her parents had not insisted that she learn English and could only assume that her father might have been unsure that the match would take place and she be whisked off to some other country for the interest of Spain.

Almost immediately she was told that Don Pedro de Ayala had called to see her.

She was delighted to meet one of her own countrymen and asked that he be sent to her immediately.

Don Ayala was elegant and gallant and he reminded her so much of home when he spoke to her in Castilian. She felt comforted to have him at her side.

'The King is eager for you to arrive in the capital as soon as possible,' he said. 'There the marriage will take place without delay. The King will meet you near London that you may be escorted there with all the deference due to an Infanta of Spain.'

'I had thought the King might have come to Plymouth,' she said.

'It is three weeks' journey from London, Infanta.'

'It does not seem that he is eager to meet me.'

'He is eager, I promise you. This is a fortunate day for you, my lady, for England and for Spain. This marriage is one of the finest things that has happened since the expulsion of the Moors from our country.'

'Surely not as important as that. I should have thought my brother's and sisters' marriages were more important than mine.'

'Nay. We need the friendship of this island. Your father-in-law is a shrewd man. He is making England a country to be reckoned with. You may find it necessary to speak with me from time to time. You may think that there are certain matters which would interest your mother and your father.'

'Am I to be a spy in my new husband's household?'

'Never that. Just a good friend to England and perhaps an even better one to Spain.'

'I cannot say,' she answered coolly. 'There is so much I have to learn.'

Dr de Puebla was announced while de Ayala was with her.

De Ayala's face crinkled in distaste.

'Must you see this man, Highness?' he asked.

'He is my father's ambassador,' she answered.

'I must warn you of him. He is a man of the people, lacking in education and manners. He is a Jew. He seems to forget his Spanish upbringing and lives like an Englishman.'

'I have been told that I must become an Englishwoman,' she replied. 'Perhaps Dr de Puebla is wise in his habits. My parents think highly of him.'

'He is on good terms with King Henry. Such good terms that he has been offered a bishopric.'

'Which he refused? Would that not have brought him in a good income?'

'It would indeed and his fingers itched to grasp it. But your father forbade it. He did not want him working entirely for the King of England.'

'Which makes me believe he is a man of sound sense. I shall receive him, Don Pedro. It would be churlish not to.'

'Then it must be, but I warn you, be careful of the man. He is of low origins and this comes out.'

De Puebla was brought in. He bowed obsequiously to Katharine and she noticed the looks he cast on de Ayala. The antagonism between these two was apparent. She would have to steer a path between them because they would be her chief advisers at the Court of England—de Puebla no less than de Ayala.

De Puebla assured her of his delight at seeing her, of the King's pleasure at the marriage and of the joy this brought all lovers of Spain.

'And of England,' said de Ayala pointedly.

'My lady Princess,' said de Puebla, 'the friendship between the two countries is the ardent wish of the Sovereigns . . . and of the King of England . . . no less. I'll swear that the joy of the bride's family equals that of the bridegroom.'

'I am very pleased that you are both here to be of service to me. I know I shall need your help.'

'It shall be my greatest desire to give it,' said de Ayala.

'And do not forget good Dr de Puebla is standing by awaiting your command.'

When they left Exeter she rode between Lord Willoughby de Broke and de Ayala; and de Puebla was furious because he had to fall in behind.

She knew that she was going to have to endure their enmity when de Ayala continued to complain about the low-born Jewish lackey and de Puebla whispered to her to have a care of de Ayala

. . . a self-seeker, a man bound by manners and customs rather than good sense, a coxcomb more interested in the cut of a jacket than matters of state.

'I will take care,' she promised both of them.

It was de Puebla who touched on those matters which de Ayala would have thought not for her ears.

De Puebla dispensed with Spanish innuendoes. An inexperienced girl of sixteen who was going to be thrust into the heart of politics needed plain speaking. She must, thought de Puebla, have some inkling of what it was all about. De Ayala thought that she was just a symbol. All she had to do in his opinion was look beautiful, charm the King and the Prince, let the former see that she had no intention of meddling and to be fruitful and within a few years have half a dozen lusty boys playing in the royal nurseries.

He said: 'Arthur will be manageable.'

'Manageable?' she asked.

De Puebla nodded. 'He will love you, I am sure. He has been told that he must, and Arthur always does as he is told. He is delicate. Pray God he lives. But he is gentle and you will have no trouble from him. The Queen is mild and does not interfere so the King is very fond of her. Arthur has two sisters and a brother but they need not concern you very much. The older sister Margaret has to go to Scotland to marry the King there. Mary the other is very young yet. Henry the brother is ten years old— rather a lusty young fellow. You can be thankful that he is not the elder. Arthur—if he were a little stronger—would be the ideal match. You'll have to watch his health a little. He's delicate and if he died it would not be so good for Spain. But your main concern is to please the King.'

'How shall I do this?'

'Oh, be docile, bear children. Take a pattern from the Queen. The King trusts nobody. He is suspicious of all. This is due to the fact that there are other claimants to the throne. Recently two impostors arose on the scene. Their claims were clearly false and he overcame them. But there was one other . . . fortunately he is no longer in a position to menace the King. But the fact that they could appear and there be people to follow them has frightened the King. He is continually on the alert and would be very resentful if he thought anyone was trying to work against him.'

'Spain would never do that.'

De Puebla smiled. 'Our two countries are friends,' he said. He moved closer to her and whispered: 'But sometimes it is necessary to be watchful of friends.'

She could see what de Ayala meant. There was something offensive about de Puebla. But he was clever—she sensed that, and her father had told her that she must listen to him and do what he asked just as she must with the ambassador de Ayala.

It was a slow journey; she was very glad sometimes to ride in the horse litter which Lord Willoughby de Broke had provided. When she was tired of the litter there was her palfrey ready for her. She certainly could not have complained of a lack of attention.

She was learning something about the people of England. They were independent and did not stand on the same ceremony that she was accustomed to. The people came out to see her as she passed and they were clearly surprised that she should be veiled. They were frankly curious about her. Why, they asked, if she has nothing to hide in her face does she hide it?

They had no natural dignity, she decided; but she rather liked that. They shouted to each other, jostled each other and called to her in a manner she believed was not as respectful as it should have been.

The amounts of food that were consumed seemed enormous; it was interesting to be housed in the mansions of the squires and knights of the places they passed through. Here there would be fires in great fireplaces and minstrels to sing for her delight.

So she learned about her new country and her conversations with both de Ayala and de Puebla gave her some indication of what she must expect.

She was most interested to hear of Arthur.

'A gentle boy,' was de Ayala's comment.

'Like a piece of clay he'll be in your hands,' said de Puebla. 'Mild as milk and sweet as honey. He's a good boy. He's caused no trouble to his father and he'll cause none to his wife.'

'Is he not very strong?' she asked.

'He is not as robust as his younger brother,' said de Ayala.

'He'll grow out of it,' said de Puebla. 'Give him a wife. That's what he needs.'

'Perhaps he seems more delicate than he is because he is constantly compared with young Henry,' commented de Ayala.

'There you speak truth,' said de Puebla in such a voice that meant 'For once.' 'I reckon they would have been happier if their roles had been reversed. Henry for King, Arthur for Church.'

'I beg you to refrain from such observations before the Infanta,' said de Ayala.

'The Infanta will forgive me,' said de Puebla '. . . particularly when she sees the truth of my remarks. My dear lady, your father has instructed me to give you an account of the English Court and that is what I must do.'

'Thank you,' said Katharine, 'you are helping me a great deal.'

De Ayala lapsed into silence. He was always annoyed when she talked with de Puebla.

When they were within fifteen leagues of London, messengers came to say that the King was on his way and was to meet the bride as soon as he arrived.

Doña Elvira said grimly: 'The King may come but he shall not meet the Infanta until after the wedding. You know it is not the custom for the bridegroom and his family to see the bride before the ceremony of marriage has taken place.'

De Ayala said: 'This is the King of England. It is not the same.'

'It *is* the same,' said Doña Elvira. 'I should consider myself unworthy of my task if I allowed it.'

Prince Arthur was riding south from Wales. His father had commanded him to come with all possible speed for he wished them to be together to greet the Infanta.

Arthur was very uneasy. He was to be married. What would that mean? What was his bride like? He was terrified of marriage. There were obligations which he might not be able to fulfil. He was tired—he had always been tired for as long as he remembered. Too much was expected of him; and when he could escape the eyes of his father and his father's ministers he was always relieved.

But all the time he had been in Wales this fate had been hanging over him. Marriage . . . It was hard enough being the Prince of Wales but to be expected to be a husband as well seemed almost too much for him to endure. He was spitting a little blood now. He did not want his father or mother to know; it drove his mother to despair and his father to look so anxious that he felt he was being reproached for his weakness.

I should never have been Prince of Wales, he often thought. How much better it would have been if Henry had been born before me. Henry could do everything that was expected of a Prince of Wales and what was so important liked doing it. Nothing pleased Henry more than to be at the centre of affairs, to have everyone looking at him; he enjoyed answering their questions; he could dance, ride, hawk, hunt . . . do anything better than Arthur. Even at his books he excelled. There was only one thing he lacked. He was not the first born. And he resented that.

Arthur had often seen the flashes of anger in his brother's eyes, that sudden pout of the rather small mouth when Arthur was given precedence, as being Prince of Wales he always was; even at three years old he had been made a Knight of the Bath and two years later Knight of the Garter.

He was better at his studies than he was at outdoor sports. It was the one field in which he could beat Henry, in spite of the fact that Henry was no dullard and his tutors spoke highly of his ability to learn. But Henry of course had interests which Arthur could never have; Arthur loved his studies, he liked nothing better than to be allowed to sit with his tutor and read and discuss what he read and studied. His father had put the blind Poet Laureate Bernard André to teach him and they had become great friends. Another tutor and friend was Dr. Linacre who was a doctor besides being a classical scholar. Arthur wondered whether his father had appointed Dr. Linacre to keep a watch on his health as well as his studies. If this was so the doctor performed this duty very discreetly. He was some forty years old at this time and he seemed to Arthur full of widsom, having travelled widely in Italy and he had even attained a degree in Padua. He was considered to be one of the most learned men in the realm.

He had dedicated a translation from the Greek into Latin of *Proclus on the Sphere* to Arthur who felt very privileged to claim such a man as his friend. Oddly enough although he felt inadequate in the company of Court gallants he was quite at home with men like Dr. Linacre and Bernard André. He wished he could go on sharing his life with such people, but he had his duties—as his father was fond of reminding him—and now those duties entailed marriage with the Spanish Princess. She had arrived in England and his sojourn in Wales had come to an end.

'I am riding from Shene to meet her,' was the command his father had sent. 'It would be well if you were to join me just before that meeting takes place.'

So he had begun the journey to London without delay, and at East Hampstead he joined his father's cavalcade.

The King was delighted with the way everything had happened. At last the Infanta was in England and there could be no turning back now. Friendship with Spain was assured; and the dowry would be useful. Henry's eyes glistened as he thought of that. His great anxiety was Arthur's health. He had been disturbed to hear that the Infanta's brother had died shortly after his marriage. Had he over-exerted himself? It was a way with these young people and if they were not very strong it could be disastrous. It was difficult to imagine Arthur's taking violent action in such a sphere but one could never be sure. This bride and bridegroom could be delayed for a little while . . . a few months . . . a year perhaps. His son the young Prince Edmund had died recently; that meant he had only two boys. True Henry was virile enough, but one could never be sure when people would sicken so he and the Queen must get more children. More boys.

When he rode into East Hampstead he was pleased to find that Arthur was there.

He watched his son approach and kneel. The greeting was formal. Henry found it difficult to be otherwise. But his smile was as warm as could be expected. Arthur looked at him almost apologetically. Did the boy know how wan he looked, that there were dark shadows under his eyes and how much the pallor of his skin alarmed the King?

'I see you in good health, my son,' he said.

'Yes, my lord,' answered Arthur a little too eagerly.

'That is well. We have some duties ahead of us. The Sovereigns will expect a fine wedding for their daughter. Are you eager to meet your bride?'

Arthur said again with that emphasis which was a little too firm: 'I am indeed, my lord.'

'That is well, and I'll swear she is as eager to meet you. We shall set out tomorrow morning at dawn . . . and we shall soon intercept her, I doubt not.'

Perhaps the boy would look better after a rest, thought the King. Of course he was tired out after the journey. Perhaps it would be better if the marriage were not consummated . . . just yet. Let them wait a year or so . . . Arthur would be stronger then.

'The Infanta is at Dogmersfield,' said the King. 'Tomorrow we shall set out to meet her. I am sure you are overcome with eagerness.'

'Yes, my lord.'

Arthur spoke quietly. He hated to lie to his father but duty demanded that he should. How could he tell his father that he hated the prospect and his dearest wish was that he could have a quiet life free from his obligations.

'Then we shall rest well tonight,' said the King, 'and set off with the dawn.'

Arthur gratefully retired. The King was very uneasy. Every time he saw Arthur he thought he looked a little more frail.

When next morning they set out it had started to rain. The

King's anxious eyes were on Arthur. The boy would get a wetting and the doctors had said that was not good for him; it started up his cough.

There was more trouble to come. Before they reached the Bishop's Palace at Dogmersfield where Katharine was spending the night, they were met by de Ayala and a group of his entourage.

De Ayala rode up to the King and the two men confronted each other in the rain.

'My lord King,' said de Ayala. 'Is it true that you are coming to visit the Infanta?'

'Indeed it is,' replied Henry. 'My son is anxious to greet his bride. You look surprised. Do you not understand that we are all eagerness to welcome the Infanta to our shores?'

'I know it so, my lord. But the Spanish law is that none shall see the Infanta unveiled until the marriage has been celebrated.'

'My lord, you cannot be telling me that I am not allowed to look on my son's bride.'

'That is what I do say, my lord, and you must forgive me but it is the law in Spain.'

'It is not in England,' said the King grimly.

'My lord, our Infanta is the daughter of the Sovereigns of Spain and she is accustomed to Spanish laws and customs.'

'She will perforce learn to accept our English ones, for when she marries she will be one of us.'

'The ceremony has not yet taken place.'

The King was aghast. He had part of the dowry. That was the first thought that struck him. What was it about the Infanta that they were afraid of his seeing? Was she deformed in some way? Was she incapable of bearing children? He must not see her! What absurd custom was this? They were behaving like infidels. Of course their country had been the home of the Moors for centuries. Perhaps some of their customs had been preserved in Spain. But this was England and he was the King and none of his subjects should defy him.

'You will understand, Don Pedro de Ayala,' he said, 'that I am unaccustomed to being forbidden to act as I will in my own country. You say this is the wish of the Sovereigns of Spain. It is certainly not my wish. I will talk with my ministers. Fortunately they are with me and if they agree that with their help I make the rules in this country and they decide that I shall see the Infanta, then so be it, I shall.'

De Ayala bowed. 'It would be against the will of my Sovereigns.'

'Then we shall see,' said the King.

He turned and addressed his followers and told them what de Ayala had said. 'I am therefore calling a council here in that field yonder and there we will determine what is to be done.'

It was an extraordinary scene with the rain now turned to fine drizzle and in the field, with Arthur beside him, Henry asked his ministers to advise him on how to act in these extraordinary circumstances.

With one accord all declared that the King was ruler in his own country and the ridiculous—one might say barbaric—law of Spain must be set aside if it were the King's will. It would be unwise to let the Sovereigns think that they could control events in England.

So they left the field and went to de Ayala who was waiting on the road.

The King told him what had happened. De Ayala bowed his head and said he would ride ahead to Dogmersfield and inform the Infanta and her household of the King's decision.

De Ayala was laughing secretly. His nature was such that he enjoyed situations such as this one. He applauded the King's decision secretly and he would have despised Henry if he had given way, but now he was eager to see what effect this would have on the Infanta's entourage and particularly on Doña Elvira who was, he had secretly thought for some time, getting a little above herself.

When he returned, the Infanta's entourage was thrown into turmoil.

'Never,' cried Elvira. 'This is a violation of custom. Queen Isabella would never forgive me . . .'

'It is perhaps a matter for the Infanta herself to decide,' suggested de Ayala.

'The Infanta! She is only a child.'

'She is soon to be a bride and she is at the centre of this storm. I see no alternative but to lay the matter before her. And it must be done with all speed as the King is even now riding this way and when he comes he will demand to see the Infanta.'

Katharine listened gravely and gave her decision.

'This is England. Their customs are not ours. The King has declared he will see me unveiled. Well, so must it be. I will receive him and the Prince as they wish.'

Elvira scolded. 'What will your gracious mother say when she hears?'

'She will understand,' said Katharine.

De Ayala watched her with admiration. She had spirit, this

princess, and as far as her looks were concerned she might not be an obvious beauty but certainly she had nothing to hide.

'*I* should be veiled,' cried Elvira. 'I should cover my face in shame.'

Katharine shrugged her shoulders and turned away. Elvira must understand that although she had an important position in the household she did not rule it.

Katharine was waiting for the King when he arrived and begged that he be brought to her without delay.

Henry entered. He came to her and stood before her. Then as she bowed he took her hands in his and kissed them.

She looked up at him and saw a man of spare figure, pale skinned, with damp reddish hair falling to his shoulders. The ermine on the sleeves of his gown was wet and bedraggled. He could not speak Spanish and it was difficult for them to talk together but he did manage to convey to her that he was delighted to see her and that he apologized for overriding the laws of her country.

All the time he was studying her intently. She looked strong and healthy. He was relieved to see that it was only a custom and that there had been no ulterior motive in keeping her face covered.

He wanted her to know that he was delighted to see her for he applauded her good sense in adjusting so quickly to English customs.

He turned to one of his attendants and said: 'Send in the Prince the moment he arrives.'

He talked to Katharine gently, quietly and although she understood little of what he said, she found him reassuring. She was glad that she had not refused to unveil; she could understand that in this country it would seem a very foolish custom. She was sure her mother would agree with her. She had been brought up to be reasonable.

There was a fanfare from without, announcing the arrival of the Prince of Wales and there he was, standing before her . . . a frail boy, smaller than herself, very damp from his ride through the rain, looking at her with apprehension in his pale blue eyes.

She smiled at him and he returned the smile.

Then remembering what was required of him he took her hand and kissed it.

He is only a boy, she thought, younger than I. There is nothing to fear from him.

The King was smiling on them benignly. There was no doubt that they had taken a fancy to each other.

Good! thought the King, but Arthur is too frail as yet for the consummation.

He hurried through the ceremony, and murmured something to Arthur's squire that the Prince should take off his damp clothes as soon as possible, be rubbed down and put into dry ones.

THE BRIDE AND THE WIDOW

They were seated at the banquet side by side, immediately good friends, their great attraction being that each of them knew there was nothing to fear from the other.

As she was residing in the Bishop's house it was she who invited the King and the Prince to her apartments to sup and the Bishop being prepared for this was determined to win the King's favour by making sure that his household provided such a meal as he would get in one of his royal palaces. Henry himself was no glutton, and in fact resented the amount of money which was wasted on food; but he was fully aware of the impression which must be made, not so much on the Princess as on her attendants who would return to Spain and report on the manner in which the Princess had been received and that would include a description of what there had been to eat at the Bishop's table.

Henry doubted if such suckling pig, chickens, beef, mutton, fish and pies could be surpassed at the Spanish Court and the Infanta certainly seemed surprised by the abundance of it and the large amounts consumed by the guests.

The Prince looked less vulnerable now that he was free of his damp clothes and wore a fine velvet gown trimmed with ermine and a beautifully embroidered shirt. His hair gleamed and his blue eyes shone with pleasure; he was clearly delighted by Katharine's gentleness.

He could not speak Spanish, but they discovered that they both understood Latin.

She would teach him Spanish, she said, and he felt excited as he always did at the prospect of studying some new subject.

He would teach her English, he promised and she told him that she had already learned a few words.

He asked her about her family and she described to him not what had happened recently but her early days when she had been the baby of a large family. She talked of her mother and he said: 'You love her dearly.' She answered that her mother was not only one of the greatest queens of Europe but she had always had time for her children. He knew that Isabella was the ruler of Spain—for although Ferdinand ruled with her it was Isabella who was the leader of the two, for Castile was so much more important than Aragon—but according to Katharine she had also found time to be the best mother in the world.

'Perhaps she will visit you here. Or perhaps we shall go to Spain.'

'Could we?'

'We shall be the King and the Queen. They do not have to ask if they may.'

For the first time in his life he wanted to be king. He was amazed. Katharine had done that for him.

As the evening wore on and the feasting was over it was time for dancing. The minstrels were there and Don Pedro de Ayala whispered to Katharine that she should show the King some of their Spanish dances.

Katharine loved to dance and summoning some of her ladies she commanded them to dance with her. The King watched her. She was strong and healthy enough. He had nothing of which to complain and he was glad he had shown the Spaniards that he would have none of their Moorish customs in England.

He was anxious though, for as the Infanta had danced, this meant that the Prince would have to do the same. Not together. That would not be discreet until they were married. It was a good thing. The little Spaniard was too agile for Arthur.

He beckoned to Lady Guildford, one of the ladies of the royal nurseries, a motherly woman who had always shown concern for the children.

'Take the Prince in the dance,' he said. He looked at her steadily. 'Do not keep him at it too long. Something short and not too lively . . .'

She understood.

So she and Arthur showed the Spanish Princess an English dance. The Prince was grateful and would have done well if he were not so short of breath.

He was greatly relieved to sit down and tried not to show how fatigued he was.

But Katharine noticed. It made her feel very tender towards him.

Prince Henry was delighted. Although he resented the fact that this was not his wedding, he was to play a big part in it. His father had chosen him to lead the Spanish Infanta first into the city and later to the altar.

He was smiling happily as his attendants gathered round him as he was dressed. He looked complacently down at his well-shaped legs in their close-fitting hose. His shirt and pourpoint were of the finest but what pleased him most was the coat—lined with ermine—and the gold chain which was placed about his neck. He would be recognized at once as a prince.

So royally clad he mounted his horse which was as grand as he was. Even his gold stirrups were decorated with jewels. He looked magnificent—older than his ten years for he was tall and broad and as he still possessed a very youthful-looking face he was certain to attract the admiration of the crowd. His usually pink cheeks were a shade deeper, and as the sun shone on the thick reddish curls which framed his face he was indeed a handsome sight.

His father himself had told him of what was expected of him. He had warned him that he must please the people. He had meant of course that he must not push himself too much to the fore, the people would not be so much interested in him as in the bride and bridegroom. He must remember to conduct himself with decorum as a prince and knight must always do.

Henry implied that he was well aware of this and added that his father would have no need to be ashamed of him.

And now here he was seated on his horse, waiting for the approach of the Spanish Princess. He had crossed London Bridge and was in St. George's Field close to Lambeth Palace from which Katharine would emerge.

He was impatient to see her. He had heard that she was handsome and not ill-formed as had been feared because at first she was reluctant to show her face. Lucky Arthur to marry the daughter of Spain! Her mother was very rich and powerful and Katharine had brought many treasures with her from Spain.

Henry's eyes sparkled at the thought of riches. Not that he would want to hoard them as it was rumoured his father did. If he had the money he would spend it on grand occasions, jousting, feasting, fine clothes and riding among the people, giving them amusements, tournaments, baiting of animals and royal pageantry, so pleasing the people.

Alas, that fate had seen fit to make him a second son.

Now he could hear the music coming from Lambeth Palace—music which had a foreign flavour—Spanish, of course. The trumpets thrilled him; he was fond of music, which gave great satisfaction to those who tutored him in that subject. So he listened with pleasure, leaning forward a little in his saddle, eager to catch a first glimpse of her.

And there she was—in the midst of the knights and squires and Spanish gentlemen—a girl on a brilliantly caparisoned mule which glittered and shone.

Her hair flowed about her shoulders—thick and auburn coloured; he could not see her face clearly for she wore a hat which reminded him of the ones Cardinals wore.

His heart beat fast as she approached and he spurred his horse forward. They were face to face. He swept off his hat and bowed and said the words he had prepared.

She replied rather stumblingly and her smile told him at once that she liked him.

He was enchanted. He thought he had never seen anyone as beautiful as the Spanish Princess.

He placed himself on her right and prepared to escort her into the city.

How proud he was to be her escort, how conscious of the sidelong glances she gave him! He guessed she was admiring him as he was admiring her.

'You will see how the city is determined to welcome you,' he said.

She lifted her shoulders and shook her head. She did not understand. He was angry with his tutors for not teaching him Spanish. Could she understand Latin? She could.

'It will be so helpful to us,' he said, and smiled.

He was able to tell her that he thought her beautiful and that her hat amused him. 'It is like those worn by cardinals,' he said.

She smiled with him.

She was not very old really. She seemed almost his own age.

'I will be your friend,' he said. 'You have nothing to fear.'

She murmured: 'Thank you.'

He felt elated. This he thought is the happiest moment of my life: and then he remembered that she was to be Arthur's bride and that Arthur would have not only herself but the crown. His happiness was immediately clouded; he forced his mouth to smile; the irrepressible Skelton had said that when he was angry his mouth betrayed him. 'That mouth will send people to the block when . . . I mean *if* you are ever king.'

So he smiled and he wondered why Skelton often talked as though he would be the King one day. If Arthur died . . . but then Arthur was going to be married and married people had sons . . . If Arthur had a son that would be the end of his hopes. And this beautiful girl would help him to get one. She was really an enemy. But he could not think of her as such.

So he smiled at the people and he was sure they had almost as much interest in him as they had in the Spanish Princess. There were wonderful pageants in the streets. Virgins and saints greeted them but what Henry liked best was the castle which had been set up near the Falcon Inn; it was so lifelike; it was a most exhilarating experience riding down Cornhill. The conduits in Chepeside were running with free wine to which the people helped themselves most liberally. Everywhere there were tributes to Arthur and his bride.

So Henry took her to the Bishop's Palace, close to the Cathedral, where she was to rest a few days before the marriage ceremony.

Then again it was Henry's turn to take her from the Bishop's palace to St Paul's.

He was delighted by her and could not take his eyes from her.

There was something so strange and exotic about her that made her different from any woman he had ever known. He thought of her spending her childhood in strange Moorish palaces; he thought of all the rich articles she had brought with her to England. He knew that they made his father's eyes gleam with pleasure and rub his hands together in an anticipation of touching them. The daughter of the Sovereigns of Spain! How truly exciting. He had heard that the wagons which had come with her were full of priceless treasure—carpets of exquisite design; beds, intricately carved; cloths of the finest texture to say nothing of jewels and plate. And all this for Arthur!

Now he could not take his eyes from her. She wore a coif of white silk with a scarf spattered with gold and stones of many colours. It covered half her face as well as a good deal of her person. She told him that it was called a mantilla. Her gown was pleated and spread out in hoops from her tiny waist. It was the first time Henry had seen the fashion which he was to see many times later as it was noticed by many of the ladies who determined to imitate it.

He enjoyed leading her to the Cathedral and all the time he was suppressing his envy of Arthur.

And there was Arthur waiting in the Cathedral dressed in white satin, looking handsome and slightly less fragile than usual.

Henry noticed that his parents were not present and tried not to look up at the latticed box from where he knew they would be watching.

And so Arthur was married to the Princess of Spain and Arthur was now taking his bride to the door of the Cathedral so that the people in the streets could see them.

The cheers were deafening. There was no doubt that the people were pleased with Prince Arthur and his Spanish Princess.

Now Henry was to the fore again for it was his task to lead the bride from the Cathedral to the Bishop's Palace where the banquet was waiting for them. His Aunt Cecilia, who had been widowed on the death of her husband Lord Wells some three years before, was one of the train bearers.

The feast had begun. There must be such a display as would impress the Spaniards and the King was determined that, much as he deplored spending the money, there should be nothing of which to complain.

And after the feasting there was the ceremony of the bedding which had been causing not only the married pair but the King and Queen so much anxiety.

First the bed must be examined for lurking weapons—knives and daggers—concealed among the feathers. The moment which Arthur and Katharine had both been dreading had arrived.

There was the usual ribaldry and Arthur was glad that Katharine could not speak the language. The bed had been scented and sprinkled with holy water and the word which was used most frequently was fruitful. Katharine had always known that the first duty of a Princess was to get children but she was afraid and knew very little of the process necessary to their production.

Katharine was undressed by her ladies and, still veiled and in her bedgown, she was conducted to the bedchamber. Arthur had been led in—having similarly been disrobed by his attendants—and the two young people stood facing each other apprehensively.

The bed curtains were drawn back. The bed was blessed and the moment had come.

The King then approached them and said in a low voice which few but the bride and groom could hear:

'You are young yet. There is plenty of time before you. You are not ready for marriage. There should be no consummation . . . until you are a little older.'

He was looking anxiously at his son. He need not have worried. Arthur was looking immensely relieved.

Katharine was smiling too.

So they were led to the bed where they lay side by side. Arthur reached for Katharine's hand and held it fast; and they talked quietly together in Latin . . . until they fell asleep.

The pageantry continued. Before Westminster Hall a tiltyard was set up. There was a loge for the King's party hung with cloth of gold; and round the entire area stages had been built for the people to sit and watch the tournament. It was received with the utmost delight. The people declared they had never seen such entertainment and they wished they had a marriage every week. It was wonderful to see the knights tilting with each other. They pointed out the famous people as they saw them. All knew the King and Queen and the royal children, of course, but figures like the Marquis of Dorset and the Earl of Essex and Lord William Courtney were names to them until they saw them take on life in the arena.

At dusk the party returned to Westminster Hall for feasting and dancing and Katharine would distribute the prizes won at the tournament.

The ladies took their places on the King's left hand—Katharine with Queen Elizabeth, and the King's mother the Countess of Richmond, the Princesses Margaret and Mary and other members of the family such as Lady Wells. On the King's right hand was Arthur, Henry and other nobles arranged according to their rank.

The pageants were beautiful and all was done in honour of the marriage; and there was much dancing and singing.

Arthur must dance, of course, and the King had suggested that his Aunt Cecilia perform with him. Always, thought Henry, he must dance with elderly people. My father is afraid that the young would dance too fast for him. Arthur, however, looked graceful in his white satin and Aunt Cecilia was certainly determined not to force him into too much exertion, cleverly giving the impression that it was for her benefit rather than his.

Young Henry was waiting his chance. When it came he would show them. There would be no need for anyone to slow him down. He had always excelled at dancing and he was going to show the assembled company how much better he could perform than his brother.

His eyes fell on his sister Margaret. He and Margaret had never been good friends, but he did admire her dancing. She was as good as he was . . . or almost. The two of them together could astonish the company.

He could not wait. He went to her and took her hand. She was longing to dance, too. She wanted some of the applause which had gone to others for doing something which she knew she could do far better.

For a second she scowled at her brother. Then she smiled. She had to admit that he could dance well too and together they would be a perfect pair.

So they danced and the musicians watching them played the

music more wildly and glancing at the King, Henry saw that his father was amused . . . more than amused . . . rather proud of these two bright healthy children of his.

'Faster, faster!' cried Henry and because his robe was encumbering him he took it off, threw it high in the air so that with greater freedom he could dance more vigorously. The company applauded as they watched the youthful pair cavorting in the centre of the hall.

At last the music stopped. The dance was over. The applause was enthusiastic and even the King was smiling.

Henry looked at Katharine. She had clapped her hands together, smiling.

Henry bowed to his parents and then to her.

I am sure, Henry was thinking, Katharine would have liked me better than Arthur.

Dudley and Empson had brought the King a valuation of the Infanta's dowry.

'Some one hundred thousand crowns, my lord,' said Dudley with satisfaction.

'A goodly sum,' mused the King, his eyes gleaming with satisfaction. His fingers moved as though to grasp those articles that he might add their value to his exchequer.

'The goods could be said to belong to you, Sire,' said Empson. 'They are after all the Princess' dowry.'

'But what were the rules laid down by the Sovereigns?'

'That the goods should remain in the possession of the Infanta until the second half of the dowry was paid.'

'That will be in a year's time.'

'True my lord, but we could make good use of those goods now. However, perhaps some advice could be sought.'

'De Ayala?' said the King and shook his head. 'De Puebla possibly.'

'We should get more satisfaction from him. I fancy he has a wish to please us for he does not stand so high in the Sovereigns' favour as does de Ayala for instance.'

'No, they like not his origins but to my mind he is an abler man than de Ayala. I will sound de Puebla.'

'It is the best solution, my lord.'

Henry lost no time in seeking out de Puebla. He did not summon him for he did not wish him to think that the matter of the dowry was a weighty one. However during the course of the conversation between them he said suddenly: 'I should like to have possession of the dowry.'

De Puebla folding his hands together, looked down at them gravely.

'The ruling was that it should remain the property of the Princess of Wales for one year after the celebration of the nuptials.'

'I know. I know . . . but in view of the fact that it is her dowry . . . which comes to me . . . to the Prince, why should we wait this year?'

De Puebla looked sly. 'My lord King,' he said, 'you know full well that I have always sought to be your friend, and that has not always been easy.'

The King nodded.

'This matter of the dowry now. . . . Am I correct in thinking you would prefer one hundred thousand crowns to the jewels and the furniture?'

'You are right.'

'It is no use trying to get the Sovereigns to pass the goods to you. They will never do that. But what if the Princess were to wear the jewels . . . use the furniture . . .'

'Why should she? She has plenty of those.'

'If she had her own Court she would need these things and the jewels are part of her state regalia.'

'What do you suggest, my friend?'

De Puebla was thoughtful. He guessed that the marriage had not been consummated. The Sovereigns would be angry if they knew this. They were as anxious as Henry was to get an heir from the union. De Puebla knew that much as Henry wanted an heir he was terrified that sexual exertion would rob Arthur of what little strength he had. De Puebla was mischievous by nature. He liked to be the innocent party who stirred up the waters in the pond and made them troubled and then run away and disclaim all knowledge of what he had done. That was how he had always worked. De Ayala despised him; well, he despised de Ayala, that cultured gallant diplomat. His methods were no way to make history.

The royal pair had not consummated the marriage because Henry did not want it consummated yet and the only reason was that he was afraid for his son's health. Let the boy take his chance, thought de Puebla, and if making love was too much for him then there would be further interesting situations to amuse de Puebla. Get the pair away from the anxious parental eye . . . and then they would see.

'Since you do me the honour of asking my opinion,' said de

Puebla, 'I will give it. This is between ourselves, Highness. Send the Prince and Princess away to a Court of their own . . . Wales, say. The people love the Prince there. They will love the Princess, too. Let them hold Court, let the Princess wear the jewels . . . use the articles of the dowry . . . then when the time comes to hand them over you will say you cannot accept second-hand goods. The furniture will have suffered, the arras . . . the tapestries will be a little worse for wear. You can then demand one hundred thousand crowns, the first half of the dowry.'

'Hm,' said the King. 'You are a devious thinker, my lord.'

'In the service of Your Highness.'

'And of your Sovereigns?'

De Puebla moved an imperceptible step nearer to the King. 'My lord, I have had good friendship from you,' he said. 'Better than . . .'

He did not finish and the King did not ask him to.

'I will think about this matter,' said the King.

A few days later it was announced that the Prince and Princess of Wales would reside for a while in Ludlow.

They were approaching the castle—Katharine with those who were left to her of the Spanish retinue she had brought with her, headed by Doña Elvira, and Arthur with a group of advisors who had been chosen by the King.

The castle was built high on a headland, its foundations grafted into the grey rock, and guarded by a deep and wide fosse. There was a vast early Norman square tower and impressive battlements which gave it a comforting air of impregnability. It was set in beautiful country overlooking the town of Ludlow; on all sides was the green countryside—woods, hills and fields rolling on to the horizon.

Katharine thought it very beautiful; she loved the greenness of everything which she had noticed on her arrival in England. She thought she would be very happy here, for she was happy with Arthur. They were good companions; they studied together; she was learning to speak English and was teaching him Spanish. She was always careful never to tire him and he was grateful because she did so unostentatiously.

The Welsh accepted them and liked them. The chieftains called at the castle. One of them brought his son hoping that he would learn to be a squire in the Prince's household. Arthur accepted him and Griffith ap Rhys became a friend of both Arthur and Katharine, greatly to the delight of the boy's father and the people of Wales.

Such happy days they were! Katharine had almost ceased to think of Spain and the longing to be with her mother was less than she had thought it possible to be.

Arthur's health seemed to improve a little. He could ride for longer hours and he and Katharine tried out a few dances together. He was so grateful because if he became breathless she always made some excuse to stop.

They were ideal companions and Arthur was deeply contented with his marriage. He was able to explain to her how he dreaded having to take part in ceremonial and she understood.

'If I am ever king I shall dispense with a great deal of it,' he told her. 'It is not necessary, you know. It does not make a good king because he has to dance and make good speeches . . .'

Katharine agreed with him.

'When we are the King and Queen we will live at Ludlow . . . oh, I know, not for *all* the time. But we could come here often could we not?'

'We will,' said Arthur.

He could talk to Katharine as he had never been able to talk to anyone before. To her he confided that he had always thought he should have been born second, Henry first. 'Henry would have made such a good king and I should have been well enough in the Church.'

'You would not have married me,' she reminded him.

'Ah,' said Arthur. 'You are right. Then I would not have anything other than it is.'

News came from the Court. There was to be a grand celebration for Arthur's sister Margaret was to be betrothed to the King of Scots. The news threw a certain gloom over the household at Ludlow. The thought of having to leave his newly found peace for the ceremonies of Court depressed Arthur.

Katharine comforted him but his depression frightened her a little. Surely their future life when Arthur was King would be a continuation of such occasions.

She would have to talk to him of this; she would have to stand beside him, help him to overcome his shyness. She was confident that together they would face whatever lay before them.

And then the good news. The King thought it was not necessary for the Prince of Wales to come to Court. His brother Henry would play his part in the ceremonies and Arthur should stay at Ludlow.

Arthur was overcome with joy and Katharine was delighted to

see him so relieved; but afterwards she thought of the matter and she knew that the reason his father had not wished him to be present was because he feared the journey to Richmond would be too strenuous for him and might have a damaging effect on his health.

She was very anxious when he looked so tired, but she assured herself that he was better since they had lived quietly at Ludlow. All was going to be well. She would look after him, make sure he did not exert himself and in time, she assured herself, his health would improve.

She must count her blessings. She was lucky. She only had to look back a little way to remember how she had been dreading her marriage; and here she was with the gentlest of husbands, who was kind and clever, interesting and tender. What good fortune was hers! She would write home and tell her mother how happy she was.

Another ceremony! How young Henry loved them—particularly, as on this occasion, when his brother was not present. That gave him added importance. He walked beside the King and was accorded the homage which would have been Arthur's if he had been present, so that he could imagine that he was the Prince of Wales—King-to-be.

And he was secretly delighted by the reason for this occasion. Margaret was to be married—by proxy it was true—to the King of Scotland. Soon his sister would depart and he would be relieved of her irritating presence. Margaret was too much like himself, too forceful, too aware of her dignity, always trying to push herself forward. Moreover she was perceptive. She saw through him too easily and often put into words something which was only a thought in his mind. It was disconcerting. She was clever and older than he was. Perhaps she wished that she had been a boy and then . . . if anything happened to Arthur . . . *she* would have been the Sovereign.

Arthur was constantly in his mind—the health of Arthur, the possibilities of his death. Such thoughts were best hidden and the notion that Margaret guessed at them disturbed him a great deal. Therefore it was comforting to reflect that Margaret was destined for Scotland. It was a pity of course that their father had decreed that she was too young to leave England immediately.

Well, she would have to go in time and Skelton had told Henry that when she did get there she would find a situation which would engage all her talents to unravel.

What did he mean by that? Winks and nudges and those intriguing innuendoes which were so characteristic of Skelton.

'James the King is a wild laddie, my lord. He abounds in love.'

'Well, is that not a good thing?'

'Love for women, my lord, reckless love for women. Mind you, none could compare with your own illustrious grandsire, so I've heard, but I'd be ready to swear James of Scotland runs him pretty close.'

'But when he is married to Margaret . . .'

'Ah, when he is married to Margaret! Marriage . . . that is the time when men repent of their sins; they have sown their wild oats and now settle down to sow a few tame ones, eh. I would I were there to see how Dame Margaret handles the Boyds, the Kennedys, the Drummonds . . . Ah, and how they handle her!'

Henry laughed. 'She will know what to do, I promise you.'

' 'Twill be a sight worth seeing I am sure.'

'And now I am to go to this matter at Richmond . . . in my brother's place.'

'It becomes you well, my lord . . . your brother's place . . .'

And there was Skelton, his expression changing from one of lewdness to speculation.

And so to Richmond and the ceremony. His father looked at him with a certain criticism as though reproaching him for his too healthy looks and his exuberant manner. The King might not like them but the people did and Henry shrewdly suspected that the people's approval was more important to him than even his father's. It was not real criticism, Henry understood. It was only the wistful thought of how pleased he would be if Arthur had one half of Henry's good health.

The Queen was looking pale though she had made attempts to disguise this. Skelton—who had a way of learning such things— said that the apothecary was constantly sending remedies to her and she often sent monks and priests to make pilgrimages to the well-known shrines of the country to pray for her.

Margaret was radiant. She had few qualms about going to Scotland. It was typical of Margaret that she could not imagine herself failing to succeed at anything. If she had heard rumours of her future husband's irregular life she gave no sign of it. She would be sure that as soon as he clapped eyes on her and realized his good fortune nothing else would be of great importance to him.

They heard Mass in the chapel and then went from the chapel

to the Queen's great chamber where the marriage by proxy would be performed.

Henry listened to the voices.

'I, Patrick, Earl of Bothwell, procurator of the right excellent, right high and mighty Prince James, by the grace of God King of Scotland, my sovereign lord, having sufficient authority power and commandment to contract matrimony, *per verba de presenti* in the name of my said sovereign Lord with thee Margaret . . .'

On and on . . . He would be glad when this was over and the feasting began. There would be jousts . . . dancing and he would excel at them all.

And now her turn; 'I, Margaret, first begotten daughter of the right excellent high and mighty Prince and Princess, Henry by the grace of God King of England and Elizabeth, Queen of the same . . .'

By the grace of God, thought Henry. Skelton said, By the grace of good fortune, Lady Luck who came to Bosworth Field.

'Good fortune was the grace of God surely,' Henry had argued.

'It is a matter which could be debated,' was the answer.

He was wicked, Skelton was. If the King knew what treason he uttered . . .

But I like him, thought Henry. No matter what he says . . . and he laughs at me sometimes . . . still for some strange reason I would have him near me.

At last . . . it was over. Now the feasting. The Queen was leading her daughter by the hand towards the dinner table. Two queens together. Henry felt a flush of anger. Margaret was a queen. Above a duke in rank, he supposed. It was insufferable.

But at the jousting and the pageants he excelled. He was sure everyone was watching him.

'A triumph, a triumph,' said Skelton later. 'The bride conducted herself with grace and charm. And now we have a queen in the nursery we must take heed of our manners.'

'Queen! It is but a proxy marriage.'

'Queen never-the-less. You will see that henceforth she will be named always as the Queen of Scotland.'

'I hope she is soon sent to Scotland. Perhaps she won't give herself such airs there.'

'Margaret will always be Margaret . . . and Henry, Henry,' said Skelton.

'They treated me as the Prince of Wales.'

'As they would, my lord . . . if the Prince himself were absent.'

'Skelton . . . I wonder . . .'

'I have had news from Ludlow. The Prince is happy with his bride. He is breathless still and I believe spits blood which he tries to hide . . . but it is hard to hide the secrets of the bedchamber from zealous servants' eyes.'

'Skelton . . . you know something . . .'

'All I know I would tell my lord.' He put his mouth close to Henry's ear. 'The love between the royal pair increases. They are very tender . . . and much in each other's company.'

'What do you mean?'

'I mean that if you put two loving people together . . . if they be man and wife . . . well, what would you . . . nature being what it is?'

'They must not have a child,' said Henry.

'Who says so? Great Harry. And he should be obeyed. But there are times when God turns a deaf ear even to princes. What we must pray for, my dear lord . . . is good fortune . . . and the grace of God.'

Spring was beautiful in England. It seemed particularly so after the dark days of winter; now the air had a balminess in it and the whole of nature seemed to be aware that spring was coming. Arthur showed Katharine wild daffodils when they rode out together and the mingling white of the daisies and gold of the dandelions seemed enchanting to her.

She was watchful of him, always declaring when she saw him begin to weary that she had been too long in the saddle and was tired. He was always solicitous but he knew that she was thinking of him and he loved her for it.

They touched hands; they kissed; sometimes he would put an arm about her and hold her to him; but their endearments never went beyond that. They were watchful, Arthur remembering his father's injunction; Katharine, aware of something she did not fully understand but fearing that it would be dangerous for Arthur, kept her emotions in check.

Perhaps it occurred to both of them that it could not last; perhaps that was why they were determined to enjoy those days to the full.

Change hit them suddenly.

One of the attendants came in to say that there was a case of sweating sickness in the town of Ludlow.

There was immediate consternation in the castle. Everyone was awaiting a summons from the King. They were sure that when the news reached him, Arthur would be removed at once.

But no message came. And then it was too late.

It was inevitable that the weakest member of the household should be the victim.

There was despair in the castle. Katharine prayed for the life of her young husband. Surely God could not be so cruel as to take him away now that they were becoming so happy together? The King would send down the finest physicians in the land. Arthur's life must be saved.

But few survived the dreaded sweating sickness. Arthur most certainly could not.

They brought the news to her. She stared at them unbelievingly. Dead! Arthur. She could not believe it. She would not believe it.

''Tis true, my lady,' they said. 'God knows what the King will do when he hears this doleful news.'

She felt bereft, desolate. A wife and no wife . . . a virgin widow.

If only the marriage had been consummated. If only she could have had Arthur's child. Then she would have had something to live for.

Now . . . she was alone.

The King was at Greenwich when he heard that Arthur's Chamberlain had arrived from Ludlow and was urgently requesting to be brought to him.

Henry was seized with trembling for a terrible foreboding had come to him.

'Bring him to me with all speed,' he said, 'and as soon as he comes.'

Arthur's Chamberlain was heavy-hearted as he rode to Greenwich where the Court was in residence. He dreaded telling the King the tragic news and he decided that he would impart it first to the Council and ask their advice as to the best way of breaking it.

The Council was dismayed and after some consultation decided that it would be best for the King's Confessor to tell him and this was arranged.

When Henry heard the discreet knock on the door he knew that it was his Confessor who stood without and, suspecting nothing, he bade him enter.

The man's woebegone expression sent quivers of alarm running through the King's mind and he immediately thought of Arthur.

'You have ill news,' he said.

The Confessor replied: 'I have, my lord, and you are going to need all the strength that God can give you.'

'It is my son,' said the King quietly.

'It is, my lord.'

'He is sick?'

The Confessor did not answer.

'Dead!' cried the King. 'Dead . . . !' He turned away. He could never bear any man to see his emotion. Why had he loved this boy who had been such a disappointment to him? All his hopes had been in Arthur although he had been frail from birth. It was a mistake to become involved with others. He had always known this and tried to avoid it. Why was Arthur the one person who had made him diverge from the path of wisdom so that he must suffer constant anxiety—as he had since the boy had been born!

Now this was the final blow.

He turned to the Confessor. 'Send the Queen to me. I must be the one to break this news to her.'

'My lord, would you wish to kneel first in prayer.'

'I would wish first to see the Queen. I would not want her to hear this news from any but myself.'

The Confessor bowed and retired and returned shortly after with the Queen.

She was alarmed. She knew from Henry's expression that something terrible had happened. He had lost something dear to him. His crown . . . his . . . son!

'What is it?' she said. 'Is it . . . ?'

He nodded. 'Arthur,' he said quietly. 'He died of the sweating sickness.'

She covered her face with her hands. Henry was so overcome with emotion that he could not speak. She lowered her hands and looked at him and saw the anguish in his face, and she knew how deeply he whose feelings were usually so well hidden was suffering, and suddenly the need to comfort him was more important to her than anything else.

'Our beloved son,' she said quietly. 'His health was always an anxiety. We were always expecting this. Henry . . . we have another son. Thank God for him. We have two fine daughters.'

'That is true,' said Henry. 'But Arthur . . .'

'Arthur was our first born . . . so gentle always. Such a good boy. But he was never strong in health. In Henry we have one who will step into his shoes. We should be thankful for that.'

'I am,' he said. 'We have one son left to us . . .'

'Your mother had but one son, and look you, he is King of

England, the comfort of his realm, the comfort of his Queen and his children.'

'Elizabeth, you are a good wife to me . . . a good mother to our children.'

'Subdue your grief, my lord. Remember God wills that we go on . . . even after such a bitter blow. We are young yet. Who knows, we may have more princes. But we have Henry and he is a fine strong boy.'

The King was silent. 'You comfort me,' he said.

And she left him for she could no longer contain her grief and when she reached her own chamber she threw herself onto her bed and gave way to it.

She had loved Arthur as much as Henry had—more tenderly, as a mother does. This was her first born. Her beloved child . . . loved, she must admit, beyond the others. Her grief was such that it overwhelmed her and when her women found her they were alarmed for her and sent for her physician.

He went to the King and told him that he must comfort the Queen.

So then it was Henry's turn and he went to her and talked to her quietly of Arthur—Arthur as a child, Arthur growing up, how delighted they had been with his cleverness, how perpetually anxious for his health.

'Somehow,' he said, 'I knew that it would happen . . . and now it has. Dear Elizabeth, we must be brave. We must go on. You were telling me this and now I am telling you. We have our son Henry. We will get more sons, and perhaps in time we shall cease to mourn so bitterly.'

There were three weeks when the Prince of Wales lay in state and then began the funeral procession from Ludlow Castle to the Cathedral at Worcester.

There was one among the mourners who wept with the others but he could not suppress the fierce joy in his heart.

This was what he had always longed for. To be the first born. But that was of no consequence now. Miraculously he was there in the place he had longed for.

No longer Duke of York, but Prince of Wales.

'Henry the King,' he murmured to himself. 'Henry the Eighth.'

He could not help studying his father, whose face was pale, whose hair was grey and whose eyes were without lustre. Arthur's death had aged him a great deal. Well, the Prince of

Wales was only eleven and even he recognized that was rather young to be a king.

'I can wait a while,' he told himself, 'knowing that one day it will come.'

THE PRINCES
IN THE TOWER

The King was weighed down with anxieties. He had lost his eldest son; the Queen was ill; but most alarming of all was the fact that his grip on the crown after seventeen years of good rule was still not firm enough to give him peace of mind.

At the heart of his insecurity was the fear that someone would arise and snatch the throne from him—someone mature, strong, able to charm the people and who was in possession of that which for all his cleverness Henry would never attain: the claim to rule by the law of hereditary accession.

There would always be whispers against him—behind his back, of course. At least none dared utter them aloud, but he was aware of them. 'Bastard sprig!' 'Was your grandmother *really* married to Owen Tudor?' 'Your mother, it is true, descended from John of Gaunt—but from his bastard family of Beauforts.' And whatever case was brought forward to prove legitimization there would always be those to shake their heads and murmur against him.

So here he was after seventeen years during which he had proved he knew how to govern since he had brought his country from near bankruptcy to financial prosperity—and yet he must live constantly with this fear that someone would one day rise against him.

In public he could snap his fingers at pretenders. He could laugh at poor simple Lambert Simnel tending his falcons and Perkin Warbeck had met his just deserts. Henry hoped by his leniency to these two—and he had been lenient even to Perkin Warbeck—that he had shown the people how little importance he attached to these impostors.

But in fact he had attached the utmost importance to them—not in themselves, of course, but what they stood for.

The young Earl of Warwick was dead. It had been a wise move to get rid of him, and to execute him openly for treason. There must be no more disappearances in the Tower. There was more to be feared from mysterious disappearances, he had learned, than from open execution. No one talked of young Warwick now. The people had accepted that he had been a menace to the peace of the country. They had not been very interested in him. Poor boy, he had been a sorry figure, a prisoner for most of his life. It would have been better for him if he had never been born.

Assessing the mood of the people Henry believed that they were not eager for rebellions; they wanted peace. They were in fact more contented with his rule than they realized. They grumbled. People always grumbled. If things went well they wanted them to go better. Give them comfort and they wanted luxuries. They did not like the taxes imposed by Empson and Dudley. Did they not see the need for a solvent exchequer? Did they not understand that a bankrupt nation could not hold off its enemies? Did they realize that their growing prosperity came from the wise calculation of the King and his able ministers? They must know that trade prospered; they cared about that. Was that why they had realized it would have been bad for the country to put a foolish youth on the throne just because his father had been the brother of Edward the Fourth?

Yet both Lambert Simnel and Perkin Warbeck had had their supporters. Lambert had been doomed to failure from the start. The idea of trying to impersonate a young man who was actually living and could be brought forth from his prison in the Tower and shown to the people was absurd. It was different with Perkin. His had been a much stronger case. For he had declared he was Richard Duke of York—the Prince who had disappeared in the Tower.

This was a lesson to all would-be pretenders. If you are going to impersonate someone let it not be one whose whereabouts are known. Choose one who has disappeared mysteriously and in this case one who, had he lived, could well be the true heir to the crown.

This struck at the heart of his acute anxieties.

Who knew when someone else would arise? At any time there could be someone with features similar to those of Edward the Fourth who would declare he was the son of that King, who would say: 'I am one of the Princes who was in the Tower and who was never accounted for.'

It was not difficult for unscrupulous people to find young men who looked like Edward the Fourth for that monarch had scattered his seed far and wide. He must have left bastards in various parts of this country and others. Wherever he went he had his women, many of whom would think it an honour to bear the King's child.

So there it was . . . the heavy shadow . . . the ghost of two little boys, who would now be young men . . . to come and haunt him and disturb his peace.

If only he could say: These boys died in the Tower. I know they died. He could not do that. He dared not answer the all-important question: How do you know?

There must be a way. He would find it.

Then the opportunity came and as soon as he realized what it could bring, he determined to seize it. It would need care; but then he was a careful man. A certain ingenuity? Oh, he would manage that.

He was careful and ingenious by nature. And there was so much at stake.

It was when the name Sir James Tyrrell was mentioned in connection with the Earl of Suffolk that the idea came to him. He was excited. It might just be possible to put an end to these fears which had haunted him ever since he had come to the throne. And if this could be done, if it were possible to work this out, he must do so. He was determined that his plan should succeed.

It had not been difficult for Edmund de la Pole, Earl of Suffolk to convince himself that he had a greater claim to the throne than Henry Tudor. He was the second son of John de la Pole, second Duke of Suffolk, and Elizabeth the sister of Edward the Fourth; and from his mother came his claim. Edmund had been twenty-one years old when his father had died and he should have succeeded to the title then because his elder brother, John, had been killed at the battle of Stoke where he had been fighting with Lambert Simnel's army. However, John had been attainted and his goods and title confiscated by the King. Edmund had become the King's ward at that time, but later Henry had given the title back to Edmund and an agreement as to the family estates had been arrived at which proved Henry's grasping nature and his determination to squeeze out every penny he could whenever the opportunity presented itself.

Consequently only a portion of the de la Pole estates were returned and in exchange for these the King demanded a payment of five thousand pounds. Edmund was appalled but the King had stated, with an air of gracious leniency, that the sum could be paid annually over a number of years.

Although Suffolk returned to Court and was present at certain ceremonies, the King's treatment of him continued to rankle. Henry believed that the young man had had a sharp lesson and would think twice before following in his brother's footsteps which he must see had led to his early death and the loss of prestige and property. His claim to the throne—flimsy though it was—caused the King to watch him with some concern, but it seemed that Suffolk had realized that his best hope of living comfortably was to be a loyal subject; he was with the army which had marched to Blackheath and dispersed the rebellious Cornishmen. Henry was pleased; perhaps he had nothing to fear from the young man; but of course he would remain watchful.

Then an unfortunate incident occurred. Suffolk had been involved in a quarrel and in the heat of passion had drawn his sword and run his adversary through the heart.

This was murder and Henry was not going to allow crimes of that nature to go unpunished.

Suffolk was enraged. It had been a fair fight, he insisted. Moreover he was royal; he did not expect to be treated as an ordinary person.

'The King has robbed me of much of my estate,' he said, 'and in doing so forgets I am of the royal House of York. Would he indict me in the King's Bench like some ordinary felon?'

'Murder is a felony,' was the King's answer to that, 'and those who commit it cannot be excused because of their royal blood.'

'Henry does not like those of us of the House of York who might be said to have more claim to the throne than an upstart Welshman,' was Suffolk's impetuous retort.

His friends warned him of talking too freely but Suffolk was recalling the loss of the large portion of his estates and he was feeling reckless.

It was inevitable that some of his words should reach the King's ear. A dangerous man, thought Henry. One who should be guarded against not so much because of his temper but because of his connection with the House of York.

Here was the old bogey rising once more. Lambert Simnel . . . and away in the distance the shadowy figures of two small boys in the Tower.

He brooded over Suffolk; he asked certain questions about his movements.

Suffolk had his friends and they advised him to get away for a while until the affair of the killing blew over and as Suffolk had no intention of standing trial, in early August, when the weather was calm, he crossed the Channel without fuss, determined the

King should not be aware of his departure until he was well away.

On arriving in France his first call was at the Castle of Guisnes near Calais. He knew he would receive a warm welcome there for the custodian of the castle was his old friend Sir James Tyrrell.

He was right. Tyrrell was in the courtyard as soon as he heard of his friend's arrival. With him was his son, Thomas, of whom he was clearly proud and understandably so. Thomas was a handsome young man and it was obvious that there was a happy relationship between him and his father.

Tyrrell called to his horsekeeper, John Dighton, to give his personal attention to their guest's stabling and Dighton, red-faced, big and broad and clearly capable, immediately set about doing his master's bidding.

Sir James then took the Earl into the castle and sent his son to give orders that nothing should be spared in providing the utmost comfort for their guest.

Then he settled down to hear an account of the Earl's abrupt departure. When he had explained, Suffolk reviled the King and brought up the old grievance of the King's taking from him the major part of his inheritance, and then giving him back a portion for which he had to pay.

'Oh the King is most gracious,' said Suffolk sarcastically. 'He has given me a period of time to pay him for my own estates. Did you ever hear of such conduct, James? And that the old miser should dare to behave so to a member of the House of York angers me beyond description.'

'His treatment of you is because you *are* of the House of York,' said Tyrrell. 'It was a sad day for us when the Tudor came and killed good King Richard.'

'I know you served him well. Rest assured that this King of ours sleeps uneasily in his bed. He is constantly on the look-out for someone to thrust a dagger into his heart or stretch out rightful hands to take the crown. You, my friend, were always loyal to our House of York.'

'King Richard's reign was too short, alas. He was our rightful King.'

'I often wonder how much truth there was in that story of Edward's precontract to Eleanor Butler,' went on Suffolk.

'There is one mystery which will never be solved.'

'And there is another. Those two little boys . . . Kings both of them if the story be true that the elder died before the younger.

King Edward the Fifth and King Richard the Fourth. They were pleasant boys. I saw them now and then when I was young. 'Tis a strange story. I wonder the King does not sift the matter, for if one of those little boys still lives he is indeed the true King. Henry cannot pronounce them bastards for if they are, so is his Queen—and how could the King of England marry a bastard!'.

''Tis a long-ago mystery,' said Tyrrell, staring straight ahead. 'Too far back in time to be settled now.'

'But one which must haunt the King . . . unless he knows the answer.'

'It may be that he does know the answer.'

'You think he may?'

Tyrrell was silent then he said, almost as though speaking to himself, 'Oh it is long ago. But you, my lord, what plans have you?'

'To rest here for a while and see how the land lies.'

'My son and I will make you welcome here for as long as you wish to stay.'

'I must not stay long. By doing so I should compromise you with the King.'

'He knows I have no plans to rise against him.'

'Then you should not be too friendly with those who have a reason for doing so.'

Tyrrell looked at Suffolk with something like wonderment.

'You, my lord . . . how?'

'Why should I not discover? It may well be that I have friends on the Continent. As for you, James, you might do well not to connect yourself too openly with me . . . until such time as it will be safe to do so.'

Tyrrell's face hardened: 'I do not fear the King,' he said.

'No, you are well away. He has been a good friend to you . . . in a manner of speaking. After all you were a strong supporter of King Richard.'

'Oh yes . . . I must say that I was forgiven my allegiance to the House of York. He made me Sheriff of Glamorgan and Morgannock and gave me the Constableship of Cardiff Castle for life with a salary of one hundred pounds a year.'

'Generous treatment for a miser. There was something behind it all. There must have been.'

'Yes,' said Tyrrell, 'there must have been.'

'The Tudor always has his reasons and he is not accustomed to giving something for nothing. He must have had a great opinion of you, James. He must have thought very highly of your services. And now you have Guisnes. Almost as though he wanted you out of the country. It shows he trusts you.'

'Yes, I think he trusts me.'

'Then you should keep it that way . . . until such a moment as you decide it is no longer necessary. One must be wily when dealing with the Tudor.'

'You are right there. Have a care, my lord.'

'You may trust me to do that.'

Shortly afterwards Suffolk left Guisnes. Tyrrell was relieved to see him go.

He had good reason to know how ruthless Henry Tudor could be.

It was then that Henry's spies on the Continent brought him news that Suffolk had stayed a while in the company of Sir James Tyrrell at Guisnes Castle. This increased Henry's uneasiness, and he decided that Suffolk must be brought back to England and if it was not possible to persuade him to come back then it would be necessary to use force.

'I will offer him a pardon to return,' said Henry to Dudley. 'I will imply that this unfortunate killing will be forgotten.'

'You think it wise, my lord?'

Henry was thoughtful. There were matters of which even Dudley knew nothing. He spoke firmly: 'Yes, I think it wise. I want Suffolk in England where we can keep our eyes on him.'

When Suffolk received the King's messengers who arrived with the pardon, he decided that his best course was to return. So far he had committed no sin against the Crown and he knew that that was what Henry really feared.

So he returned and was received by the King.

Henry studied him warily, wondering about his activities on the Continent. Enemies of the House of Tudor abounded there, but he was not unduly disturbed about Suffolk's attempts to raise an army against him. He believed that would meet with little success. He did wonder though what Suffolk and Sir James Tyrrell had talked about when they were together.

'Well,' said Henry affably, 'that matter of affray in which a man was killed . . . we will choose to forget it.'

'I am glad of that. There was nothing else I could have done. I was insulted.'

'These moments arise and in the heat of them . . . well, it is understandable.'

Suffolk thought: Cold-blooded fish. Who could imagine his ever being caught up in the heat of any passion? His eyes were a cold pale blue—how different from Edward who would have blazed out, shouted and then in a short time they would have been laughing and drinking one another's health. A man knew where he was with Edward. With the Tudor he could never be sure.

'So you visited Tyrrell at Guisnes,' said the King quietly.

'It was the first port of call, my lord.'

'And how was the custodian of that castle?'

'In good health I think. His son is with him—a fine upstanding young man.'

'Yes, yes. It is good to have sons. Is he content with his life there?'

'It would appear so.'

'You must have had a great deal to talk of. I know what it is when a man meets someone from home. Did he talk of England . . . of his past life here?'

'Not much. We were not together very long.'

Henry was trying to probe the thoughts of the other. Had Tyrrell said anything? Of course he hadn't. He wouldn't be such a fool.

He changed the subject. He did not want Suffolk to suspect he was over-interested in James Tyrrell.

He brought the meeting to a close. It was significant now that the rift between Henry and Suffolk was over, but with each a little wary of the other.

That had happened just before the young Duke of Warwick was brought to the block and beheaded. Shortly before Perkin Warbeck paid the penalty for his recklessness.

After Warwick's execution Suffolk became uneasy. Warwick had died because of his claim to the throne. His, Suffolk's, was not so strong but it existed; and he had already shown his antipathy to Henry Tudor.

He thought it might be wise to slip out of the country again with his friends. In secret he had discussed his dissatisfaction with the Tudor rule and it had been suggested to him that the Emperor Maximilian would delight in the discomfiture of the English King and it seemed feasible that he might be ready to help in his downfall.

Suffolk thought: Why should not I be the one to bring about this happy result? I am of the House of York. Ours is the true reigning house.

Moreover Henry Tudor might be a good administrator but he was no soldier. He might know how to fill the exchequer by taking those goods and lands which belonged to others but he would not find it easy to raise an army of inspired men, to be that leader whom people admired and followed without question.

It was not long before the Earl of Suffolk was at the Court of Maximilian where to his great delight he was received as an honoured guest and listened to most sympathetically.

This was not quite the same as providing an army which was what Suffolk had hoped for, and although Maximilian would like to see Henry discomfited, when it came to providing the necessary arms and men that was another matter.

Maximilian sighed and prevaricated. It would be most difficult for him to do anything at the moment. Then he had an idea. He would invite the Count of Hardeck to meet the Earl.

'There is a man who loves causes . . . if they appeal to him,' said Maximilian. 'He will be sympathetic to you, I am sure, and if that sympathy goes deep enough . . . well, Hardeck is a man with the means.'

Hardeck was young and enthusiastic. He listened to Suffolk's account of how Henry had robbed him of his estates, and how England was groaning under the taxes imposed by Dudley and Empson; he was appalled by the subjugation of the noble House of York and that the Queen was not given her true rights and must always be subjected to the will of Lancaster.

The young Count would lend Suffolk twenty thousand gulden and this could be paid back with interest when Suffolk had achieved his goal.

'You should return to England,' Maximilian advised the Earl. 'Find out how many men will be ready to stand with you. Find out whether if you raise an army the Tudor could stand against you.'

Suffolk decided he would do so. Hardeck would be repaid, he promised him, and his payment would be double that which he had lent; and as surety Hardeck's son should go with Suffolk to England.

This was success such as Suffolk had scarcely dared hope for. Hardeck had come in at the right moment when Maximilian was slipping away.

So, with his friends, he came to England.

Had he been wiser he would have known that Henry would not be ignorant of what was going on. The King did in fact know every twist and turn of the negotiations with Maximilian and was amused at Suffolk's temerity and naivety in imagining that the Emperor would involve himself in such a hopeless cause. On the other hand Suffolk had found support and that must not be lightly shrugged aside.

It was not really Suffolk with whom he was concerned. Suffolk was a fool and could easily be dealt with. As soon as he stepped on English soil he was arrested on a charge of plotting treason and in a short time he was lodged in the Tower. With him were arrested his brother Lord William de la Pole and Lord William Courtenay, another Yorkist who had married one of the daughters of Edward the Fourth.

That attempted revolt was stifled almost before it had begun and the King had cause for gratification.

But the idea which had come to him when he had heard Suffolk had called at Guisnes Castle was still with him. It had obsessed him and he saw a way of bringing about that satisfaction which he had long sought.

He sent for Sir Richard Guildford, his master of ordnance, and with him came Richard Hatton, a man whom he had reason to trust.

'I want you to bring Sir James Tyrrell and his son and his master of horse John Dighton to England,' he said. 'It will be necessary to practise a little deception because I want them to come willingly.'

'Your orders shall be carried out, my lord,' promised Guildford.

'As soon as they are safely in the country, they are all three to be immediately lodged in the Tower. It may be necessary to tell Tyrrell that I wish to speak with him on a matter which is too secret to be imparted to anyone. I think that will bring him without delay. Let it appear that I am indeed his friend and wish to reward him, and make sure that he brings with him his horsekeeper and his son, who is at present in residence in the castle.'

The men departed and Henry, trying to curb his impatience, eagerly awaited their arrival.

Tyrrell was wary. Suffolk had been arrested. He was glad he had not been involved in that. Suffolk was hot-headed, impulsive, not the man who should attempt to pit his wits against shrewd Henry Tudor. His planned insurrection had been doomed to failure before it had begun. How wise he had been to keep clear of that! It was a pity that Suffolk had visited him—but his stay had been brief and he could prove that nothing treasonable had happened between them.

When he wakened one morning to find the castle surrounded, he was horrified. It could mean only one thing. He was about to be arrested and the only reason could be implication with Suffolk. When he saw the Calais garrison were stationed outside the castle, his first thought was that he would hold out. He had the necessary stores, men and arms to withstand a long siege and he would do so until he knew why his castle was being besieged.

He did not have to wait long. A messenger came to tell him that Sir Thomas Lovell, the Chancellor of the Exchequer, was aboard the ship which lay at anchor and he wished to have a private word with Sir James Tyrrell. He came from the King and he was in fact commanding Sir James to come to meet him.

It was no use asking the messenger for what purpose, but he had brought with him a safe conduct.

Tyrrell guessed that the King had discovered what Suffolk was doing and that he was going to be accused of complicity. He sent for his son.

'Thomas,' he said, 'this messenger comes from Sir Thomas Lovell, who wishes to have speech with me.'

'You should not go, Father. You should not leave the castle.'

'I shall, my son. I have safe conduct and while I am gone I leave you in charge of the castle. Hold the siege and take no orders that do not come from me. Do you understand?'

Thomas said he did.

So Sir James left with the messenger and went aboard to meet Sir Thomas Lovell.

As soon as he was ushered into his presence he knew he had been foolish to come, for Lovell lost no time in accusing Tyrrell, in the name of the King, of high treason.

'This is monstrous,' said Tyrrell. 'I am entirely guiltless.'

'It will be necessary for you to return to England with me.'

'I was promised safe conduct. I am not afraid of answering my accuser but I shall go back to the castle to put my affairs in order there. Then I will return to England to answer these false charges.'

'You will at once send a message to your son. The castle is to be surrendered without delay.'

'I shall send no such message.'

'I think you will, Sir James. If you do not you will be promptly thrown into the sea.'

'On whose orders?'

'From one who must not be disobeyed.'

'You mean . . . the King?'

'I did not say that. I have orders to take you back to England . . . I was not told whether you were to be alive or dead . . . only to bring you at any cost.'

'Let me go back to the castle. Let me make ready to leave.'

Lovell shook his head. 'The castle is to surrender. You will send a message to your son.'

He signed to two strong men who came forward at once and seized Tyrrell.

'Are you prepared to sign that order? The sea is rough today. Accoutred as you are you would have little chance of surviving.'

They really mean it, thought Tyrrell. What is behind all this? Why did not the King send me a simple command to return? I should have done so. I have nothing to fear from him. Or . . . have I? No, he could not. He would not dare. What I could tell . . .

He was seized with a fit of shivering. He seemed to see Henry Tudor's cold eyes staring at him.

He said: 'I will sign the order for the surrender of the castle. Only my signature will satisfy my son.'

Lovell smiled and bowed his head.

He summoned a messenger. 'Take this order at once to the castle. Thomas Tyrrell and John Dighton are to join us here on the ship without delay.'

'My son knows nothing of . . . of anything you may be accusing me of.'

'We have our orders,' smiled Lovell. 'And we intend to obey them to the letter.'

In a very short time Thomas Tyrrell and John Dighton joined Sir James on the ship.

Before he reached England Tyrrell knew that he had been a fool to leave the castle. If he had not done so he would be there now . . . defending it against the Calais garrison. He had been tricked. He should never have obeyed the summons to see Lovell. And now what? He knew he was going to be accused with Suffolk. He had committed no treason. It was true that Suffolk had visited him but they had not even talked of treason. If he had a fair trial he could prove this. Suffolk would exonerate him for Suffolk was a man of honour even though he was impulsive and hotheaded.

We shall be all right, thought Tyrrell. We must for we have done nothing.

His great concern was for his son Thomas. Thomas was completely innocent. It was wicked to have dragged him into this. Whatever happened, Thomas must not be made to suffer.

It was spring but there was a chill in the air. He was closely guarded and with him Thomas and John Dighton. They were taken to London and when he saw the great grey edifice ahead of him and realized that it was to be his destination he was filled with cold horror.

He was the King's prisoner. What could they prove against him? Nothing. He deluded himself. The King's men could always prove what they wanted to and something told him that there was more in this accusation than he had at first thought.

He was right. The trial had been quick. They had judged him, and with Thomas and Dighton he had been found guilty. The case was that Suffolk had sought aid to come against the King, he had received certain monies, he had planned rebellion, and Sir James Tyrrell had been his accomplice.

Where was Suffolk? He heard that he had been arrested and accused at Paul's Cross as a traitor with William de la Pole and William Courtenay. They were in confinement somewhere. He did not know where.

But he, Tyrrell, had been condemned to death. It was strange that Suffolk and his accomplices had not been sentenced, yet James Tyrrell who had played no part in the rebellion and whose only sin was that he had received an old friend who called on him, should be condemned to death.

The next day he was to be taken out to Tower Green and there he would suffer the fate of traitors. He should be grateful that it was to be the axe and not that worse fate which was reserved for some.

It was dusk when the door of his cell was opened. No word was said but a figure heavily cloaked came into his cell and stood watching him.

The door of the cell was shut behind him and the two of them were alone.

A shiver ran down Tyrrell's spine. He thought it was the angel of death already come for him.

Then a voice said: 'James Tyrrell, you are to die tomorrow.'

'Who are you?' he asked.

'No matter. You are to die and your son with you.'

'I am innocent of what I am accused. I may have committed crimes in my life but I had no part in Suffolk's plan. As for my son, he is completely innocent of anything that could be brought against him. He is wrongfully accused . . .'

'He will meet his death tomorrow . . . unless you save him.'

'Save him. How?'

'It is not impossible.'

'Have you come to help him?'

'I will make a bargain with you. You can save your son's life.'

'How? How?'

'It is easy. You cannot save your own life. That would be too difficult to achieve, but you can save your son's.'

'Only a pardon from the King could do that.'

'I could get that pardon.'

'Who are you?'

'Shall we say that I come from one who can pardon your son.'

Tyrrell was silent. His heart was beating wildly. It could not be . . . but perhaps it was.

'What . . . what should I have to do?'

'To confess to something . . . something that happened a few years ago.'

Tyrrell was silent. He felt his hair beginning to rise on his scalp; it seemed to him that the walls of his cell were closing in on him. Whenever he passed this place he had felt uneasy and it was ever since . . .

But that was long ago. That was another man's crime. Could he be blamed for seeing that it was carried out? He had had to do so. So much depended on it . . . his future . . . his family . . . his beloved son . . .

'What is wanted is a confession from you, James Tyrrell.'

'What . . . must I confess?'

'You know, do you not? Cast your mind back . . . Remember Dighton . . . Miles Forrest . . . remember that night . . . two little boys . . . innocent young boys whose existence could have started a civil war. They had to go. You realized that. You helped them to it, Tyrrell. What you have to do is tell the story. Make a confession. It is what you would wish to do, is it not? You are shortly to leave this world. Can you go to your Maker with that sin on your conscience?'

'Who are you?' said Tyrrell again. There was no answer and he went on: 'I do not hold myself guilty . . . completely . . . not as guilty as he who instigated the crime. I arranged for it to be carried out. But the heaviest guilt does not rest with me. It is that one to whose advantage it was to have those two boys removed.'

'You did what you did for gain, Tyrrell.'

'My gain was not to be compared with that of another.'

'Was it not? It was your whole life. You did not want to live as an outcast, Tyrrell. You wanted your share of the good things that are given to faithful servants. You are guilty, Tyrrell, as guilty as any man . . . as guilty as Forrest or Dighton . . . You would have to confess your guilt.'

'The King would not wish that.'

'The King does wish it.'

Tyrrell caught his breath. Could it indeed be the one he thought it was who stood before him wrapped in concealment?

'The life of your son, Tyrrell. His estates will be restored to him. He will go on living . . . His only sorrow will be that his father lost his head because he had played the traitor. Will you do this for your son?'

'How can I be sure?'

'You cannot be entirely sure. But you can be sure of one thing. If you do not, your son will surely die with you.'

For a few moments there was silence in the cell. Tyrrell was thinking, I will do it. What harm can it do me? It is well that people should know.

He said: 'I will do it. For my son's life I will do it.'

'That is good. Tell me the story as it happened. Make your confession now. Shall I prompt your memory? It was in the summer of the year 1483 . . .'

'No . . . no . . . much later.'

'Let us say it was in the summer of 1483. Richard of Gloucester knew that he must kill his nephews to make the crown secure for himself.'

'The crown was secure. He had proclaimed them bastards.'

'We are going to make our confession, Tyrrell, if we are going to save your son. In that summer Richard of Gloucester sent a certain John Greene to the Tower with a note for the Constable, Sir Robert Brackenbury, with the order that he should put the Princes to death. Sir Robert was an honest man who refused to do it. Richard was furiously angry. "Whom can a man trust?" he cried and one of his pages answered: "I know, Sire, one whom you can trust." And he gave him your name.'

'This is false.'

'Remember your son's life is in danger. You were a very ambitious young man at that time. You were jealous of the favour Catesby and Ratcliffe enjoyed from the King. You were eager to curry favour with Richard who ordered Brackenbury to give you the keys of the Tower for one night. So you, a nameless page before that time, sprang into favour because you were ready to do the King's bidding after Brackenbury refused.'

'I am a sinner,' said Tyrrell. 'I would be counted a murderer, but this is not true. I was no nameless page. I was a trusted servant of the King. I had received my knighthood at Tewkesbury in 1471. I was the King's Master of Henchman and Horse. I will confess . . . but I must confess the truth.'

'You will make the confession you are told to make.'

'But this is foolish. It does not carry conviction. Do you say King Richard sent a note to Brackenbury ordering him to murder the Princes and that he refused? If that were true how could

Richard have allowed him to live after such a thing? Brackenbury was an honest man. No one ever denied that. Yet he remained Richard's friend. He died beside him at Bosworth Field.'

'We are not concerned with Brackenbury's death. Only with your confession.'

'You would have me say that which is false.'

'Did you arrange for the murder of the Princes in the Tower?'

'I did.'

'And did your henchmen Miles Forrest and John Dighton perform the deed?'

'They did.'

'And were the Princes smothered in their beds?'

Tyrrell put his hands over his face. 'Their deaths were quick,' he said. 'Poor innocent children, they knew nothing of what was happening. The felt no pain. They had to die. Their deaths may have saved the lives of thousands.'

'True.' There was a certain warmth now in the cold voice of the stranger. 'It was necessary. A hideous deed, but out of evil, good can come. It had to be, Tyrrell, it had to be. Now you arranged for their deaths, did you not?'

'I did.'

'Tell the story as it happened. We disagree on but a few details. Never mind. They can be put right. It happened earlier than you say.'

'I know when it happened. I am perfectly clear about that.'

'You are being recalcitrant and there is very little time left for us. It is a matter of whether you want to save your son's life.'

'I see that the guilt is to be shifted to King Richard.'

'The guilt was King Richard's. He had taken the crown . . . usurped it from his nephews.'

'He believed them to be bastards.'

'Oh come. They were a threat nevertheless and he decided to remove them. It was as we have said. Brackenbury refused and you took over the Tower for a night. Forrest and Dighton obeyed your orders. The children were stifled and buried under a stairway in the Tower.'

'It does not agree with the facts. I am the only one of King Richard's faithful servants who has been able to live successfully during the present reign. People will say: Why was this so? It could only be that although I served Richard well I also performed a great service for King Henry.'

'The confession of a man just before death will convince them that you speak the truth.'

'How can I be sure that my son's life will be saved?'

'The King is not a bloodthirsty man. He does not like to shed men's blood and only does so when it is for the good of the country.'

'And mine is for the good of the country?'

'Traitors cannot be allowed to live.'

'I took no part in Suffolk's rebellion.'

'You are judged guilty.'

'Not for this . . . for another crime of which I was only an instrument used to carry it out.'

'The death of the two young boys in the Tower doubtless saved a civil war which could have cost the country thousands of lives . . . and its prosperity. That has been avoided. And no one must be allowed again to rise in their name.'

'Ah,' said Tyrrell. 'I begin to understand. When it is proved that they are dead none will rise in their name, and I can prove that they are dead by telling the truth.'

'What you consider to be the truth would not save your son.'

'It would prevent men from impersonating the Princes.'

'You know what is required. It is for you to choose.'

'I will make the confession.'

'As is desired?'

'As is desired,' said Tyrrell.

The next day Sir James Tyrrell was taken out to Tower Green and his head laid on the block. He died with the comfort of knowing that he had saved his son's life.

The following day Thomas Tyrrell was found guilty of treason but his sentence was delayed and finally he was freed and his estates were not confiscated.

John Dighton, who had been named as one of the men who had taken an active part in that mysterious murder, was not hanged but kept in the Tower. After a while he was freed although he, too, was alleged to have confessed to his share in the murder of the Princes.

Nothing had been written down about the confession, but a few weeks after the death of Tyrrell, the King let it be known that Sir James Tyrrell had made a confession that the Princes had been murdered in the Tower on the orders of Richard the Third and that Tyrrell and his manservants had played a part in it.

The news was gradually allowed to seep out, almost as though no great effort was made to bring it to the notice of the people.

John Dighton, who had made a lucky escape from death, was one of those chosen to circulate the story, which he did.

Lord William de la Pole and Lord William Courtenay remained the King's prisoners; but Suffolk, the leader of the hoped-for insurrection, was merely exiled to Aix.

The King liked it to be known that he was not vindictive. It was not the will of a just king to shed blood in anger. He wanted all men to know—and this was an obvious truth—that he only did so when expediency demanded that he should. If a person was a menace to the Crown—and the Crown of course meant Henry—then it was often wiser to remove that man. He did not want revenge. He wanted peace and prosperity during his reign. It was what he strove for. He wanted a secure throne for his House and that was the best thing possible for England.

In time people began to accept the story of the death of the Princes in the Tower. They had been murdered by Richard the Third who was emerging as something of a monster. It was amazing how little interest people felt for what did not actually concern themselves. No one picked up any discrepancies in the story. No one asked for instance why that good honest man Brackenbury, who was alleged openly to have refused to help his master commit murder, should have continued to be the friend of the King whom he had admired and beside whom he died fighting at Bosworth. No one asked why Tyrrell should have been the one to lose his head when he had played no part—at the least a very small one—in Suffolk's treason and why Suffolk should get off with exile.

Nobody cared very much. Nobody wanted risings and rebellions. The Princes were dead. Murdered by their wicked uncle. It had all happened long ago and most people who were concerned in it were dead.

BIRTH AND DEATH

The Queen was feeling ill. She was pregnant and although she would not admit this to anyone she was dreading her confinement. Only those in her intimate circle must know how weak she was, and she was particularly anxious that the King should not be told.

'He has enough anxieties apart from worrying about me,' she confided to her sister, Lady Katharine Courtenay, who had troubles of her own, for her husband had been in the Tower in captivity since his complicity in the Suffolk case.

'There seems to be nothing but anxieties,' agreed Katharine. 'It has always been so with us. Sometimes I think it must be a great comfort to be poor and of no consequence at all.'

'I daresay the poor have their trials,' said Elizabeth. 'I think I have been fortunate. I have a good husband and a fine family. They bring their sorrows though. I don't think I shall ever get over the death of Arthur.'

'Poor boy. He was always ailing.'

'My first born, Katharine, and I will say to you what I would say to no one else . . . my favourite.'

'Perhaps it is a lesson to us. We should not have favourites among our children.'

'It may well be. I shall be losing Margaret soon to Scotland. Then it will be Mary.'

'You will have Henry and the children he will have. Be thankful for that, Elizabeth.'

'I am. Life did not turn out so badly for us, did it? When you think of all the twists and turns of fate it is amazing that we have come out of it all so satisfactorily. On our father's death . . .'

Katharine laid a hand over her sister's. 'Let us not brood on it. It is so long ago. Here we are now. You are the Queen, you have a kind husband and children of whom you can be proud. It would be hard to find three more handsome and lively children than your Henry, Margaret and Mary.'

'I agree. I agree. I trust the new one will be a son. It is what the King wants. I know we have Henry and he is strong and healthy but ever since the death of Arthur, the King has had this fear.'

'Henry is too fearful. I suppose it is inevitable that he should worry about the succession when . . . But no matter. I wonder what will happen to the Spanish Princess now. Poor child. It has been a tragedy for her. I believe she was very fond of Arthur.'

'Who would not be fond of Arthur? He was such a gentle person. Oh it is cruel . . . cruel . . . to take him from us.'

'Hush, sister. You must not upset yourself. Remember the child.'

Remember the child. Elizabeth had been remembering the child all through her married life it seemed. No sooner was one pregnancy over than there must be another. It was necessary to fill the nurseries and when children died it was a great tragedy. She had lost little Edmund and Elizabeth . . . but that Arthur should be taken from her was the greatest tragedy of her life. Arthur who had grown to maturity, who had been a husband though in name only.

She was thinking of that other Katharine, the little Princess from Spain, and she was filled with pity.

While the sisters were talking the King arrived at Richmond. There was the usual flurry of excitement which his presence engendered and when he made his way to the Queen's apartments Elizabeth wondered what had brought him to her at this time of day. It must be something of importance, she was sure.

He came to her apartments and Lady Courtenay bowed as he entered and looked askance at the Queen who glanced at the King. He nodded and Lady Katharine slipped away.

'It is rare that I see you at such an hour,' said the Queen. 'I trust all is well.'

'I am a little concerned. It is about the Spanish Princess. I think you could be of help in a . . . somewhat delicate matter.'

The Queen waited.

'I believe you have sent an invitation to her to visit you here?'

'I thought it the best. Poor child, she must be feeling desolate.'

'Poor child indeed. And I know you will do everything possible to cheer her up.'

'I shall try. I have had a litter made for her by my tailor and I thought that Croydon Palace would be a good residence for her. She will be most unhappy if she stays on at Ludlow.'

'So you will soon see her.'

'In a day or so I believe. As soon as she has made the journey.'

The King was thoughtful. 'It has thrown so much into confusion . . . The position of the Princess here . . .'

'Yes, I suppose Ferdinand and Isabella will expect her to go back to Spain now.'

'That is what I want to avoid. If they take her back they will want her dowry, too.'

'I see.'

'I have no mind to part with so much.'

The Queen was about to interject when she thought better of it. It was unwise to argue about money and possessions with Henry; he had a great reverence for them and regarded them with the utmost seriousness.

'I have been turning over in my mind . . . and discussing the matter with my ministers. There is a way to keep the dowry in the country.'

She looked at him questioningly. Was he going to suggest keeping it now that it was in his hands? Surely he could not be so unscrupulous.

But of course that was not it. Henry would always have a clever reason why things should be as he wanted them to be.

'We must keep Katharine in the country. There is one way of doing this and that is to marry her to Henry.'

'Henry? But that is surely not possible?'

'Why not?' asked the King with a coldness in his voice which she had rarely heard. That was because she questioned his actions so infrequently.

'Well,' she stammered. 'He is five years younger.'

'Five years younger? What has that to do with the matter? I have never yet known a matter of five years prevent a marriage which will bring great good to all parties.'

'She was married to Henry's brother. It would not be considered legal.'

'A dispensation would settle that.'

'And you think the Pope would give it?'

'The Pope will do what seems best for him. You may depend upon that.'

'But is it not against the laws of the Church for a woman to marry her husband's brother?'

'If the marriage was not consummated I see no reason that this should be so.'

'But the marriage was very likely consummated. They were two young people . . . together . . . fond of each other.'

'I think it most unlikely that it was consummated. I gave orders that it should not be and Arthur would never disobey me.'

The Queen realized that the King was faintly irritated because she showed signs of disagreeing with him. She was amazed that she had done so, though mildly; perhaps it was because the idea was repugnant to her and she felt sorry for the young Princess who was being bandied from the dead brother to the living one.

'What is the delicate matter you wish me to do?'

'Find out from Katharine's own lips whether or not the marriage was consummated.'

'And if it were not?'

'Then, as I see it, there is no obstacle to the marriage of Katharine and Henry. You will ask her this question and if the answer is no, then we may go ahead with negotiations.'

'And if it has been?'

'Then we will keep the matter to ourselves. I shall consider what can best be done.'

'I see you are determined that she shall have Henry.'

'I see no other way of keeping her dowry in the country,' said the King with a wry smile.

Katharine was indeed in an unhappy state. She was feeling quite bewildered. It seemed strange that a short while before she had been the wife of the heir to the throne, queen-to-be and now she was a widow . . . a stranger in a strange country and she did not know what would become of her.

Her great hope was that she would go home. They would make another match for her, of course, but at least for a while she would be with her mother. She did not want another match. She had realized how lucky she had been to come to Arthur who was so kind and whom she had grown to love during the short time they had been together.

The Queen had been kind to her, too. She had written to her and said she must not stay at Ludlow. There would be too many memories there and it would be better for her to take up her residence in an entirely new place.

'I am having the Palace of Croydon prepared for you,' wrote the Queen, 'and my tailor John Cope is making a litter which will convey you to Croydon. It will be a most suitable vehicle of conveyance for it will be made of black velvet and black cloth and trimmed with black valances.'

It sounded funereal but of course she was in deep and bitter mourning.

The Queen was right; she did feel a little better in Croydon but as her grief for the loss of Arthur lifted a little, her apprehension regarding her own future increased.

At first few people came to Croydon. This was the period of her mourning; but one day she received a letter from the Queen at Richmond asking that she come to see her.

'I myself am somewhat indisposed,' wrote the Queen. 'It is for this reason that I ask you to come to me.'

In her litter of black velvet Katharine set out from Croydon and when she arrived at Richmond was warmly embraced by the Queen.

'My dear dear child!' cried the Queen. 'You look so sad. Let us mingle our tears. I believe he was as dear to you as he was to me.'

Katharine bowed her head and the Queen held the young girl in her arms.

'He loved you dearly,' went on the Queen. 'I was so happy to see you together because it was clear to me that you would be just the wife he needed. He was so gentle . . . so modest . . . and that is rare in those of his rank.'

Katharine said: 'He was all that I looked for in a husband.'

'And your union so brief. Oh, it is a cruel world we live in. But we have to go on whatever our sorrow. You have a happy future before you, my child.'

'I long to see my mother,' said Katharine. 'My lady, can you tell me when I may expect to go to her?'

The Queen was silent. Then she took Katharine's hands. 'You love her dearly, I know.'

Katharine nodded silently.

'There will be another marriage for you.'

'Oh no . . . not, not yet . . . perhaps never.'

'You are the daughter of a great King and Queen, and there will be those to seek your hand. There will certainly be another marriage for you. You have had one marriage and are so young to be a widow. Forgive my asking this question, my dear, but was that a true marriage?

Katharine stared at her mother-in-law uncomprehendingly.

'Well,' the Queen stumbled on, 'when two people marry, the Church tells us that one of the main reasons for doing so is for the procreation of children. Is there any hope that you . . . might be bearing Arthur's child?'

'Oh no . . . no . . .' cried Katharine. 'That would be impossible.'

'Impossible because you and Arthur . . . did not consummate the marriage?'

'It would be quite impossible,' said Katharine.

'I see. You were both so young . . . and he was not well . . .

and the King had feared for his health and that was why he was against the consummation of the marriage. You understand that, Katharine?'

'I understand.'

'And so it is impossible for there to be a child of the marriage because it was not consummated.'

Katharine nodded.

'Thank you, my dear. I hope you do not want to leave us.'

'You have been so kind to me . . . in particular you, my lady.'

'My dear daughter, I want to go on being kind to you for as long as we both shall live.'

'I shall go back to Spain. I am sure my parents will send for me . . . soon.'

The Queen hesitated. She was taking a good deal on herself but she felt rebellious, which was rare with her. She was sorry for this young girl who had been sent to England away from her friends and now was being bartered so blatantly, passed from one brother to another for the sake of the thousands of crowns which made up her dowry.

She said: 'The King and I have grown very fond of you since you have been among us.'

Katharine did not believe for one moment that the King had grown fond of her. It was hard to imagine his being fond of anyone.

'We should be very sorry to see you go,' went on the Queen. 'And there is one other among us. No doubt you have noticed the warm regard of our son Henry.'

Alarm showed itself in Katharine's eyes. She half guessed what was coming. Oh no. She could not bear it. She wanted to go home to her mother. She had been reconciled to Arthur because he was kind and gentle and life had been so much happier with him than she had dared hope it would be. But to be passed over to his brother . . . that young boy . . . She had been a little older than Arthur even. Oh, how desperately she wanted to go home.

'The King would give his consent to a match between you and our son Henry.'

'Henry is but a boy.'

'Boys grow up. He is old for his age. He could marry at sixteen . . . fifteen perhaps.'

'I do not think my parents would agree,' said Katharine.

'There could of course be no match without their agreement,' the Queen answered. She laid a hand on Katharine's arm. 'Say nothing of this. I told you because I thought you should know what is in the King's mind.'

The two looked at each other for a few moments and then Elizabeth opened her arms and Katharine went to her. They stood for a few moments in a close embrace.

It was only a few days later when the King sent for her. He greeted her with a show of affection which was rare with him, and it was obvious that he was very pleased about something.

'My dear daughter,' he said.'I have good news for you. I have heard from your parents.'

Her face lighted up. They were going to send for her. They would never agree to her marrying young Henry. It was wrong according to the laws of the Church and none could uphold the Church more strongly than her mother. Henry was her brother-in-law. That was the important fact, not that he was five years younger than she was. That meant nothing to them.

The King's next words dashed her hopes. 'They agree to a marriage between you and Prince Henry.'

'But . . . that is . . . impossible. I was his brother's wife.'

'No, my dear child, the marriage was not consummated. That makes all the difference. All we need is a dispensation from the Pope. And we can rest assured that if I wish it and if your parents wish it there will be no obstacles to that.'

'I . . . I . . . I do not wish . . .'

'I know your feelings. You have so shortly become a widow. You loved Arthur. My dear child, you know nothing of marriage. That will come . . . in due course. You will be betrothed to Henry and when he is of an age to marry the ceremony shall take place. You will be the Queen of England one day.'

'Does Henry know of this?'

'He does and he is overjoyed.'

'He is too young . . .'

'Nay, he understands well. He was, to confess it, a little jealous of his brother's good fortune.'

The King's face was twisted into a smile as he tried to look jovial. Katharine thought it was as though his features resented being distorted into such unusual lines.

'It will be a long time . . . yet,' said Katharine faintly.

'Ah, time passes quickly. It gives me great pleasure to convey to you this excellent news.'

He rubbed his hands together and his eyes glinted.

He is seeing one hundred thousand crowns which have already been paid to him and is congratulating himself that he will not have to part with them, thought Katharine. And he is seeing the hundred thousand coming to me when I marry Henry.

The King put his lips to her cheek and she was dismissed.

In her apartment she called for writing materials.

She wanted to write to her mother but she could not do this. Everything she wrote would be seen by both her parents and she knew her father would be angry if she pleaded with her mother and excluded him.

Nevertheless, she must relieve her feelings in some way.

'I have no inclination for a second marriage in England . . .'

Her mother would understand that that was a cry for help.

Then she thought of the rules of obedience which had always been adhered to; one must never think of oneself but of the good of the country. If her parents wished it she would have to take Henry. Perhaps they could be happy together; he had always shown an interest in her. She would have to be resigned to her fate if it were her parents' wish that she should accept what they planned for her.

She added: 'I know that my tastes and conveniences cannot be considered and you will in all things act as is best.'

When she had written and dispatched the letter she lay down on her bed and staring dry-eyed before her murmured: 'Please dearest mother, send for me. Dear God, let me go home.'

It was late January when the Queen in the company of her ladies was rowed from Richmond to the Tower where she had decided her child should be born.

Her sister Katharine was very anxious about her for Elizabeth had had such a difficult pregnancy and was scarcely strong enough for the ordeal before her.

People stood about on the river bank to watch the Queen's barge and to give a cheer for the poor lady who looked as though she would give birth at any moment.

The chamber in the Tower had been prepared and to this the Queen went immediately. Her women gathered about her helping her to bed and making sure of her comforts. Lady Courtenay sat by her bed, ever watchful of her sister and wondering about her husband who was incarcerated in this very Tower. She had been anxious ever since the execution of Sir James Tyrrell who had had very little to do with the planned rising. She wondered why Suffolk and her husband had got off so lightly. It was no use asking Elizabeth. The Queen knew so little of the King's affairs which Katharine Courtenay believed were very devious indeed.

February had come, bleak and bitterly cold when the Queen's

pains started and on Candlemas Day, the second of that month, the child was born.

Katharine Courtenay felt sad when she saw that the child was a girl. Dear Elizabeth, she had so longed for a boy. Perhaps if there had been a boy, Katharine thought, there could have been a rest from this incessant childbearing which was undoubtedly having dire effects on the Queen's health.

The child was sound but a little frail. As she held the baby in her arms she heard the Queen's voice calling her.

She went to the bed. 'A dear little girl, Elizabeth,' she said.

Elizabeth closed her eyes for one despairing moment. Then she opened them and she was smiling.

'She is . . . healthy?'

'Yes,' said Katharine, and put the child in her arms.

After a while she took the baby from its mother who fell into a sleep of exhaustion. This time next year, thought Katharine, we shall doubtless be in a similar situation. Will it go on and on until they get a boy? And how will Elizabeth endure it? She won't admit it but she is less strong after each confinement.

The midwife was looking anxious.

'Why are you worried? asked Katharine.

'The Queen is not strong enough,' said the midwife. 'This should be the last.'

'I will talk to her.'

'Someone should talk to the King.'

Why not? thought Katharine. He had a son and now three daughters. That must be enough.

When the Queen was rested Katharine sat at her bedside and they talked together.

'She is a beautiful child, I hear,' said the Queen. 'They would not deceive me, would they?'

'Why should they? You have three other beautiful children, sister.'

'Arthur was weak and they kept that from me for several days.'

'You brood too much on Arthur. You have Henry. You could not have a son who was more full of strength and vitality.'

'It is true. You have been a great comfort to me, Katharine, and I know you have troubles of your own. I am going to call this little one Katharine . . . after you.'

'Then I am honoured, dear sister.'

As Katharine bent over the bed and kissed the Queen, she was a little startled by the clammy coldness of her skin.

Within a week the Queen was dead. Her passing was not only

a matter of great sorrow but of amazement. She had appeared to recover from the ordeal of childbirth and it was not until six days later that the fatal symptoms appeared.

When Katharine Courtenay had found her in a terrifyingly weak state she had sent a messenger at once to the King and when Henry arrived he was horrified. He had sent with all speed for his physician, who believing that the Queen was on the way to recovery, had left the Tower for his home in Gravesend.

The news of the deterioration of the Queen's health spread rapidly as Dr Hallyswurth came hurrying through the night with the help of guides and torches to speed his coming, and people were already in the streets whispering of the mortal sickness which had come to the Queen.

She died on the eleventh of February, nine days after the birth of the child. It was her own birthday and she was thirty-eight years old.

In all the churches in the city the bells were tolling.

Crowds watched while spices, sweet wine-gums and balms with ells of Holland cloth were taken into the Tower and they knew that these things were for the dismal purpose of embalming the Queen.

From her apartments she was taken to the chapel in the Tower and there she lay in state for twelve days after which her body was put in a velvet carriage and taken to Westminster. An effigy in robes of state and crown was put in a chair on the coffin and it was said that this bore a startling resemblance to the Queen at her most beautiful. It was a day of great mourning.

The King was genuinely stricken with grief. Although he knew that Elizabeth had been in ill health for some time he had not expected her to die. She had recovered from the birth of the child and everyone had believed she would soon leave her bed. It was a bitter blow; but being Henry he was immediately facing the grim fact that now he had no wife and only one son to follow him. Margaret was already the Queen of Scotland. He needed children. And Elizabeth who was to have provided them was dead.

The Prince of Wales was equally bewildered. He had loved his mother. She had been very beautiful and he was susceptible to beauty. That she should have died so suddenly was disturbing. He felt bereft. He had not loved her as he had Anne Oxenbrigge, but now he was growing up he was becoming very much aware of his royal dignity and he would not admit that a nursemaid had been so very important to him. His mother had seemed remote but good and beautiful and she had been the daughter of a king. As a Tudor he attached great importance to that. And now she was dead.

He was twelve years old now and he was going to be betrothed. He looked at the Spanish Princess. She was wary and did not meet his eyes.

Poor Katharine, she must admire him very much. Well, she was pretty and he had envied Arthur. It was strange how everything that he had envied was now coming to him.

Katharine looked very sad. She was realizing that if her parents decided she must stay here she had just lost one who would have been a good friend to her.

Henry was looking at her, smiling faintly.

She returned the smile. She would have to please him, she supposed. If she did not, what would happen to her?

She looked about her. Here was genuine sorrow. Even the King looked older and more grey. As for the Lady Courtenay, she was quite distraught as she with the Queen's sisters laid their palls on the coffin.

What will become of us all? wondered Katharine. She will not be here to see.

A few days later the child Katharine, who had cost the Queen her life, was stricken with a grievous illness and within a short time she was dead.

THE SEARCH
FOR A QUEEN

The King was restive. He had lost his queen but he could not afford to waste time in grief. He was not yet so old that he was beyond getting children. He was forty-six—a mature age, it was true—but he was by no means impotent. His life with the Queen had shown that. He could convince himself that he was a comparatively young man and therefore he must at once make plans to remarry.

The Spanish Sovereigns were being awkward about the dowry. Ferdinand was a wily man to deal with and Henry did not trust him. Isabella was a great queen but she was concerned for her daughter and Henry believed that Katharine might have written to her expressing repugnance for the match with young Henry. He knew of course that that would carry little weight with Ferdinand but with Isabella it might be another matter.

But suppose he had a more dazzling proposition to put before the Sovereigns? He sent for de Puebla, a clever man who delighted in intrigue and was not averse to a little sharp practice. He was the sort of fellow who could always be safely sounded out and who for considerations could be counted on to give consideration to every scheme—however shocking it might appear to some.

Henry said: 'The Sovereigns are no doubt a little concerned about their daughter's future.'

'Why, my lord, they know that she is to have Prince Henry. That seems to them a sensible and happy conclusion to the Infanta's matrimonial affairs.'

'Henry is only a boy, not yet twelve years old. I fancy that the Sovereigns are concerned about waiting for him to come of age before the final ceremony can take place. I have another idea. How would they feel about seeing their daughter Queen of England immediately?'

'My lord!'

'Why not? I am free to marry.'

'And you would take your son's widow!' Even the worldly de Puebla was taken aback.

'It seems reasonable. Katharine is here. There would not be the expense of bringing her over. She is a widow. I am a widower.'

'I do not know how it would be regarded,' said de Puebla.'But it can be put to the Sovereigns.'

'We could marry almost immediately. I have always held the Princess Katharine in high regard.'

Why, thought de Puebla, she could be in childbed before the year is out . . . she might manage even that. No time wasted between the birth of the little Princess and the birth of the next child even though there had to be a change of queens. Even by de Puebla's standards there was something very cynical about this king.

'Well?' said the King.

'I will put the notion to the Sovereigns without delay.'

'Do that,' said the King. 'We do not wish for unnecessary delay.'

De Puebla could not resist the chance to break the news to Katharine. Moreover he felt that by so doing he might ingratiate himself with her. He wanted to assure her that he was working for her, so he called on her.

'My lady Princess,' he said, 'I have news which I thought I should impart to you without delay. I have this day written to your noble parents.'

'Written of me?' she asked, growing pale.

'Yes, at the request of King Henry.'

'Of what does he wish them to know?'

'He is sending them a proposition. He is asking for your hand . . .'

'For Prince Henry, I know. That has been decided.'

'No . . . for himself.'

Katharine stared at him. She could not have heard correctly.

'The King . . .'

' 'Tis so. The King would make you his queen . . . without delay.'

'I can't believe this. The Queen has not been dead two months.'

'The King is in a hurry.' He came closer to her. 'He is obsessed by the need to get heirs. Elizabeth gave him several but too many died. He wants you who are young and strong to take the place of the Queen in his bed.'

De Puebla was smiling in a way which nauseated her. Horrible pictures sprang into her mind . . . images of something she did not understand and which made her uneasy, more than that—terrified her.

'No,' she said. 'No. I shall never agree.'

'I have been ordered by the King to write to your parents.'

'Oh no, no,' she cried. 'Not that . . . anything but that . . .'

'I believe Queen Isabella has decided you shall have Prince Henry. My Princess, when I hear from her I shall come straight to you. I thought it best to warn you . . . that you may be prepared.'

She stood staring straight before her and de Puebla, bowing low, asked leave to retire.

Poor girl! If the Sovereigns decided it would be expedient for her to take old Henry she would have to. And he fancied Ferdinand would rather like the idea of seeing his daughter Queen of England now . . . even though he would have to pay the second half of the dowry.

When she was alone Katharine went to her apartments and shut herself in. Doña Elvira tried to discover what ailed her but she would tell no one. She wanted to be alone with her horror.

Fervently she prayed, calling on God to save her, calling on her mother to come to her aid.

The days began to pass slowly.

Whenever she was in the company of the King, which she thanked God was rarely, she saw his eyes on her. They were not lascivious, speculative rather, as though he were assessing how fit she was to bear children. She compared him with Arthur and weeping afresh for her young husband, she longed above everything else for home, to be able to tell her mother of her fears, to see those dear kind eyes filled with understanding. If she could but see her mother, explain to her, she was sure that no matter how advantageous this marriage would be to Spain, Isabella would never allow it to take place.

What if she wrote to her mother? But de Puebla had told her in confidence. Her father might see the letter. Henry might learn that she begged not to be married to him. She could visualize all sorts of dire results; and she decided that nothing could be done but hope and pray.

Henry himself was restive. He was not well and the arrogance of his young son irritated him now and then. He should of course be grateful for having such a son who was so suited to being a king; but sometimes the boy behaved as though he were already one and he wondered whether young Henry was looking forward with a little too much zeal to the day when he would ascend the throne. Sometimes those rather small but intensely alert blue eyes would be caught studying his father as though, thought the King, he were summing up my ability to cling to life, and assessing how many more years were left to him.

The prospect of a crown was too glittering for a young boy of Henry's temperament to reconcile himself to waiting patiently until it could be justly put upon his head.

The King gave a great deal of thought to his son and the Prince of Wales was not the least of his anxieties. The boy had to be kept on a firm rein and the King fervently prayed that more years might be granted him so that he did not leave the country in the hands of this exuberant boy until he had attained some maturity.

The King had dismissed John Skelton from the Prince's household for he had come to believe that the poet tutor had a bad influence on the Prince. In a way the King admired Skelton. He was a poet of some ability and above all he was a fearless man. He had shown that in his verses about the Court which he had portrayed quite derisively. But Henry believed he was too worldly to be the daily companion of a young impressionable boy, and fancied he had probably already initiated the Prince into the enjoyment of pleasure between the sexes and that, unlike in his own case, these pleasures would be very much to young Henry's taste.

Well, Skelton had gone; Henry did not want to be unjust to any man. He had no desire to be harsh and rarely acted so except when common sense demanded it. So although Skelton had lost his post as tutor to the Prince of Wales he was given the living of Diss in Norfolk and in addition to this Henry gave him forty shillings a year in recognition of his service in the royal household. Therefore Skelton had done rather well for himself, for the pension added to his stipend put him in a position to be envied by other less fortunate priests.

Skelton had settled down to write more scandalous poems and young Henry had a new tutor, William Hone. The Prince had greeted the change with a certain resentment. If he had been a little older and more sure of himself there would have been open rebellion, the King believed; and it was one of the factors which added to his uneasiness.

Hone was a meek man. Perhaps the difference from Skelton was too marked, and young Henry became quickly reconciled because he found William Hone very easy to handle.

The fact was young Henry was finding people generally easy to handle—largely, the King suspected, because those around him had their eyes on the future. They would be thinking: How much longer is the old lion going to last? Then it will be the young cub's turn. Therefore, wise far-seeing young men that they were, they made sure to keep in the prospective King's good graces.

It was an uneasy situation and one entirely distasteful to the King but he was too much of a realist not to see that it could not be otherwise.

He would have to content himself with keeping an eye on his son and when he thought a man was too dangerous—as in the case of Skelton—discreetly getting rid of him.

He often considered the young men who were the Prince's particular friends. There was Charles Brandon . . . something of a rake and five years Henry's senior which was a matter for some concern. Brandon was making Henry grow up too quickly. He was turning the young Prince into a sophisticate . . . and he not twelve years old yet! There was a world of difference between twelve and seventeen but Brandon had been brought to Court because of the gratitude Henry owed his father. The King liked to reward those who had been with him at Bosworth Field where Brandon's father had been his standard bearer and had died standing steadfastly with Henry. So Charles Brandon was there . . . at Court . . . young Henry's companion and confidant. But he must be watched . . . in spite of his father's loyal service on that decisive field of battle.

Then there was young Edward Neville—tall as Henry with the same fair skin and reddish hair, a fine boy, but of course belonging to one of those families who had made a great deal of trouble in the land. One who was descended from Warwick the Kingmaker would have to be watched.

Henry Courtenay was another boy. He was younger than Henry and was at Court because his mother was there, sister to the late Queen; but his father was now in the Tower on account of complicity with Suffolk which had resulted in the execution of Sir James Tyrrell. The late Queen had said that it was her duty to look after her Courtenay nephews and nieces. And Henry could not very well turn them away in view of their relationship to the Queen. Moreover, children should not be blamed for the sins of their fathers.

Yes, the King would have liked to make a change in those surrounding his son; but he had other matters on his mind now and he had at least sent Skelton away.

Perhaps he was too sensitive about his son's ambitions. After all, the boy had to be brought up to kingship. There was some small comfort in the fact that he knew he would inherit the throne. That was so much more to be desired than coming to it suddenly. No, young Henry was preparing himself for the role and the King should be pleased that he took to it with such alacrity.

Pray God he himself could live for a few more years until Henry was of a sober age. The King had no doubt that with maturity would come some suppression of that egoism which was so much a part of his son's nature. All young men could be unwise. He will settle to it, thought the King. He just needs a firm hand now.

The sound of voices below broke into his reverie and, going to the window, he saw a group of young people at play. He was alert immediately because he caught sight of young Henry among them. His son was on horseback for the game—as most games played by the boys—was a military as well as an equestrian exercise. Henry stood out among them—although he was younger than most. The King could not repress his parental pride. He will soon be taller than I am, he thought, half resentfully, half fondly. And the boy glowed with health as his father had never done.

He would look the part, and he would play it to the full, but would he have the stability, the cunning . . . the King reproached himself. Young Henry was but a boy yet. The correct training, the moulding, the watchfulness would shape him into the sort of king his father wanted him to be and whom the country needed.

The game was that which was a favourite of the young: quintain. On a pivot stood a figure in the form of a knight in armour. It was life-sized and fixed to one hand was a sandbag. The player must ride at full gallop to the figure, attack it and retreat before the arm shot up when the sandbag could hit the rider. Like all such games there was a strong element of danger in it, for the rider who was not quick enough in getting away could receive such a blow from the sandbag as would unseat him, and there had been accidents—one or two fatal.

Although the King was nervous about his son's taking part in dangerous games he knew that he must do so; and this favourite one of quintain would not have interested the boys at all but for the danger they had to avoid.

He watched them for a while. He noted that young Henry had more turns than the others, that the applause which greeted his successes was more vociferous than that awarded to the others.

Inevitable, thought the King. But I must be watchful of him. If I had another son . . .

His expression lightened. Katharine was here . . . on the spot, and if there were objections he would impress on his ministers the need for another male heir. It is never wise to have but one. Henry seemed healthy but let them remember the Black Prince and the disaster his death had brought with the accession of the boy Richard.

Katharine had not been tested for fertility yet, and he had to be thankful that she had not, for if the union with Arthur had been consummated that might have made marriage with him too distasteful to be accepted. But as it was he saw no reason why she should not be his wife. She had married his son it was true, but it had been no physical marriage.

He had hopes of Ferdinand. Of Isabella he was not so sure.

Even as he watched his son at play he heard the sounds of approaching hoofbeats and glancing away from the game in the opposite direction he saw that the visitor was de Puebla and he guessed that the Spaniard brought news from his Sovereigns.

A faint pulse beat in his temple. He found that he was quite excited. There should be as little delay as possible. There would be a lavish wedding to satisfy the people's love of ceremony . . . and then . . . the consummation and the results.

One of his squires was at the door to tell him that Dr. de Puebla was below and seeking an audience.

'I will see him now,' said the King.

De Puebla came in and bowed. He looked grave and knowing the man well the King's spirits sank. There were going to be obstacles. That much was apparent.

'You have heard from the King and Queen?' asked the King.

'My lord, I have heard from Queen Isabella.'

The King was even more dismayed. It was from that quarter that he expected opposition. Ferdinand was much more likely to agree if the match was advantageous enough. Isabella was too emotional and feminine, too much the doting mother, which was strange in a woman of her ambitions and abilities. And Isabella was Castile and Ferdinand Aragon, and Castile was the more important. Ferdinand in a way owed his greatness to Isabella and loving wife and mother though she was, Isabella never forgot it.

'She refuses sanction for your marriage with the Infanta,' said de Puebla.

'Refuses? But she must see the advantages.'

'She says it is against the laws of nature. The Pope would not agree.'

'The Pope will agree if we explain to him his need to do so,' said Henry tersely.

'But Isabella will doubtless explain his need not to grant a dispensation,' said de Puebla slyly.

Henry disliked the man although it was to his advantage to cultivate him. He was a good go-between, serving Henry almost as much as the Sovereigns. It was for this reason that he had done so well in England and that his rival had been recalled.

'My lord,' went on de Puebla, 'the Queen is very firm. She says no to such a marriage. She is surprised that it should be suggested.'

'And Ferdinand?'

'You know, my lord, that he could not act without Isabella.'

Henry nodded.

'Perhaps we should not give up hope. But I deplore the wasting of time.'

De Puebla smiled again with that sly look. 'None could accuse you, my lord, of doing that. I must tell you truly that the tone of Queen Isabella's letter is very strong. I know my mistress well. She is not pleased that the possibility of marriage should even have been suggested. She says that Katharine is to marry the Prince of Wales and she desires that the binding ceremony of betrothal takes place without delay. If this is not done she demands the return of the half of the dowry which was sent on Katharine's marriage to Prince Arthur.'

Henry was silent. He was astute enough to know that in asking for the hand of Katharine so soon after his wife's death he had made a grave error.

De Puebla went on: 'The Queen, however, understands your need for a wife and she would draw your attention to the recently widowed Queen of Naples.'

'The Queen of Naples?'

'Young, comely . . . and a queen,' said de Puebla.

Henry was silent and de Puebla went on: 'If you should need my services, Sire, I should be happy to give them.'

'Thank you,' murmured the King. He felt old and tired. But he was not one to waste time in regrets.

Already his mind had turned from Katharine of Aragon to the Queen of Naples.

When de Puebla presented himself to Katharine a few days after his audience with the King he came to her smiling enigmatically. He felt the good news would be more appreciated if she suffered a few moments of anxiety first.

'You have news from my mother?' cried Katharine.

'My lady, I have indeed such news.'

He paused, allowing a smile to creep slowly across his face. She was waiting breathlessly and he realized he could delay no longer.

'The Queen, your noble mother, refused to allow a match between you and the King.'

Overcome by relief, Katharine covered her face with her hands. She should have known. How she thanked God for her beloved mother! While she was there, steadfast and caring, there could be little to fear.

'She is, however, eager for a binding contract between you and the Prince of Wales and is insisting that this be settled within the next few months.'

Katharine could not speak. The Prince of Wales seemed a good prospect compared with his father; but mainly she supposed because marriage with him must necessarily be postponed until he was of a marriageable age. He was not quite twelve so there would be at least two years' freedom. Oh, this was good news indeed.

'I am aware that you are pleased with your mother's refusal.'

'I am so recently widowed. I have no wish to marry again . . . yet.'

'You will have to wait a while for the Prince to grow up,' de Puebla was smiling. He had a little commission from the King and he was wondering how best he could put it to Katharine. He went on: 'Your mother has suggested that the young Queen of Naples would be a suitable match for the King. She is recently widowed and some twenty-seven years of age.'

'She would be more suitable in age than I, most certainly.'

'Your mother would expect you to write a note of condolence

to the Queen of Naples. She has just lost her husband and you, so recently widowed yourself, would understand her melancholy.'

'I will of course do so.'

'That is good. And it shall be delivered into the hands of the Queen of Naples herself.'

'Was that my mother's only request?'

'Yes. But I have letters from her for you.'

Katharine reached out to seize them eagerly and after handing them to her de Puebla bowed himself out.

Eagerly she read the letters. They assured her of her mother's love and care. Isabella never ceased to think of her although so many miles divided them. She would soon be the betrothed of the Prince of Wales, and one day, Queen of England. She must always remember that she was Spanish by origin even though by marriage she became English. She must never forget that her mother thought of her constantly, cared for her and was working all the time for her good.

Katharine kissed the letters; re-read them many times, wrote her letter to the Queen of Naples and settled down to enjoy her feelings of immense relief.

The King received the messengers immediately on their return from Naples. They had had instructions that letters written by the Princess Katharine were to be delivered into the hands of no one but the Queen.

Now they returned with an account of what they had seen.

'Tell me of the Queen,' said Henry, coming straight to the point. 'She is twenty-seven years of age, I know. Does she look so? Is she comely?'

'She looks young for her age, Sire, and she is comely. But it was not easy to see for every time we were in her presence she wore a great mantle which revealed only her face. But she appeared to be handsome . . . as far as we could see.'

'Is she tall or short?'

'My lord, we could not see her feet and the height of her shoes. From what we did see it would appear she is of middle height.'

'Tell me how was her skin? Not blotched or marked?'

'No, my lord. Fair and clear . . . as far as we could see.'

'What colour hair?'

'Judging by what we could see—and the colour of her brows—it would be brown. Her eyes are brown . . . with a touch of grey.'

'Her teeth?'

'Fair and clear and well set. Her lips round and thickish. As for her nose . . .'

They hesitated and the King said quickly: 'Yes, yes, her nose?'

'It is a little rising in the middle and a little coming and bowing at the end. She is well nosed.'

'Ah,' said the King. 'But what of her breasts?'

'They are somewhat great and full, my lord. They are well trussed up after the fashion of the country which makes them seem fuller than they are in truth and her neck appears shorter.'

'Has she hair on her lips?'

'No, my lord.'

'Tell me, did you get near enough to discover whether her breath was sweet?'

'We believe so, my lord.'

'Did you speak with her after she had fasted?'

'We could not come to her at such time, my lord, nor could we have been sure that she had fasted. We can only say that her skin was fair and clear and we detected no unpleasant odours in her presence.'

'Ah,' said the King. 'She seems worthy.'

He dismissed the ambassadors and thought about the new wife he would have.

She must be possessed of all the good qualities he had been so eager to confirm. He had to get children and he could so easily find the process repulsive if his new wife failed to comply with the necessary requirements. Queen Elizabeth had been one of the most beautiful women in the country and he had felt no over-whelming desire; but he had always done his duty although he had to confess that he experienced a certain relief when his Queen was pregnant and the need for marital practices was removed.

And now . . . this new wife. The Queen of Naples. Naples was worth a good deal. He would go ahead with proposals for the marriage. He was sure that the people of Naples would be delighted to ally itself with England, which under its wise king was fast becoming a power on the European scene.

But there were other ambassadors whose account was even more important to Henry than his wife's appearance. They had done their work well and were eager to tell him of their findings.

The news they brought was disquieting. Ferdinand had acted quickly on the death of the King of Naples and the Queen was now of very little importance. Her property had been confiscated and she was left with very little. She depended on Ferdinand of Aragon for the small income she received.

Henry sweated with horror when he heard this report. Had Isabella made the suggestion ironically—a little mischievously? He knew he had a reputation for being grasping and setting great store on possessions. He had just made up his mind that the Queen of Naples would do very well as the next Queen of England and had in fact been on the point of drafting out a request for her hand.

This changed everything.

Clear of skin and sweet of breath the Queen of Naples might be, but if she was penniless and her title was an empty one, she was no fit bride for Henry Tudor.

It was disappointing. Two brides lost in a very short time.

But he was not one to despair. The hunt for the new Queen of England would go on.

There was now no longer any excuse for delay. The betrothal ceremony was to take place and that was binding. Katharine must accept it; it was what she must take if she were to escape from marriage to the King.

There were several reasons why she must accept her fate besides that it was the wish of her parents. She was living in Durham House and she often wondered how she was going to find the money to pay her servants. Poverty made her feel that she was an exile. She had never experienced the lack of money before she came to England. Indeed she had never thought of money. It was different now. Her parents sent her nothing. Why should they? They had paid one hundred thousand crowns as the first part of her dowry and would pay the other half after her marriage. They were not going to send more which would be used by Henry. It was his duty now to make sure that his son's widow had adequate funds.

But Henry was not one to part easily with money and there was nothing coming from him. The gowns which she had brought with her from Spain were beginning to lose their freshness and some were even becoming threadbare, but the King considered that no concern of his. He had made a good proposition to her parents and it had been rejected. At the moment she was merely the widow of the Prince of Wales with a dowry only half of which had been paid and over that her parents were haggling.

Katharine was beginning to see that only by becoming the prospective wife of the heir to the throne could she expect to live in comfort.

Therefore, she must forget that she had no great desire for this alliance, but the main reason was that her partner in it was only a boy.

On the other hand Henry was looking forward to the ceremony. He was always delighted by such and when he was the centre of them his pleasure was greatly increased.

Margaret was subdued at this time. She had been boastful and arrogant and had never lost an opportunity of scoring over him, but now the prospect of going into Scotland was alarming her. She had grown quiet, less demanding; and Henry felt a little sorry for her. How glad he was that as King-to-be he would stay in his own country, at his own Court, surrounded by those who made much of him. That they did so because they feared to do otherwise he knew in his heart, but he liked that, too. One of the best things in life was power. He had known that when he was a baby, holding sway over Anne Oxenbrigge because she loved him. But power which came through fear was equally exciting and desirable.

Yes, Henry was very pleased. How delighted Katharine must be. Poor girl! She had thought she was well set up in life when she married Arthur. But Henry secretly believed she had compared the two brothers and if she had, she must have known how much more attractive Henry was.

But she had seemed to like Arthur. Ah, but that was because she had not known then that there might be a chance of getting Henry.

Again he wished he were older. 'The years seem as though they'll never pass,' he commented to Charles Brandon who as a mature seventeen-year-old replied that they went fast enough for him.

Perhaps they did. He had reached the golden age. When I am seventeen where shall I be? wondered Henry.

Margaret came to see him. Her departure for Scotland was imminent and she wanted this brash brother of hers, of whom she was exceedingly jealous, mainly because he was to stay in England, to lose a little of his assurance.

He looked splendid, of course he did. He had good looks and in spite of his youth a certain stature. He was taller than all of his companions who were of his age, and he was, of course, too sure of himself. It would give her satisfaction to prick that conceit if it were possible, it would be a little balm to her sorrow. Besides, she told herself virtuously, it would be good for Henry.

'So . . . our boy is going to be a bridegroom,' she said. 'Ah, but that won't be for a while will it? Our boy has to grow up first.'

'At least I'll stay here in England. I haven't to go to some bleak dour old country.'

As usual they sought and found the other's most vulnerable spot.

'I believe my husband eagerly awaits me,' said Margaret.

'No doubt he will be there to greet you if he can spare the time from his mistresses.'

'I shall know how to deal with them.'

'Make sure they do not know how to deal with you.'

'I will come to my brother for advice. He is so knowledgeable, being eleven years of age he knows everything.'

'I am twelve.'

'Not for a few days.'

'I am mistaken for older.'

'Who makes that mistake? Everybody knows when our noble heir to the throne was born. They all mourn the loss of Arthur. He was the one who was the real Prince of Wales.'

'People seem to think I am more suitable for a king,' said Henry almost modestly.

'Because you're here . . . that's why. They loved poor Arthur. We all did. Particularly Katharine.'

'Katharine will have a new husband now.'

'Poor Katharine. She cannot like the change to a little boy.'

'How do you know?'

'I listen. She has asked her mother to take her away from here . . . to take her home . . . so that she doesn't have to marry you.'

'She wants to marry me.'

'Oh no, she does not. I know she has written to her mother asking to be taken home.'

His eyes narrowed. It couldn't be true. He was feeling gallant. He would have smiled at her, pressed her hand reassuringly. He liked to play the noble knight. That was what he had been taught to believe in. Chivalry. It was so necessary to knighthood. He had been thinking that he was rescuing Katharine from poverty at

Durham House, making her important because of her alliance with him . . . and all the time she was writing to her mother begging to be taken home!

He would have liked to appear in her eyes as the chivalric knight who was going to rescue her from poverty and uncertainty, who was going to protect her from her fate. It should all have been very much in the knightly tradition and she had spoilt it all by writing to her mother and begging her to take her away.

She was seventeen years old. It was a mature age of course but that had not deterred him. He had cast his eyes on many a woman of her age who had been ready to fondle him. Charles Brandon had talked to him of his adventures with women and Charles had already a reputation of being a rake.

So it was not her age. And to think that he . . . Henry the Prince of Wales, King-to-be, did not appear in an attractive light to this woman who was so sorely in need of his protection.

His grandmother had explained to him how important the ceremony was. She often talked to him in place of his father who was too busy to do so. His father believed that the Countess of Richmond, being a woman and an extremely clever one, would understand children better than he did.

She was fifty-eight years old, for she had been barely fourteen when her son Henry Tudor had been born so that there was not a great difference in their ages. She seemed very old to Young Henry; she was small and thin and very austere looking; and rarely wore anything but the black and white of a nun. She was very religious, attended Mass five times a day, and spent a great time on her knees praying although she confessed that this resulted in excruciating back pains.

Skelton had said ironically: 'That will increase her reward in Heaven.' And Henry had laughed as he always had laughed with Skelton. But he was in awe of his grandmother all the same.

Yet she adored him. He sensed that and he loved her for it. Not that she actually put her adoration into words. That would not have been her way. But her assiduous care for him and the manner in which she looked at him—when she thought he was not aware of it—betrayed her. He was strong, healthy and vigorous and she liked it. Of course Arthur had been something of a paragon with his quiet and studious ways, but he had made them anxious in a way he, Henry, never had.

His grandmother's piety impressed the people although Henry

perceived that they did not greatly like her. It was the same with his father. Serious-minded men knew that Henry the Seventh had done a great deal for the country's prosperity, but they did not like him all the same.

Henry was constantly hearing about his maternal grandfather, Edward the Fourth. There was a king they liked. He had heard the whispered comments of those who had grandparents old enough to remember. 'When he came riding through the town the citizens hid their daughters.'

There was a king. Large, handsome and romantic.

Henry thought that when he was a king he would like to resemble his maternal grandfather rather than his father.

Meanwhile he was only twelve years old and he had to attend his betrothal to his brother's widow.

His grandmother explained to him. 'This betrothal will be *per verba de presenti* which means that it is binding. In fact some of the marriage service will be included in the ceremony.'

'So,' said Henry, 'I shall be married to Katharine of Aragon.'

'No, not exactly married. But you will have gone through this form of betrothal.'

'Does it mean that we shall most certainly be married later?'

His grandmother hesitated. She knew what was in the King's mind and that he was determined to leave a loophole of escape so that he might keep the Spanish Sovereigns on tenterhooks— and at the same time keep that part of the dowry which they had already paid.

Henry noticed her hesitation and was nonplussed. 'Why do we go through with such a ceremony if it is not really a marriage?' he demanded.

'The Spaniards want it.'

'Ah, they think I am a desirable husband, do they?'

His grandmother gave one of her wintry smiles which sat oddly on her austere features.

'They know, my boy,' she said firmly, 'that you are one of the most desirable *partis* in the whole of Europe.'

'Who are the others equally so?' cried Henry, who could not bear competition without the immediate desire to eliminate it.

'Oh, we cannot go into that,' said his grandmother. 'There are a few princes with hopes of inheritance. But you will be the King of England.'

Her face darkened for she thought immediately that he could only be so on the death of his father and her love for her son was almost fanatical and far exceeded even that she felt for her grandchildren.

Henry watched her thoughtfully. He was longing for the day when the crown would be placed on his head; but he realized that it should not be just yet. If it were now there would be too many surrounding him telling him what to do. He wanted that day to come when he would be an unshackled king—when everyone— even his grandmother—must bow to his word. Alas, that day had not yet come; and here he was again chafing against the slothful passage of time.

He was in a sullen mood when he arrrived at the Bishop's House in Fleet Street where the formal betrothal was to take place. It did not diminish even when he saw Katharine looking beautiful in an elegant dress which was not quite in the style to which he was accustomed and all the more attractive for that. He couldn't help thinking that the hooped petticoat over which the dress fell in alluring folds was interesting, just as the cardinal's hat she had worn on their first meeting had been.

She intrigued him in a way because she was different from the other ladies of the Court; he had liked the way she had spoken English and he had fancied that she had liked him very much when she had first come. He knew that she was anxious about her future and that quite a number of her attendants were too, for he had made a point of discovering all about her that her servants could tell him and the latter always liked to have an answer for him. He knew for instance that it was a long time since she had had a new dress and even this one she was wearing for such an important ceremony was one she had brought with her from Spain.

His father was present with his grandmother. They both looked stern and serious. He would have liked to say: 'I will not betroth myself to this Princess who prefers her own Court of Spain to mine.'

To mine! His father would be angry at that. He had reminded him once or twice that he was not King yet.

He took Katharine's right hand and said the lines he had had to learn off by heart to make sure that he did not leave out anything and that he said them in the right manner.

He rejoiced, he said, to contract matrimony with Katharine and to have her for his wife, forsaking all others during the term of their lives.

Katharine had turned to him and she was saying the same thing in rather halting English which in a way was endearing.

Then she smiled at him, a little fearfully, almost appealingly and all his rancour vanished.

She was beautiful; he liked her maturity; more fervently than ever he wished he were seventeen. Alas, he was a few days from twelve and he must needs wait, but his feelings of chivalry had overcome his resentment. He was foolish to listen to Margaret. She was just annoyed because she had to go away to Scotland.

Katharine was his affianced wife; she looked to him for protection, and chivalrous knight that he was, she should not look in vain.

Henry's moods changed quickly and it was in one of pride and joy that hand in hand with Katharine he emerged from the Bishop's House into the sunshine of Fleet Street on that June day.

THE PRINCE
DISCOVERS HIS
CONSCIENCE

A few days later another important event occurred. This was the departure of the Princess Margaret—now known as the Queen of Scotland. On that lovely June day the calvacade set out from Richmond Palace and beside Margaret rode the King. The people flocked into the streets to cheer the pretty Princess as she took her farewell of her country.

She was indeed charming, dressed in green velvet and seated on a white palfrey, and her entourage was magnificent. It was one of those occasions when Dudley and Empson had persuaded the King that to be parsimonious about the Princess' equipage would be a false economy. They must remember that it was a political occasion and the Scots must realize that the King of England—miser though he might be called—was very rich indeed.

Margaret revelled in the splendour. If she were a little apprehensive about meeting her future husband she forgot that in the pleasure of the moment. She had a litter covered with gold, trimmed with silk and gold fringe, and embroidered with the arms of England; and the men who carried the litter had been provided with new special livery in green and black. She had a chariot lined with bear skins and the trappings of the horses and the hammer cloths were made of black and crimson velvet. Lords, knights and ladies accompanied her, all splendidly attired.

Prince Henry was accompanying the party as far as Colley Weston where he and his father would say goodbye to Margaret after they had stayed a few days at the home of Margaret, Countess of Richmond, who had left the Court a little beforehand so that she might be in her home to greet them when they arrived.

The Princess Margaret was glad that her brother was present so that he could see all the splendour of her equipment and realize that he was not the only important member of the household.

She was amused, contemplating his envy. But then of course he would remember that there would be far more splendid occasions in store for him; and once he was King—and that would mean that he had escaped from his father's restraining hands—the money so carefully preserved by their father would doubtless be recklessly spent.

But she found there was little time to gloat over Henry's envy; at the moment she was at the centre of events and she must enjoy every minute.

At Colley Weston in Northamptonshire her grandmother was waiting to receive the party. She embraced her son with that emotion which neither of them showed for anyone else. And the Countess then turned to her granddaughter and there was a look of pride in her eyes as they rested on the beautiful girl.

She was congratulating herself that the Tudors were strong now. She wished that the King could cast aside his uncertainty. Nothing could come against them. They had a fine Prince of Wales. It was a pity that they had not another boy just in case, but it seemed ridiculous to imagine that anything could happen to Henry. Well, the King must remarry soon and if he had another son . . .

But this was Margaret's matter; and very satisfactory it was that she should go into Scotland for the union should assure peace at the Borders.

In due course Margaret said goodbye to her family. The King gave her his blessing and warned her to take every care in the manner in which she conducted herself at her husband's Court. She must remember always that she was her father's daughter and that it was her duty to prevent trouble arising to his detriment.

Margaret, a little tearful now at the parting, was longing nevertheless to be free from restraint; she promised that she would remember what her father had said and that he could rely on her to do all that she could for his good.

The journey through England was exhilarating. Everywhere she was greeted with affection and admiration. She smiled and waved and when she could, talked to the people; she revelled in the fine garments which had been provided for her, she lingered as long as possible for she was in no hurry to end this triumphant journey. The people loved her and she loved the people; their admiration made her eyes sparkle and brought bright colour to her cheeks making her more beautiful than ever. If her father could have seen her he would have agreed that Dudley and Empson were right. It was money well spent.

So she travelled northwards. In the city of York there were special celebrations which started from the moment when the gates were flung open to welcome her. She began her stay by attending Mass and then receiving the nobility who had gathered there to await her arrival.

There were banquets and as she was noted for her skill in dancing many balls were held in her honour. Life was wonderful and she was able to push aside that faint apprehension which attacked her from time to time when she thought of crossing the Border into that land which she had heard—and which her brother Henry had said—was dour and populated by barbarians.

And in due course she came to that wild border country and she was told: 'My lady, you have now left England. This is the country of which you are Queen.'

She looked around her. She would not have known that she had crossed a border if she had not been told it was so, for the grass and trees and lanes were similar to those of England. But when they arrived at Lammermuir and the local nobility came to greet her, she noticed a difference. They stared more openly; they did not bow with the same grace; their clothes were not quite so fine and though made of good materials they lacked a certain elegance.

It was sad to say goodbye to the English noblemen who had accompanied her and her exuberance began to fade a little, but she was glad to move on from Lammermuir and when she reached Fastcastle and was warmly welcomed by Lord and Lady Home she felt her spirits lift a little. The stay was brief, however, and after one night they were on their way to Haddington.

The King, impatient to see his bride, was travelling to Dalkeith, and Margaret, having heard that she would no doubt meet her husband there, was determined to be prepared. She had changed into her most becoming dress and had asked her attendant Lady Guildford twenty times how she looked. Her heart was beating wildly; the next hour could be the most important of the whole journey. This would decide her future.

She stood in her apartment waiting. From the bustle below she knew that he had arrived. She knew that he was coming nearer. At any moment now.

The door was opened and a man stood on the threshold.

There was colour in his cheeks and his eyes shone with excitement. They surveyed each other quickly . . . and then they were smiling.

She saw a handsome man, with dark auburn hair and hazel eyes, well-shaped features, handsome bearing and above all an indefinable charm.

He saw a beautiful young girl and he was very susceptible to female beauty. She was enchanting—pretty, young, fresh and eager to please—all this and the daughter of Henry Tudor.

This was a happy moment for Scotland and its King.

He took her hand and kissed it; while he held it to his lips their eyes met and it was almost a look of understanding which passed between them.

Then he bowed and turned to her attendants, kissing the ladies and speaking to the men.

Conveying a certain relief as though to say: Now I have done my duty and I can return to pleasure, he came back to Margaret.

'At last,' he said, 'you have come to me. I began to fear that you never would.'

'But we have been betrothed for a long time.'

'It seems an age . . . but now you are here. Do you think that you can love me?'

'Oh yes. I wondered whether you were the handsomest king in the world.'

'Is that what you heard of me?'

'It was.'

He grimaced. 'I am glad I did not know it. I should have been most fearful of disappointing you.'

'Oh you do not. They spoke truth.'

'And they told me you were the most beautiful of princesses and they spoke truth also.'

'Oh it has all ended so happily.'

'By sweet St. Ninian, my Queen, it is only beginning.'

He was thinking: She is charming. It will not be difficult. I should count myself lucky.

But he laughed ironically at the thought. For he could not rid himself of memories of that other Margaret. Of all his mistresses Margaret Drummond had been his favourite. But she was dead . . . foully murdered by some person or persons unknown. He would never forget Margaret. He had had countless other mistresses but Margaret had been all that he could have wished in a woman. Had she been his wife he would have been faithful to her . . . he was sure of that though no one else would believe it.

It had been said of him that he would never marry while Margaret Drummond was with him. And one morning she with her two sisters was found dead. They had been poisoned. By whom? No one had ever discovered or if they had discovered had not disclosed.

It might have been some of his ministers who had thought her influence on him was too strong; it might have been some jealous woman . . .

Who could say? But the fact remained that Margaret was dead and here was another in her place.

He was smiling at her, pressing her hand. She was ready to be loved, he could see that. Very young but ready, very ready.

He was fortunate. He must remember that. For all that latent passion which he as a connoisseur of women could detect, there was an innocence about her, a romanticism which perhaps most girls of her age would have before they came into contact with the world.

In time she would discover. Janet Kennedy would see to that and he doubted he would be ready to give up Janet for a pretty young girl, delightful though she might be.

But that was for the future. Perhaps the new Queen of Scotland could be made to accept the inevitable.

All James must concern himself with now was to conduct his bride to Holyrood where in the church of that palace the ceremony of their marriage would take place.

Katharine's position had changed. As the future Queen of England she could no longer live in obscurity. She would come to Court and as it was no exaggeration to say that the clothes which she had brought with her from Spain were decidedly shabby, the King was obliged, though reluctantly, to make her an allowance.

Katharine's first need was to pay her servants and when that was done—for their wages were very much in arrears—there was not a great deal left for clothes. But still it was an improvement and the future seemed a little more secure. In two or three years she should be truly married to the Prince of Wales and then the King must give her an adequate allowance.

She had written to her mother and what joy it had been to receive a reply in that dear and familiar handwriting. The words were warm and loving. Katharine must never doubt that her mother watched over her and was determined to do everything in her power to promote her well-being. She would see that the best thing that could happen to her, since Prince Arthur was dead, was marriage with the new Prince of Wales. And Katharine being her own good and docile daughter would realize that such a marriage would be to Spain's advantage. Isabella was sorry that Katharine had such difficulty in meeting the needs of her household. 'We cannot send you money, dear daughter. We need all we have for the war. It is swallowing up far more than we anticipated. Moreover it is the duty of your future father-in-law to make you an adequate allowance. He is reputed to be extremely rich. He doubtless would like us to support you, but this is a matter of state, dear daughter, and I am sure your father would agree with me that it would be foolish of us—even if we had the means—to take over the commitments of the King of England. Be patient, dear daughter, and know that your mother loves you and will always watch over you.'

Katharine wept when she read that letter. She must not complain. She was the most fortunate of daughters to possess such a mother.

The idea came to her that if she pawned her jewellery it should fetch a great deal. It was part of her dowry and the King had said that she should wear her jewellery and de Puebla had hinted that the King was in due course going to reject it as part of the dowry.

Doña Elvira was horrified at the idea of pawning the jewellery.

'I must pay my servants,' cried Katharine. 'And I cannot appear at Court in threadbare gowns.'

'But this is the dowry you will bring to your husband.'

'My late husband's revenues have not come to me. The King has taken them. I have nothing but the King's small allowance. I must do something. When I am married to the Prince I shall be able to redeem the jewels.'

Doña Elvira shrugged her shoulders.

It was all very bewildering and it was true that Katharine must find money somewhere.

It will pass, thought Katharine. In two . . . perhaps three years I shall be married. Then all will be well. As my mother says I must be patient.

I will, she thought. I can be because I know that she is there . . . always loving and kind and watching over me.

De Puebla called at Durham House. Looking very sombre he asked for an immediate audience with the Princess.

As soon as he came into her presence Katharine was filled with a terrible fear.

'What is wrong?' she cried.

'News from Spain,' he said.

'My mother . . .'

He nodded and was silent.

'News? What news? Tell me quickly.'

'My dear lady, you must prepare yourself for a great shock.'

'Is it my mother . . . my father . . . ?'

Again that nod and silence. It was more than Katharine could endure.

'It is my mother,' she said blankly. 'She is ill . . .'

He looked at her beseechingly. It was odd to see the sly de Puebla so moved.

Then he said clearly and with the greatest compassion in his voice: 'Queen Isabella is dead, my lady.'

'Dead!'

She was trying to grasp what this meant and at the same time trying not to, for she could not bear to contemplate a world without her mother.

De Puebla was saying: 'She had been ill for some time. The tertian fever it was said . . . and dropsy. Her last thoughts were for you . . . and your sisters.'

'Dear mother,' munnured Katharine. 'It cannot be . . . it *must* not be . . .'

'One of the last things she did was to have the Bull of Dispensation brought to her. She wanted to see it for herself. She wanted to assure herself that your betrothal to the Prince of Wales would go forward and none could dispute it.'

Katharine covered her face with her hands.

'I will send for your ladies,' said de Puebla. 'My lady, it grieves me to have to bring you such news.'

'I know,' said Katharine. 'Leave me . . . please. I would be alone.'

Alone! she thought. That is what I am now. She is gone. Alone . . . yes, alone in a hostile world.

Katharine was not the only one to be deeply affected by the death of Isabella. The King immediately realized what a difference this could make to his own position.

Without delay he sent for Empson and Dudley, those two who because of their wizardry with figures were more in his confidence than any others.

'I had thought, naturally,' he said to them when the three of them were alone, 'that Ferdinand's power would have been increased by the death of his wife.'

'Isabella was a shrewd woman. She loved Ferdinand as a husband—strange that such a woman could have such a feeling for her family—but as a ruler she was fully aware of his deficiencies.'

Henry nodded. 'And now Ferdinand has lost a great deal of that power which was his when his wife was alive.'

'For all her devotion to her family, she was always the one who held the power. She never forgot her position and was determined that it should not be passed on to Ferdinand.'

'Well, let us look at the facts,' said Henry. 'She is dead and she has appointed her daughter Juana Queen Proprietor, and Castile is settled on her and Philip her husband.'

'One can be sure that the Archduke will take every advantage of the position.'

'She does say until the majority of her grandson Charles.'

'That is some time yet. He cannot be more than four years old.'

'The Lady Katharine is not such a good match as we had first thought,' mused the King.

'No, her position has changed considerably. It is a pity that she is betrothed to the Prince.'

Henry was thoughtful. 'Oh,' he said, 'there are loopholes. I saw to that. I have a feeling that that marriage may not take place. I agreed to the ceremony, yes . . . because the Sovereigns were getting restive and there was the dowry to be considered, but it must necessarily be some time before a marriage could take place and a great deal can happen in that time. See how the position has changed now with the death of Isabella.'

'My lord, what is to be done?'

'I have no doubt,' said the King, 'that we shall put our heads together and discover how best to settle that matter. In the meantime I have decided that the Prince of Wales shall not go to Ludlow.'

His ministers looked at him in surprise. It was customary for the Princes of Wales to reside at Ludlow. The people of Wales expected it.

'I have decided,' went on the King, 'that there is much that the Prince of Wales must learn and he will do that best at my side. I want him to learn the art of kingship. I think he will learn well enough . . . in the right environment.'

The ministers nodded.

'And the commitment to the Lady Katharine?'

'Of that more later.'

The King sent for his son. Young Henry was not very pleased with his father. He had greatly looked forward to setting up his own household at Ludlow and he had been curtly informed that he was not to go there; his father believed that he could be more profitably engaged at his side. This was all very well, but at Ludlow Henry could have played at being King; at his father's side he was always of secondary importance and the King had a way of treating him as though he were still a boy—and was not always careful of his manner towards his son in the presence of others.

It seemed that the older he grew the more he chafed against the restraints of youth. He was nearly fourteen and two years had passed since his formal betrothal to Katharine of Aragon. He had been very interested in her naturally as she was his future wife, but he was not sure whether he was pleased about that or not. Sometimes he was, and sometimes he was not. He liked women very much. He talked about them incessantly with Charles Brandon and Lord Mountjoy. He had joined them in certain adventures—most illuminating and gratifying. There were many beautiful ladies at the Court and he liked to write verses about them and sometimes set them to music and strum them on his lute. All those about him declared he had a wonderful talent and he liked to think he had.

Well, he would be married very soon now—a year or two. Perhaps when he was fifteen. That would be an experience. He was not sure whether he wanted to marry Katharine or not. At times he did very much, when he thought of her poor and rather lonely, perhaps longing for the day when he would release her from her poverty and loneliness. He liked to think of coming to her rescue—true knight that he was—and in spite of the temptations of so many beautiful women—who were all eager to be honoured by the Prince of Wales, he would marry her. 'I gave you my promise,' he said in his fantasies about himself, 'and I will remain steadfast to you.'

Therefore when he heard what proposition the King had to lay before him, he was astonished and completely taken off his guard.

'My son,' said the King, 'you are aware of the change in Spanish affairs.'

'Yes, my lord,' answered the Prince.

'Ferdinand does not hold the same power since Queen Isabella died. When your brother married Katharine it was indeed the best of matches. Times change.'

The Prince listened intently. He knew that his father had behaved in a very parsimonious manner towards Katharine; he knew that she was always short of money. That was part of another of his fantasies. He had imagined himself showering riches on her at which she cried: 'You are the most wonderful of beings. I am the luckiest Princess in the world and quite unworthy of your greatness.' He was rather glad therefore that she was in this position. It made his gesture all the more wonderful.

'It is fortunate,' went on the King, 'that it was not in fact a true ceremony that was held in the Bishop's house.'

'But . . . it was like a marriage ceremony. We signed our names . . .'

'Henry, you must be able to adjust your thoughts. That is what being a good king means. If a marriage such as this one could bring no good to our country . . . and might bring harm . . . then the best thing possible is to repudiate it.'

'But how can we repudiate that which has in fact taken place, when there is evidence to prove it?'

'You have to disregard such sentiments if you are to keep the country prosperous and the crown on your head. This Spanish marriage is no longer necessary nor desirable to us.'

'But if it has already taken place.'

'It has not taken place. You are not married to the Lady Katharine and we are going to have another ceremony in which you repudiate that previous one.'

'My lord, it seems to me that in all honour . . .'

'What it seems to you, my son, is not important. She will understand for I believe her to be a sensible girl. Moreover she will know nothing of it . . . yet.'

'To repudiate a promise, my lord, and particularly one given so solemnly seems to me not to be in keeping with knightly honour.'

'Henry, you are obtuse. No more of this, you will obey my orders.'

'My lord . . .'

'Silence. Don't show your childishness.'

Henry disliked his father at that moment, for he knew that he would have to obey. He would have to do as they wanted. It was a reminder of his youth.

'We will settle this matter without delay,' said the King.

'You mean there will not be a ceremony like that other . . .'

'Of course there will not be. This is a secret matter. The Bishop of Winchester awaits us below.'

'What do you want me to do?' asked Henry sullenly.

'You will not have to learn your words. They will be handed to you. You will read them and then they will be signed in the presence of the Bishop.'

'I like it not . . .'

'It is not for you to like or dislike. You must make it clear now that you do not consider the contract with Katharine of Aragon valid and you will make a statement to this effect.'

Henry, his mouth tight and sullen, his little blue eyes veiled, followed his father down from the apartments to a room below the kitchens. There was no window in this room and Henry realized at once that the King was determined they should not be seen.

There were present Richard Bishop of Winchester, Giles Daubeney, Charles Somerset, Earl of Worcester, and the King's secretary.

They were all men, the Prince noticed, who had served his father well and before he came to the throne. Therefore he would be sure of their loyalty.

'Are we ready?' said the King.

It was agreed that they were.

Henry was told to stand before the company and a paper was thrust into his hand.

'Read,' commanded the King.

Henry started: 'Before you reverend lord and father in Christ, Richard Lord Bishop of Winchester, I Henry, Prince of Wales . . . declare that while of tender years and being to all knowledge below the age of manhood contracted a *de facto* marriage with her most Serene Highness Katharine daughter of the King of Spain and although that contract, because of my minority, is in itself already invalid, imperfect and of no force or effect nevertheless . . . I being on the verge of manhood declare that I do not intend in any way to approve, validate or ratify that pretended contract . . . Now in this present document induced by no force, trickery or prayer but willingly and freely and in no way compelled, I denounce the contract and dissent therefrom . . .'

He went on reading and his heart was saying: But I was forced. I was told I must do this. It is not my fault that I am breaking vows . . .

He had come to the end. The paper lay on a table and under the King's scrutiny they all signed after Henry had done so.

They came out into the sunshine. Young Henry was resentful. He did not feel that he had acted as a chivalrous knight.

Henry had lost a certain pleasure in himself. The perfect knight had broken his vows; he had acted in a way which the laws of chivalry would have condemned as debasing; and he had acted so because he had been afraid to do otherwise. He could not forget Katharine in her well-worn gowns looking to him, he fancied, with an appeal in her eyes. She had looked to him as her saviour and he had repudiated her.

It was not the role in which he saw himself. Usually he could lead his mind away from thoughts of disloyalty to himself. But there was the evidence in very fact; he had signed his name to that paper indicating that he did not consider himself bound to Katharine.

It was policy. His father had insisted and he had to obey his father who was more than an ordinary father; he was the King. A true knight obeyed his king without question. No, not when the case was a dishonourable one. Then a good and true knight rebelled. He served God first, the King second. Whichever way Henry looked at it he came up against his conscience.

It was the first time in his life that he realized what a strong force that was with him. He wanted to be above all other men and recognized to be so. He had little patience with the saints. He wanted to be a man. He must be the superior every time—in stature, in looks, in skill both mental and physical. He must excel at the joust; he was always to be the victor; he must win every battle against his adversaries. He must possess the best qualities of all his most illustrious ancestors. He must tower above them all in every way.

He wanted people to admire him. To look up to him. To say: There is a king victorious always, never failing in war . . . in peace . . . in honour.

There was the rub. He had gone through what was tantamount to a marriage ceremony with Katharine; and now he had denied it; and he knew why. It was because her mother was dead and the Kingdom of Castile had not passed to Katharine's father Ferdinand (which would have meant Katharine remained an important factor in policy making) but had gone to Isabella's sister who had an ambitious husband. Therefore Katharine was no longer to be considered so the King had forced his son most cynically to repudiate her.

And I did it, thought Henry.

Katharine was never far from his thoughts. He was ashamed of his action and as it was against his policy ever to be in the wrong he began to look for excuses for his conduct. It was no use telling himself that his father had forced him to do it, because it destroyed his image of himself if he allowed himself to be forced. That was why the matter was so disturbing. There had to be a reason why he had done what he had and it had to be a good one. His conscience demanded that.

It came in due course.

It was Charles Brandon who found it for him—not that Charles knew it. Charles was a gossip and took great delight in gathering the secrets of those about him. He had always been particularly interested in Katharine not only because she was affianced to

Henry and was destined to become the future Queen, but because she belonged to one of the most important Houses in Europe.

Now he talked a great deal about the death of Isabella and the difference this would make in Spain.

'They say the Princess Katharine is desolate. She and her mother were on the best of terms.'

Henry frowned; he remembered that Katharine had asked her mother to send for her, to take her back to Spain, which meant of course that she preferred that to marrying him.

That had been unflattering; but it was not enough excuse for breaking his sworn promise to her. His conscience would not accept that—although he had tried hard to make it do so.

'And the Kingdom of Castile goes to Katharine's sister . . . mad Juana, they call her.'

'Is she truly mad?'

'Mad indeed. There is madness in the family.'

Hope shone in Henry's eyes, but this was dispelled immediately by Brandon's light remark: 'Well, is there not madness somewhere in most families?'

'It is a wonder,' said Henry, 'that they allowed her to marry.'

'Who would not marry a mad woman for the sake of a crown?'

Henry shivered.

'Philip has her under control. They say he is extremely handsome.'

'Is he, do you think?'

'Oh yes. Undoubtedly so. Juana is possessively in love. She cannot bear him out of her sight.'

'She is a warm-hearted lady.'

'My dear Prince, she burns with passion.' Charles laughed. 'I should like to meet her. Do you know the latest story about her? I have it on good authority and can swear to the truth of it. Philip indulges himself, you know. He is not the man to content himself with one woman . . . even if she had been a paragon of the virtues . . . which Juana is not.'

'She loves him passionately, you say?'

'Passionate possessive love becomes cloying . . . as no doubt you will learn one day, my Prince. There is no doubt that you are going to be the target of much tender passion.'

Henry glowed with pleasure at the prospect.

'But steer clear of women like Juana.'

'What is this story you have heard?'

'Oh it is about Philip's mistress. She was very very beautiful with the longest most luxuriant golden hair ever seen in the land.

Philip doted on her and Juana was furiously jealous. Well, Philip had to leave Court for a while. Juana then . . . remember she is the Queen in her own right and I'll swear she has inherited something of her mother's authoritative ways . . . well, she summoned the woman to her palace.'

'And the woman went?'

'It was impossible for her to do otherwise. How could she disobey the royal command?'

'And then?'

'Juana had her bound hand and foot, called in the barbers and had them cut off that beautiful golden hair. In fact they shaved her head . . .'

Henry was aghast. 'She did that. And Philip . . . what of Philip?'

'When he came back he was horrified. I think it was the end of that mistress. Hair takes a long time to grow and he is not a man to stand still, they say. But it did not endear his wife to him . . . and everyone who knows her says she is quite insane . . .'

'And this is Katharine's sister . . .'

'Katharine is quite different. Juana is the only one to inherit the madness. There is nothing of the wild woman about Katharine. I hear she is very devout and spends a great deal of time on her knees. I even hear that she expressed a desire to give herself up to a life of prayer.'

'What when she marries?'

Brandon laughed aloud. 'Alas, her poor husband! But I'll swear if he is the man I believe him to be he will see that she gives up quite a bit of time to other activities.'

Henry laughed with Brandon but he was thinking: A life of prayer! How could a woman do her duty to her husband and the state by living like a nun? It would be a good excuse for not marrying at all.

His conscience liked the idea. He brooded on it. What Katharine had said—or what he had heard she had said—meant that the life she would prefer was that of a nun.

He had no intention of telling anyone what he was thinking. He did not want an avowal from Katharine that the stories circulated about her were untrue and that she was ready to be all that was expected of a wife when the time came.

Henry wanted to put it on paper that he had had a good reason for doing what he did. He wanted to be able to proclaim to the world that the marriage with Katharine of Aragon would not be good for the state. He had not repudiated her for any personal reasons and certainly not because he was afraid to stand up to his father for what was right.

Then the idea came to him. He would write to the Pope. He would tell no one. But his letter would be there on record if ever he was called on to answer for his action.

He made several drafts of the letter and finally produced one which he could send. In it he told Pope Julius that Katharine had made a vow dedicating herself to an austere life. She would fast, and give up her time to prayers and pilgrimages. He asked the Pope to forbid her to do this as such practices would injure her health and possibly affect her ability to bear children. He was deeply concerned about this as it would in time be his duty to get heirs for England; and if Katharine would not give up this way of life, marriage would be impossible.

He waited in trepidation for the reply; but he was at peace with his conscience. He had had a very good reason for signing that document which, while it did not actually annul the ceremony through which he and Katharine had gone, did give him a loophole to escape if necessary.

The Pope treated his letter with the utmost seriousness and replied that any vows Katharine had made which might affect the health of her body could be revoked by her husband.

The husband was master of the wife and the procreation of children was the very special blessing of matrimony and Henry had the Church's full permission to restrain his wife and to prevent her from carrying out any vows she might have made which would endanger her ability to perform those functions which were the duty of a wife.

Henry was delighted. Now if he should not wish—or not be allowed—to marry Katharine he had a very good excuse for not doing so. He could produce a copy of the letter he had sent to the Pope's reply. He could say Katharine's way of life had made marriage with her unsuitable and it was for this reason that he had signed the repudiation—not because his father had forced him to.

He became happy again.

But he had discovered his conscience and he knew that forever more it would be necessary to placate it.

The King was still looking for a wife and his eyes had turned to France. The Comte d'Angoulême had died leaving a widow with two children, François and Marguerite. It seemed that the son François had a chance of reaching the throne of France for he was the nephew of Louis the Twelfth. The widowed Comtesse was considered to be very beautiful and gifted and her daughter

Marguerite, who was about a year younger than Henry, had a reputation for a beauty and intelligence which equalled that of her mother.

So the King's eyes had turned to this family.

Why not the mother for him and the daughter for Henry?

Young Henry was told by his father that emissaries had been sent to Angoulême to discover the state of affairs there. The King thought the match would be an ideal one for it did appear that the Spanish connection was becoming weaker every month.

The Prince was very interested in Marguerite and wanted to hear all that he could about her. He had decided that Katharine had ruined her health by her refusal to lead the life of an ordinary Court lady. He shut his eyes to the fact that she was too short of money to do so, and he refused to listen to those who hinted that something should be done about this. It was for her family to help her, he reasoned. The dowry . . . well that had not been paid and he had heard that a great part of the first installment had been in jewelery which she had pawned.

He pretended to be rather shocked by that. For did the jewelery indeed belong to Katharine?

He was building up quite a little bank of excuses why he should not marry her.

And here was Marguerite—younger than he was which was better than being five years older. She was very beautiful. He liked that. She was very clever. He liked that less. He did not want a wife who thought herself as clever as he was. Still Marguerite sounded most exciting.

He questioned one of the men who had gone to the Court of Angoulême because he wanted to hear a first-hand account of someone who had actually seen her.

'I would like you to tell me the absolute truth,' he said. 'Hold nothing back. I shall take it ill if I find that you have given me too glowing a picture that was not true.'

'I would not dream of doing so, my lord,' was the answer. 'But I can tell you that Marguerite of Angoulême is one of the most beautiful ladies I have ever seen. She is brilliantly clever. She writes poetry and enjoys the company of poets. She is the constant companion of her brother, the young Duc d'Angoulême.'

'And what of him?'

'He is handsome, gracious, sparkling, my lord.'

Henry frowned; he did not like other people to be too brilliant.

'They are indeed a most beautiful trio.'

'Trio?'

'The mother, the brother, and the sister. They are always together but the object of their adoration is Duc François.'

'He is younger than I.'

'Yes, my lord, by a few years. He loves his sister dearly and she loves him. She is probably the more cultivated of the two—very learned in Greek, Latin and Philosophy. It is clear that the Duchess hopes her son will be the King of France. She calls him her king, her lord and her Caesar.'

Henry was envious. He would have enjoyed being so adored. He thought of his sister—another Margaret—who had pretended to be contemptuous of him. And there was certainly no adoration from his father; as for his mother, she had been kind and tender, but he could not imagine her calling him Caesar.

He began to feel mildly irritated with these perfect beings.

'And Marguerite, what does she call this wonder brother of hers?'

'Caesar indeed. All their hopes and dreams and love are centred on that boy. I wonder he has not more conceit of himself than he has . . . but that is great enough. His mother talks of nothing else but the wonders of this boy . . . nor does the sister. It seems that a short while ago he let loose a wild boar in the courtyard at Amboise which set the palace guards to flight but François himself chased the boar up the apartments, killed it with his sword and sent it rolling down the great staircase to the courtyard. They speak of all he does as though they were the greatest deeds worthy of the Court of King Arthur. I tell you, my lord, what the mother and sister feel for François of Angoulême is sheer idolatry. They think there is no one in the world like him . . . nor ever will be.'

'I daresay Madame Marguerite is of the opinion that no man can match her brother.'

'That is so, my lord. It is the law at Angoulême.'

Indeed, was it! The more he heard of this Marguerite the less inclined he felt to take her.

He was rather glad when no more was heard of the possibility. It might be that wily old Louis the Twelfth had put a stop to it.

But it made Henry thoughtful. Katharine, meek, turning to prayer because she felt frustrated and may possibly have heard of that rather shameful repudiation of her, seemed rather attractive.

How grateful she would be if in spite of everything he married her. How different from flamboyant Marguerite. He imagined her coming to the Court. All the time she would be comparing him to this brother of hers. Caesar indeed! Oh yes, there was much to be said for meek and grateful women.

He began to think of Katharine somewhat romantically. He visualized himself going to her and saying: 'They were against our marriage. When I was young they forced me to sign a paper. I did so, but I had no intention of breaking my promises. And here I am, Katharine, ready to rescue you and make you my ever-loving queen.'

She would never forget what he had done. She would realize that he was a very perfect knight whose honour prevailed through all vicissitudes.

She would be grateful to him for the rest of their lives.

His conscience was so happy that it was lying dormant.

I shall marry Katharine, he told himself, no matter what the opposition.

And he looked ahead into a misty future. It might well be that when the time came there would be no one to go against his wishes.

The future looked glorious and rosy. He would dream of Katharine and the chivalrous rescue.

SHIPWRECK

That winter of the year 1506 was a bleak one. Katharine had suffered miserably from the cold. Her position had certainly not improved and since the death of her mother she had become an encumbrance in Spain as well as in England.

She very much feared the King; she felt that his attitude towards her was entirely cynical. He, who had professed affection for her and such delight when she had come to marry Arthur, was now grudging her the small allowance he had made her and letting her see that he very much regretted that she had ever come to England.

Life was so cruel. She was in this position through a sudden twist of fate. If Arthur had lived she might now be the happy mother of children, the future Queen. If her mother had lived none would have dared treat her in this way. She often wondered if her father had ever really cared for her at all. It seemed to her that his children had been merely the means of helping him to increase his power. She knew that was inevitable to a certain extent but when one of them was placed in a position such as she was, surely some family feeling might have been revived to help that unfortunate one.

She had pawned so many of her jewels that she was afraid they would not last much longer. The Prince of Wales would be fifteen in June. That had once been the time considered possible for his wedding.

Would it take place? If it did she would be lifted out of her misery. It *must* take place.

For the last year her life had gone from bad to worse. The King was displeased with her father and the alliance between them which had begun with the marriage of Katharine and Arthur was severely strained. There were the perpetual differences about Katharine's dowry, and both of them refusing to help her, each using the other as an excuse. So it seems that I, thought Katharine, am of no importance to either of them.

They were both acquisitive; they were both ruthless in their

269

determination to achieve power and hold it. What did they care for a poor defenceless girl? It had been so different when Queen Isabella was alive.

In the previous year Ferdinand had remarried. Katharine had been shocked when she heard for she could not bear to think of another in her mother's place, particularly as he had married a young girl and rumour said he doted on her. Katharine believed he had always been a little jealous of Isabella. She had been his superior in every way, mentally as well as in her possessions, but they had appeared to be fond of each other. Isabella certainly had been of him, but always she had realized his weaknesses and always he had resented her power.

Now he had a young girl, Germaine de Foix, and this fact brought anxious furrows to the brow of the King of England for Germaine de Foix was a niece of Louis the Twelfth of France, which must mean bonds of friendship between Spain and Henry's old enemy, France.

Henry had not said definitely that there would be no marriage with the Prince of Wales. He did not want to do that. In fact to have abandoned her altogether would have meant a return of her dowry and he was not prepared to let that go out of the country. But she knew that he was sending out feelers for a possible bride for the Prince of Wales. She knew that Marguerite of Angoulême had been suggested for young Henry and her mother Louise of Savoy for the elder.

She fancied that rejection from Angoulême had been the reason for these propositions coming to nothing, and she had heard that Louise had seen a picture of the King and found it repulsive, as no doubt she did his parsimonious habits. The real reason perhaps was that she was so wrapped up in her son François, the young Duke whom she called her Caesar, that she could not bear to be parted from him; and the same applied to Marguerite.

In any case the King was still seeking a bride and there had been no further suggestions for the Prince of Wales.

Just before Christmas she begged an audience with the King and after a while this was granted.

She was amazed by his frail looks. He was thin and there was a yellowish tinge to his skin, but his eyes were sharp and shrewd-looking as ever.

'My lord,' she said, 'I cannot go on as I am. I have had no new clothes for two years; my servants are not paid. I must be able to live with dignity.'

'Have you applied to your father?' he asked.

'My father says I should apply to you.'

He lifted his shoulders. 'You are his daughter.'

'I am yours, too. I was Arthur's wife.'

'That was scarcely a marriage, dear lady. Your father does not behave in a seemly fashion I hear.'

She began to feel hysterical. She must have help from somewhere. She could not go on in this way. Her apartments were cold and there was no means of heating them.

She told him this; her voice was raised and she was near to tears.

The King looked shocked.

'Pray calm yourself, my lady,' he said. 'I think that you forget what is due from us both.'

She had clenched her fists together, 'I am desperate . . . desperate. Either help me or send me to my father.'

The King said: 'For the moment you should go back to your apartments. You are overwrought. I will do something to relieve your situation.'

What he had done was to invite her to come to Court for Christmas. This had disconcerted her. How could she mingle with the fine ladies of the Court in her threadbare gowns? Yet how could she spend the money which such a visit would necessarily require?

But because it was the King's command that she should go to Court she must do so, and when she was installed in a small apartment there one of the King's ambassadors came to her. He came, he said, on the command of the King to discuss her difficulties. She should rejoice for the King had given the matter his consideration.

She was tremendously relieved . . . but only for a few moments. When she heard the King's solution, she was overcome with dismay.

'My lady, the King realizes that the upkeep of Durham House is beyond your means. Therefore he offers you a home here at Court. He is dismissing the members of your household whom you will no longer need. He says it is small wonder that you cannot pay your servants. The answer is that you have far too many. He is dismissing all but five of your ladies, and he is leaving you your Master of Hall, your treasurer and your physician. Then you will have your apartments here at Court. Thus you will be in a position to live in accordance with your means.'

She was dumbfounded. He had helped her by taking away most of those who were her friends.

She was so distraught that she sent at once for her Confessor.

She wanted to pray with him, to ask him to help her to bear this fresh burden which had been put upon her by a cynical king.

He could not be found and when she sent for her physician he told her that her Spanish Confessor was one of those who had been dismissed.

So here she was at Court—even more wretched than she had been at Durham House. Her expenses might have decreased but her misery had intensified.

There was only one ray of hope at that time. On occasions she saw the Prince of Wales. He was always aware of her, she knew. Sometimes their eyes would meet and in his would be a smile which was almost conspiratorial.

What did that mean? she wondered.

She looked for him on every occasion. She felt happier when he was there.

There was only one way she could escape from this intolerable situation. That would be through marriage with the Prince of Wales.

The King was by no means a happy man. He was still unmarried and he had one son only. True, Henry was growing into splendid manhood. He was already taller than his father, he was outstandingly handsome and with his light auburn hair and fair skin he was admired wherever he went. He took great care always to be dressed to the best advantage. He liked to show off his well-shaped legs and the sumptuous velvets and brocades of his garments were the talk of the Court.

All very well, thought the King, but I hope the boy is not going to be extravagant.

Certainly that could be curbed while the King lived but as Henry said to Dudley and Empson, it would be intolerable if the Prince believed that when he came to the throne he could plunge into that storehouse of carefully built-up treasure and squander it.

Everyone made excuses for him. He was young yet. He had great charm and good looks; he was admired by the people. When he grew older he would realize his responsibilities.

But would he?

The King watched his son closely, curbed his exuberance, keeping him at his side. He was determined that the Prince should not yet be allowed to set up a household at Ludlow but remain at the King's Court.

The rift with Ferdinand was growing. Henry was in fact seeking friendship with Philip, Juana's husband, who, since the death of Queen Isabella, had become virtually ruler of Castile.

(Juana was the Queen but women did not count, certainly not one who was half mad and at the same time besottedly in love with her husband so that he could do anything he would with her.) When Philip's father Maximilian died Philip would be the most powerful man in Europe. He was therefore a man to be cultivated and the deeper the rift between Henry and Ferdinand the more Henry would need Philip's friendship to stand against the French. Moreover Ferdinand's marriage with the niece of the King of France had made this more important than ever.

Henry's fury with Ferdinand was increased when English merchants trading in Castile were refused the privileges they had enjoyed for some time under Isabella's rule and were unable to do business. Consequently they returned with their cargo of cloth and did not bring back the wine and oil which the country needed. Ferdinand swore that this was no fault of his. It had been his government who had refused the English merchants permission to do business. He had done his best to persuade them to allow the trade to proceed as before but they had refused. The English merchants had come to Richmond to complain to the King and they were in a very angry mood. Henry hated to see business deals frustrated; he had great difficulty in placating the merchants and although he was not to blame, people had looked to him to make the country prosperous and if he failed to do so he would be the one to answer for the failure.

Indeed he needed to court the friendship of Philip who would be only too ready to go against his father-in-law, for Ferdinand was very resentful that Isabella should have declared her mad daughter Juana Queen of Castile, for that meant handing over that country to Juana's husband Philip.

But there was one other matter which made Henry feel he needed Philip's friendship.

At the time of the rebellion of Edmund de la Pole, Earl of Suffolk, which had given the King the opportunity to dispose of Sir James Tyrell and thus put an end to that spectre which had haunted him for a long time, the Earl had been exiled.

Perhaps it was a mistake to send people into exile. One never knew what they were plotting there. On the other hand Henry always avoided bloodshed except when he considered it absolutely necessary.

Four years had passed since Suffolk was brought to trial and during that time he had been in Aix. It was dangerous of course. But Henry had expected that and he watched the antics of his enemy very closely. At the time of Suffolk's trial he had thought his claim to the throne was too remote to be of great importance.

After all it came through his mother's being sister to Edward the Fourth. Henry now realized that he should have been more careful and he would give a great deal to have Suffolk safely in the Tower.

He had signed a treaty with the Emperor Maximilian, father of Philip, in which Maximilian had promised he would not help English rebels, even though these rebels should claim the title of duke.

Suffolk had clearly been meant in this for he regarded himself as a duke even though his titles had been confiscated.

In spite of this Suffolk stayed at Aix for two years and when he did finally go after having been promised safe conduct, he was arrested in Gelderland and imprisoned in the Castle of Hattem. Shortly after his incarceration there, this castle had been captured by Philip; thus Suffolk had passed into the hands of the man whose friendship Henry now so ardently sought and one of the main reasons for this was Philip's possession of Suffolk.

There were so many things in Henry's mind. His spirits would have been considerably lifted if he could have found a bride. He missed Elizabeth more than he had thought possible. She had been so docile, never complaining, accepting his superior wisdom in all things. Having enjoyed the company of such a wife it was not surprising that he missed it and desperately longed to replace her.

The country was prospering as never before and his ministers thought it rather foolish of him to be so constantly worrying about a claimant to the throne springing up. It was due to those alarming insurrections of Lambert Simnel and Perkin Warbeck . . . and of course the continued fears concerning the Princes in the Tower. They had coloured his outlook to such an extent that there were times when they dominated all else.

But his ministers were right. He had nothing to fear. Nevertheless he would do what he could to cultivate Philip's friendship, and he would seek a bride and remarry which would remind himself that he was young yet. He would watch over the development of young Henry and mould him as the king he would one day be. And as for his son's marriage, well, if an opportunity turned up he was free to take it. He kept telling himself that he was in no way bound to the marriage with Katharine of Aragon.

But the woman was an incessant nuisance. She was constantly grumbling and even now that she had free quarters at Court she went round like a messenger of doom trying to win the sympathy of those about her.

She had no money to buy clothes; she could not pay her

servants; the few women who were left to her could not marry because she could not provide them with dowries; her undergarments had been mended so many times that there was nothing left of them but patches.

She was in a sorry state and worst of all she did not know whether she was the prospective Princess of Wales or not.

'We are not committed,' said the King. 'Let her understand that.'

He had little thought to waste on her; he was wondering how he could best cultivate the friendship of Philip.

Then fate played into his hands.

That January the greatest storm the English ever remembered struck the island; the gale raged all through the day and night; even in London roofs blew from houses and it was unsafe to be in the streets. Among other buildings, St. Paul's Cathedral was damaged, but all this was nothing compared with the fury of the gale along the coasts.

It so happened that Philip with his wife Juana was at this time on the high seas. They were on their way to claim the crown of Castile and were making the journey by sea because the King of France would not permit them to cross his land.

So Philip had set sail from the Netherlands with his army and was in the English Channel when the full force of the storm struck his fleet. It was scattered; ships were sunk and some were washed ashore along the English coast.

With Philip was his wife Juana whom he would have preferred to be without. Philip was twenty-eight years old; he had already earned the title of Philip the Handsome and it fitted him. His long golden hair and fine features gave him the appearance of a Greek god and his large blue eyes and skin were fresh and healthy. If he was not tall, he was not short—perhaps slightly above medium height. Perhaps if he were older those perfect features might have been spoiled by marks of debauchery, but at this time, in spite of the life he led, they remained unsullied.

He had married Juana for Castile and he always said they might have lived together in reasonable harmony if she had not become so enamoured of him that she could not bear him out of her sight and when they were together she could not prevent herself showing in every possible way her passionate devotion to him. As she was more than a little unbalanced, this passion for her husband—particularly in view of the life he liked to lead—assumed violent demonstrations. The incident of the cropped-haired mistress was but one. Her desire for Philip was insatiable and the stronger it grew so did his revulsion for her.

It was a very unhappy state of affairs but on this occasion he had to endure her company for they were on their way to Castile where she would have to claim the crown of Castile.

He had often wondered whether he could put her away. That she was mad, many would be ready to admit if they dared. But surely, as admitting it was so would please him very much, they need have little fear from that. He always had to remember though that the crown came through her. She would be ready to give him all power in Castile but in exchange she would want him with her night and day.

It is too big a price to ask, he thought, even for Castile.

The marriage had been fruitful so Philip had done his duty by the woman. Their son Charles would be one of the most powerful men in Europe one day but his father would take that role before him. On the death of the Emperor, now that he had Castile as well, much of Europe would fall into Philip's hands.

He had thought that once Juana had children he would be able to escape from her wearying passion. It was not so. She was proud of them, of course, loved them in fact, but she made it clear that all her passionate desire was still concentrated on her husband.

Of course he was attractive—one of the most desirable men in the world, and he had evidence of that for he could not remember one woman who had denied him once he made his wishes known. But Juana's passion for him, to which her madness seemed to add a dangerous fuel, did not abate. He had begun to fear it never would.

Ever since they had left the land he had had to endure her company. Wherever he went she was after him and it was not easy to hide oneself on board a ship. He had consoled himself: Soon we shall be in Castile. Soon the crown will be handed to her. He could already feel it on his head.

And now . . . this storm. Was it the end? He had been a fool to bring his army to sea. But what else could he do? He did not want to appear without it . . . and Ferdinand had no right to make treaties with the King of France, allying himself with France through that marriage with the French King's niece. Artful old devil, thought Philip. He would probably be delighted if they perished at sea. Then he would get his hands on the baby Charles and bring him up as he thought he should be.

God forbid!

Once Juana had the crown perhaps he could put her away. Heaven knew, her conduct should not make that difficult.

But now all his plans were to come to nothing. Here he was at sea, and with every passing moment the storm was rising.

He was shouting orders to his men. They were afraid, he knew that. Only those who knew the sea could understand how terrible it could be. Philip was brought face to face with that knowledge and he could only fear that he had come to the end.

Someone had brought him an inflated jacket. It might be necessary to leave the ship, my lord, he was told.

'Leave the ship? I never will. Where are my other ships?'

'They are no longer with us, my lord. Some may have been lost . . . others blown to land somewhere. We are in the English Channel. Thank Heaven the English coast cannot be far away.'

Juana came rushing up to him. She was dressed in a furred robe and about her was strapped a purse.

She laughed at him and held out her arms. 'We shall die together, my beloved,' she cried. 'I ask nothing more.'

She would embrace him but he threw her aside.

'This is no moment,' he said. 'We have to be prepared. We may have to abandon ship.'

'Ah, for the sea's embrace,' cried Juana. 'I trow it will be a little more welcoming than yours, my cruel lord.'

'Try to be sensible,' said Philip angrily. 'At such a time . . . Have you no sense?'

'None at all,' she cried. 'None where you are concerned, most beautiful and cruel of men.'

He had turned away. 'What now?' he said to the men who, in spite of the situation, could not help gazing at Juana in astonishment. 'Could we land?' asked Philip.

'We could try. If the ship will hold out long enough . . .'

'England,' said Philip. 'Well, better than a watery grave mayhap.'

Juana had flung herself at him once more and was clinging to him.

'Let us die together, sweet husband,' she cried dramatically, and again he flung her from him.

'Death!' he cried in a fury. 'At least it would be escape from you.'

Then he had left her and staggered onto the deck.

Juana who had fallen, partly due to Philip's rough treatment and partly due to the violent movement of the ship, half-raised herself and sat rocking to and fro.

'Oh my love . . . my love!'' she cried. 'Will you ever love

me? I will stay with you forever. You will never be rid of me never . . . never.'

Her women were running round her. They were frightened out of their wits—not by her strangeness, they were accustomed to that—but at the prospect of death at sea.

The thunder roared and the lightning was terrifying.

'Philip,' screamed Juana. 'Where are you, my love, my husband. Come to me. Let us die in each other's arms.'

One of her women knelt beside her.

'You are frightened, woman,' said Juana. 'You tremble. We are going to die, are we not? I wonder what it is like to drown. Death comes quickly some say and in this sea surely so. I am not afraid of dying. There is only one thing in this world that I am afraid of . . . losing him . . . losing my beloved . . .'

She looked at them . . . these women who were clustering round her. They were in greater need of comfort than she was. She spoke truthfully when she said she was not afraid. If she could be with Philip that was all she asked.

The ship was lurching violently and as Juana tried to get to her feet, she heard a voice crying out: 'Land! Land. The lord be praised, it's land.'

Philip shouted: 'Can we make it?'

'We have to, my lord. This ship can't carry us further . . . It's land or death in the sea.'

'Go for the land then,' said Philip.

He was thinking that he would have to throw himself on the hospitality of Henry. Was that wise? Most unwise, he thought. He would be more or less Henry's prisoner. Here he was with only a few seamen at the mercy of one who might befriend him if it were expedient to do so.

But it was that or death by drowning, so there was only one course to take.

Juana was on her feet. She staggered on deck and stood beside Philip. She looked incongruous in her fine gown with her purse of gold strapped about her waist and her long hair flying in the wind. She was beautiful; there was no denying that and in her wildness she was like some sea goddess rather than a normal woman. Philip looked at her in momentary admiration. She had shown less fear than any of them at the prospect of drowning.

'Philip,' she cried. 'We are together. . . We have come through this.'

She clasped his arm and he did not throw her off. Perhaps it was too solemn a moment and he was too relieved that land was in sight and that death was not imminent.

'I think,' he said slowly, 'that we may be safe.'

As they came nearer to the land they saw that people were waiting there. In the early morning light this was a frightening sight for some of those people carried bows and arrows and others had farming instruments which they could be intending to use as weapons. They looked menacing.

The ship had ground to a halt and some of the men were wading ashore.

Philip heard one shout, 'This is the Archduke of Austria and King of Castile, with his Duchess and Queen. We beg for refuge.'

There was a chorus of 'Come ashore.'

We must, thought Philip wryly. There is nothing else we can do.

It was not long before, with Juana beside him, he was standing on dry land.

One man had put himself in front of the crowd and it was clear that he was a person of some authority.

'I am Sir John Trenchard,' he said. 'Squire of these lands. I welcome you ashore.'

'Thank you,' said Philip. 'Tell me where we are?'

'You have landed at Melcombe Regis . . . you just missed Weymouth. All along the coast your ships have been watched. There'll not be many which have escaped the storm I fear, my lord Archduke. I thank God that you are safe. My house and household will be at your service and I doubt not you would wish to come with me right away.'

'There is nothing I should desire more,' said Philip.

'Then let us go. We are close by. You can have food and shelter at least.'

The manor house was warm and cosy after the rigours of the night and Philip could not feel anything but relief and an overpowering joy that his life had been saved. The savoury smells of roasting meat filled the hall and he gave himself up to the pleasure of taking advantage of the comforts his host had to offer.

Lady Trenchard was giving urgent orders in the kitchens and throughout the household, while her husband dispatched a messenger to Windsor that the King might know without delay what an important visitor Sir John had in his house.

The King received the news with an excitement so intense that for once he felt unable to hide it. Philip in England! Shipwrecked! At his mercy in a way. Fortune could not have been more favourable.

The weather was bad; the heavy rain was causing floods all over the country and although the violent wind had abated a little it was still wreaking damage throughout the land.

Henry blessed the storm. Nothing could have worked more favourably for him. Philip must be accorded a royal welcome, he said. He should be met and brought to the Court where Henry would devise such hospitality which would astonish all those who were aware of his reluctance to spend money. He was sure Dudley and Empson would agree with him that this was one of those occasions when it was necessary to spend.

He sent for young Henry.

The Prince had a faintly resentful look in his eyes. The King knew what that meant. He would soon be fifteen years of age and he resented being kept so closely under his father's surveillance.

Often the King had impressed on his son how much depended on him, what great responsibilities would be his, and it was then that he grew faintly uneasy because he saw that faraway look in the boy's eyes, which meant that he was seeing the time when he would be King and imagining what he would do when his father was no longer there to restrain him.

'Be thankful, my lord, for the Prince's good health and looks and his popularity with the people,' said his ministers.

'I am,' replied the King, 'but sometimes I think it would be better if he were a little more like his brother Arthur was.'

'The Prince will be strong, my lord. Have no fear of that.'

And he sighed and supposed they were right. He knew that some of those who wished him well believed that he looked for trouble; he was never at ease and was always expecting disaster. Well, that was so; but then it was due to the way in which he had come to the crown.

Now he looked at his son.

'You have heard the news doubtless. The Archduke Philip has been shipwrecked on our shores. He is at Melcombe Regis with his wife.'

'Yes,' said Henry. 'I have heard it. Philip and Katharine's sister.'

The King frowned. He would have to pay a little more respect to Katharine now that her sister and brother-in-law were here, he supposed. But he was faintly irritated that his son should mention her.

'You are always saying that you are not allowed to take a big enough part in important matters. Well, my son, here is your chance. Philip must be welcomed to our shores. Quite clearly I cannot go to meet him. I do not want to treat him as though he is a conqueror, do I? But I wish to show him honour. I intend to make this visit memorable . . . for myself as well as for him. So I shall send you, my son, to welcome him. You will go at the head of a party and greet him in my name.'

Henry's eyes sparkled. How he loves taking a prominent part! thought the King. How different from Arthur!

'You will treat Philip with every respect. You will welcome him warmly. You will tell him of our pleasure in his coming. Now go and prepare to leave. I will see you before you set out and will prime you in what you will have to say to our visitor.'

Henry said: 'Yes, my lord.'

He was all impatience to be gone, thinking: What shall I wear? What shall I say? Philip of Austria . . . son of Maximilian . . . one of the most important men in Europe, one whose friendship his father was eager to cultivate. He would excel. He would show everyone how he would handle delicate matters . . .

'You may go now,' said the King. 'I will see you before you leave.'

Henry was off, calling to Charles Brandon, Mountjoy . . . all his friends.

An important mission entrusted to him at last!

In her apartments Katharine heard the news. Her sufferings had not diminished since she came to Court. In fact she thought that they had become more humiliating; for here she must live close to the rich and observe that the humblest squire was more comfortably situated than she was. It was amazing how quickly servants realized the contempt of their masters and lost no time in reflecting it. True she and her attendants were served food from the King's kitchens but it was always cold when it reached them and was obviously those scraps which were considered unfit for the royal table.

She was eating scarcely anything. Pride forbade her. Moreover she found that her appetite had diminished; she was in such a state of perpetual anxiety. Her father did not reply to her entreaties and she knew it was no use appealing to King Henry.

All her hopes were centred on the Prince of Wales for he always had a kindly smile for her when they saw each other. It was a little patronizing perhaps, and in it there was an assumption of superiority but there was something protective in his smile and Katharine was in sore need of protection.

Therefore, when the news reached her that her sister and brother-in-law were in the country wild hope seized her. It was years since she had seen Juana but to see her again would be wonderful. She could talk to her. She would make her understand what her position here was like. Juana was important now: Queen of Castile. Juana could help her.

This could be deliverance.

It was in a state of hopeful expectation that she awaited the arrival of her sister and brother-in-law.

A place of meeting had been arranged. It was to be at Winchester. Richard Fox, Bishop of Winchester had already been warned that when Philip arrived he was to be treated to the very best and most lavish hospitality. Philip was to be made to feel that there was no suggestion whatsoever of his being a prisoner. He was an honoured guest.

Philip had arrived at Winchester feeling rather pleased with the turn of events. He had heard by now that not all his ships had been lost. Many of them had been able to get into port and although damaged could be refitted and made seaworthy. In the meantime he was in England, about to meet the wily King; he was very much looking forward to that encounter.

Moreover he was feeling particularly pleased because he had left Juana behind him at Wolverton Manor in Dorset whither they had travelled from Melcombe Regis and where they were—since it was the wish of the King—entertained with as much splendour as it was possible to muster.

Juana had protested. She wished to accompany him. She did not want to let him out of her sight. But he had been adamant. The shipwreck had affected her more than she realized. She was distraught. She was overwrought. She was in a weak state. He feared for her health.

She had watched him through narrowed eyes and he had been forced to threaten her. If she did not agree to stay and rest he would have her put away. She suffered from periodic madness and the whole world knew it. He would have no difficulty in making people believe that her violence had become so dangerous to others that she must be put under restraint.

That threat could calm her better than anything, for although she was the Queen of Castile, Philip was more powerful and every member of her household would agree with him that she suffered from bouts of madness.

He soothed her; he was gentle with her; he spent the night with her—which could soften her more than anything; and in the morning he was able to leave alone for Winchester having warned her attendants that she was to have a long rest before setting out to make the journey to Windsor.

Savouring his freedom from the cloying devotion of his wife he was in excellent form, ready to enjoy the adventure; and when he heard that the Prince of Wales was on his way to meet him in the king's name he was greatly amused. The boy was not quite fifteen, full of life, straining at the leash. Philip looked forward to an entertaining encounter.

Young Henry meanwhile was rehearsing what he would say to Philip. Philip was handsome and therefore vain, he presumed. Philip was important to his father; therefore he must treat him with the utmost respect. At the same time he must let the Archduke know that he was of no small importance himself: Prince of Wales, King-to-be, someone to be reckoned with for the future.

They met at the Bishop's Palace and stood face to face, smiling at each other. The speeches Henry had rehearsed were forgotten. He said: 'Why, my lord Archduke, you are indeed as handsome as they say.'

Philip was amused. 'My lord Prince,' he said, 'I see you have heard tales of me similar to those I have heard of you. And I will say with you . . . they do not lie. You are all that I heard of you though I'll confess I did believe it was largely flattery.'

There could not have been a better beginning. Philip knew exactly how to please the boy and he set out with all his considerable charm to do so.

As for young Henry he was delighted; he felt he was making a supreme success of his first diplomatic mission.

Before they sat down to the lavish banquet the Bishop's servants had prepared they were the best of friends. Philip had explained that he had left Juana behind to recuperate after the fearful ordeal at sea. Henry wanted to hear about the shipwreck and listened entranced to Philip's account.

It was dramatic. Henry could see the young man—who was already a hero to him—giving orders on the deck.

'We believed our last moment had come. I prayed then to God. I went on my knees and asked for my life to be spared. I believe—but you may think I am wrong—that I have work to do here on Earth and the time has not yet come for me to leave it.'

Henry protested that he did not think the Archduke was wrong at all and God must have realized that.

'I swore to the Virgin Mary that I would make two pilgrimages if she would intercede for me. I promised her I would go to her churches of Montserrat and Guadalupe and there do homage to her if she would but plead with God to save my life.'

'And she did,' said Henry, his eyes glistening with religious fervour. Knights were the more to be admired if they combined piety with bravery.

'From that moment the wind dropped. The rain abated so that we could see the outline of the English coast,' went on Philip.

It was not quite true but Philip could not resist dramatizing the story for such an entranced listener.

'Heaven intervened,' said Henry piously.

'That is so, my Prince. We came ashore although I must confess that the inhabitants looked a little fierce at first.'

'They should be punished for it,' said Henry, his little mouth hardening.

'Nay, nay. They were protecting the shores of their country. How were they to know that I was a friend? I could have been an invader. Do not blame your good people, my lord Prince. Rather thank them. They would guard your island well. And the best gift a ruler can have from his people is loyalty.'

'I think the people will be loyal to me.'

Philip laid his hand on the boy's arm. 'You have the makings of a great ruler. That is clearer to me than is this goblet of wine.'

How Henry glowed! How he admired the Archduke! He was so good looking, so charming, and Henry was glad to know although he himself was not yet fifteen and could be expected to put on a few more inches, he was already as tall as Philip.

He asked about Juana. Philip explained that she was suffering from exhaustion and that he had insisted that she remain behind for a while and take the journey to Windsor more slowly.

Henry said: 'I look forward to meeting the lady Katharine's sister.'

'Ah . . . indeed yes.'

Henry shut his lips firmly together. He had been warned by his father not to speak of Katharine. These were her close relations and the subject of her treatment in England could be a dangerous one.

Henry wondered fleetingly what the King intended to do about Katharine; but he was too involved with this fascinating companion to let her intrude into the conversation. Besides she was a forbidden subject. But the very fact of that made him feel he wanted to talk of her.

'Your wife has brought you great possessions,' said Henry; and it occurred to him that if Katharine had been the elder she could have brought Castile to him. He was sure then there would not have been all this uncertainty about his marriage.

At length they retired for the night for they were to leave early next morning. By that time the excellent camaraderie between them was noted by all around them.

It was as though the Archduke of Austria and the Prince of Wales had been friends all their lives and none would have guessed that they had met for the first time only the day before.

It was a pleasant journey. They were both young and healthy enough not to be disturbed by the wintry weather and as they approached Windsor they perceived King Henry with a magnificently attired entourage riding towards them.

King Henry, regal in purple velvet, made a striking contrast to the black-clad Archduke and his rather sombre attendants. The King swept off his cap and was glad that he had taken the precaution of wearing a hood with the cap on top so that it could be removed leaving his ears covered, for the icy wind was penetrating and he was plagued by many rheumatic aches and pains these days.

'It is too cold to linger here,' he said to Philip, 'but I would say to you that I, rejoice to see you. You are as welcome as my son here. He, I and my whole kingdom are at your service.'

Philip replied that he was deeply moved by such a touching welcome and taking his place between the King and the Prince of Wales he rode with them towards the castle.

From a window Katharine was watching. She had hoped to be there in the great hall to greet her sister and her husband but it had not been suggested that she should, so fearing a rebuff she had remained in her apartments.

But I shall see Juana, she told herself. Something must come of that.

She looked from the window. She saw the three men. But where was Juana? She was terribly afraid. Why was it that people always whispered about her sister? She knew Juana was wild. She had always been so. Only their mother had known how to deal with her. But there were times when Juana had been a loving sister, kind and even gentle, always ready to listen to other people's problems.

But where was Juana now?

There was a scratching at her door and a young girl came in. This was the Princess Mary—the King's youngest daughter who was some ten years old. Mary had become very beautiful—perhaps the most beautiful of all the King's children. That beauty had come down through the House of York and with it a vitality which had shown itself in Henry, Margaret and Mary.

Mary was tender-hearted, more affectionate than her sister Margaret had been and she had shown friendship for Katharine for whom she was vaguely sorry—mainly because she never had any new clothes and she was in some sort of disgrace, it seemed to Mary—disgrace which was not of her own making.

Now Mary was very excited. 'They're here,' she cried. 'There is to be a grand banquet. I am to go. I have my father's permission. I shall play the lute and the clavichord and everyone will say how clever I am. Perhaps I shall dance. Perhaps Henry will dance with me.'

Mary was silent. She had been tactless again. She shouldn't have mentioned Henry because Katharine wanted to marry him and she was not sure that he wanted to marry her and there was a lot of fuss about some dowry which upset Katharine a great deal.

'I was hoping to see my sister,' said Katharine. 'She is not with the party?'

'Oh, Queen Juana . . .' Mary was just about to say mad Juana and remembered in time that she was Katharine's sister. 'She is staying behind . . . She has to rest . . .'

Mary's voice trailed off. Then she was at the window.

'They look very dull,' she said, 'except my father . . . and Henry of course . . .'

Katharine was thinking: What if I am invited to the banquet? Is my ruby brooch big enough to hide the darn in my velvet gown?

But she was not thinking very seriously about what she would wear. The one thought which kept hammering in her mind was: Where is Juana?

The King led his guest into the castle. As they walked he congratulated the Archduke on his escape and assured him of his own delight in the outcome.

'I have long desired to talk with you, my lord Archduke, and now fate in this rather churlish way has gratified my desire.'

Philip replied as graciously. He could only rejoice in his shipwreck since it had brought about this happy meeting.

The state apartments of the castle were magnificent and Philip admired them. Then Philip was conducted to the most splendid apartment of them all, hung with cloth of gold and crimson velvet, and as it was lavishly decorated with Tudor roses Philip realized that the King was giving up the royal bedchamber to him.

It had been the custom of kings during the ages when they wished to show especial honour that they gave up this most intimate of their apartments. In medieval times often the guest had been expected to share the King's bed. Later this custom had been altered a little and now it was customary to relieve the guest from sharing and offer only the bedchamber.

But it was indeed the ultimate honour and Philip was delighted.

The King had realized that it would not be possible to exclude Katharine from the celebrations; but the fact that her sister Juana had been left behind to follow later was an indication that he need not worry too much about the treatment the Princess had received in England.

With his usual shrewdness he had summed up Philip. Ambitious, wily to an extent, luxury loving, something of a libertine, a young man whom it should not be difficult for such as himself to handle, and he intended to get the most advantage from the visit.

Young Henry had already succumbed to the visitor's charm. There had been no need to warn him to flatter the young man; he was doing that unconsciously. The King thought uneasily: There is a similarity between them. Will Henry be like Philip when he comes to the throne?

But that was a long way ahead, the King hoped, although his rheumatism was dreadfully painful particularly in such inclement weather as this. But he had time ahead of him; if he could get a wife he would feel renewed.

Katharine received the message. She was to appear at the banquet.

Her hopes were raised by Henry's changed attitude towards her when she was presented to her brother-in-law; Philip embraced her and those hopes soared. She wondered when she would have an opportunity to talk to him.

She was grateful that she still had some jewels out of pawn and she had managed to keep one black velvet dress in moderately good condition. When she was dressed in it and put on her jewels she believed she successfully hid her poverty.

Henry proudly presented his daughter Mary to the Archduke, and even his expression softened a little at the sight of the delightful creature. He could not help being proud of his children. The urge was strong in him to get more. Perhaps he could talk to Philip about a bride. Philip's sister Margaret's name had been mentioned before. Perhaps he could get the matter settled quickly for it would be an ideal match.

He was affable to Katharine, calling her his daughter, which all about him noticed and they wondered whether this was an indication that there was still a possibility of her marriage with the Prince of Wales or whether it was merely done for Philip's benefit.

So the banquet began and conversation flowed with the utmost affability between Philip and his attendants and the King and the Prince of Wales and all those nobles who were fully aware of the King's desire for friendship with the visitor.

The Princess Mary enchanted the company with her lute and clavichord as she had said she would; and she danced to the admiration of all. The King suggested that Katharine dance one of her Spanish dances and that one of her ladies should accompany her in the dance.

It was like those pleasant days of long ago for Katharine when she was treated according to her rank.

Mary had come to her after the dance and taking her hand led her to the dais at the end of the hall on which the royal party were seated. The King made no objection but included her in the smile he bestowed on his daughter.

Young Henry smiled at her, almost possessively and perhaps with real love. She was happier than she had been for a long time.

She sat beside Philip and her heart beat fast with hope. He was smiling at her in a rather vague way as though his thoughts were elsewhere.

'I was dismayed not to see my sister,' she said.

His voice was cold. 'She was indisposed after such an ordeal. I was concerned for her health and insisted that she rest before making the journey.'

It sounded as though he cared very much for Juana, and Katharine warmed towards him.

'I shall look forward to seeing her. I doubt not she will join us soon.'

'It will be so, doubtless,' he said.

She thought: If I could speak to him in secret. If I could ask him to convey a message to my father . . . one which the King might not know of. Perhaps he could bring me some relief. If my father knew how short of money I am kept . . .

She would try. But how speak to him alone? In the dance, perhaps?

'My lord Archduke,' she said quietly, 'I should be greatly honoured if you and I could dance together.'

He turned to her; his eyes were cold. 'My lady, I am but a plain sailor. You would not have me dance with you!'

There was a brief silence. Katharine felt the blood rush into her face. It was an insult—and deliberately given.

The silence on the dais was brief. The Prince of Wales looked dismayed. He felt protective towards Katharine; on the other hand he was completely fascinated by his new friend. Katharine should not have asked him to dance; she should have waited for Philip to ask her. Henry preferred to forget the incident.

The King had been very much aware of it. It told him a good

deal. Philip had escaped from Juana; he had treated Katharine as though he regarded her as of little importance.

That was revealing. Then he need not be too careful of her either and he was glad of that. He had been a little uneasy about what the sisters might discuss if they were together. He believed now that there would be no protest from Philip if he sent Katharine away. But perhaps he should allow her the briefest encounter with her sister.

On the following day the Princess Mary came to Katharine's apartments. She was pouting slightly and Katharine wondered what had offended her, for she was inclined to be spoilt at the Court—like her brother and elder sister Margaret, she was fond of her own way. Now something had upset her and clearly she had come to tell Katharine about it.

Soon it came out. 'I am to leave for Richmond at the end of the week.'

'Oh . . . but you love Richmond.'

'I love Richmond but not when there is all this entertainment going on at Windsor. The Archduke will be here and there will be balls and banquets and all sorts of exciting things going on and I shall not be here to enjoy them.' She looked quickly at Katharine. 'And,' she added, 'nor will you.'

Katharine looked at her in amazement.

'Because,' went on Mary, 'you are to come with me. We are to leave together . . . for Richmond.'

'But who has said this?'

'It is my father's wish that we should go.'

'But . . . my sister will be coming . . .'

'I know. But we are to go. Perhaps your sister will come to Richmond to see you.'

'She will come here . . . and I shall not be here to see her. Oh, it is so unfair. Why is everything done to hurt me?'

Mary came to Katharine and put her arm round her.

'I don't want to go to Richmond either,' she said.

Katharine looked at the beautiful little pouting face. No, Mary did not want to miss the balls and banquets. But *I* shall not see my sister, thought Katharine.

Then a horrible suspicion came to her that it had been planned because the King did not wish her to see her sister. He would know how bitterly she would complain. Had she not on many occasions brought her sorry condition to his ears? Not that he had listened.

Oh, life was cruel. It could not be that now she was going to be denied a meeting with Juana.

A few days passed in the most lavish revelry and still Juana did not come. Philip's servants had certainly respected his wishes that Juana's journey to join him should be a very slow one. She did not arrive until the day before Katharine and Mary were to leave for Richmond.

Fortune is a little on my side at last, thought Katharine. At least I shall see her.

With great joy she greeted her sister.

They looked at each other for some time in astonishment. They had both changed a good deal since they had last met. Katharine noticed the wildness in Juana's eyes. She had seen it before but now it was more marked. Her sister had aged considerably. Of course she would change; she had been a young girl when she had left home to marry Philip.

Juana saw a new Katharine too. Was this Catalina, the rather quiet little sister who had always been so terrified of the future which would take her away from her mother's side? Poor sad little widow! She really did look as though she were in mourning.

'We must be together . . . we must talk,' said Katharine. 'There is so much I have to say to you. You will be going to Castile.'

'Yes,' said Juana. 'We are going to claim the crown which is now mine.'

'You are Queen of Castile, Juana, as our mother was. It is hard to imagine anyone in her place.'

'Our father has replaced her in his bed,' said Juana with a laugh. 'They say his new wife is young and beautiful and he is rather a doting husband.'

Katharine shivered.

'I wish him joy of her,' cried Juana. 'I have the crown. He cannot take that.'

'Juana, when you see our father I want you to speak to him for me.'

'What think you of Philip?' said Juana. 'Did you ever see a man so handsome?'

'He is certainly very good looking. You see, Juana, I have no state here. They say I am to marry the Prince of Wales. We have gone through a ceremony . . . but shall I? What does our father say of this matter?'

'He has said nothing as far as I know.'

'But . . . I am his daughter.'

'I think he is not pleased that I have the crown. He always wanted it, you know. He married our mother for it. But I have it now . . . and I have Philip. Philip loves me . . . because I have the crown of Castile.' She caught Katharine's arm and held it tightly. 'If I did not have the crown of Castile he would cast me off tomorrow.'

'Oh no . . .'

'Yes, yes,' cried Juana. The wildness in her eyes was very evident. 'Oh he is so beautiful, Katharine. He is the most beautiful creature on Earth. You have no idea. What have you known of men such as he is? Your Arthur . . . what sort of man was he?'

'He was good and kind,' said Katharine quickly; she was becoming alarmed by this wildness in Juana. She always had been. When they were in the royal nurseries in their childhood their mother would come when the attacks started. She was always able to soothe Juana.

'I am not to be lightly set aside,' said Juana. Then she began to tell Katharine how she had cut off Philip's mistress' golden hair. She began laughing immoderately. 'I shaved her head. You should have seen her when we had finished with her. We bound her hand and foot. Her shrieks were such as would have led anyone to believe we were cutting off her head instead of her hair. She looked so odd . . . when we'd finished. We shaved it all off. Oh it was so funny . . .'

'Juana, Juana, do not laugh so loudly. Juana, be calm. I want to talk to you. I want you to speak to our father . . . I want him to know how I live here. I cannot go on like this . . . He must do something. Help me, Juana. Help me.'

A dreamy expression had come into Juana's eyes. 'He will not escape me,' she said. 'He cannot, can he? Not while I have the crown of Castile. He threatened me. Oh little Catalina, you have no idea . . . he would put me away . . . if he could. He will try to . . . but I won't let him. I am the Queen of Castile. I . . . I . . . I . . .'

Katharine closed her eyes; she did not want to look at her sister. She knew that it was hopeless to look for help from her. Perhaps it was as well that the next day she would be leaving for Richmond.

The King was relieved to see Katharine depart. He did not think there was much danger to be expected from her but he was a cautious man and he did not take risks. Philip was clearly not inclined to listen to her complaints and as for her sister she was not in a state to. Still it was as well not to have her at Court. She was an embarrassment in any case; and her clothes were decidedly shabby. He did not want unpleasant questions raised.

There were other things to discuss. He did not see why Philip should not make some definite matrimonial arrangements for him before he left. Philip had a rich sister Margaret. Her name had been mentioned before but there had been the usual prevarications. Then there was another matter. Even more important. He would not really feel at ease until Edmund de la Pole was safe in the Tower. It was alarming to have him wandering about on the Continent. One could never be sure who would rally to his cause if he attempted to get back and claim the throne.

A heaven-sent opportunity had brought Philip to these shores. He would not have been Henry Tudor if he had not made the most of that good fortune.

First of all he must make Philip his friend. Young, good looking, susceptible to flattery, it should not be difficult. Young Henry was very useful. The two of them went hawking and hunting the wild boar together; they seemed to understand each other very well. The Prince of Wales had grown up in the last few months. Fifteen this year. A little young for marriage perhaps, but it might be that he and Philip could discuss the boy's marriage. After all Philip was not on the best of terms with Ferdinand even though he was his father-in-law; and he certainly showed no sympathy for Katharine. There were numerous possibilities and the King decided to try them all.

First he was going to bestow on the Archduke the greatest honour he possibly could. He was going to create him a Knight of the Garter.

Philip was enchanted, and ready to discuss all that Henry wished and proved himself to be very ready to concede the King's requests.

He would be delighted, he said, for Henry to have his sister Margaret Archduchess of Savoy and he believed she would be overjoyed to come to England.

'I am sure that Maximilian would never allow his daughter to come without a dowry.'

'My father would insist on giving her a dowry worthy of her rank.'

Henry's eyes gleamed. He could not resist tentatively suggesting a figure.

'Somewhere in the region of thirty thousand crowns,' he murmured.

Philip did not flinch. It seemed to him a likely figure, he said.

Oh yes, surely such a guest was worthy of the Garter.

In St. George's Chapel the ceremony took place and young Henry had the honour of fastening the insignia about Philip's leg;

and the friendship was sealed more firmly when the marriage contract between Henry and the Archduchess Margaret was signed.

It had indeed been a memorable visit.

But there was one question which Philip evaded; and that was the return of the Earl of Suffolk.

It was a matter which he would have to discuss with the Emperor, he said.

'Oh my lord,' laughed Henry, 'it is you who would have the last word, eh?'

Philip hated to admit that this was not so.

'It is for you to say,' went on Henry. 'We know that your word is law. Suffolk is a traitor. I would have him here under lock and key.'

Philip appeared to consider and a vague look came into his eyes. At length, he said lightly, 'I have no doubt, my lord, that you could persuade Suffolk to return.'

'I'll swear he would wish to come back. To be exiled from one's country . . . unable to return . . .' Henry paused significantly. 'Well, you are here now . . . held by the bonds of friendship and you can well imagine how you would feel if for some reason you could not return to your country.'

Philip was alert immediately. He had long realized that Henry was a sly old fox. Was there a hint behind that bland expression? What did all this friendship mean? Philip had never had any great illusions about it. He had been delighted by his reception because he had known that it meant Henry regarded him as a great power in Europe. But he could change. Philip saw himself held here for ransom. How much would his father be prepared to pay to rescue him? A great deal no doubt, and Henry had a reputation for loving money more than he loved most things.

Philip appeared to consider. He said slowly: 'Well, I have no doubt that something could be done about that. Suffolk was my father's guest. He found it hard to refuse him refuge . . . but I have no doubt whatsoever . . .'

'It would be pleasant to have this little matter settled once and for all. I always did abhor a traitor.'

Which, thought Philip, is exactly what King Richard would have called you.

But that was long ago. Henry had the power to hold him here and Philip was counting on leaving England very soon. His ships were made ready. The pleasant interlude was coming to an end and now the Tudor was beginning to show himself other than the kindly host.

What did Suffolk matter? Let him take his chance. Philip could feel cold with fear at the prospect of being a prisoner here.

He had given way to the marriage, although he could imagine his sister would probably refuse her ageing suitor. What did that matter; he had said he would arrange the settlement. He could do no more than that. And now Suffolk.

'I'll swear,' he said, 'that if you would promise to spare his life he would not try to escape when we told him he was no longer welcome.'

Henry smiled. He did not wish publicly to execute Suffolk. He wanted the man here in England under lock and key. To have him a prisoner in the Tower would do very well to begin with.

'I'll strike a bargain,' said Henry. 'I will promise to spare his life. But I want him here.'

'I am sure that could be arranged,' said Philip.

'My good friend, I knew I could rely on you.'

Philip said the friendship must grow stronger between them and he was happy to say that he and the Prince of Wales had been on the best of terms from the very beginning of their acquaintance. It would grieve him greatly to leave these friendly shores but Henry would understand a man in his position could not neglect his duty however strong the temptation to do so.

With the coming of the better weather Philip made his preparations to depart; Henry had given him a written promise that Suffolk's life should be spared, and Philip sent emissaries on ahead to deal with the matter.

At the end of March Suffolk returned to England and Henry had him paraded through the streets of London on his way to the Tower. He wanted to impress on the people that it was folly to attempt to revolt against a strong king.

When Suffolk was safe in the Tower he sent for the Prince of Wales and talked to him alone.

'Another enemy safe under lock and key,' he said, 'or as safe as lock and key can be.'

'Only when a man has lost his head can he cease to be a menace,' said young Henry, his lips tightly pursed. He was always deeply concerned about anyone who had attempted to take the crown.

'I have given my promise that he shall live,' said the King. 'Philip insisted.'

'I suppose he had promised safe conduct to Suffolk.'

Henry was simple in a way, thought the King. He was unaware as yet of the deviousness of men. He had set Philip up as a hero and that meant that he could not suspect him of acting dishonourably in any way. It was a pleasant trait in some respects and he would learn and grow out of it. At the moment it was endearing and perhaps should be allowed to persist . . . for a while. Let the boy learn his own bitter lessons.

'I gave him my promise,' said the King. 'My promise . . . but *you* have made no promises.'

The Prince was a little puzzled. The King hated to refer to his own death but there were times when it was necessary and when it must be impressed on young Henry that one day he would take over the reins of government.

'It is never wise to leave those living who imagine they have a claim to the throne—especially when they are related to a royal house as Suffolk is.'

'You mean . . .'

'I have given my promise. You have not given yours . . . If it should be a matter for you to decide . . . Henry, my son, try to rid yourself of any who can make a nuisance of themselves and so obstruct the path to good government.'

Henry nodded slowly. What his father was saying was: When I am dead and you are King get rid of Suffolk . . . and anyone who through royal blood thinks he or she has a claim to the throne.

THE END OF A REIGN

Life had returned to normal for Katharine. The hopes which had arisen with the visit of Philip and Juana to England had come to nothing. The only consolation was that prevailing conditions could not last much longer. The Prince of Wales was now fifteen—an age when he could be expected to marry. If he married someone else what would she do? What could she do? She imagined that all that would be left to her would be to go into a convent and give herself up to prayer and meditation.

Devout as she was, she did not want that. She wanted children, a happy married life, and she knew that her only hope was the Prince of Wales.

Whenever she saw him he was aware of her; he smiled at her possessively but she fancied there was that in his eyes which demanded gratitude. She *was* grateful, for she knew that by being kind to her he went against his father's wishes; but common sense told her that even the Prince of Wales must know that he would marry her only if some other irresistible project did not turn up. She had heard it whispered that Eleanor of Castile was being suggested for him.

The only consolation was that she would know soon.

Then came the terrible news from Spain. Philip and Juana had arrived in Castile where the Cortes had accepted Juana as the Queen; Philip was given the rank only of consort which would not please him. In vain had he protested that Juana was mad; the people of Castile accepted her as the daughter of the great Queen Isabella, their true Queen. Philip had to realize, Archduke of Austria that he was, that he was only the consort of the Queen of Castile.

There was another menacing figure in the background too. That was Ferdinand. Henry had often smiled to himself as he contemplated his old enemy. How did Ferdinand feel—he who, through Isabella, had been King of Castile, and now found himself only King of Aragon?

Philip undoubtedly had his enemies, and tragedy struck him at

Burgos. No one was quite sure how it happened, but it was believed that it started at a ball game—at which Philip excelled. Being hot from the game, he called for refreshment and drank very deeply from the cup which was brought to him. Soon afterwards he began to feel ill, and when people asked each other who had brought that cup to him, no one could remember. Philip was very ill and remained so for some days. Juana herself had nursed him. Katharine heard that she had changed during that time of sickness. Intense as her anxiety was, yet she grew calm and nursed Philip night and day allowing none but herself to supervise the preparation of his food. In spite of her care, one morning she discovered black spots on his body and during that day he died.

They said he had died of a fever but everyone suspected poison. The matter was not investigated very thoroughly because it was remembered that Ferdinand's envoy had been in Burgos at that time; and with Philip dead, Charles a child, and Juana mad, Ferdinand would become Regent of Castile.

King Henry was astounded by the news. The Prince of Wales shed tears. Philip had been so young, so handsome, so vital, that it was impossible to think of him dead . . . and almost certainly by poisoning. Young Henry wanted to go to Burgos to sift the matter, to find the murderer and inflict terrible tortures on him. 'He was my friend,' he said. 'We loved each other.'

Charles Brandon was a little cynical, but he did not voice his thoughts. People were beginning to be careful what they said to the Prince.

The King was thinking: That schemer Ferdinand will be in control now. And he wondered what would happen about those plans he had discussed with Philip during his enforced stay in England. What of the bonds of friendship; what of the marriage with Archduchess Margaret?

He was soon to hear that Margaret did not wish to marry the ageing King of England, and he was sure that the proposed marriage between Eleanor of Castile and young Henry would be pushed aside now that Ferdinand would be in control.

What had come out of all the lavish entertainments given to Philip? Henry groaned at the thought of the cost. And what had been gained? He had spent so much time, energy and above all money cultivating the friendship of a man who had died before the year was out.

It seemed that all the good that had come out of that visit was the return of Edmund de la Pole, who was now the King's prisoner in the Tower.

The King was feeling very weary. His rheumatism was worse; his skin was turning yellow; and he felt ill for a great part of the time.

If I could find a wife, he thought, I should be rejuvenated. It was amazing that with all he had to offer—a crown no less—it should be so difficult to find anyone who wanted it.

Why? Was this an indication of what people were thinking about his hold on that glittering and most desired object?

His friends and ministers implied that he was not his usual wise self in allowing this obsession with holding the crown to play such a big part in his life. They had implied that he had it firmly in his grasp. He had brought much good to England. He had taxed the rich until they groaned and complained bitterly; but he had a strong economy; he had a prosperous country; and if he demanded taxes from all those who could afford to pay them—as well as from those who could not—he had never lived extravagantly. None could say that the money squeezed from his longsuffering subjects was spent on his own amusements. He was never extravagant unless deep consideration told him that it was wise to be so. Money was only spent if it could bring back gains which exceeded the expense.

And then suddenly he had the idea. Juana! She was a widow now. She was very attractive—quite a beauty in fact. She was Queen of Castile. Why should she not come back to England as his bride?

He sent for Dr. de Puebla and sounded him.

De Puebla had aged considerably and the damp climate of England had not been good for his health. Yet he stayed on knowing that his position as the go-between and friend of the King of England, though he served a Spanish master, was more interesting and remunerative than anything he could have attained in Castile.

De Puebla was a little taken aback at the King's suggestion.

'My lord . . . she is but recently widowed. She is not quite balanced as you saw for yourself. Moreover she remains so enamoured of her late husband that she has had him embalmed and carries his coffin about with her wherever she goes. She has just given birth to a daughter . . . It seems hardly the time . . .'

Hardly the time! Time was a sore point with the King. He could feel it slipping away from him. He must get a wife quickly.

'She has shown that she is fertile,' said the King. 'She is beautiful. She pleases me very much.'

'My lord, you know of her mental instability.'

'Mental instability does not prevent the bearing of children. I want sons, and I want a wife quickly to bear them for me.'

'I will acquaint King Ferdinand with your wishes,' said de Puebla.

'And you will tell him what an excellent prospect this is for his daughter. She will be Queen of England.'

'A title he hoped for another of his daughters,' said de Puebla. He had long deplored his inability to bring about that marriage. He knew that Ferdinand relied on him to do so; but all he had been able to report was the continual bickering about the dowry.

'That is another matter,' went on the King. 'If Ferdinand will not pay the remainder of that long-overdue dowry I shall have to consider the match between his daughter Katharine and my son at an end.'

Ah, thought de Puebla. He desperately wants marriage with Juana. Can this be used as a bait to bring about the marriage between Katharine and the Prince of Wales?

Katharine was cheered a little during those months. The King had written to her saying that he loved her and could not endure to think of her worried about money; he enclosed two hundred pounds which he trusted would be of some help to her.

Katharine smiled wanly. She knew what was going on. Scraps of gossip came to her. The King was hoping to marry Juana and was in correspondence with her father because of this. The long-standing trouble about the non-payment of the dowry would be revived and it was clear that hoping for Juana, the King was realizing that he must still hold out the possibility of a marriage between Katharine and the Prince of Wales.

It was all very cynical but she supposed she must be grateful for help, for whatever reason it was given.

Ferdinand, long disappointed and suspicious of de Puebla, replaced him by Don Gutierro Gomez de Fuensalida who was very different from his predecessor—elegant, courtly, in fact what was expected of a Spanish ambassador, and one who had already served Ferdinand at the Courts of Maximilian and Philip, so he was known to be skilled in diplomacy.

Negotiations dragged on. Ferdinand sent word that Juana who was after all Queen of Castile refused to be parted from her late husband's coffin and wherever she went it was taken with her. She could scarcely be expected to consider another marriage while she was in that state.

But the King continued to plan. It was as though he were

clinging to Juana as his last hope. He was quite ill during the beginning of the year and the Prince of Wales began to behave as though he already wore the crown. He was no longer a boy and people were saying it could not be long now before he was the King.

If the older Henry was hoping desperately for a bride the young one was longing to put the crown on his own head.

Maximilian agreed that his grandson Charles should have the King's youngest daughter, Mary. There were grand celebrations because of this and Katharine was seen in the tiltyard seated beside the King and he was heard to refer to her as his daughter.

It was spring of the year 1508 when the English emissary, whom Henry had sent to Castile to find the real truth behind the diplomacy, returned with the news that Ferdinand had secretly announced that he had no intention of allowing Juana to marry anyone. She was mad; and he was going to rule Castile in her name.

Henry was incensed.

He was feeling more and more wretched. He had emerged from the winter more or less crippled with rheumatism; he was in constant pain and none of his physicians could alleviate it. His temper, which for so long he had kept admirably under control, broke out.

The Prince of Wales came to him one day and found him glowering over one of the dispatches which had just arrived from his man in Castile.

He began to shout suddenly. 'Ferdinand is playing with me. He has no intention of sending Juana here. He has cheated me . . . lied to me. Katharine has not helped. She has been telling her father of my ill treatment. They have no intention of giving me my bride.'

The Prince of Wales looked at the poor man his father had become. He was no longer afraid of him. The crown was fast slipping out of the old man's grasp. That which he had feared ever since he had seized it was about to come to pass, only it was not some claimant to the throne who would snatch it from him. It was Death.

I am all but King, thought young Henry. It cannot be long now.

He said: 'It seemed clear from the start that Ferdinand would not agree to the match . . . nor would Juana.'

'What do you mean?' cried the King. 'We have been negotiating . . .'

'But never seriously on their side. Ferdinand had no intention . . .'

'What do you know of these matters? You are but a boy.'

'A boy no longer, my lord.' Henry looked pityingly at the shrunken man with the swollen joints who moved so painfully in his chair and he felt his own glorious youth urging him to escape his shackles. 'I am aware of what goes on. And of what importance is this Spanish marriage? Juana is mad and you, my lord, are too old for marriage.'

'Too . . . old for marriage . . .' sputtered the King.

'Indeed it is so. It is . . .'

The Prince stopped short, suddenly halted by the look of intense fury in his father's pale eyes.

'How dare you!' cried the King. 'You . . . you . . . young coxcomb . . . how dare you!'

'I . . . I . . . only spoke what I thought to be the truth.'

'Go from me,' said the King. 'You have too high an opinion of yourself. You are a brash boy . . . nothing more. Take care. I am not yet in my grave remember, and the crown is not yet on your head. Go, I say. You offend me.'

The Prince retired with all speed. He was alarmed. He had felt the power of the King in that cold gaze and he was afraid that he was planning to take some action against him.

After his son had gone the King sat for a long time in silence, staring ahead of him.

The King's health improved a little. The Prince was docile, making sure to obey his father in every respect. Nothing was said of that scene between them; but the two of them watched each other warily.

The King was too much of a realist not to admire his son. Henry had the makings of a king and he should be grateful for that. He would consolidate the House of Tudor. If he could curb his vanity, his extravagance, learn the true value of money, he would do well enough.

As for the Prince he admired his father; he knew that he had been a great king and had laboured under great odds. He disapproved of almost everything his father had done while at the same time he knew that his miserliness had enriched the country.

When my time comes, he thought, I will enjoy life. I will make the people happy. I will give them ceremonies and entertainments . . . jousts . . . tourneys and the conduits flowing with free wine. I will not be hampered by those old misers, Dudley and Empson. I shall know how to please the people.

The following June he would be eighteen years old; a man, and what a man—over six feet in height, towering above others, so handsome that women's eyes sparkled as they looked at him—good at sport and at learning, a poet, a musician. He had everything.

He fancied that the whole country was waiting for that glorious moment when he should be proclaimed the King.

There were revelries at Court that Christmas and the King presided over them, seeming a little better. It was only in the clear light of morning that the yellowness of his skin was apparent. During the winter he suffered cruelly from his rheumatism and he was still looking for a bride.

The hard winter was at last over and it was April. But spring had come too late for the King in that year of 1509.

The Prince of Wales was summoned to the King's bedchamber in Richmond Palace and everyone knew that the end was near.

Kneeling by the bed was the King's mother—small and wizened, praying for the soul of her son.

She might have wondered how she would live without him who had been the whole meaning of life to her but it was not necessary, for she felt her own death was very close. It would be a gracious act of fate to take her with her son.

The Prince had come in. Oh, he was beautiful, she thought. Thank God for young Henry. This is not death when Henry is left to wear the crown, to populate the House of Tudor with illustrious sons.

The King was fighting for his breath, and thinking of his sins. There were many of them, he feared, but perhaps he had some virtues. He had killed . . . but only, he could say, when it was for the betterment of England and if it was also for his own good, well then he would say that.

He would ask the Virgin to intercede for him and to plead that what he had done he had done for his country.

His mother was looking at him. She was assuring him that he had done well, that he had no need to fear death.

And there was young Henry . . . sad because death was sad. And yet there was a shine about him. He could feel the crown on his golden head now and that was satisfaction to him . . . as it had been to his father.

It was young Henry they should be praying for, not the old man. He was past praying for now.

'My lord.' It was the Archbishop putting his face close to the dying man's. 'The marriage of the Prince . . . Do you have any command?'

There was a brief silence. For a moment the King seemed to

be more alive. His eyes sought those of his son. His lips moved. 'The Prince will decide . . .' he said.

That was how it would be. When he was no longer there, when Henry was the King, he would do exactly what he pleased. He must not hamper the boy by making commands which he would disobey and then have to think up some elaborate reason to explain that he had not acted disobediently. Let him make his choice . . . freely . . . as he would in any case.

Moreover he had been cruel to Katharine. His conscience which had been so quiet until now was beginning to raise its head reproachfully.

He closed his eyes. They were watching him intently.

Then young Henry stood up. He knew that he was no longer Prince of Wales. He was the King.

KING HENRY
THE EIGHTH

They were all coming to pay homage to the new King.

He detained Katharine for he said he would speak with her.

She thought how handsome he was with his newly acquired dignity and his endearing delight in it.

He took her hands and kissed them.

'I had always intended that you should be my Queen,' he said.

Waves of gladness swept over her. It was truly so. He was smiling, well pleased, loving himself as well as her. She thought how charming he was . . . how young. All the miseries of the last years were falling away from her. This young man with those few words and looks of tenderness in his eyes had brushed them aside.

She would never forget. She would be grateful for ever.

There were tears in his eyes. He saw them and they pleased him. He was the perfect chivalrous knight rescuing the lady in distress. It was a role he loved so well and had often played it in his imagination.

'That pleases you?' he asked.

She turned her head away to hide her emotion; and he liked that too.

He put his arms about her and kissed her.

'I shall never forget this moment,' she said. 'I shall love you until the day I die.'

She heard a chaffinch sing in the gardens. Then the bells were pealing. In the streets the people were waiting to see him and his chosen bride.

'The King is dead,' they would say. 'Gone is the old miser and in this place this handsome young man, this golden boy, every inch of him a king.'

Already they were proclaiming him.

'God bless the King. God save King Henry the Eighth.'

BIBLIOGRAPHY

Aubrey, William Hickman Smith — *National and Domestic History England*

Bruce, Marie Louise — *The Making of Henry VIII*

Chrimes, S. B. — *Henry VII*

Gairdner, James — *Henry VII*

Gairdner, James — *History and Life and Reign of Richard III*

Gairdner, James — *Life and Papers of Richard III*

Green, John Richard — *History of England*

Green, Mary Anne Everett — *Lives of the Princesses of England*

Guizot, M. Translated by Robert Black — *History of France*

Halsted, Caroline A. — *Richard III*

Hume, David — *History of England from the Invasion of Julius Caesar to the Revolution*

Hume, Martin A. S. — *Spain: Its Greatness and Decay*

Jenkins, Elizabeth — *The Princes in the Tower*

Kendall, Paul Murray — *Richard III*

Luke, Mary M. — *Catherine the Queen*

Mattingly, Garrett — *Catherine of Aragon*

More, Sir Thomas — *Life of Richard III*

Prescott, William H. Edited by John Foster Kirk — *History of the Reign of Ferdinand and Isabella the Catholic*

Ramsey, J. H. — *Lancaster and York*

Stephen, Sir Leslie and Lee, Sir Sydney — *The Dictionary of National Biography*

Strickland, Agnes — *The Lives of the Queens of England*

Timbs, John and Gunn, Alexander — *Abbeys, Castles and Ancient Halls of England and Wales*

Wade, John — *British History*

Walpole, Horace — *Historic Doubts on the Life of Richard III*

Williams, Charles — *Henry VII*

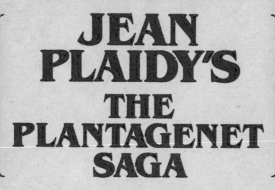

By the year 2000, 2 out of 3 Americans could be illiterate.

It's true.

Today, 75 million adults...about one American in three, can't read adequately. And by the year 2000, U.S. News & World Report envisions an America with a literacy rate of only 30%.

Before that America comes to be, you can stop it...by joining the fight against illiteracy today.

Call the Coalition for Literacy at toll-free **1-800-228-8813** and volunteer.

Volunteer Against Illiteracy. The only degree you need is a degree of caring.

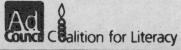

Ad Council Coalition for Literacy

LV-2